W9-ARK-089

DISCARD

THE HERZOG LEGACY

By Gertrude Schweitzer

THE HERZOG LEGACY
BEFORE HONOR
SHADOWS ON THE LEFT BANK
THE LEDGE
SO MANY VOICES
BORN
THE YOUNG PEOPLE

THE HERZOG LEGACY

by
GERTRUDE SCHWEITZER

Doubleday & Company, Inc., Garden City, New York
1976

All the characters in this book are fictitious,
and any resemblance to actual persons,
living or dead, is purely coincidental.

Library of Congress Cataloging in Publication Data

Schweitzer, Gertrude, 1909–
The herzog legacy.

I. Title.
PZ3.S4143Pap   [PS3537.C816]   813'.5'4
ISBN: 0-385-03897-6
Library of Congress Catalog Card Number: 75-21245

For
Carolyn, Bart, Jeffrey, and Todd

THE HERZOG LEGACY

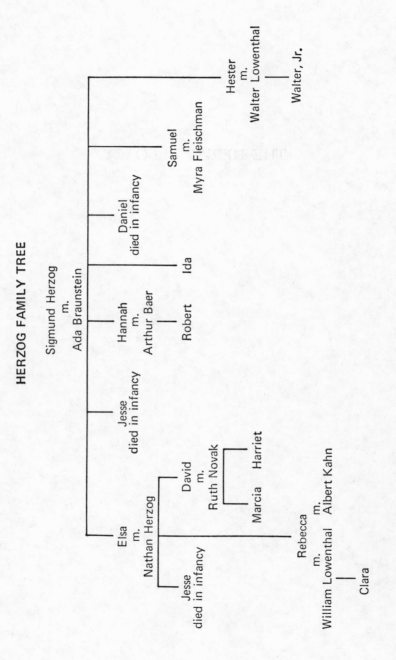

HERZOG FAMILY TREE

PROLOGUE

In 1844 Sigmund Herzog tried to persuade his father to enroll in the project that was to take emigrants from Germany and settle them in the Republic of Texas. Herr Herzog had no wish to leave Frankfurt, where even a Jew, if he was a clothing manufacturer like Herzog, could live in comfort, relatively free from harassment, for the unknown hazards of a strange land. When the Texas project collapsed, leaving hundreds of refugees stranded, he trusted that he had heard the last of this nonsense of Sigmund's.

He had not, although it was five years before the subject came up again. Sigmund, with typical tenacity, renounced many of the pleasures of youth in order to save the money he made working for his father. In 1848, when he was twenty-two years old, he said good-by to his family and set sail for America.

Sigmund spoke no English. After paying for his passage, he had little money left. If he had dreamed of prospecting for gold in the pavements of the New World, he was disappointed. Many like him gave up and went home, but even if Sigmund could have bought his passage back he would not have gone. He was too stubborn.

He was also handsome and, even as a young man, compelling. All the Herzogs had finely etched, imperious faces, with brilliant, large eyes of blue, gray, or green, and, with few exceptions, great personal magnetism. They tended to be clever as well. Within several months, Sigmund had put aside sufficient money from various menial jobs to equip a pushcart and had picked up enough of the language to convince prospective customers of the superiority of his merchandise. He began by selling cheap household items to the poor in the streets of New York, but before long he was able to upgrade his stock and take it into the homes of middle-class women, who found him as attractive as they did his prices and what he had to sell.

Eight years after he landed in America, Sigmund opened a

women's clothing store in Baltimore. He detested the business and disliked the city, but he had significant reasons for enduring both. While showing his wares in a fine house in New York one day, he had excited the interest of a girl who was visiting there from out of town. Her name was Ada Braunstein. Her father had brought the family to Baltimore from Munich in 1839 to escape the harsh property laws for Jews in Bavaria. As a physician and man of education who spoke fluent English, Dr. Braunstein had had little difficulty establishing himself in the new land. By the time Sigmund and Ada met, he had a successful practice among the upper-middle-class Jews of Baltimore.

Ada was a gentle, unadventurous girl, but love emboldened her. She became a steady customer of Sigmund's while she was in New York, and so managed to see a good deal of him. When her father came to take her home, she dared to present the young peddler to him by making much of something Sigmund had once let drop: a distant family connection with a Baron von Herzog, who had been a field marshal in the Prussian Army against Napoleon. The young man's bearing and manners made such a relationship believable. Dr. Braunstein had once hoped for a prosperous match for his daughter, but Ada was a rather dumpy girl with little to say for herself, and although she was almost twenty-one, no serious suitors, wealthy or otherwise, had appeared. This fine-looking, intelligent, soft-spoken descendant of a baron and field marshal—never mind his temporary occupation as a common peddler—might do very well.

It was at Dr. Braunstein's suggestion that Sigmund sold out his stock at an excellent profit, bought himself a good suit, and moved to Baltimore. Sigmund loved New York, but he did not love peddling, as good as he was at it. He did not love treating as his betters people to whom he felt superior. With Ada and her father— especially with her father—he was at home. Dr. Braunstein understood politics as well as music and was an omnivorous reader. He and Sigmund had long discussions, always in English, which Sigmund spoke with less of an accent than did the doctor. Ada once suggested that Sigmund came to their house more to see her father than to see her. In a sense it was true. She was a sweet, loving girl, and a lady, but she was not stimulating company. A man did not, of course, expect mental stimulation from a woman.

Sigmund worked as a salesman in a women's clothing store for a year. Then Dr. Braunstein loaned him the money to open a store of his own. It did well almost from the first, but before long Sigmund decided that what he was engaged in was only a socially acceptable form of peddling and was no more congenial to him than pushing a cart. By then, he and Ada were married and living in a house on Eutaw Place, a wedding present from the doctor, and Ada was expecting a child. If it had not been for three widely disparate events, he might have been trapped for life in what came to be known, generations later, as "the rag business." One of these events was the arrival in Baltimore of a young man named Nathan Herzog. Another was Dr. Braunstein's sudden death of a heart attack. The third was the Civil War.

Nathan Herzog came to see Sigmund at the store, which was prematurely and hopefully called Herzog & Sons. He had just arrived from Stuttgart and he wanted a job. His personal references were excellent. In addition, he claimed to be a distant cousin. Sigmund knew of no relatives in Württemberg, but he liked the looks and the enterprise of this nineteen-year-old fellow. It was possible to find in him the fine bone structure, fair coloring, and aristocratic bearing of the Baron von Herzog Herzogs. And Sigmund wanted to find them. However long it might take to train Nathan to take over from Sigmund some of the onerous responsibilities of running the business, it would be many years shorter than waiting for the hypothetical sons. Sigmund gave him a job as a stock boy and, since no stranger could qualify for the rapid advancement he planned for Nathan, accepted him at his word as a member of the family.

Dr. Braunstein, who kept a paternal eye on things, might have interfered with Sigmund's plans. Or tried to. Sigmund had begun to chafe under that constant watchfulness. He was no longer awed by his father-in-law's attainments. In some respects he had not only equaled them but, he felt, gone beyond them. He had made a success of the store; wealthy women came from as far away as Georgetown to shop at Herzog & Sons. He had founded the Hebrew-American Literary Society of Baltimore, and his opening address, in English as flawless as Dr. Braunstein's and far richer, had been published in the newspaper. He was as well known and respected as his father-in-law, even though he was much younger and had come to Baltimore many years later. When Sigmund walked to the synagogue on Saturday mornings, he was stopped so often by people who wanted to greet him that he was hard pressed to get there on time and maintain his reputation for strict punctuality. No, he did not

3

any longer require Dr. Braunstein's advice and guidance, and he resented being forced to accept them.

Thus, although Sigmund was shocked and saddened by his father-in-law's sudden death, he could not view it as an unrelieved disaster. It was not as advantageous financially as Sigmund might have hoped (for all his show of affluence, Dr. Braunstein left little more than the money needed to keep his widow in modest comfort) but he was considerably consoled by the knowledge that the man who had set himself up as his mentor had apparently been foolishly improvident. Very likely Sigmund would have done as he pleased, even if Ada's father had lived, but now he could do it without constraint—without anyone's looking over his shoulder.

In April 1861 the Confederates fired on Fort Sumter. Maryland was technically a Northern state, but Baltimore's sympathies were violently pro-Southern. Later that month a Baltimore mob attacked the 6th Massachusetts regiment and shot Union troops to death. President Lincoln issued a call for volunteers.

Sigmund hated the whole thing. His own sympathies were with the North, something about which he and his father-in-law had had many long and sometimes acrimonious arguments, but he was not prepared to shoot his neighbors over it. He was not, in fact, prepared to shoot or be shot at for any reason. No one expected a married man of thirty-five with one small daughter and another child on the way to volunteer for either army. By the end of 1862, however, there were rumors that the Union was about to conscript all able-bodied men between twenty and forty-five, and some of Sigmund's friends, even those with family responsibilities, promptly enlisted in the Confederate Army.

This seemed to Sigmund an ideal time to visit his aging parents in Frankfurt and have them meet their daughter-in-law and grand-daughter before they died. He and Ada, who was six months pregnant, and two-and-a-half-year-old Elsa sailed on the Great Eastern in February 1863, leaving Nathan in charge of Herzog & Sons, with a small interest in the profits to encourage good management. In March the Union conscription act that would have made Sigmund liable for military service went into effect, but with it a provision that any drafted man who could provide an acceptable substitute or pay the government three hundred dollars would be excused.

Since Sigmund could now avoid conscription, Ada wanted to return home at once. She did not like the cold, ugly city of Frankfurt, and she found the Herzogs en masse overpowering. Sigmund, although he himself felt oddly alien in his native land, had no intention of going back so soon. Buying his way out of the Union Army was not enough to assure him of the old admiration and respect in a community of hotly partisan Southern sympathizers. Besides, it was a daily joy to him to wake up and realize that he did not have to go to the store.

He did not, of course, try to explain these subtleties to Ada. He simply assured her that it would be better for her to wait until after the birth of the baby, and ignored her tears. Women, like children, were always weeping for one reason or another. Paying attention simply encouraged them to weep more.

Only Ada was unhappy in the house of Sigmund's parents. Elsa, doted on by grandparents, aunts, and uncles, had a fine time and was soon chirping away in German as glibly as in English. Sigmund was out most of the day. He had fallen into conversation with a printer in a coffee shop and been invited to come around to see the operation. Since then, he had gone to the plant several times a week, fascinated by the skill and speed of the typesetters, the workings of the rotary press, the whole concept, never before experienced at first hand, of almost instantly transforming ideas into print for hundreds, even thousands, to read. This, not selling clothes to empty-headed women, was the kind of thing he should be doing. A man should do what interests him. Sigmund's interests had always been in the world of words, ideas. He would find out everything possible about this printing business, and perhaps never go back to Herzog & Sons.

Ada gave birth to a son in the bed in which Sigmund had been born. They called him Jesse, after Sigmund's grandfather. An hour later Ada was asking Sigmund how soon they could go home to Baltimore. Sigmund had no intention of returning to America until after the war, but this was no time to upset her. He told her they would go as soon as the baby was strong enough. From time to time afterward, he wondered whether God had punished him for lying, but this occurred to him only in his lowest moments.

Jesse was a tiny, frail baby, so frail that he was almost three weeks old before he could be circumcised. The long voyage across the ocean would certainly be too much for him. Aside from his feeble health, there was the matter of his feeding. Ada, who had nursed Elsa for nine months, lost her milk when Jesse was six weeks old, and it had been hard to find the right wet nurse. They could not risk taking him from her.

They stayed in Frankfurt for more than two years. From time to time, when Jesse seemed better, Ada suggested that they might be able to go home, and Sigmund agreed that they might. The improvement never lasted long enough to make other excuses necessary. In March 1865, three months before his second birthday, Jesse died. The war ended in April. In May, Sigmund and Ada returned to Baltimore as they had left, with one daughter, Elsa, now five, and Ada again pregnant.

Sigmund intended to stay in Baltimore only long enough to make arrangements with Nathan for the sale of the store and to sell the house on Eutaw Place. Nathan's reports about ever-increasing profits suggested to Sigmund that, even with his small interest in the store, Nathan might now, perhaps with the help of a bank loan, be in a position to buy Sigmund out.

From the beginning, probably because he wanted to see in him a way out of the trap of Herzog & Sons, Sigmund had overestimated Nathan. Nathan was a pleasant young man, honest, reasonably intelligent. With Sigmund in charge, he had done well enough. He knew how to follow orders and he got along with people. But he was not equipped for the role in which Sigmund had cast him. He lacked the initiative, the imagination, the authority, the drive to guide a business or direct a staff, even in normal times, much less during the chaos of the war. It was typical of him that all the while the store was showing greater and greater losses, he wrote to Sigmund of increasing profits. He did this not to deceive Sigmund for his own ends, not to aggrandize his accomplishments, but because he thought it was what Sigmund would want to hear. The fact that the deception must eventually be discovered did not trouble him much, even though he was afraid of Sigmund. That was all in the future. Nathan thought very little about the future.

Sigmund's furies were rare, for as a rule no one frustrated him to the point of fury; no one dared. But when he discovered the truth about the store and Nathan, he could not contain his rage, which he directed not only at Nathan but at everybody around him. He even, in annoyance at some foolish female remark, threw a sofa pillow at his pregnant wife, though he had never before raised a hand to anyone in violence. Elsa saw him do it and never forgot it.

Part of Sigmund's anger was, of course, directed at himself for his

6

misjudgment of Nathan. If he could have denied the blood relationship, he would have done so at once, but he had embraced it too openly, with too much conviction. To repudiate it now would make him appear even more of a fool. He was stuck with Nathan. What was still more infuriating was that he was apparently stuck with the store. He had planned to sell his interest and buy into a printing plant in New York. Now his interest was worthless; there were only debts. When he had paid them off, he would be a poor man once more. It would take him years to build up Herzog & Sons again. He might never be able to make it what it had been. He had been away a long time, and there were other, bigger stores now. Besides, what little heart he had ever had for the business had dried up, shriveled by a burning dream.

All at once he saw what he had to do—how to free himself and render justice to Nathan at the same time. As scrupulously as he had always done, he would pay every outstanding debt. He would then generously sign over his interest in the store to Nathan. What more could a man be expected to do for a distant relative? If Nathan, inevitably, ran Herzog & Sons into the ground, it would have nothing to do with Sigmund. Nathan would be the Herzog, his the putative sons. As long as Sigmund had to start over again anyway, why should he go back to peddling?

Ada cried almost as much as she had cried in Frankfurt. She wanted to stay in Baltimore, among her friends and relatives. She did not pretend to understand why Sigmund suddenly longed to be a printer (*were* there Jewish printers?), but men were strange creatures and wives had to go along with their vagaries. Why, though, could he not be a printer in Baltimore? Sigmund had never told her that Baltimore was too provincial, too parochial, for his taste, that his city was New York. Ada cried and cried. She begged Sigmund at least to wait so that this baby could be born in the house on Eutaw Place. But Sigmund was afraid to wait; afraid, remembering Jesse, of what might turn into an extended postponement of his dream. He had waited long enough.

The house Sigmund bought in New York belied any true expectation of a return to humble beginnings. It was a large brownstone in the same upper-middle-class neighborhood as the house where Ada had been visiting when he first met her. They maintained it through all the struggles of the next years. Sigmund saw nothing incongruous in coming into such a house with his compositor's pay and his ink-stained fingers, nothing remarkable in Ada's management. It was a gentleman's home, and he had always been a gentleman, even when he wheeled a pushcart. As for Ada, she managed on the money he gave her, like any good wife.

Her baby, the first born in that house, was a girl, Hannah. There was another girl, Ida, and another boy, who died at birth, before Sigmund finally got a son, Samuel, who lived. One more daughter, Hester, was born after him. Ada was forty-two by then, and her childbearing days were over.

One son and four daughters. One son. Clearly, Herzog & Sons had never been meant for Sigmund. It was good to remember that when word came from Baltimore that in the booming postwar economy even Nathan was doing well, while Sigmund's own future was uncertain. By the time his son, Samuel, was born, in 1872, he had opened a small job printing shop. It was moderately successful, but his ambitions had soared beyond the mechanics of reproducing words in type. At forty-six he was no longer a young man. There were moments when he wondered if it was not too late.

The incident that finally propelled him toward his goal was a curious triumph for integrity. When, in 1872, Horace Greeley announced his candidacy for the presidency, Sigmund considered writing him a letter of support. Sigmund's letters, marvels of literary style, were likely to attract attention. If the founder of the New York *Tribune* became interested in him . . .

But he could not bring himself to support Greeley. Although he agreed with Greeley's pacifism and his opposition to slavery, Sigmund considered outrageous his advocacy of such notions as organized labor, women's rights, and communal living. In fact, the more Sigmund thought about it, the more outraged he became, until, unable to contain himself, he sat down and penned a letter in his beautiful, shaded hand, telling Greeley exactly what he thought of his radical views.

Even the genial, accessible Greeley might well have made no more than a token response to a letter of support, however gracefully written. Who, after all, was Sigmund Herzog? But an outraged Sigmund Herzog, blistering the pages with such challenges as: *Do you propose, sir, to sweep the Family, foundation of Civilization, into innocuous desuetude?* could not be shrugged off so readily. Greeley answered. Sigmund wrote again. Greeley suggested that Sigmund write an article for the paper, and Sigmund soon became a regular contributor.

Some years afterward, when the two men finally met, they were entertained by the parallels, from a certain point on, between their careers. Greeley, too, had started as a compositor and job printer. His regular articles in the *Daily Whig*, like Sigmund's in the *Tribune*, had aroused the interest of influential men who encouraged him to edit his own newspaper. The Paper, with a capital P, as everyone in the family was always to speak of it, might never reach the eminence of the New York *Tribune*. But it was, after all, a harder climb from a factory in Frankfurt, Germany, than from a farm in Amherst, New Hampshire.

BOOK I
1890—1918

1

Hester was sitting on the floor, writing a note to her father. By rights she should have had the desk, because all Ida did at the desk was use it to spread out her pictures and pamphlets—never to write, which was what a desk was for. But Hester knew what would happen if she said anything.

"Never mind," Ida would sing. She had been doing that for almost a week now—singing her words instead of speaking them in a normal way. "Never mind. Remember, Hester, I am a young lady and you are only a chee-ild."

It was no answer. Nothing Ida said was ever an answer to anything. But Mama would support her just the same. "If Ida wants to use the desk, sweetheart, it's her privilege; she's eight years older. When she gets married, you'll have it all to yourself, the whole room."

Nobody was going to marry Ida any more now. She was too old, twenty-three; Elsa and Hannah had both been married before they were twenty. Besides, Ida was peculiar. She talked to God all the time. Not in prayers or in the synagogue, like other people, but in ordinary conversation, as if He were a friend of hers who lived next door.

Dear Papa, Hester wrote,

I think you should put something in the paper about letting women vote. It is foolish that no matter how stupid a man is, he can vote, and no matter how smart a woman is, she can't . . .

Nobody would marry Hester either. She was too clever. Boys didn't like clever girls. Elsa was clever too, but look who had married Elsa. A relative, old enough to be her father. Hester would never marry a man that old. She would never marry anybody. Nowadays there were plenty of other things a woman could do, and if she became important enough, people wouldn't smirk and call her an old maid, the way they were beginning to do with Ida . . .

"What are you writing? Another of your poems?"

Hester looked up to find Ida's vague gaze somewhere between her ear and the floor. Ida never met anyone's eyes, which infuriated Papa. The last thing Ida must have wanted to do was get Papa going; she was terrified of him (they all were, even Elsa; all except Hester) but she couldn't seem to help herself.

"As I've told you twenty times," Hester said with mock patience, "I don't write poems any more. This is a note to Papa."

"Oh, another of your notes to Papa," Ida trilled.

"You needn't sound like that. He likes my notes. You heard him say Samuel could learn something from me about expressing himself."

A little color came into Ida's sallow cheeks. All the girls had Mama's coloring, even Elsa, who was the prettiest. Instead of proposing to Elsa outright, Nathan had sung her a popular song, "I Love a Little Yaller Gal," and almost lost her until he pointed out that the reference was to the yellow dress she wore, not her complexion. Only Samuel was light, like Papa, and not short or inclined to plumpness, the way Mama and the girls were. It didn't seem fair.

"There isn't anything wrong," Ida said indignantly, "with the way Samuel expresses himself."

Everybody in the family doted on Samuel except Papa. People took it for granted that Samuel, since he was the only boy, must be Papa's favorite, but he wasn't.

"Papa just meant in writing," Hester said. "He would be pleased to get notes from Samuel, but of course Samuel hates to write. Listen to this," she added quickly, seeing Ida's brief attention flag. "What do you think of this?"

Hester read what she had written. Almost at once she heard the revival of Ida's interest, in the shape of a gasp.

"You can't send him that!"

"Why not?"

Ida leaned forward, raining hairpins. Papa always told Ida she looked like Medusa, the way her hair slithered all over. Hester was glad her own hair was thick. When she was allowed to put it up next year, it would stay up.

"Why *not?*" Ida sang, up the scale. "Because you *know* how he feels. You *know* it's the *last* thing—" She choked a little, her slightly protuberant eyes watering, and went on in a high voice. "Haven't you heard that *letter* often enough? The one about—"

"Sweeping the Family into 'innocuous desuetude.' I love that. *Innocuous desuetude.* Doesn't it have a beautiful sound?" Hester tilted her head as if listening to the words, and then straightened and said briskly, "Anyway, I intend to change Papa's mind. What you heard is only the beginning. When he reads all my arguments, he'll realize he's behind the times."

"Realize? Change his mind? Papa? He won't read past the first sentence."

"He will. Anything he starts to read, he finishes. If Samuel doesn't like the beginning of anything, he stops reading, but I'm like Papa. I don't care. I have to know how it comes out."

Ida was no longer listening. She had moved to the open window and stood gazing out through the heavy white curtains that hung limp in the breathless July air.

"Stop her, if you please, God, from sending that note to Papa," Ida murmured, as if she saw Him out there walking along West End Avenue. "But should you not want to stop her, please give me a headache so that I don't feel well enough to go down for supper."

If Hester had needed a headache, she wouldn't have gone through all that; she would simply have said she had one, whether she did or not. Probably Ida—and Elsa and Hannah, too—thought they would be struck dead, or at least dumb. Papa had hinted as much (whether he or God would do the striking was not clear) but Hester had found out a long time before that if you were good enough at it, nothing at all happened when you lied, because nobody could tell, maybe not even God. And as Samuel said, you could save yourself a lot of trouble.

She went back to her note:

Samuel isn't stupid, but would you rather let him vote than me?

She crossed that out. It would only make Papa angrier at Samuel than he was all the time anyhow, and it would not help to persuade him. Hester did not really expect to persuade him. She knew as well as Ida what he thought of women's rights. Although she had not been born at the time, she knew what he was supposed to have said when he heard Horace Greeley had died insane.

"Ah, well, that accounts for a great deal. I never understood how a fine, intelligent gentleman like Mr. Greeley could lend his support to such monkeyshines as woman suffrage. Now I know the poor man's mind was trembling on the verge of madness."

Since then, Papa's statements on the subject of women's rights and their advocates had only become more scathing. In the Paper's brief news item a few weeks before about the newly formed National American Woman Suffrage Association, the president had been referred to twice as Mr. Elizabeth Cady Stanton. Papa had pretended to think it was the compositor's carelessness, and to be annoyed, but he had winked at Hester.

Hester had thought the "misprint" a good joke. There was no reason she could see why women should not be allowed to vote, but she was not impassioned about it. Maybe she would be when she was old enough to vote herself, but that was a long way off, 1896. By then women probably would have won the vote anyhow, without her bothering about it. In the meantime she might as well laugh at *Mr.* Elizabeth Cady Stanton, who was as plump as Mama and looked more like a round, white-haired rubber doll than a *Mr.* You could not imagine her saying such things as that marriage was nothing except legalized prostitution, but she had said it, and since then Papa had never stopped going after her in the Paper.

In place of what Hester had crossed out about Samuel, she wrote:

If *"the gentler sex"* had the vote, it would help to stop wars and strikes and crooked politics, because women are more against those things than men are.

That would appeal to Papa. He always said women were the gentler sex, and he hated war, strikes, and anything crooked even more than he hated the idea of woman suffrage. He might even smile when he read that part.

It would be lovely if something she said could sway him, because it would affect not only Papa but also the Paper and the thousands who read it. Imagine a girl of fifteen influencing all those people!

But Hester knew Papa would not be swayed. He might even be furious, as Ida feared, and get into one of what Mama called his "states." The fury would not be directed at Hester, though; it never was. She had been writing her notes to him since she was nine years old, and while some of them had enraged him, he had not once blamed Hester. No matter how much he disagreed with what she wrote, and pulled it to pieces for syntax, he was proud of her for writing it. Which was why she did it.

That first time, when she was nine, she did it because Samuel, who was twelve, dared her. It was just before *Pesach,* and Samuel was rehearsing the four questions he had to ask at the Seder.

"You'd think you'd know them by now, after all the times you've done them," Hester said. "*I* know them: '*Mah Nishtana.*' "

"You're so smart," Samuel broke in. "I could remember them if I wanted to, but who cares about those stupid questions?"

"I ought to be asking them anyhow. I'm the youngest."

"A girl can't ask them, stupid. It has to be the youngest *male.*"

"Oh, I know, but that's silly. I could do it much better, and you don't even want to."

"That doesn't matter. It's the Law."

"Papa could change the Law. If he knew how well I could do it, with expression—"

"Why don't you tell him?"

"What?"

"Go on. Ask him if he'll let you ask the questions. I dare you!"

When Samuel knew she was really going to take the dare, he tried to dissuade her. Then he made her swear on the Bible that she would never tell Papa he had said the questions were stupid or that he didn't want to ask them. He was much more frightened than she was. After she got the idea of writing Papa a note instead of asking him face to face, she was not frightened at all.

"This is an example of the ideas that are put into the heads of the young these days," Papa had said, looking sternly at Mama as though she were responsible.

"Now, Papa," Mama had said in alarm.

It was what she always said when she thought Papa was getting into a "state." Papa noticed no more than if she had sneezed.

"Loose women like that Victoria Woodhull and her cronies," he had continued, "telling little girls to abjure their shyness, their gentleness, their modesty, their very femininity, and to conduct themselves like boys. Do you know what abjure means, Hester?"

"No, Papa."

"Look it up. I'll expect you to use it in a sentence this evening."

Victoria Woodhull had left the country by then, married and settled down in England, but that made no difference to Papa, once he was warmed up. He carried on about her as though she had personally told Hester to engage in free love, believe in spiritualism, and demand her woman's right to ask the questions at the Seder.

Papa's "states" were unique to Papa. He never raised his voice. In fact, he spoke more softly than usual, and even more elegantly. He seldom made a direct attack on anybody in the family. If Samuel brought home poor marks from school, Papa said nothing to Samuel. Instead, at the next family meal, he went on about the importance of education and the wicked stupidity of anyone who failed to take advantage of it. He made all the others, not just Samuel, feel at fault. Only Hester was immune. His blue eyes, so frosted over they looked gray, skipped her face and rested on the faces of the others in turn, "freezing our spines," as Samuel put it.

"You've stopped writing," Ida said, turning away from the window. "You're not going to send it."

"Of course I am." Hester signed the note, *Your loving daughter, Hester*, as she always did. "I've just finished it."

"Please don't send it," Ida whispered, forgetting to sing. "I'll give you something nice if you don't."

"What?"

"I'll have to think." Ida's vague glance drifted to the opposite wall. "You ought to get up from there. You're too big to sit on the floor."

Hester lay down flat on her back on the rush mat that replaced the rug in summer. "It's the coolest place in the room. What will you give me?"

"One of my pictures."

Hester made an unladylike sound. Ida's pictures were a family joke. She cut them out of magazines and pamphlets, pasted them on cardboard, and framed them with *passe partout*. Then she stored them in a large envelope, taking them out regularly to gaze at them and rearrange them. Most were pictures of angels or of soulful-looking men and women who would probably be angels in time. She even had a picture of Jesus. She kept it hidden, but Hester had seen it. If Hester ever needed anything from Ida, all she would have to do was threaten to tell Papa Ida kept a picture of Jesus.

"Don't deride what you don't understand," Ida sang.

Ida always made it seem as if there were something wonderful and special about the pictures that only she knew, but even Mama thought they were a joke.

"You shouldn't tease her," Mama told Hester and Samuel. "In some way, the pictures are important to her." But she smiled and shook her head as if to say, "Heaven knows why!"

Hester thought it was part of the same queerness that made Ida talk out loud to God. Both with the pictures and with God, her face got what Hester thought of as its smeary look; like the Cheshire cat just before it started to disappear, only without the smile.

"I'm going," Hester said, getting up from the floor.

Ida put her hand to her throat. "Where?"

"To put the note under Papa's door before he wakes up."

"I'll give you one of the lace handkerchiefs Hannah brought me from Venice."

"Pooh!"

"No, Hester, wait. My cameo pin. You always liked my cameo pin."

"Did I?" Hester, her hand on the doorknob, shrugged. "I don't like it any more. Now I like emeralds. Do you have any emeralds?"

"Oh! You're just a horrid little—"

Hester did not wait to hear what Ida thought she was. She went out of the room and closed the door, and then had to stand in the hall a minute, until she could stop giggling.

She wished Samuel were home, so she could tell him how easily she had guyed Ida again. He would nod and laugh and pat her on the shoulder, and it would be twice as much fun. Everything was twice as much fun once Samuel was in on it. But he was never home on Sunday afternoons any more. Now that he was eighteen, he and his friends took girls riding in carriages in Central Park every Sunday. Mama and Papa thought there were always chaperones along, but Hester knew some of the girls went out alone with the boys. Some of them, Samuel had told her, were not even Jewish.

She tiptoed down the long, dim hall to the door of the big bedroom where Mama and Papa slept. There was no sound from inside. Papa took a nap every Sunday between three and five. During those two hours, nobody dared to disturb him for anything except some emergency at the Paper. On the minute of five, he would get up as if somebody had called him, and be down for supper at five-fifteen, not the tiniest spot or wrinkle anywhere on his clothes, every hair of his head and his beard combed perfectly straight and smooth. Right after supper he would go downtown to the Paper and stay there until the Monday edition went to press. But he would find time to read Hester's note and speak about it. He always did.

After she had slipped the note under the door, she went looking for Mama. She went all the way down to the kitchen, but there was nobody there except Mary, sitting with a bowl in her lap, stringing beans. When Hester asked her where Mama was, she only turned dark red and looked at the floor with her mouth open. She was a greenhorn from Ireland, less than a month in America, and frightened of everything and everybody but Mama. She seemed hopeless to Hester—Mama had even had to hold her hands to show her how to sweep—but Mama said she would make a good servant. It was better to train them from the beginning, Mama said. Then they had no notions of their own, but learned your ways.

Hester tried again. "Mary, you don't have to be afraid of me. I'm only fifteen years old. That's even younger than you, isn't it? All you have to do is tell me where my mama is."

Mary bent her head a little lower, as though searching the floor for a dropped string bean.

"You don't even," Hester persisted, "have to say anything. I'll ask you some questions, and all you have to do is shake your head yes or no. Now. Is my mama home?"

Mary did not move.

"Well, I know she's home, so the way you answer that is to nod your head up and down. I'll show you."

As she reached out for Mary's head, the girl leaped out of her chair with a mouselike squeak and scuttled into a corner of the kitchen, spilling the beans all over the floor. In the midst of this, Mama came in.

"Oh, what a shame, Mary!" she said, and smiled at the cowering girl as though she loved her. "Well, there's no great harm done, is there? If you wash the beans very carefully, it will be as if it never happened. Help her pick them up, Hester, and then come upstairs and see me in the sewing room."

Hester knew Mama was angry. Papa always said Mama never got angry, but it wasn't true. He couldn't tell, that was all. Hester could. Mama was angry now, but Hester didn't see why.

"I'm sorry I frightened you," she said to Mary. "If Mama asks, you can tell her I said I didn't mean to frighten you and I'm very sorry."

Mama was at the sewing machine, hemming a skirt. Miss Daschner, the seamstress, came once a month, but Mama had to do a lot of hemming in between, because ladies' skirts were always catching in something. Hester had heard Mama tell Miss Daschner that one thing she agreed with those new, modern women about was that it would be more sensible and sanitary to raise skirts a little so they didn't sweep the streets and get into everything. That was the first time Hester knew that Mama had any ideas she did not get from Papa.

Hester came into the narrow room and stood at the door, breathing a little hard from her climb to the third story. Sometimes Mama seemed to be getting slightly deaf, but she had heard Hester knock, even over the noise of the machine. She told her to sit down and wait a minute.

Hester sat on the footstool, the way she had done as a small child. She smoothed her dress over her knees and folded her hands in her lap. The stiff taffeta bow that held her hair back felt hot and scratchy against her neck. She kept her eyes on Mama's foot working the treadle of the sewing machine.

In a few minutes Mama sighed, turned around, and spoke in her low voice. "Well, Hester?"

Hester raised her eyes and widened them. Neither she nor Hannah had the light, clear Herzog eyes, but Hester's dark ones were almost as large as Elsa's, and she had even longer lashes. "What, Mama?"

"Now, sweetheart." Mama's spectacles slipped down her nose. She pushed them back with one finger. In a few minutes it would happen again. Her nose was short and soft and seemed not to have enough bone to hold up spectacles. "You know very well what. You were badgering Mary, weren't you?"

"Oh, no, Mama. I only asked her where you were, and she got frightened. Everything frightens her."

Mama shook her head. Her gray hair was as fine as Ida's, but it was twisted too tight to come down, except for a few soft wisps around her face. "That's all that happened, Hester? You asked her where I was, and that made her jump up and run into the corner?"

"Well, I began asking her questions she could just answer yes or no, and I explained to her about shaking her head so she wouldn't even have to speak."

"Yes, I see. You explained. And did you touch her?"

"Oh, no, Mama. She may have thought—I don't know. Maybe she thought I was going to, but I didn't. I wouldn't. You told me about her being afraid people might hit her." Hester stopped to catch her breath. "Anyway, I told her I was very sorry if I frightened her. You can ask her if I didn't tell her that."

"Sweetheart, a lady doesn't ask a servant to verify what her daughter says." Mama sighed again. "That isn't the point, anyhow. I know you aren't always truthful, and it troubles me, but what troubles me more is that you aren't always kind."

Some awful sort of wave swept over Hester. She felt that if she called out through it, Mama would not hear her; nobody would hear her or see her. "Mama," she said. "Mama."

"I love you anyhow, sweetheart. I'll never stop loving you," Mama said. "But I'm your mother."

Hester ran out of the room and closed herself in one of the spare rooms on the floor below. She flung herself down on the unmade bed, on the damp, musty-smelling mattress, and cried until, like a small child, she fell asleep.

The clang of the supper bell woke her. She sat up, dazed for a moment, wondering what she was doing in this room. When she remembered, she was puzzled. Why had she cried like that? Why had what Mama said made her feel so awful? When she thought back on it, she didn't understand it.

"You're late, Hester," Papa said.

"I'm sorry, Papa." Hester slipped into her chair at the table. "I was reading and lost track of the time. Then when the bell rang I had to stop to wash my hands and brush my hair."

"My insistence on punctuality is not a caprice. Time is valuable. Anyone who is late steals it from others." Papa looked around the table at Mama, Ida, and Samuel, and then went on ladling the soup. "What were you reading, Hester?"

"*A Connecticut Yankee in King Arthur's Court,* Papa. It's the new book by Mark Twain."

During the soup, there was no general conversation. Papa thought people should concentrate on what they were eating. He said it was better both for the digestion and for proper appreciation of the food.

When everyone had finished, Papa rang a little hand bell and Mary came upstairs from the kitchen. She was still too timid to come into the dining room, so she stood outside the door and Mama handed her the dishes.

"Well, now, Ida, how did you spend the afternoon?" Papa inquired.

"I—well, it was very warm—"

"Look at me, kindly, Ida, when you address me."

Ida tried, but in a few seconds her glance slid away again. "It was —quite hot today, Papa."

22

"I'm not aware that I inquired about the weather. I asked you how you spent your time."

Samuel's eyes swiveled sideways, in Hester's direction. She blinked twice, not looking at him. If she looked at him, she would giggle.

"Arranging," Ida said. After a pause, she added, "Some of my things." She waited, but there was still only silence from Papa. "I also prayed," she said despairingly.

Papa smiled. Ida made a sound something like a groan. It seemed to echo around the table.

"Why do you say it with such trepidation, Ida?" Papa's eyes looked bluer when he smiled. His teeth shone. They were all his own teeth, though he was sixty-four years old. "Surely you don't think I would disapprove of orderliness or piety?"

"No, Papa." Ida smiled too. For a minute she looked almost gay. "No, of course not."

"You're a good girl, Ida," Papa said gently. "A good, sweet young lady." He glanced first at Mama and then at Samuel. "A person who fails to look others in the eye gives the impression that he has something to hide. Samuel?"

"Yes, Papa?"

Samuel was almost as afraid of Papa as Ida was, but it didn't show. There was something about Samuel that made everything he said sound a little mocking, even when he didn't mean it to be. Part of it was the way he looked, like an exaggeration of Papa. He was enough handsomer, enough more elegant, to seem slightly overdrawn. He smiled even less often than Papa did, but he always appeared to be suppressing laughter. His voice was still softer than Papa's, so soft that people often failed to hear him, and got the impression, when they asked him to repeat, that he did not, that he had said something altogether different, something impolite or shocking, the first time.

"You spent your afternoon in what manner?" Papa asked him.

"I and one of my friends took two young ladies for a drive in the park, Papa."

"One of my friends and I."

Samuel murmured something. Even Hester, who was sitting next to him, could not catch it. Papa leaned forward a little.

"What was that, Samuel?"

Samuel looked at him solemnly. "I was just repeating what you said, Papa. One of my friends and I."

Hester, though she had not quite heard him, did not think Samuel had repeated Papa's words. Papa did not seem to think so either. He stayed without moving for a minute, looking at Samuel, who looked straight back. Samuel always looked straight back. He had once told Hester that the way he could do it was to stare so hard that Papa's face went out of focus.

Papa sat straight again. "Perhaps your grammar will improve during the course of your studies at Columbia College, though I am not unduly optimistic. I sometimes think," he said, his eyes moving from Samuel to the others, "that there are young men, even future journalists, on whom education may be wasted."

Samuel seemed about to speak. Hester knew what he wanted to say. "The next time he talks about me being too stupid for college, I'm going to tell him, Hester, I swear I am, that I don't *want* to go to college. Not Columbia, anyhow. Harvard, yes, maybe, because I could get away from here, but he won't let me get away. He wants me here, working on the Paper. Shall I tell you something, Hester? I *hate* the Paper. And I swear, the next time . . ."

But Samuel said nothing now, and Hester knew he never would. Tomorrow he would go back to his summer job as a copy boy on the Paper, and in the fall he would go to Columbia and work on the Paper after classes, because that was the way Papa wanted it.

"What friend?" Papa was asking.

The only one who did not look bewildered at the question was Ida. She was smiling a little, her eyes somewhere between the sideboard and the china closet, seeing something that was invisible to the others.

"Samuel, I asked you a question," Papa said. "In the event that your hearing has suddenly failed you, I shall repeat it. What friend?"

"I beg your pardon, Papa?"

Papa sighed. "You say that you and one of your friends went driving this afternoon with two young ladies. I am asking you to tell me the name of the friend."

"Oh." Samuel brightened. "His name is Walter Lowenthal."

"Lowenthal." Papa nodded. The name was satisfactory. "What Lowenthal?"

"His father's name is Benjamin. I think he's a jeweler or something."

"A jeweler or something. Yes, no doubt. If he is not a jeweler, he

24

is certainly something else. Is your knowledge equally precise on the question of Mr. Benjamin Lowenthal's birthplace?"

Hester was sure Samuel would not know where Mr. Lowenthal was born. Papa was sure too. But they were wrong.

"He was born right here in America, Papa," Samuel said. "So was his father." A pink glow came into Samuel's cheeks. "His father fought the Indians under General Anthony Wayne."

"Ah! Your friend, then, is a fourth-generation American. Yes. Quite unusual." He smiled at Samuel, who turned even pinker. Papa did not often smile at Samuel. "One could wish, of course," he added, the smile fading, "that his grandfather had engaged himself otherwise than in slaughtering the natives of this continent."

A gentle shuffling behind the dining-room door announced Mary's arrival with the next course. Supper was the same every Sunday: soup, and the beef from which the soup had been made, served with hot potato salad. The beef was a special cut. Years before, Mama had explained to Mr. Mittelman, the kosher butcher, that it was the only cut to Papa's taste. Mr. Mittelman had begun calling it "Papa's Meat," and now that was how it was known to all his customers, who would come in and ask for "three pounds of Papa's Meat."

When everyone had finished eating, Papa took a cigar from his vest pocket, clipped off the tip with his cigar cutter, and lit it. He puffed at it for a few minutes, and then held it between his thumb and first two fingers. Hester thought he looked especially elegant and important with his cigar in his long, slender hand, the rich-smelling blue smoke framing his face. Mama and Ida did not like the smell; it made their eyes water. But Papa never noticed.

"I have an announcement to make," Papa said. "News of significance to all of us. Mama and I have known of it as a possibility for some little while. Now it is an accomplished fact, and time for you children to be informed. It has to do with your sister Elsa and her family." He looked around the table. "Ida? Are you listening?"

Ida wrenched her gaze from the opposite wall and rested it on Papa's ear. "Oh, yes, Papa." She swallowed. "Elsa."

"As you may or may not be aware," Papa went on, "I made it quite clear to Elsa before she married Nathan that I did not consider him a judicious choice as a husband." He looked at Mama, who had made a soft sound. "You wish to say something, Mama?"

"I was only wondering whether, under the circumstances, it was necessary to tell the children—" Mama raised one plump hand and then let it fall back into her lap. All at once she sounded like Ida. "About Nathan. Your opinion, that is—"

"What I am telling them, Mama, is the truth. I know of no reason to withhold the truth." He cleared his throat. "I did not expressly forbid your sister Elsa to marry Nathan. Naturally, if I had, she would not have married him. Perhaps I should have forbidden her, but I did not feel that I could, in conscience, do so. He was, after all, a Herzog. He was well able, at that time, to support a family. His age was not necessarily a drawback. Elsa has always been mature and sensible beyond her years and might have found a young man childish."

What, Hester wondered, was Papa leading up to? Had Nathan done something terrible? Was Elsa leaving him? Were they going to get a *divorce?* Hester felt a queer little inside shiver. She had never known a divorced lady, but she had read about them. The picture in her mind was nothing like Elsa. Maybe Elsa had changed, though. Hester had not seen her in a long time, not since she had brought her younger baby to New York right after he was born, six years previously. The girls in school would be intrigued by the idea of knowing somebody whose sister was divorced. They would ask Hester all sorts of questions. She would have to make them promise not to tell their parents.

"However, I warned her," Papa was saying. "I pointed out to her that Nathan is not a man of substance, not a man to perform well under pressure or to deal practically and forthrightly with problems. Elsa chose not to heed my warning. As a result, she is suffering now. In fact, she has been suffering for some time, but she chose not to tell us until the situation had deteriorated to the point where she could no longer conceal it from us. The point where Herzog & Sons, Nathan's store, is in bankruptcy and Nathan is all but penniless." Papa took another puff of his cigar and then held it up, examining it as though looking for some flaw in the leaves. "He and Elsa and the children are coming to New York next week to live with us."

"Only for a time," Mama murmured. "Only until Nathan can get on his feet again and they can find another place to live."

Papa did not seem to hear her. "I shall of course have to give Nathan something to do on the Paper," he said. "*If any provide not for his own, and specially for those of his own house, he hath denied the faith. . . .* That happens to be from the *New* Testament, but it is valid nevertheless, and I want you children to remember it. No matter what the provocation, we Herzogs do not turn away from each other. We take care of our own."

Hester was a little disappointed that Elsa was not, after all, going to be a divorced woman, but she soon forgot about that. It would be exciting to have four new people living in the house. Elsa was not really new, of course, but Hester could not remember her living there. She had been only three when Elsa married Nathan and went to Baltimore. It would be a change not to be the youngest any more, to have two younger children around who would look up to her and do what she told them.

"I'm glad they're coming, Papa," Hester said.

Papa smiled. "When everyone else is struck dumb, our Hester can be counted upon to speak." He looked around the table. "Not everyone who uses words well uses them also wisely. I have, for example, read good, clear prose employed in the interest of unworthy or trivial causes such as woman suffrage." He looked at Ida. "Would you care to have the vote, Ida, my dear?"

"Oh, no, Papa."

"No, I should think not." Papa's eyes went to the ceiling, where the smoke hung in the still air. "If you were to have it, Heaven help us!"

Papa was making fun of Hester as well as of Ida, but Hester didn't care. *Good, clear prose,* he had said. He had never complimented her like that before.

"Well." He pushed back from the table, took his watch out of his vest pocket to look at it, and then said what he always said: "Well, I must go and give New York the news for breakfast.

2

Elsa thought at the time, and often afterward, that she was never closer to despair in her life than on the trip from Baltimore to New York. The death of her first child had grieved her, but not for long. He had scarcely been a person, only three weeks old, and at nineteen she had plenty of time to have other sons. The last years in Baltimore, with the store's business declining and the debts accumulating, had been a constant worry, but she had never expected life to be easy, or thought of the good years as anything but a temporary respite, and she had been sure she could manage, whatever happened.

When Nathan told her he was giving up, that there was no way he could start over on his own, and that no one would hire a man his age, she accepted it. There was nothing else she could do. He was her husband.

"Write to your father," he said. "Tell him you have nowhere to turn but to him."

Elsa wrote. She was not as humble as her husband had suggested. "Nathan has many assets that will be of use in New York. Like you, Papa, I think he was miscast as a Baltimore merchant."

But even when the reply came, even while she was packing, Elsa did not believe they were going. It was only on the train that it finally became real to her. Then she felt that she had always known it would happen, the way an escaped prisoner knows he will be caught someday and taken back.

The motion of the train made David sick, and she could not get the smell washed out of his blouse. Rebecca ran up and down the aisle making a nuisance of herself, screaming with fury when Elsa stopped her.

"Oh, leave her alone. She is just naturally high-spirited," Nathan said.

If it was Nature that made Rebecca so difficult, it was Nathan who defeated any attempt to modify her behavior. He was entranced by her beauty and amused at her antics. When she became too trying even for him, he went somewhere else.

On the train, he got into conversation with a man traveling alone, and sat beside him during most of the journey. Elsa, struggling with the children, could hear them talking and laughing up ahead. Strangers always exhilarated Nathan, but he had been in good spirits anyway, ever since the letter from Papa telling them to come to New York.

"I consider this very fine of him, don't you, Elsa? Offering us a home, as well as promising me employment? Very fine and generous indeed."

"Nathan, we can find our own place. It doesn't matter where or how small. We can manage until things are better again."

"But that's foolishness, Elsa. Why should we scrape and scrimp in some miserable hole when your father is opening his arms to us?"

She could not answer him. She could not tell anyone what nightly in her childhood prayers she had asked to be forgiven for, and daily had repeated in her heart. After she married Nathan and went away, she almost forgot it. When her first-born child died, it did not occur to her—not then—that this was the punishment she had been expecting. But she thought of it on the train that was taking her back to her father's house. She thought of everything then.

The man Nathan had been sitting beside came down the aisle with his valise while they were still getting their things together. He was a tall, well-dressed man who sounded almost British when he spoke.

"Good-by, Mr. Hart," he said. "Pleasure to have talked with you."

"Good-by to you, Mr. Lowell," Nathan said. "A most enjoyable conversation for me as well."

Elsa was trying to get some of her smelling salts out of the bottle to rub on David's blouse. She did not look up.

"That man called you Mr. Hart, Papa," Rebecca said.

"Did he, *Liebchen?* I suppose he must have misunderstood me when I introduced myself."

Nathan followed the porter with their baggage along the platform, but after a moment he dropped back to where Elsa was dragging David and restraining Rebecca.

"That was a very fine gentleman, a Mr. Lowell from Boston," he said. "We had a most interesting conversation."

"Yes," Elsa said.

"It isn't always wise, Elsa, to give one's correct name to strangers on a train."

"No," Elsa said.

Her father had told her, before she married Nathan, that there was doubt about his being one of *their* Herzogs. Papa, trying to discourage her from marrying him, had implied that Nathan had wormed his way into the family through a deception. Out of curiosity alone—she would have married him if he had admitted to being Bluebeard—Elsa had asked Nathan about it. Nathan was astonished. He gave her a box full of records he had brought from Germany that clearly traced the relationship.

"Has Papa seen these, Nathan?"

"No."

"Why not?"

"I told him we were related. He accepted my word. The question of proof didn't arise."

Elsa had taken the records and shown them to her father, who had muttered over them for a long time before flinging them away from him.

"Well, I only hope," he had said, "that you don't live to regret that he is one of us."

At the time, Elsa thought of it as just another of Papa's unpleasant remarks, but there were moments later, like that moment on the station platform, when she understood what he meant.

She had met Nathan when she was eighteen, on a visit to relatives of Mama's in Baltimore. Several much younger men had been attentive to her, but she had seen at once that they were in no hurry and that Nathan was. He had considered himself a confirmed bachelor. The moment he saw Elsa, he reconsidered, and, at thirty-eight, suddenly heard time ticking on.

Elsa was perfectly clear about him. He was handsome, amiable, and charming. Even his accent, still heavy after all his years in America, had a certain charm. He was also well off, with no one but himself dependent on his earnings. Inside, he was like a doll she had had as a child, a doll through whose parted lips she had fed a cup of milk, only to have it gush out of the hollow body through a dozen sprung cracks.

It made no difference to Elsa. She had kept and cherished the doll, and she would keep and cherish Nathan. The night he played the piano and sang, "I Love a Little Yaller Gal," she knew it was the end of her time in that house in New York. She pretended to be angry, to mistake the meaning of Nathan's song, because she understood in some instinctive way that this would only intensify his eagerness, but she was elated. Her looks had never been important to her before, but now she saw the use of them. They had set her free.

Then, that day, twelve years later, she went back with Nathan and the children. She had been back before, on a visit, but this was different. This felt like forever. She was a grown woman, thirty years old, with a husband and two children, and yet it felt like everything all over again, Papa and the Paper and all of it, forever.

"The old house looks just the same," Nathan said.

She was surprised to see that it was like all the other houses on the block. She had remembered it standing alone, unique in its brownstoned, high-stooped ugliness, but they were all the same.

"Is that our house, Mama? Is that where we're going to live?" David squeaked.

Elsa felt that she might turn and run, simply run down the street and away. But Rebecca had already rushed up the steps and was boldly ringing the doorbell. Nothing frightened Rebecca.

It was strange, during that terrible time on the way back, how little Elsa had thought about Mama. Only when she and Mama were alone in the sewing room did all that part of it come back to her.

The sewing room was Mama's, except for the one day a month Miss Daschner, the seamstress, came. No other room in the house was closed off in the daytime, but this one was. To go in, it was necessary to knock on the door and wait for Mama's low, sweet voice to say, "Come." It was the one room Papa never entered.

"You are my right hand, Elsa," Mama used to say.

Elsa had not remembered that in years, but it was there, in the sewing room, like a sampler on the wall.

"Everything looks just the same," Elsa said.

"Yes." Mama pushed her glasses back from the end of her nose. "The old change slowly. A few more wrinkles and gray hairs each year . . ." She smiled down at her plump little folded hands. "Papa doesn't like me to speak of age. He frowns at himself in the mirror sometimes as if he can't recall who that is in there, that white-haired, white-bearded gentleman who looks somewhat familiar. I think he still feels like a young man."

"Was he ever a young man, Mama?"

Mama did not answer. She leaned forward and lightly stroked the fabric of Elsa's full gray skirt. "That's a becoming dress, a very fine silk. Is it new?"

"New? No, Mama, made over. I've become adept at making over."

"It's becoming," Mama said again. "Very pretty."

Elsa shrugged. "Nathan likes me to dress well."

They were talking as they always had, all around the edges of what they wanted to say. It reminded Elsa of the day before her wedding, when Mama had sent for her to come up to the sewing room, and Elsa had thought that at last she was to learn about the terrifying mysteries that awaited her the following night.

Mama had talked about the wedding and how gentle Nathan was and about the duty of a wife to please her husband. At the end she had taken Elsa's hands and said:

"Don't be afraid, sweetheart. Nathan is an older man. That will make it easier for you."

And Elsa, with no more idea than before what "it" was, had been too frightened by Mama's compassion to enjoy the wedding.

"Everything in your room is the same except the bed," Mama said. "I thought of having it painted. The new style here is to paint all the walnut wainscoting white; I don't know if it's the same in Baltimore. But then I decided you'd prefer it the way it always was." She blinked at Elsa over the top of her slipped-down spectacles. "I hope that's right."

"I've seen a white drawing room and thought it was quite cheerful," Elsa said. "I doubt if it would be restful for a bedroom."

She had become as adept at this way of avoiding a lie as at making over clothes. Mama had a picture in her head, and Elsa had no intention of disturbing it. Even as a child, she had not wept in Mama's lap, but alone.

"Anyway, you'll have a place of your own again before long," Mama said. "It's going to be lovely having you here, like old times, but I know it's only until Nathan gets back on his feet. I know a woman wants a place of her own."

"Has Papa said what he plans to have Nathan do on the Paper?" Elsa asked, though she knew it was a foolish question. Papa would not have said.

"Not exactly," Mama replied, which meant not at all. "But don't worry. Papa always takes care of his own."

"I know he does." Elsa was afraid, from the way Mama looked at her, that maybe the bleakness had come through into her voice.

But Mama only said, "He did mention that he wants to take Nathan down to the Paper right away, tonight, to show him through. At that time I'm sure he'll explain what work he wants Nathan to do."

It was Hester who said all the things Mama could not say, asked all the questions Mama did not know how to ask. Hester, the baby, who had never been a baby, any more than Papa had ever been a young man.

"Nathan's so *old*, Elsa. Isn't it funny to be married to a man that old?"

"I don't think about his being old or young. He's my husband."

"Does he make you happy?"

"I don't think anybody can make happiness for anybody else. I think you have to do it for yourself. Besides, I'm not sure what it means to be happy, or how important it is."

Hester pounded on the big bed that was the one new thing in the room of Elsa's childhood.

"Don't talk like that, like a book. That's the way people talk when they don't want to say anything. Why can't you tell me about you and Nathan? It's important for me to know."

Elsa laughed. Even at three, Hester had had that piercing impatience. Rebecca had it too, but hers was in part physical. Hester's impatience was entirely of the mind.

"How can it be important, Hester? Nathan and I aren't your concern."

"Everybody's my concern. I want to know everything about everybody."

"You ought to be on the Paper, then."

"When I'm older, I will be."

"How will you manage that? Surely Papa still believes ladies don't belong there."

"I'll make him see I do."

"Make him, Hester? Make Papa?"

Hester leaned back on her elbows and smiled at the ceiling. "He won't know it's happening, of course."

Elsa looked at her. Outwardly, Hester was more like Mama than any of them, shorter than her sisters, darker, her features softer. She had lost the baby fat she had had when Elsa had been there six years before, only to exchange it for the ripe plumpness of what, in Mama, was a comfortable maturity. But there was nothing comfortable about Hester.

"Papa always knows what's happening," Elsa said.

Hester sat up. No, her eyes were not like Mama's, not at all, except for the color. There was no softness in Hester's eyes. They were, it seemed to Elsa, eyes she had never seen before. But why did she expect them to be familiar? She had been away from this house a long time. All she knew of Hester was through the generalized blur of Mama's letters. "You don't like Papa, do you?" Hester said.

Elsa felt her legs go rigid. She said, "Hester," testing her voice, and then again, improving on it, "Hester, that's a sinful thing to say."

"Oh, sinful! You can't help it if you don't like him, can you?"

"He's my father."

"Well, it's not your fault. You didn't ask for him."

33

Elsa's temples were pounding. "Stop it. Stop. You'll be— punished."

"Why? I'm not the one who doesn't like him. I'm his favorite." She watched Elsa's face for an instant, and then leaned forward and stroked her skirt, just as Mama had done. "That's pretty. I didn't think you'd have clothes like that. Papa said you were poor."

"This is a dress from when we weren't poor."

"You must hate to be poor and have to live here on Papa's charity."

Elsa was afraid to ask whether those were Papa's words. She was afraid of what might come into her voice. She was afraid to know.

When Hester had left, she took off her dress and lay down on the bed in her dressing gown. Perhaps nobody would come for a while. The children were in the kitchen with Mary, the servant girl. Nathan had gone for a walk to familiarize himself with the neighborhood. Maybe if she could sleep a little, she would feel better.

Half sleeping, half waking, she thought of Ida, who had seemed diffident, ill at ease, as though it were she, rather than Hester, who had been too remote in age from Elsa to remember her. But Ida had always been strange. Her face, with its large, misty eyes, floated in the darkness behind Elsa's closed lids, wavered like a reflection in a wind-riffled pond, became the seamy face of old Rabbi Tallheimer, with whom Elsa had studied the Talmud in Baltimore. The rabbi's voice crashed in her ears, then changed to a whisper:

Whoso curseth his father, his lamp shall be put out in obscure darkness.

It was Nathan who was whispering. "I'll have to light the lamp, Elsa. A storm has come up. It's as dark as night in here."

Elsa sat up shivering. "How much cooler it is!"

"No, the breeze isn't coming this way, fortunately, or the room would be flooded. I got home just in time to avoid being drenched myself."

Home. All the Baltimore years gone with a snap of the fingers. Home is another man's house.

Elsa watched Nathan as he talked, telling her what he had seen on his walk, how pleasant the neighborhood was, how much he thought he was going to enjoy it. He was almost fifty years old, and looked older, but he talked like a man starting out in life, fresh and eager.

"Papa's taking you down to the Paper," she told him. "To show you through."

Nathan smiled a great deal. Sometimes, as now, she could tell he meant to stop smiling, but forgot. "When?"

"Tonight. Right after dinner."

Nathan got up and opened a drawer of the chiffonier that had been Hannah's during the years she had shared this room with Elsa. He took out a clean collar and began inserting the collar buttons. "I want you to come along," he said.

Elsa fixed her eyes on the spot at the back of his head where the gray-streaked hair was thinnest. "Why?"

"That's neither here nor there. I want you to come."

"Papa won't hear of it."

"Tell him you've always longed to see the inner workings of the Paper, and now that you're a married woman, and your husband will soon—"

"That would be a lie."

"Nonsense. The Paper? Of course you must long to see it all. I'm sure if Sigmund is convinced of that, he'll be glad to have you along."

"Please, Nathan—"

That was a mistake. He enjoyed indulging her on his own initiative, in his own way. To submit to pleading or cajolery was, in his mind, a show of weakness. "Let's hear no more about it." His voice edged on shrillness. "This is my wish, and I expect you to persuade your father of it."

"Very well, Nathan."

He turned his smile around to her. "That's my good wife."

But she would not lie. She told Papa that Nathan wanted her to see where he was to work, and that since she had never, in all these years, known what it was like down there where Papa made the Paper, perhaps he would let her come.

It was not a lie, but it felt like one.

"I don't make the Paper, my child," Papa said. "Not alone, at any rate."

If he had ever before called her "my child," Elsa did not remember it. She had tried for so long, so frantically, to please him, and then stopped trying, and now she had done it, at least for the moment, with what felt like a lie.

"I suppose there will be no lasting harm in your coming," Papa said, "as long as your husband approves."

"May I come too, Papa, please? I don't know what it's like down there where you make the Paper either."

"You certainly may not." Papa's voice was different when he talked to Hester, like someone else playing Papa's part. "I sometimes wonder," he said, frowning from face to face, "where a well-reared girl gets such hoydenish ideas."

It came back to Elsa like the sourness of a badly digested meal, that way Papa had of blaming them all for the fault of one of them. Perhaps none of the others minded.

Mama looked bland, but she had looked that way even when Papa threw the cushion at her, just before Hannah's birth. Elsa had been a small girl, but she still remembered screaming with fright, less at what had happened than at Mama's behaving as though it hadn't.

Ida was dreaming, deaf, away. Was she in love? That, apparently, was a condition that removed its victims from themselves, transferred them to some hazy otherness controlled by someone else. It was a state Elsa was grateful never to have experienced.

"Is it true, Papa," Samuel asked, "that one of the foreign correspondents at the *Times* is a woman?"

Samuel. He had been six when Elsa left to marry Nathan; a docile little boy, Papa's only son and pet. Mama's formless letters had suggested he was docile still, home a good deal, industriously and happily working for Papa and the Paper when he was not at school. But he did not seem docile to Elsa, this almost man with the Herzog fair good looks. And that he was no longer Papa's pet was evident in the soft contempt of Papa's answer.

"What absurdities are listened to by an undiscriminating ear!" he said to the others around the table. "Even if it were so, which of course it is not, the aberrations of Mr. Jones and the newspaper he is swiftly running into the ground would not be worth discussing."

Samuel reached for his water goblet and almost upset it. Something in the configuration of his lips, in the slight slant of his eyes, made him look as though he might burst into laughter. He murmured several indistinguishable words. Papa's white lion head turned slowly in his direction.

"What was that, Samuel?"

Samuel stared into his face. "I said I should have known better, Papa."

Elsa did not think that was what Samuel had said. She had a moment of painful excitement, a burning to know what the words really had been. But even if he would tell her, she could not ask him. The onus would not be lightened by sharing, only compounded.

"That particular lament," Papa said, "is the whine of fools."

Only Hannah had escaped, Hannah in her grand Fifth Avenue house with her prosperous husband who had no need of Papa or the Paper. Except that Nathan now sat in Hannah's place, nothing had changed. If Elsa closed her eyes, she could imagine that she had never left this table, that this was where she had lived her life, experiencing Papa. It was hard to believe that she had attended school, played with other children, visited with Mama, met young men, married, and gone away, existed in a world without him. Even here, he had been largely absent. She had scarcely seen him, except when he sat at the head of this table. Yet now that she was back again, it was as if she had seen no one and nothing else.

Papa hired a carriage to take them downtown. He and Nathan would have gone by surface car, but Papa considered a private conveyance more suitable for a lady. He pointed out the sights as they drove along.

"You must be bewildered by so many vehicles. Baltimore is, of course, a small town in comparison. We now have nearly one-and-a-half million inhabitants living on Manhattan Island alone. About ninety thousand more live in the Annexed District." He spoke as though he had spawned them all. "Of this total, more than fifty thousand read the Paper."

"That's truly amazing, Sigmund," Nathan said. "Wonderful."

It may have been only because the horses were traversing a patch of roughness in the road that Papa's voice shook. "You are not required, Nathan, to mouth meaningless admiring phrases," he said. "There is nothing wonderful about it. Reasonably satisfactory, perhaps. For the moment. But considering that a building we will soon pass houses a newspaper with a circulation of more than twice that number, and that the building we are passing now—" He broke off to indicate with his cane the tallest structure Elsa had ever seen. "That's the Tower Building, eleven stories high."

"Is it safe, Papa?"

"Oh, yes, quite safe. We have others even taller now. Skyscrapers, we call them."

Again, as with the population, he had the air of a creator.

"The Tower of Babel was only seven stories high," she said.

He seemed, for an instant, almost confused. "Ah, well, yes. I, for one, have nothing to fear, however," he said, and made the clogged, throaty sound that was his version of a chuckle. "The Paper comes into being in a four-story building."

"I am most eager to see it," Nathan said.

Papa looked at him as if he had forgotten he was there. "Are you? Yes, I remember that eagerness of yours. You were once eager to see Herzog & Sons."

Elsa could not bear Nathan's sick smile. Words rushed from her throat, from her mouth, like vomit. "Don't belittle Nathan, Papa. Your largess gives you no right to do that. I won't have it."

The words seemed to hang there, echoed by the clicking rhythm of the horses' hoofs. Papa's face was turned toward her, but she saw it as a shadowed blur. Nathan murmured something that she did not try to hear. It felt like a long time before Papa spoke.

"So," he said softly. "Our gentle, compliant Elsa won't have it. She tells her father what he has and has not a right to do. Is that how you train your wife, Nathan?"

"Certainly not. I'm as amazed as you are." Nathan looked at her without quite finding her eyes. There were lines in his face that she had never noticed. Most of the Herzogs wore well, but Nathan would soon appear as old as Papa. "Elsa, I'll speak to you later," he said.

"I hope you will." Papa held his cane at his side like a scepter. "I hope you will express your gratitude."

"What?" Nathan said, but Papa did not repeat himself.

"A good wife cleaves to her husband, and does him good all the days of her life."

"What?" Nathan said again.

"Elsa," Papa said, "you will now kindly apologize for your disrespect to your father."

The words belonged to her childhood, as ritualistic as the mumbo jumbo of words of "counting out." "I apologize, Papa."

"Your apology is accepted. How you will make amends to a Higher Power is, of course, between you and your conscience."

But her conscience, that iron ingot that had weighed her down for as long as she could remember, felt, for the moment, marvelously light.

Papa pointed out another tall newspaper building on a street called Park Row. A little farther on, the carriage stopped in a much narrower street, in front of a large, squarish structure of dirty gray stone. A steady, pounding noise came from somewhere in its bowels.

"What you hear," Papa said, "are the presses, the sound that carries the news from all over the world to nearly sixty thousand readers."

Inside, it smelled of newsprint, cigar smoke, and perspiration. Papa led the way to the second floor, leaping up the stairs ahead of them. Elsa, trying to hold her skirts above the filthy steps, went slowly, but Nathan lagged behind her. Once, when she turned to look at him, he muttered:

"I hope I'm not expected to know anything about this business. After all, I'm a merchant."

As though he had somehow been wheedled into leaving a thriving store and contributing his talents to an unknown venture.

"Of course you're not, Nathan. Simply look and listen and say very little, and it will be all right."

"I suppose he'll have to start me somewhat down the ladder. For the look of things. But he surely won't keep me there long, a man of my age who headed his own enterprise for so many years."

"Come along," Papa called from the head of the stairs. "Step lively!"

They entered a room so fogged with smoke that at first Elsa could scarcely see. It appeared to be filled with nothing but rows of empty desks, like a deserted schoolroom. Gradually she made out the shapes of men. One was writing in pencil, jabbing at the yellow paper in front of him as though he were attacking it. One was operating one of the three typewriters in the room. It seemed to Elsa that he went more slowly than the man with the pencil. Two men sat expectantly near the two silent telephones. Several in the back of the room were reading rival newspapers or, apparently, dozing. Some of the men were in shirt sleeves.

"Good evening, gentlemen," Papa said.

Elsa would not have been surprised to see them leap to their feet and respond in unison, but there was only a generalized rumble. They did rise when they saw her. Those who had shed their jackets put them on.

"As you see, I've brought visitors. My eldest daughter, Mrs. Nathan Herzog, and her husband, a distant cousin, who will soon be coming to work on the Paper. They're here to observe us, so kindly continue in your usual manner. This, Nathan, Elsa, is the newsroom

at that period in the ordinary day that we speak of as the doldrums."
It was Papa's voice, and yet not. There was something added to it,
some vibrancy she did not recognize. "Boy!" he called.

Elsa did not see where he came from, the young man about Samuel's age who rushed up to Papa. "Yes, Mr. Herzog?"

"You're the new copy boy, aren't you? Jimmy?"

The young man blushed. "That's right, Mr. Herzog."

"Get me the layout of page one, Jimmy." The boy darted off.
"Willis!" Papa was across the room now, talking to the man with
the jabbing pencil. "Is this the material on the Sherman Silver
Purchase Act? Is it ready? I'm going to run my editorial on the new
tariff legislation in the next edition."

No one, now, read or dozed. Papa was everywhere. He had not put
down his cane, but used it as a pointer or rested it on someone's bent
shoulder or thumped it on the floor in rhythm with something he
was saying. When one of the telephones rang, he was there before
the man at the desk had picked up the receiver, saying, "Well?
What?" before the man had finished hanging up.

He had forgotten Elsa and Nathan. Elsa had the curious feeling
that he had never known them, this man who bounded around the
room, his face alive, his voice resonating. She felt that if she called
him "Papa" he would look at her in astonishment, and chuckle, and
it would not be the hard, clogged chuckle she knew.

She leaned against the wall, feeling a little faint. No one in the
smoky, stuffy room had offered her a chair. The men at the desks
behaved as Papa had told them to do, as though she were not there.
Nathan, his mouth set in what looked more like a rictus than a
smile, was trying to follow Papa around. Or the man who resembled
Papa.

In fancy, she had had an image of a vast, empty hall, with Papa a
Juggernaut in the center from which the Paper issued. In childhood
dreams, she had confused the Paper with a tunnel into which Papa
stepped at the end of their street and disappeared. Sometimes she
had followed him in, run after him and, lost in the darkness,
pounded on the walls of the tunnel until she woke. She had dreamed
it occasionally even when she was grown, even after she was married.
Now she thought she might wake to find herself in the tunnel, this
the dream.

"Well, Elsa, I trust you are convinced." It was Papa's soft, dry voice, Papa's marble face. He had come to where she stood supported by the wall. "I trust you have had enough."

Elsa straightened. "Of what, Papa?"

"Judging by the pallor of your cheeks, I am certain you are ready to concede that this is no place for a woman." He turned to Nathan, who was at his heels. "Kindly take your wife home now, where she belongs."

"You're not coming, Sigmund?"

Papa looked at Nathan as though he had gone mad. "I? Leave at this hour? How do you imagine New York would have the news for breakfast?"

3

College was not as unpleasant as Samuel had anticipated. Being a Columbia man gave him prestige in the right quarters. Also, he discovered early that he did not have to work hard to get by. He had a good memory and the knack of stretching a little knowledge. It occurred to him for the first time that perhaps he was clever, or could be if he put his mind to it. He had other objectives. Still, he was entertained by the thought that his father might be wrong about him. Papa did not like to be wrong, even when it was to his advantage.

Samuel also found it entertaining that Papa approved of his best friend, Walter Lowenthal. Papa admired Walter's brilliance and was pleased by his manners and his family background. It surprised him that a young man of this caliber had chosen Samuel as a friend. Papa intimated that it must be less because of Samuel himself than because there was a certain cachet in associating with the son of the editor of the Paper.

What amused Samuel was that if Papa had known a little more about Walter, he would have whistled a very different tune. Whenever Papa praised Walter's virtues at the dinner table, in order to point out to the family Samuel's lack of them, it was all Samuel could do to keep from exploding with delight.

Walter was in Samuel's class at Columbia, though he was a year younger. He worked no harder than Samuel did, but the knowledge he acquired was formidable. By some process not available to ordinary minds, he could skim over a page, or half listen to a lecture, and absorb the content, analyze it, and repeat it with his own embellishments, either orally or in writing, never pausing for a word. These gifts gave him the necessary free time to explore and introduce Samuel to some of the diversions New York had to offer adventurous young men.

It was Walter who got hold of the girls for those relatively innocent Sunday drives in Central Park, when he was seventeen and Samuel eighteen. Samuel would not have known where to find such girls, but Walter's precocity was not limited to book learning.

"You have to pretend to think they're ladies," Walter explained. "Some of them almost are. Not in our sense, of course, but as gentile girls go." Samuel understood that. Everybody knew gentile girls were much likelier to be fast. "The thing is to treat them very politely until the last minute."

The last minute, on those Sunday drives, involved a tentative search under the carriage robe, followed by varying degrees of protest. Samuel's partners were rarely as co-operative as Walter's.

"You've got to be commanding," Walter told him. "Women like that."

No one who lived with Papa could be commanding.

To begin with, Walter *looked* commanding. He was very tall and broad and, even at seventeen, slightly stoop-shouldered; somehow the stoop made him even more imposing. He had a large head with an immensely high forehead, deep-set blue eyes that were as piercing as Papa's, and a great prow of a nose. No one could have thought him handsome, yet women were more attracted to him than to Samuel, who could see for himself his own good looks. Samuel resembled Papa, but in him everything was fined down, so that while Papa, too, looked commanding, Samuel did not.

There were moments when Samuel wondered whether he really liked Walter. Even at seventeen, Walter was overpowering. His energy was inexhaustible. He was so full of plans and projects that just hearing about them made Samuel tired. Sometimes, away from him, Samuel's head seemed to echo with the sound of Walter's voice, the endless flow of his words, and he would almost wish that he need not ever hear them again.

But Papa would never in the world believe that it was Samuel who had tired of Walter.

Besides, Samuel could not have done on his own the things he did with Walter. He could not even have thought them up.

Walter's store of information was a constant source of astonishment to Samuel. He was not yet out of his teens when he first took

Samuel to a house in the Tenderloin district. The way to recognize such houses, he explained, was by the board fences enclosing the stoops. He pointed out one that he said was operated by a woman named Georgiana Hastings, whose clients included some of the wealthiest and most prominent men in the city. Someday, he said, when he and Samuel were older, and wealthy and prominent themselves, they would go there.

Walter walked down the street with his long, rapid gait, his head thrust a little forward, looking, as he always did, eager to get on to whatever was next. Samuel, imagining grimy skin and used sheets, hung back.

"Come along. What are you dawdling for?" Walter called.

"Where did you hear about this place?"

Walter gave his loud, baying laugh. "Don't you read your own newspaper? Your father's been crusading against the Tenderloin for weeks. He might as well publish a directory."

It took some doing to work on the Paper two nights a week and every day during the summer without reading it, but Samuel managed. He read what was necessary for his classes, and little else. But even if he had been a great reader, he would not have read the Paper.

"What does Papa say about it?" he asked Walter, hurrying to catch up with him.

Walter quoted at length as they went along. Samuel was sure he was repeating Papa's exact words. "A rot at the core of our fair city, a source of shame to every decent citizen . . ." Samuel stopped listening and tried to match his shorter stride to Walter's. He would say he preferred the lights out. In the dark, the state of the sheets or her skin would not matter. A few moments earlier he had been terrified of being unable to function, but now he felt certain encouraging stirrings.

"I know Papa would appreciate what I'm doing tonight," he said, "believing as he does in firsthand reporting."

The joke lasted them most of that year. Lasted Samuel, at any rate. Walter's amusement at the conceit that their visits to the brothels, saloons, and gambling houses of the Tenderloin were in the interests of journalism could not have been as exquisite as Samuel's.

"Where do you and Walter go all the time?" Hester asked him one night. "Out with girls?"

If he could have told anyone in the family, he would have told

Hester. It was not, of course, a fit subject for discussion with a decent Jewish girl. Still, he thought Hester would have appreciated the humor of it.

"Yes, that's right," he said. "Out with girls."

"Where do you take them?"

"Oh, the Plaza, Delmonico's—"

"On the wages Papa pays you? Piffle!"

"You don't know how much Papa pays me."

"I know Papa."

It was a warm spring night. Hester had followed Samuel out to the front stoop, where he was sitting while he waited for Walter. According to Mama, refined people did not sit on their front stoops in full view of every passer-by, but Mama was not home. She and Elsa had gone across town to visit Hannah, who had sent the carriage for them.

"Anyhow," Hester said, "I wish you'd take me sometimes."

Samuel was not listening intently. He was thinking about Flora, who danced in the variety show at the Haymarket. She was prettier and daintier than the other girls, and she had shown a preference for him. "You're more elegant than your friend," she had told him. "I'm fond of elegant men." Samuel had dressed with even more care tonight than he usually did, in preparation for seeing her again.

"Don't be silly," he said to Hester, thinking, as he had several times before, that *elegant* was an adjective that suited him very well. "A man doesn't take out his little sister."

"I'm not little. I'm almost eighteen," Hester said. "Elsa was engaged when she was my age. Besides, it wouldn't be you who would be taking me out; it would be Walter."

Samuel emerged from his reverie and looked at her. It seemed to him that he must not have looked at her for some time, because he had not noticed that her hair was up and that she had grown as high as his shoulder. He supposed she was pretty—all the Herzogs had good features—though his own taste ran to slim, well-proportioned girls with delicate skin. Walter, on the other hand, preferred the big, buxom type—

What was he thinking of, comparing Hester, his sister, with the girls from the Tenderloin?

"You're blushing," she said. "I don't know why the idea of my going out with Walter should embarrass you."

"It doesn't embarrass me. I was just wondering why you should have any interest in him."

Samuel was wondering, on the contrary, why Walter should have any interest in Hester, but he was too fond of her to say so.

"He's the only man I know who's smarter than I am," she said. "I don't think my brains would bother him."

"Well, but you see, Hester, brains aren't exactly what men look for in a girl," Samuel explained in a kindly voice. "You might do better to conceal yours a bit and cultivate other, more feminine traits."

Hester sat down on the stone balustrade, hitching her skirt up to her surprisingly slim ankles. Samuel frowned and looked away. "I won't do any such thing," she said. "If men don't like it, they can lump it. That's why I want you to arrange something with Walter. I think he's different."

"I assure you he's not. Anyway, pull down your skirt, because here he comes now."

Hester laughed. "I thought it was my brains I was supposed to conceal."

At the last minute, though, as Walter came bounding up the steps, she did, to Samuel's relief, pull down her skirt.

"Good evening, Walter," she said, looking straight at him, the way another man might have done.

Walter swept off his hat and bowed. "Good evening, Miss Hester. I'm happy to see you looking so well."

Walter, Samuel noticed, was carrying a walking stick with an ornate silver head. He had finally won at cards after weeks of bad luck. Samuel, who had done better, had loaned him the money to play. Walter had made no mention, after the game, of paying him back, and Samuel wondered whether to bring it up. If their positions were reversed, he was sure Walter would let the debt go, probably forget all about it. Walter was careless with money, as though it had no importance—an attitude that shocked Samuel. But he decided there was not much use in asking Walter for repayment, because by now the money was certainly gone. The cane alone would have taken most of it.

Hester and Walter were exchanging small talk to which Samuel did not listen, but now he heard Hester ask:

"Do you think Mr. Harrison will be re-elected?"

"It's possible," Walter said. "One can't overestimate the stupidity of the people. If some of them happen to understand the danger of

our protective tariffs, or of purchasing too much silver, they don't realize we'll never get rid of such evils while Harrison is President."

"Why don't you stump for Mr. Cleveland, then?"

"I? A man still in college? I won't even be old enough to vote until
the election after this one."

"Well, write something. Maybe Papa will print it in the Paper."

Walter was stooped over her, his head thrust even further forward
than usual, so that his face was only a few inches from hers. He
looked, Samuel thought, like an eagle about to peck.

"Write an article in support of Cleveland, do you mean?"

Hester nodded. "Explaining about the tariffs, too, and the danger
of undermining the gold standard. Saying the McKinley Act and the
Sherman Silver Purchase Act ought to be repealed. Papa's of the
same opinion, so he'll consider it favorably." She leaned back in such
a way that the fabric of her dress tightened against her body. "I'd
write it myself, but Papa would never put it in the Paper. He thinks
it's unladylike for a woman to engage in journalism."

Samuel knew very little about the relative merits of Mr. Harrison
and Mr. Cleveland, and nothing at all about the tariffs. He could
not imagine how Hester knew, or why she should be interested. But
of two things he was certain. One, Papa would no more print anything Walter might write on the subject than he would anything of
Hester's. Two, Hester was perfectly aware of it.

"I want a word with my sister. A family matter," Samuel said to
Walter as they were preparing to leave. "I'll catch up with you." He
waited until Walter was halfway to the next corner before asking
Hester what she was up to. "He'll do it, you know. Write about all
that you were discussing. Tonight, probably, after he gets home, even
if it's almost morning. What are you going to tell him when Papa
sneers at it?"

"Papa won't sneer at Walter."

"Well, maybe not, but he won't print it either. He wouldn't print
it if Mr. Cleveland wrote it himself. Nobody but Papa writes editorials for the Paper. You know that as well as I do. Why let Walter
think—?"

"Never mind. I have my reasons. And don't you say anything to
Walter or I'll never speak to you again, Samuel Herzog!"

"He's my friend. I don't like him to be deceived."

"It will turn out well for him, Samuel, I promise." She trailed

46

Samuel part way down the steps. "And remember about getting him to take me out. That's very important."

Samuel raised his eyebrows. "Important!"

"Yes, very. As much so for Walter as for me. You needn't believe it, but it's true." She put her hand on his sleeve. "I'll give you a pair of real gold cuff links for your birthday. With your initials."

"You needn't bribe me," Samuel muttered. "Anyway, where would you get the money for gold cuff links?"

"Never mind. I'll get it."

She would, too, Samuel thought, as he went to join Walter, though he had no idea how. And if she gave him the cuff links for his birthday, Papa could not rant about his foppish tastes. But persuading Walter to take Hester out was another matter. Samuel could think of nothing that would make him willing to do it.

As they rode down Ninth Avenue toward the Haymarket, Walter talked steadily about the article Hester had suggested he write. He was totally caught up in the idea, as Samuel had known he would be, as he was caught up in any new plan or challenge. If he remembered it had come from Hester, he ignored the fact. It was all his now. The words slid off his tongue. He put down his walking stick to gesticulate with both hands, picked it up again to use as a baton marking the rhythm of his phrases. He sat on the edge of his seat, the forward thrust of his head suggesting that he was looking for the best spot to leap to from the moving carriage.

"After it appears in the Paper, it could well be expanded into a book, Samuel. The definitive book on Acts of Congress that have placed our country in peril. It would add interest, I think, to explore the minds of the men behind such Acts: John Sherman, in competition for fame with his brother, William Tecumseh, for example—"

Samuel, feeling as battered by Walter's voice as though it were a fist, interrupted in desperation. "It sounds brilliant. It will probably be a great success. Hester was telling me, before you came, how much she admires your intelligence."

Walter frowned. "Hester?" For a moment he seemed not to know whom Samuel meant. He was quite capable of leaving it at that and going straight on with his monologue. But then his face changed and he gave a little nod of approval. "Yes, well, she's rather intelligent herself, especially for a girl."

"She finds you attractive, too."

"Yes," Walter said again, as though that were only to be expected.

"I think she'd like to come out with us some evening. That is, you would take Hester and I'd take some other girl."

Walter seemed not at all startled. He folded his large hands over the head of his walking stick and looked out at the street for a moment, appearing to observe the passing carriages.

"A concert," he said finally. "That would be suitable." He looked at Samuel. "What girl will you take?"

Samuel, who had been prepared for a struggle, and probable failure in the end, stammered foolishly, "Do you mean—are you consenting to take Hester?"

"Why not? It's time we spent an occasional evening with respectable girls. After all, we'll have to settle down before long. We can't sow our wild oats forever."

"That's a dismal thought," Samuel said.

The projected evening sounded dismal too. Music in an Eighth Avenue concert hall was one thing, but Samuel knew that was not the kind of concert Walter meant. And a girl who would scream if he as much as put his arm around her waist.

"I don't know any girl to take," he said.

"You see? That's what I mean. We've neglected that aspect of our lives." Walter had a way of pushing his lips in and out when he was thinking. "It's too bad I have only brothers. But I'll find you someone."

"I wish I could take Flora. Dress her appropriately, have her leave the paint off her face, and pass her off as a nice girl—" Samuel chuckled. "Do you suppose—?" For an instant it seemed conceivable, the kind of prankish idea he and Walter often thought up. Then he sighed. "No, I guess not. Not with Hester along."

"Certainly not," Walter said severely. "I'm trying to make you understand that it's time to look for a girl who can do you some good."

Samuel was not sure he knew what Walter meant, but he did not ask. The carriage had drawn up to the Haymarket, whose doors were open to admit a party of boisterous middle-aged men. Loud laughter and louder music issued from the brightly lit interior. Samuel could hear a voice he thought was Flora's singing:

> "Georgie, Georgie, pray give over;
> Georgie, Georgie, you're too free. . . ."

If Flora was as interested in him as she had appeared to be the last time, she would do him the only kind of good he cared about.

Sometimes, in a mood of passing penitence—especially after he had lost a sizable sum at the poker table—Samuel blamed Papa and the Paper for his profligacy. If he had not had to endure that equivalent of penal servitude, it would not have been necessary to seek relief in such extravagant pleasures.

"When you're a reporter, Samuel, you'll like it better," Mama said.

He had never told her how he felt about the Paper. He had never told anyone except Hester. But Mama was surprising. She seemed to know little about anything outside her immediate household and social concerns. She talked little. When Papa was around, she was so overshadowed by him that it was almost as though she did not exist. But suddenly she would say something like this.

"He's never going to let me be a reporter," Samuel answered.

"Who is *he?* The cat's father?"

Samuel laughed. "Mama, I'm not a little boy any more."

"That doesn't mean you shouldn't have respect for your father."

"All right. Papa is never going to let me be a reporter."

"Of course he is. He's grooming you to take his place someday."

"Oh, no, Mama. He wouldn't want me to take his place. Not me."

"Who else? You're the only son, aren't you? He won't turn it over to anyone outside the family, so who else? Nathan? No." She patted his hand. "You'll be a fine newspaperman, the same as Papa, once you put your mind to it."

There was no use telling her that he did not want to put his mind to it; that even if Papa made him a reporter the next day it would make no difference. In fact, there were certain advantages in staying a copy boy. It was demeaning, but it was easy. He carried copy and ran errands and, when Papa was not there, played cards with members of the staff. Most of them liked him and tried to treat him like one of them, as if his name were not Herzog.

On a rival newspaper, maybe he could have stood it. He might even, like most copy boys hopeful of advancement, have written something once in a while; he could write rather well if he had to, though only his professors at Columbia knew it, and he was not, after all, especially interested in, or fitted for, anything else.

But he hated the Paper. He hated the squat old building near Park Row, the rickety staircase and the big, dusty, noisy newsroom; the call of "Boy!" like calling a dog; the smell of printer's ink and sweat; and Papa, immaculate and cool, everywhere Samuel looked, everywhere at once; and waiting, with his breath lodged somewhere between his lungs and his throat, for the dog call on Papa's lips, Papa's special way of exploding the "B" so it sounded like spitting . . .

"Boy!"

"Yes, sir?"

Once, Samuel had said, "Yes, Papa?" and the blue eyes had frosted over with a kind of glaze of non-recognition. "In this office, boy, I am your employer, pure and simple."

Samuel did not make that slip again.

"Boy!"

"Yes, sir?"

"Take this copy to the composing room. And see you come straight back."

Papa often went down to the composing room himself to make changes, but he had never appeared when Samuel was there. He had no way of knowing why Samuel, when sent, did not quickly return. Yet Samuel felt that Papa did know. At the age of fourteen, while saying his nightly prayers, it had come to Samuel that the forbidding and omniscient God he was trying to appease bore a strong resemblance to Papa.

Old Charley, the foreman, was the reason why Samuel lingered in the composing room. Charley had once worked on the *Tribune* for Horace Greeley. He claimed to have been the only man who had ever been able to decipher Greeley's handwriting, and that when Greeley sent a note accepting his nomination for President of the United States, Charley had to be called in to read it. Charley had an endless supply of stories, some fantastic, some believable, many slyly off-color. Samuel took to jotting the best ones down in a little black notebook that he always carried with him. It became the basis for his reputation, in later years, as a raconteur and wit.

"It seems to me I told you to come straight back from the composing room."

"I'm sorry, sir. I had to obey the call of nature."

Even Papa could not command nature. Instead, he had a mechanical copy box installed which, upon the ringing of a bell, slid copy directly to the composing room. Soon after that, he began sending Samuel out to cover fires and accidents.

"I told you Papa would make you a reporter," Mama said. "Now you'll be happier."

"Yes, Mama," Samuel said.

He had never been so miserable. Even as a child, he had diligently avoided physical discomfort. Now he had to go out in all kinds of weather, stand near burning buildings in the heat of summer, stand in frigid December winds where a skater had fallen through the ice of the Central Park lake, stand in the rain, stand in the snow, stand, stand, until he had to wear larger shoes to relieve the aching of his elegantly slim feet.

The things he had to look at sickened him. He never became hardened to the sight of dead or maimed bodies. Sometimes he shut his eyes. Once, he pretended to have been at the scene when he was not. Samuel did not know how Papa could tell that his story was imaginary, but he could.

"Where did you go tonight, Samuel?"

"To the fire on Fourteenth Street, Papa. You have my story."

"I have a fictional story about a fictional fire."

"No, Papa."

"No? In that case, rewrite the lead. 'Soon after nine o'clock tonight' is not the correct way to begin a newspaper story."

He made Samuel rewrite the lead twice, and the body of the story three times.

"Now you have learned to write a passable story," Papa said finally, and tore the sheets of copy slowly into pieces. "Since you are not paid for practicing, however, but for reporting the news, you will receive no salary for today."

Papa did not treat the rest of the staff, not even Nathan, the way he treated Samuel. Nathan worked on the rewrite desk, cutting unneeded verbiage out of the copy reporters turned in. He complained (but not to Papa) that it was monotonous, unrewarding, and a misuse of the talents of a man who had owned and managed a successful department store. But he did not have to be out, standing, in terrible weather, seeing terrible things. And although Papa largely ignored him, he did not persecute him.

"It must be wonderfully exciting to work on a newspaper," Myra Fleischman said.

Myra was the girl who had gone to the concert with Samuel, Walter, and Hester. She was the daughter of a friend of Walter's mother, a fresh-faced girl with freckles and a wide-mouthed smile. Hester said she looked like a horse, but Walter told Samuel that was jealousy. Sisters, he said, often resented girls who interested their only brothers. Samuel did not know how Walter knew this, but he thought it might have been true, because Myra really did not look like a horse.

"I suppose it is exciting," he said to her. "One is in on all the great events of the day before the public hears anything about them. Of course, I've been at it for so long now that I don't think much about that aspect of it. I just do my job."

"My papa says yours is one of the most influential newspapers in New York."

"I suppose it is."

"He says you can influence what will happen in the whole country, who will be President, things like that."

Samuel did not mind talking about the Paper to Myra. When he was with her, it became something else. Papa shrank. Samuel changed into a bold and brilliant recorder of dramatic events, a molder of public opinion. He liked the way her eyes fixed on him with total attention and something close to awe. She had large, rather pretty eyes, though he could never remember their color when he was away from her.

All that summer, Samuel and Myra and Walter and Hester went out together, attending concerts, the theater, the opera, and riding in Central Park on Sundays. Toward the end of the summer, Myra let Samuel hold her hand in the carriage, though she kept her glove on.

Samuel seldom made plans. It seemed to him that things happened of themselves, or through the machinations of other people, and that they would happen regardless of him. He had not sought out Myra, but now she had become a quite agreeable part of his life. He had not sought out the girls in the Tenderloin either, nor gone there to look for gambling casinos, yet once introduced to these pleasures, he took them with enthusiasm. Such plans as he made were principally concerned with juggling his time so as to accommodate Myra, the Tenderloin, the Paper and, for the few remaining months of his senior year at Columbia, his studies.

He was graduated just below the middle of his class. Walter, who was in the top quarter, regretted somewhat wistfully that he had not bothered to take first place so that he could have given the valedictory. The two of them celebrated their liberation for several jubilant nights, but the night the brothel on Forty-sixth Street and Seventh Avenue was raided, Samuel was there without Walter.

"I want to speak to your father about something," Walter said when he came to the house. "I suggest you go on ahead, because it may take some time. If I can, I'll meet you later."

Samuel did not ask what Walter wanted to say to Papa. Walter and Papa often had long discussions, usually about politics. Discussions, especially about politics, bored Samuel. He left them to it and hurried off, hoping to find unoccupied a particular dark, petite girl who was said to be French and therefore endowed with certain exotic accomplishments.

Raids in the Tenderloin were periodic and well publicized, conducted for the purpose of exhibiting the earnest efforts of the police to clean out the district. Customarily, everything proceeded in an orderly manner, with a minimum of pain or embarrassment for anyone. The girls were arraigned in Jefferson Market Court, bailed out by a Tammany district leader, and back at work in a few hours. No one took any notice of the patrons.

On this occasion, however, an enterprising young reporter from the *Herald* recognized Samuel and scented a pungent tidbit that Mr. Bennett, his scandal-mongering editor, would relish.

Papa spent the first part of every business day closed off in his office reading through the other New York morning newspapers. It did not take him long. He was one of those readers who could glance down the middle of a column of type and see every word in the column. At intervals, if he came upon an item that the Paper had omitted, or found a piece of writing to use as an object lesson, he would erupt into the newsroom, waving the page in question, and either hold forth to the room in general or single out an appropriate member of the staff.

On this occasion, he stood empty-handed in the doorway until he caught Samuel's eye. Samuel, while waiting for an assignment, was engaged in figuring certain odds relevant to filling an inside straight. Such problems entertained him. He had covered one side of a sheet of paper with jottings and begun on the other side when he felt a compulsion to raise his head. His eyes collided with Papa's, jolting him out of his seat.

"Yes, sir?" he said, though Papa had not spoken a word.

"Kindly come into my office," Papa said.

Papa sat down behind his desk. Samuel stood in front of it. He looked down at Papa, but that was not how it felt. Papa's face extracted his juice, diminishing him like a squeezed orange. Silently, Papa handed him a page from the *Herald*.

The phrases seemed to separate themselves from the page and shimmer in the air before Samuel's eyes:

. . . seen leaving the premises in haste . . . clothing dishevelled and awry . . . apparent disagreement with his father's opinion that it is "a source of shame to every decent citizen. . . ."

It was a long time before Papa spoke.

"Until now, you have done nothing to make me proud," he said finally. "Now you have disgraced yourself and humiliated me and the Paper."

Samuel's head began to pound so violently that he thought it might break apart. He distinctly saw himself lean across the desk, grab the lapels of Papa's coat, hurl shouted words into the rock-hard face until it cracked. So distinctly that when Papa said: "Well? Have you nothing to say for yourself?" he was bewildered to find that he had not moved or opened his mouth. The words he spoke had no conscious connection with his will.

"I'm sorry."

"For what, Samuel? For being found out?"

"For going to a place like that and—and embarrassing you."

"Why did you go?"

"I—a man has needs, Papa."

"Ah!" Papa sat back with a little smile. "Are you now presuming to instruct me in the characteristics of a man? Because if you are, I had better inform you that your knowledge of the subject is sadly limited." The smile dissolved. "A man has needs, yes. But a *man* does not succumb to them like an animal. A *Jew* heeds the warning in Proverbs that the house of a harlot 'is the way to hell, going down to the chambers of death.'" He paused, and his voice, which he had not raised, grew softer still. "Aside from this—aside from the effects of your behavior on me and on the Paper—I wonder how, having so defiled yourself, you can ever again look Mama or your sisters or Myra Fleischman in the eye."

Myra. What did Papa know about Myra? Samuel could not recall that he had ever met her.

"You appear stunned," Papa said. "Did you imagine it could be kept from them? If they don't read about it themselves, it will be told to them by others. Mr. Fleischman may well forbid his daughter to see you again—that is, assuming she would have any wish to do so." Papa, at a sound from Samuel, sat forward again. "What did you say?"

"Nothing, Papa. That is, I only said this was the first time."

"Ah! And if you were to kill someone, would you imagine that your guilt was mitigated because you had never done it before?"

"No, Papa."

"Very well. Now. I consider it only just, in view of the damage you have done to the Paper, that you be required to make some material amends. To that end, your salary will be reduced eight dollars a week. This will also serve to put the iron into your moral fiber that I fear it lacks. On the money that remains to you, I think you will find it impossible to indulge yourself."

Samuel waited. "Is there anything else, Papa?"

"No. You may go." As Samuel reached the door, Papa said, "Incidentally, Walter Lowenthal will be coming to work on the Paper tomorrow, as a political reporter. I'd like you to show him around and acquaint him with the routine of the newsroom."

Samuel was too shaken by what had gone before to mask his surprise. "Walter? On the Paper? He never told me he wanted to—"

"Of course he didn't," Papa interrupted. "Walter is too honorable to use his friendship with you. He said nothing whatever until I made the suggestion. Only at that point did he admit that one of the dearest wishes of his life has been to work on the Paper. I think he will go far." Papa paused. "In fact, if certain changes and improvements fail to occur, I can envision his eventually succeeding me."

Samuel knew when to call a bluff. "Mama says you'll never turn the Paper over to anyone outside the family."

"I never will," Papa said. "Walter is soon to become a member of the family. He asked me last night for your sister Hester's hand in marriage."

Walter was indignant when Samuel suggested that he had fooled Papa about how honorable he was.

"It's absolutely true," Walter said. "I've never tried to trade on our friendship. I've impressed your father simply by letting him judge my merits for himself."

"You wouldn't have had the chance if we weren't friends. You wouldn't even have met him."

"Are you suggesting that I deliberately sought you out and cultivated your good will so I could meet your father? I didn't even know, at first, who you were. I certainly had no idea then that I wanted to work on a newspaper. It never occurred to me until very recently."

Samuel laughed. "You told Papa it has been the dearest wish of your life."

"Well, it has been. I didn't tell him for how long."

They were in Samuel's room. Samuel was half lying on the bed, his feet on the floor so as not to crease his trousers. Walter paced, his head thrust forward, his large hands making large gestures. One of Samuel's professors at Columbia, named Brander Matthews, had once described to the class Sir Henry Irving's appearance and grandiloquence as Hamlet. Samuel thought the actor must have resembled Walter.

"How long was it?"

"Oh, probably the idea has been in my mind for some time, without my being aware of it. I've admired your father, enjoyed talking to him, found myself fascinated by the things he has told me about the Paper, its romance, its power. Then, recently, I decided to jot down some thoughts I had about the issues in the coming presidential election, and it developed, rather astonishingly, into what was obviously an excellent editorial. Naturally I showed it to your father, not with any notion that he would publish it, since I knew he writes all the editorials for the Paper himself, but for his opinion. He told me that my talent and ability were unmistakable, and asked me whether I had ever considered becoming a newspaperman. It was at that moment I realized this was, indeed, the dearest wish of my life."

Walter paused in his pacing long enough to give Samuel the beaming look of a man who has brought something, whether a piece of work or a good meal, to a satisfactory conclusion. Samuel looked up at him in astonishment. "That editorial," Samuel said. "Isn't that the one you were talking of expanding into a book?"

"Yes, of course. I forgot you knew about it."

"Did you also forget it was Hester's idea, not yours? And that it was she, not you, who showed it to Papa?"

Walter waved an impatient hand. "What possible difference do these petty details make? The important thing is that I've discovered my true vocation."

"I wonder," Samuel said, "about that moment of discovery. Was it before or after you decided to marry Hester?"

"I don't understand what you're driving at."

"Well, this all started with a discussion of how honorable you are."

Walter scowled. Now, with his big head between his hunched shoulders, he looked, Samuel thought, not like Sir Henry Irving but like an angry, intelligent baboon.

"Now, listen, Samuel, I don't care for your insinuations."

Samuel grinned, stretching his arms lazily over his head. "There's no need to get in a state. I'm pulling your leg. Do you think it matters to me if Papa is fooled by you?"

"But I won't stand for your saying I've fooled him. I have never, for one minute, tried—"

"All right, all right. I don't want to quarrel." Samuel raised himself on his elbows to peer out the window at the fading daylight. "Look, it's almost sundown. Doesn't it say something in the Bible about not quarreling on the Sabbath?"

Walter's belligerence slid away. "It says not to profane it, which I suppose amounts to the same thing." He spoke absently, began pacing again, and then stopped and sat down in a chair with his hands on his knees. "Listen, Samuel, have you given any thought to how you'll manage on the pittance your father has cut you down to?"

Samuel shrugged. "What can I do, except try to be lucky at poker?"

"That's a start. It's not a permanent solution."

"There is no permanent solution."

"But there is."

Walter hitched his chair closer to the bed. He lowered his voice, although there was no one but Samuel anywhere nearby. Papa had not yet come home. The women were downstairs making preparations for the Sabbath. Walter, who always spoke rapidly, now put on a spurt of speed that made it difficult for Samuel to follow him. In a little while they would be called downstairs for the lighting of the *Shabbes* candles and the recital of the blessing, and then they would go with Papa to the synagogue and return for the *Shabbes* meal, which Walter had been invited to share with his prospective new family. He seemed to believe that if he did not tell his scheme to Samuel first, he would never have another chance.

As far as Samuel could make out, Walter had read in the Paper about a meeting of stockholders in a horsecar company at which somebody had complained of the high annual figure for feed for the horses, and an officer of the company had explained that this was due to the unavoidable waste of oats by spillage in the feeding process. What was obviously needed, according to Walter, was an automatic oats dispenser that would release measured amounts as the horses ate. Not being of a mechanical turn of mind himself, he proposed to turn over the invention of this device to a young man he had heard of who tinkered with such things as a hobby and would certainly be glad to come in with them for a small percentage of the profits.

"We'll begin by selling it to livery stables at a cheap, introductory price, and wait until the horsecar companies begin clamoring for it. At that point, we'll be able to charge almost any amount we like. Our profits, on an absurdly small initial investment, will be enormous. We'll be rich, Samuel." He was so close, now, that Samuel could feel his breath. Walter, when he was not pacing as he talked, habitually imprisoned his listener with his physical presence. "You'll be able to do anything you want—even leave the Paper."

Samuel tried to sit up, but Walter was in the way. The best he could do was move his head a little to the side.

"This initial investment you're talking about," he said, "is to come from my winnings at cards? Suppose I lose."

"We can't advance our plan," Walter said irritably, "by supposing that."

"Well, if I do win, and the investment is all mine," Samuel said, "then I should get the major share of the profits."

Walter was shocked to his feet. "You surprise me, Samuel. You really surprise me," he said. "You must know that the major investment—without which there would be no profits, no business, in fact, no automatic oats dispenser at all—is my brains. The money means little to me compared to the realization that you, my friend, my future brother-in-law, want to cheat me out of it."

Samuel slipped off the bed and put on his coat, pulling down his shirt sleeves to show a few inches of stiff, glossy cuff, adorned with the gold links Hester had given him for his birthday. He brushed his blond hair vigorously with two silver-back brushes and, appearing to smile at Walter in the mirror, smiled at his own handsome image.

"Walter, you never know when you're being joshed," he said. "If I win any money, I'll need it just to keep myself in collars and have a little fun."

Walter began talking again, but Samuel scarcely listened. Most of what his friend had said was already drifting from his mind. *You'll be able to do anything you like—even leave the Paper.* Those words he remembered. It was too bad, he thought wistfully, that Walter's ingenious schemes were never feasible. In a week, this one would be forgotten and another would be on Walter's indefatigable tongue.

"I've tried to give you a practical solution," Walter was saying now, rather sulkily. "If you refuse to accept it, I really don't see how you expect to get out of your dilemma."

"Something will happen," Samuel said. "It always does."

He had no idea at the time, or even until almost the last minute, what it would be. When he received the invitation to attend a ball in honor of Myra Fleischman's eighteenth birthday, his reaction was surprise. He had not attempted to see Myra since his name had appeared in the newspaper in connection with the Tenderloin raid. He had never expected to see her again. After he accepted the invitation, he had moments of such alarm that, though he seldom perspired, moisture seemed to stream from all his pores. What if Myra and her family heard the account for the first time from guests at the ball, and he was publicly ordered to leave . . . ?

He did not seriously suppose this would happen, but he knew too little about the Fleischmans to be certain. Although he had, of course, called on Myra and met her parents, they were hazy figures to him. He was not one to observe or to occupy himself with what did not immediately concern him. Until the night of the ball, it had occurred to him only fleetingly, if at all, that Myra's father was a very rich man.

That night, in the gilded ballroom of the Fleischmans' Fifth Avenue house, Mrs. Fleischman's diamond necklace blazing under the lights from the crystal chandelier, a nine-piece orchestra playing for the quadrilles and cotillions, and French champagne flowing, even Samuel could not remain unconscious of Mr. Fleischman's wealth.

It did not show on Myra, except for the string of pearls she wore for the occasion, a birthday gift from her father.

"Papa likes to spoil me," she told Samuel. "I don't really care very much for jewelry. Shall I tell you a secret?" She stood on tiptoe to whisper into his ear, creating a warm, tickling little breeze. "I like your gift the best of any I received."

He had given her, at Walter's suggestion, a book of Tennyson's poems. Young ladies, according to Walter, liked the idea of poetry, even if they did not read it.

"I've always thought of you," Samuel said to Myra, "as someone with a sensitive appreciation of the finer things in life. I'm glad my judgment proved correct."

He could see that she was as impressed with this speech as he was himself. Her eyes took on a look that made him think of caramels on a warm day. Why could he never remember that her eyes were the color of caramels? When she came into his mind, it was her freckles and her wide, somewhat toothy smile he recalled, and the way she sometimes looked at his mouth as he talked, as though watching eagerly for the next word.

"I was beginning to believe you had stopped thinking of me at all." Her eyes were cast down now, and she spoke in a low voice. They stood in a relatively secluded corner of the ballroom, between dances, but still Samuel had to bend his head close to hear her over the chatter and the laughter. "I was beginning to wonder if I would ever see you again."

Samuel mumbled something about his increasingly important and time-consuming duties on the Paper, but she went on as though he had not spoken. He was uneasily aware of a woman at a little distance who had smiled in their direction and begun whispering to her companion. If she was whispering about him, about his exposure in a brothel, surely she would not have smiled in that benign way.

"Papa says you showed a gentlemanly delicacy," Myra was murmuring.

"Pardon me?"

"In staying away for a time." Her eyelids fluttered up at him and down again. "Is that why you did stay away, Samuel?"

He could not believe she meant what she seemed to mean, but he said, "Yes, certainly."

Myra gave a soft little sigh. "I'm glad. I was afraid it might be because you no longer cared for me."

"Oh, no!"

"Then you needn't be bothered about that other business. I won't be."

Samuel still doubted that she could be referring to something of which young ladies were surely ignorant.

"Really not?" he asked cautiously.

She shook her head. "Papa explained to me that when a man cares for a nice girl, those other women protect her purity before marriage."

It took Samuel a little while to untangle this. By the time he had sorted it out, he understood that events were shaping his life again and that all he had to do was go along. At that moment, it looked to him as though his imprisonment by Papa and the Paper might be over. It was all to the good that Myra took his enthusiasm as evidence of the passion he had properly diverted elsewhere until the appropriate time.

4

Sigmund sat in his office, blinking at the hole he had just made with his fist in the front page of the New York *Journal*. Only once or twice before in his life had his anger exploded into even such minimal physical violence. He found it difficult to believe himself capable of it.

His abhorrence of violence, in fact, was the cause of his fury at the letter Mr. Hearst had printed in his outrageous newspaper. Between that scoundrel and his equally unprincipled rival, Mr. Pulitzer, both of whom would go to any lengths to increase their circulation, the country was being steam-rollered into a senseless war. Most of the other newspapers were accessories, copying, if they did not invent, the exaggerations, the misstatements, the inflammatory headlines in the *Journal* and the *World*. Sigmund's editorials, vigorously opposing intervention in Spain's squabbles with the Cuban revolutionists, were cries in the wilderness.

He sighed, pieced together the torn center of the *Journal*'s front page, and went on reading.

Before long, he knew, Walter would telephone him from Washington to comment on Hearst's publication of the letter. Walter was enamored of the telephone, using it not only for the communication of news but on any pretext that occurred to him. Sigmund had sent him to Washington because it was the obvious spot for a political reporter. He had also sent him there to be rid of the sound of his voice. In the latter purpose he had failed. Walter used the telephone constantly and interminably, and because frequently there were golden nuggets of information to be mined from the verbiage, Sigmund had to pay attention.

This time, as Sigmund had expected, Walter began by pointing out that the Paper could have scooped Mr. Hearst on the letter. Since Sigmund already knew the facts that Walter would review for several moments, it was not necessary to listen. He put the receiver down on his desk and went on with his work, occasionally, when the crackling from the receiver paused, offering an ambiguous "Yes" into the mouthpiece.

Walter, who was as ingenious as any of Hearst's ferrets, had known and told Sigmund two days before about the letter from the Spanish minister in Washington to a friend in Cuba expressing contempt for President McKinley. Walter's disappointed amazement at Sigmund's refusal to print it had throbbed over the wire at eloquent length.

"Yes, Walter, I'm aware that it may have news value," Sigmund had said when he could inject a word. "The sort of noxious news value of which the Paper will never take advantage while I am alive . . . noxious, yes, you heard correctly. The public is sufficiently inflamed against Spain without reading a Spanish denigration of the President to incite it further."

"The public will read it willy nilly, Papa." Sigmund could not have said why it irritated him to be called "Papa" by Walter. "If we don't print it first, others will."

"I am responsible only for what I print. I will never print anything deliberately designed to lead our country into war."

Now Sigmund, judging by the sounds emerging from the receiver on his desk that Walter had approached the end of his peroration, put the instrument to his ear.

". . . and our circulation will suffer," Walter was saying.

"No doubt. However, it will revive. Have you anything for the next edition, Walter? If so, I'll have you switched to Nathan. I'm rather busy at the moment."

This reminded Walter that he did not like the way Nathan tampered with his stories. What he did to them, according to Walter, amounted to mayhem. "Absolute mayhem, Papa. He cuts the heart out of them. Nathan, if I may say so, has no sense of the beauty or rhythm of a phrase."

Sigmund did not remind Walter that beauty and rhythm, especially when there was as much of it as Walter spouted, sometimes had to be sacrificed to the demands of space and import. Walter was in many ways a brilliant newspaperman, an asset to the Paper, and it was necessary to put up with him. "I'll see to it," Sigmund said, which was vague enough not to be a lie.

Walter rang off finally, but not before mentioning, as he had on other occasions, that Hester was becoming increasingly restless, that she insisted she was cut out for something other than to be a housewife, and that a letter from her father, whom she greatly respected, might bring her to her senses.

"I realize she has an excellent mind and may someday find uses for it outside the home," Walter said. "At the proper time I will certainly not object. But first, very naturally, I want a family, a son, Walter, Jr., and she must understand—"

"It's regrettable," Sigmund broke in. There were times when an interruption was the only possible defense against Walter. "However, I'm afraid it is no longer my responsibility to keep your wife in line."

Sigmund cradled the receiver and pushed the telephone away as though it were Walter himself. He had thought, in the beginning, that Walter was the man to manage Hester, but he had been wrong. Probably no one could—no one except perhaps her papa—and he was not going to try to do it by mail. She should certainly have settled down and had one or two babies by now, after four years of marriage, but Hester had never done anything simply because she should.

It was not possible, of course, to understand God's ways, but in the matter of Sigmund's children, He seemed especially inscrutable. He had given to Hester the qualities a father had reason to expect in a son, and withheld them from the only male child of Sigmund's whom He had permitted to live. Sigmund had tried to make a man of Samuel. He had never been soft with him. He had never allowed him to shirk a task because it was distasteful to him, nor given him a penny or a promotion that he had not earned. Nothing had changed Samuel. He had been a weak, lazy, devious boy who cared for nothing but his own gratification. He was the same as a man: a pleasure-seeking dandy, unwilling to exert even enough energy to get out from under his wife's thumb.

From the day Sigmund had started the Paper, he had determined that it would never pass out of the hands of his family. It was so provided in his will. Now, at an age when many men were mumbling by their firesides, he had no apparent successor. Even if Samuel had had the ability, or the wish, to become anything beyond an adequate telegraph editor, Sigmund would have had no confidence that he would not somehow circumvent the will and divest himself of the Paper for the immediate gains. Nathan, surprisingly, was a first-class copy reader, who could put other men's thoughts into clear, sharp newspaper prose, but he had no ideas of his own, no initiative, no capacity for leadership. And Walter, for all his brilliance, lacked the stable judgment to run a newspaper and control its policy.

Sigmund, who had already lived beyond his three score and ten, would simply have to live considerably longer, in the hope that one of his descendants would provide him with an able, dedicated successor.

The existing possibilities were not encouraging. Elsa's son, David, gave evidence, at fourteen, of turning into another, less affable, Nathan. Sigmund exerted what influence he could, but he was doubtful of its effect on the curious, stubborn strain of weakness that seemed to run through the male Herzog line. The only other male thus far was Hannah's nine-year-old Robert, who would no doubt go into his father's banking business. Samuel and Myra had no children. Sigmund suspected that Samuel was sterile; it would have been in character. Ida . . .

The only explanation for Ida was lunacy, though there had never been any such thing in either Sigmund's family or Ada's. He had thought her a good, biddable girl, with no defects more serious than a tendency to dream too much, and a disinclination, which he had put down to an excess of feminine shyness, to look people in the eye. One morning, soon after Hester's marriage, she had not come down to breakfast. Ada had found her bed not slept in, her clothes and possessions gone, and a note on her dresser—the note, surely, of a madwoman.

> *Dear Mama and Papa:*
> *I am going out West to join the Bahai faith. "Ye are all the fruits of one tree and the leaves of one branch. Walk, then, with perfect charity, concord, affection and agreement."*
> > *Your loving daughter in Abraham,*
> > *Christ, Mohammed and Baha Ullah,*
> > > *Ida*

Since then she had written once or twice a year, almost as briefly, saying she was well and happy and enclosing what Sigmund supposed were religious tracts; he had them burned without reading them. Had he not felt she was suffering from brain fever, and so not responsible for her actions, he would have disclaimed her as his daughter and forbidden mention of her name. In any case, there was nothing to be hoped for from Ida.

If only Hester had been born a boy! Sigmund had heard his own father say that his children were all alike to him, fingers on his hands; to prefer one over the other would be a sin. In the beginning, Sigmund had prayed that he might feel the same fondness for Elsa, Hannah, Ida, and Samuel as he felt for Hester, but he had given it up. If God had not wanted him to have a preference, He would not have made Hester so unlike the others. Why He had created her female, only He knew.

The only one of his grandchildren who had any obvious promise was also female: Rebecca, daughter of Elsa and Nathan. She was a striking beauty in a family of handsome people—tall and black-haired with fine green Herzog eyes and a naturally queenly carriage. She was also intelligent and spirited. As a young child, she had been almost unmanageable. Once, when Sigmund had pinned her arms to prevent her from throwing the bric-a-brac from the mantelpiece in a temper, she had spit in his face. Her explanation, which he had demanded after she had been suitably punished, still made him chuckle after seven years.

"How else could I defend myself? It wouldn't have done any good to kick you. I had no shoes on."

He had not, of course, chuckled openly then, but he had had a feeling she knew.

If she married a man who could handle her, he might be right for the Paper, but such a man was even less likely to exist than in Hester's case. Hester was attractive enough, but Rebecca, even at sixteen, had the kind of beauty that turned sensible men into fools.

Still, she was probably Sigmund's best hope. It was partly because of her that he had kept Elsa and Nathan in his home all these years. The arrangement suited Nathan, who could not have afforded to live so well and was happy to avoid the responsibility of maintaining a house. Whether or not it suited Elsa, Sigmund did not know. Elsa kept her own counsel. She was an admirable woman, a great help and comfort to Ada, but if she revealed herself to anyone, it was not to Sigmund.

He looked up briefly from the newspapers, which he was able to scan and assimilate while part of his mind went elsewhere. From the window of his office he could see across to Park Row and the buildings of some of his competitors. Others had moved farther uptown.

He was often urged to do the same. His staff complained that this old structure, which had housed the Paper since its inception, was too cramped now and was crumbling around them, that it was a poor monument to a great enterprise. But Sigmund liked the familiar. When, on occasion, the lights failed at night, he could walk unerringly through all these rooms, from floor to floor, as though it were daytime. He liked that. He saw no reason to spend money on a more expensive street. He had always been willing to spend it for the finest available equipment, and for higher salaries to attract the best staff he could get. But a building was a shell, an outer covering. The only monument the Paper needed was the Paper itself.

Yes, he would have to live many more years if he was to find someone in the family to carry it on. Fortunately he was descended from long-lived stock. He did not feel seventy-two. It surprised him to come upon his face in the mirror, still firm and only lightly lined, yet unmistakably the face of an old man. He could not remember seeing his beard and hair turning gray, but they were pure white now. He was old, yet it did not seem to him he had ever had any greater vigor, moved with any more elasticity. He could still, if need be, work ten hours a day. Most of his contemporaries were dead, but he must not die for a long time. Surely God, Whom he worshiped so faithfully, would see to it.

There was a knock on his door, permissible at this hour only for urgent news or business that could not wait. Before he could acknowledge it, the door opened and a modishly dressed young woman, plump, but with a tiny waist, walked boldly in. Her gown was of some stiff, silky brown fabric, its sleeves ballooning at the shoulders and tight at the wrists. The lower part of the floor-length skirt was adorned with five layers of ruffles.

"What's the matter, Papa? Don't you recognize me?"

Sigmund sat back in his chair and looked up at her. She had Ada's sallow skin, like all the Herzog women except Rebecca, in whom it was modified to a warm olive, but at the moment her cheeks were becomingly flushed.

"I'm not accustomed to receiving fashionable young ladies in my office," he said. "I'm also understandably startled to see you here when I assumed you were in Washington. Especially so since I spoke to your husband on the telephone not an hour ago, and although he mentioned you, he didn't say you were on your way to New York."

"He didn't know," Hester said.

Sigmund raised heavy white eyebrows. "You'd better sit down and explain yourself. Be careful of your gown. There's a great deal of dust in a newspaper office."

"Oh, my gown!" She plumped down into a chair with scornful unconcern. "Walter bought it for me. Heaven knows what it cost, but price never troubles Walter. He says it's essential for the wife of a man in his position to dress well." She gave a small, unladylike snort. "I'm sure I don't know what position he's talking about."

"It's in very questionable taste, Hester, for a wife to speak so slightingly of her husband."

Sigmund had always been stern with his children, as his father before him had been with his. Unlike his father, he had never raised a hand to any of them. They nevertheless had had, and still did have, a proper awe of him. All except Hester. Hester, and now his granddaughter Rebecca, against whom his severity invariably glanced off and lost its shape.

In this instance, Hester laughed. For him, her laugh was teasing, affectionate, but he had heard a less attractive note in it for others.

"You're old-fashioned, Papa. Wives aren't so docile any more. This is almost the twentieth century."

"I'm well aware of what century it is. I'm also aware that there is, and always has been, a raffish element in our society that attempts to pave the way for any sort of loose attitude or behavior by suggesting it's the modern trend and those who don't go along are behind the times." He stopped to take a breath, thinking that he was becoming as prolix as Walter. "What I am not aware of, still, is what you are doing here without your husband's knowledge."

She looked down at her skirt, took a bit of the fabric between her thumb and forefinger as if to test its quality, and then let it go and looked up at Sigmund again. "Papa, I'm miserable in Washington. I don't know anyone. Walter is hardly ever home. I spend most of my evenings alone. The other evenings we go to receptions or dinners, where the men discuss politics after the ladies have withdrawn. The ladies discuss their social conquests. One asked me recently whether I had ever been to any of Mrs. Astor's annual balls, and when I said no, that as far as I was aware, there were no Jewish families among the Four Hundred, she turned pale." Hester's lips twitched. "I told her she needn't worry about my being Jewish, that it wasn't contagious. It was the only moment of the evening I enjoyed, but Walter said I might have damaged his career."

"So you might. A newspaper correspondent must be in favor with the right people. Often a remark dropped at a reception or a dinner can furnish the nucleus for a story no other journalist has wind of."

Hester flounced in her chair and frowned. For the moment, in spite of her fashionable clothes, she looked to Sigmund more like a child than a young woman of twenty-three.

"I can't simper along with those people. Those stuffed dolls. Those—those *shiksas*. I won't, Papa."

Sigmund sighed. "Hester, you are inventing troubles to fill your time. Go home and have a baby. Busy yourself with raising a family and running a household and you won't have the leisure to brood about nothing."

"Papa, listen," she said. "Please, Papa." She leaned forward, toward him. The deepening flush in her cheeks, the brilliance of her eyes, made her seem almost as pretty as Rebecca. "I will. I'll have a baby. But I need a little time first. A year? That isn't much, is it?"

"Time for what, Hester?"

"To live."

"To live," he repeated, nodding slowly. "Of course you must realize I haven't the faintest notion what you are talking about, why you are pleading with me. Apparently for permission, but to do what? Whatever it is, you're a married woman. The man to ask for permission is your husband."

She was still sitting in the same feverish attitude, impervious to his lack of sympathy, no doubt sensing its falseness. "You do know, Papa. You must know what I'm asking you. Please," she said, "let me work on the Paper. Let me live at home with you again, and work here. I'll do anything. Sweep the floor, if you think that's all I'm good for. You don't even have to pay me. I just want to be part of it. Part of the Paper. When the year's over, I'll go back to Washington and have a baby and be a good wife to Walter. I'll even be sweet to the *shiksas*."

He answered her in his softest voice, because now he was angry. She was a poor target for his anger, because it was not her fault, but he could not be angry with God.

"I think you must be as mad as your sister Ida," he said. "Even if I were not as opposed as you know me to be to women in newspaper offices—especially one of my own family—what you ask would be outrageous. You're suggesting that I encourage you to leave your husband's house by harboring you in mine, giving you work to do as a

68

substitute for your responsibilities to your husband. What sort of man—what sort of father—do you take me for?" He brought both hands together on the top of his desk. "Go back to Walter, Hester. I have nothing more to say to you."

He had never succeeded in deflating her, and she was not deflated now. She relaxed, giving her shoulders a little shrug, and said: "All right, Papa. I'm sorry. I thought there was no harm in trying." She paused. "Would you mind very much if I stayed overnight? The train ride was long and tiring. I'd hate to have to go straight back."

"You should have thought of that before you came."

"There's only one more train. It will be dark when it gets to Washington. A young lady alone—"

"Did you bring a valise?"

"Yes."

"Where is it?"

"Well—I left it off before I came here."

"At the house?"

She nodded, smiling.

"Hester, I have work to do. I'll see you at supper."

When she had gone, he tried to reach Walter at the Washington office, but he was not there. In any case, it was only a question of time before Walter would reach him. Sigmund put the episode out of his mind until then. He had a newspaper to run.

Most publishers were no longer editors as well. Some never had been. Many, though they knew good journalistic writing when they saw it and could instantly detect an inexact word or an awkward phrase, could not themselves have written a paragraph fit to appear in the first-class newspaper.

Sigmund was competent to do the work of almost any man on his staff. They were good men, and he rarely had to interfere with them, but he still kept his hand in, whether it was to suggest an idea for a news story or to put a head into type in the composing room. There was no aspect of getting out a newspaper that did not enthrall him still. But above all, the direct and regular expression of his views in the pages of the Paper seemed to him imperative. It was his newspaper, and it was only proper that he should be its spokesman, not only through the policies he had instituted and controlled, not only through the columns others wrote and he endorsed, but with his own words.

He let no one read his editorials before they appeared. Some said it was because he could imagine no valid criticism, and would not accept any if it were offered. It had never greatly troubled Sigmund to have his motives misunderstood, as long as he himself knew they were creditable. As long as God knew. In this case, he wanted nothing he wrote to influence the presentation of the news. Every man on the staff was aware that an expression of opinion in a news story was grounds for instant dismissal, but it was possible, for a reporter who had just read Sigmund's viewpoint, unconsciously to slant a story to conform with it.

He glanced up at the framed statement of purpose that hung on the wall over his desk: the same statement that hung on the wall of every room in the building—even the pressroom in the basement and the composing room on the top floor—and appeared each day under the masthead of the Paper.

Independent of any man or party, to print all the news accurately, impartially, intelligently, decently, and without fear.

Every newspaper in the city affirmed some similar purpose. Few adhered to it. But Sigmund's readers had learned that the Paper meant what it said. They had had their initial lesson eleven months after the first issue had appeared.

Those had been the days when personal journalism was at its peak. Sigmund, outraged by the hypocrisy of an editor on another newspaper who crusaded against the city's vice in his columns while himself enthusiastically indulging in several forms of it, had written a denunciatory and explicit editorial on the subject. The editor, a notoriously hotheaded man, had rushed to Sigmund's office shouting that his reputation and his marriage had been ruined by Sigmund's lies.

"If they are lies," Sigmund had suggested coolly to the purple-faced editor, "you should by all means sue me for libel."

"I'll do better than that!" The man had plunged his hand into his pocket and brought it out with a gun, which he had proceeded to wave under Sigmund's nose. "I'll see to it that you don't ruin anyone else's life with your damnable moralizing. I'm going to shoot you, and any jury in the country will say I'm justified."

Whether he would actually have pulled the trigger or was merely trying to frighten Sigmund (in which purpose, at least, he thoroughly succeeded) no one ever knew. His professed intention, announced in a loud and carrying voice, brought several men hurrying from the newsroom to overpower him. He had gone on threatening vengeance as they dragged him out.

Sigmund had reported the entire incident in the Paper the following day, repeating and enlarging upon his charges against the man and giving definitive proofs.

"In like manner," he had concluded, "this newspaper will continue fearlessly to offer viewpoints and report the news, in accordance with the statement of purpose under the masthead. If for so doing, any individual writer becomes the victim of violence, another will instantly take his place in the pursuit of that purpose."

It had been some time before Sigmund felt entirely safe, but the editor, even if he had intended to shoot Sigmund, evidently accepted the suggestion that he would then have to shoot every member of the staff in turn, and had no stomach for such massacre. His newspaper survived the episode by less than six months, and he himself faded from the journalistic scene. In the same period, the Paper's circulation soared.

But integrity was not always so profitable. The *Journal* and the *World*, vying with each other in screaming, colored headlines, catering to the public appetite for scandal, violence, and melodrama, were leaving the Paper behind. It was not only the ignorant masses who slavered over their sensational and often inaccurate columns. Yellow journalism—so called after Mr. Hearst's shapelessly garbed comic-strip character "The Yellow Kid"—evidently had appeal for even some of the well educated, who bought and read the vulgar newspapers when their peers were not looking.

Sigmund editorialized steadily against the folly of sending troops to liberate Cuba from Spanish control. The *Post* and the *World* played on the sympathies of Americans for a people seeking their independence, whipping up hatred for Spain with letters such as the one from the Spanish ambassador in that morning's *Journal*. When the facts were too inconclusive, they invented suitable horrors. Today Mr. Hearst had seven ships in Cuban waters filled with correspondents adept at concocting stories out of fragments of truth. There was no telling what Mr. Pulitzer would do tomorrow. In this cynical battle for readers, Sigmund lost circulation daily. The circulation of the *Post* and the *Journal* had gone beyond a million.

Sigmund heard the exact figures at the daily noon staff conference in his office. This was not, as on some newspapers, a conference of the editorial staff alone. The business manager and advertising director were always present, and, on occasion, the mechanical supervisor or the foreman of the composing room.

"Every department head on the Paper has a voice in how the Paper is run," Sigmund had originally told his staff. "The only difference between you and me is that I have the *final* voice."

He had intended a touch of humor in making his point, but no one had smiled. People did not expect humor from him, or know how to take it when he attempted it. Few were altogether at ease in his presence. There were publishers whose affability and charm attracted the city's and the world's celebrities. Sigmund left what he called the "personality-purveying" to executives on his staff who were better qualified and had more taste for it.

Whether or not he was liked was of little importance to him. His personal interest in anyone outside his own family was minimal. He treated the men who worked for him with courtesy, consideration, appreciation of merit, and absolute fairness. In exchange he got respect and admiration, and demanded first-class work and devotion to the Paper. It seemed to him a satisfactory bargain.

Ben Roemer, a small, balding man who had been in charge of the Paper's advertising for seven years, had an air of gloom even when the figures were excellent. Part of this was due to some peculiarity in his voice which gave it a hollow sound, like that of a stage ghost.

"I've heard from Mr. Hammond again," he intoned now. "It looks as if his threat to cancel is more than talk. He's losing a fortune on his investments in Cuba."

"And I am to advocate American intervention in the affairs of another country in order to save Mr. Hammond's fortune, or he will take his advertising elsewhere." Sigmund's eyes rested as coldly on Ben's face as though it were Hammond's. "I trust you left no room for discussion."

"Of course I didn't, Mr. Herzog. I told him the Paper's policies can't be bought."

Ben had not, Sigmund knew, told the advertiser any such thing. Sigmund thought Ben would rather have killed a man than risk offending him. It was an irritating trait, but perhaps one that made him successful at his job. In any event, Ben knew now, if he had not before, that he could not temporize with Hammond and at the same time preserve Sigmund's good will.

Miles MacRae expressed the opinion that intervention, and war, could no longer be stopped, even by President McKinley, who was strongly against it.

"There's too much momentum now. It's like a train that has gone out of the engineer's control and is hurtling downhill," he said. "We'd be well advised to prepare for it, Mr. Herzog. I'd like to have correspondents on the spot beforehand."

Sigmund seldom opposed his managing editor. MacRae was the man on his staff whom he most respected, whose views and habits and utter dedication to the Paper were closest to his own. It was curious that this should be so, that this forty-year-old pipe-smoking Scotch Presbyterian, who looked like a college professor, should have more in common with the German-born Jew than did Sigmund's own son. Curious and sad. Because MacRae's was the position on the Paper that Sigmund had once dreamed would in time be Samuel's, on his way to the top.

MacRae's judgment was almost invariably correct. Sigmund thought it was probably correct now. Nevertheless he refused to let him send reporters to Cuba.

"Once we do that, gentlemen," he said to the men around his desk, "we are acknowledging to the world that we consider war imminent; we are tossing another psychological weight into the balance that may tip the country toward it. I'm unwilling to add that weight."

"But the news—" an assistant editor began.

"We'll continue to get the news from the Associated Press. If war does, indeed, break out, we will, of course, send men to cover it and give us firsthand stories. Meanwhile, I will not lend the smallest support to the possibility of war."

Henry Sheldon, the business manager, grumbled that such tactics were not going to help circulation. It was a pro forma grumble to which he expected no reply. They had all been on the Paper long enough to know when it was a waste of time to argue with Sigmund.

They went on to a discussion of what news should be covered that day. MacRae lingered behind for a moment, after the others had gone, to suggest that one of the assistant editors, an old man who had been with the Paper since the beginning, be pensioned off.

"It won't be for long, I'm afraid," MacRae said. "He's drinking so steadily now that he's in a stupor most of the time."

Sigmund gave his approval to whatever arrangement MacRae felt was proper. When he was alone again, he reflected for a moment on the peculiarities of drink. Most newspapermen drank heavily. Also numbers of Irishmen. It was said to have a particularly virulent effect on American Indians. Jews, as a rule, drank moderately. Even Samuel, who selected the most rowdyish reporters on the staff as his companions, did not share their inordinate taste for alcohol. Sigmund wondered if there might not be the nucleus of a story in this somewhere, perhaps in connection with the shenanigans of the Anti-Saloon League . . .

The telephone rang before he could give shape to the idea. It was Walter, his rapid-fire phrases shooting over the wire almost before Sigmund had the receiver to his ear.

"Is Hester there, Papa? Yes, I know she is. That is, not there in your office, necessarily, but in New York. She left me a note to that effect. I stopped at home to change my clothes and found it waiting for me. I immediately went to the telephone, intending to speak to you, but I realized it was noon and you would be holding your conference."

He paused briefly to give Sigmund time to say, "That was thoughtful of you," and then went on again at once.

"As I told you only this morning, Papa, she has been restless for some time, but it didn't for a moment occur to me that she would actually leave. For a short while, her note says. To get her bearings. What she may mean by that, I have no notion, have you? Her bearings. I can assure you I've provided for her comfort and happiness in every way. Within my means, that is. Socially, she has access, through me, to the best circles. As I believe you know, I can say, with all due modesty, that I am welcome everywhere . . ."

He was, Sigmund thought as Walter went on and on, but it was often difficult to understand why. His reputation was that of a sparkling conversationalist. The word, by definition, signified an exchange. Perhaps in other company he paused more frequently to listen. In the family, he had become a sort of scourge. Even Ada, whose threshold of tolerance was notably high, had said before one of his visits: "My head aches a little tonight. Please keep Walter away from me."

It was several minutes, now, before he finally asked Sigmund whether he had seen Hester and what she had said.

"She asked me to let her work on the Paper," Sigmund told him. "She has, of course, been asking me that at intervals since she was old enough to understand what a newspaper is. I have given her permission to stay with us overnight, since the last train to Washington arrives after dark. She will return to you on the first train in the morning."

"Yes, thank you, Papa, but perhaps that's not best," Walter said. "She will only leave again, in the end."

Sigmund saw, then, that Walter had not called simply to make sure of Hester's safe arrival, nor even to express bewilderment about her behavior. There was something else, something toward which all the rest had been leading.

"What do you propose, Walter? To let her stay here with us?"

"In my opinion, Papa, that would be only a stop-gap." Walter cleared his throat. "She seems to be most eager to go abroad. For some time she has been saying that the world is not limited to New York and Washington, and that she wants to see something of it before she becomes trapped—that's the word she uses, Papa, trapped—in housewifery and motherhood. Now, whatever you and I may think of that, I'm afraid she will never settle down until she satisfies her—"

"Hester said nothing to me," Sigmund broke in, "about wanting to go abroad. As I told you, she pleaded with me to give her work here, any sort of work, as long as she could be part of the Paper. That doesn't seem to me to coincide with your idea that she longs for a trip to Europe."

"Of course she would rather work on the Paper, Papa. That goes without saying. But I think she knows you're unlikely to change your mind, and I believe, once she has gone abroad, fluttered her wings a little, she'll be willing to forget the notion and come home and have a family and behave herself. She is not, you see, Papa, like other women. She is like a colt that must be allowed to run free for a time, to work off her high spirits, or she will kick down the door of her stall."

"A colt is male. I think the word you want is filly. And I believe it is customary not to let them run free, but, rather, to break them."

Walter, whose factual knowledge on most subjects was prodigious, said stiffly, "Yes, well, of course I'm aware of all that. I wasn't attempting to employ an exact metaphor."

"I was," Sigmund said. "In my opinion, the more freedom Hester is allowed, the more she will want. Besides, you were not, surely, thinking of permitting her to go abroad alone?"

"No, of course not, Papa. That's precisely the point. I, certainly, am not free to take her, even if I had any wish to go, which I have not. But an opportunity, a unique opportunity, has presented itself." Walter cleared his throat. When he resumed, the booming of his voice was such that Sigmund had to hold the receiver several inches from his ear. "I have naturally become acquainted here in Washington with a number of people in the State Department, among them Graham Phelps, who has just been appointed to our consular service in Germany. Hester and the Phelpses' daughter, who is two or three years younger, are the best of friends. In fact, the Phelps girl—her name is Susanna—seems to prefer Hester to the young society women with whom she grew up. *Does* prefer her, I should say. Obviously, since it is Hester she has invited to accompany her and her family to Germany, and to remain with them for a month, until Susanna begins to feel more at home in a strange land. At that time, fortuitously, another Washington couple of our acquaintance will be returning home from France, and the Phelpses would arrange for Hester to—"

"Walter," Sigmund said, "I appreciate your detailing the logistics for me, but it is quite unnecessary. If these arrangements are satisfactory to you, well and good. Hester is your wife."

"Yes." Walter cleared his throat again. "It would be, I feel, an ideal solution. These are people, you understand, Papa, of the highest order. The Phelpses. Socially, influentially, politically, we could do no better than to cultivate them. If Hester goes with them to Germany, practically as a member of the family, it can be of inestimable value in many ways—even to the Paper."

"Surely you hope for too much from a member of the consular service," Sigmund said. "However, that is neither here nor there. I'm delighted that you have so readily solved your difficulties with Hester. Is it my blessing you want? For an ideal solution, how can I fail to give it?"

"Irony won't help Hester, Papa," Walter said crossly. "This is, I assure you, a crisis. In Hester's life and in our marriage. She has run away from me. My only chance to get her back, as a true wife and a mother to our future children, is to let her fly a little now."

"Then, by all means, let her."

Walter's sigh came over the wire like a gust of wind. "If only I could!"

"Ah!" Sigmund said. "Now, at last, I imagine, we are approaching the heart of the matter. All I need do is ask the obvious question. Why, Walter, can you not?"

"Papa, my work is well regarded in the field, you know. I have been approached by other publishers and editors."

"Is this relevant to our conversation? It scarcely seems so. But I congratulate you in any case, and suggest you seriously consider such offers."

"I'm not thinking of doing that, Papa. I'm quite happy on the Paper. I meant simply to indicate that I am treated with respect in the outside world and should be entitled to it in the family."

"The connection appears to me to be tenuous. However, let's get to the point, Walter. I have a newspaper to run. What do you want?"

"If we're going to be blunt, Papa, my expenses here in Washington—you have no idea, I'm sure, how enormous they are. Entertaining people who may be helpful in my work for the Paper. Gowns for Hester, so that she—"

"Blunt, Walter."

"Very well, then." Walter's tone edged on petulance. "The fact is that I can't possibly afford the cost of Hester's passage to Germany."

"I'm sorry to hear that. Having found the ideal solution, it must be very disappointing to you to be forced to let it slip."

"Papa." Walter cleared his throat. "I know Hester's happiness means a great deal to you. I thought perhaps you would consent to underwrite the voyage. As a loan, of course."

"Yes," Sigmund said. "I thought you thought so."

Walter maintained the longest silence in Sigmund's memory. Finally his voice burst with the burden, cannonading into Sigmund's ear before he had a chance to withdraw the receiver.

"And will you, Papa?"

Sigmund longed to say no. It would have been a satisfying ending to what he felt was, on his part, a well-managed dialogue. But there were other things to be considered. "I don't know," he said. "I shall have to think it over."

Immediately upon hanging up, he pushed the matter to the back of his mind and concentrated on his editorial. It was another attempt to counter with reason the flamboyant jingoism of Hearst and Pulitzer, and he knew as he wrote it that it was probably futile; that, as MacRae had said, the momentum toward war could no longer be stopped. The public was largely beyond reason now, and Sigmund's

77

cool appraisal of the results of intervention, his cold scorn of the methods of his competitors, were not popular. He was losing readers. Although he had assured Walter that morning that the lost circulation would be regained, he was not as confident as he wanted his staff to believe.

In view of the rapid growth and success of the Paper, the impression was general that Sigmund had become an extremely wealthy man. He knew there were whispers—even, probably, within his own family—about his niggardliness. He had never moved, like others in his position, from the brownstone near West End Avenue to a more fashionable neighborhood. Until very recently, he had not owned a carriage. He kept only one servant, the same Irish Mary who had come to the Herzogs' as a greenhorn. Everybody was aware that other successful New York newspapers were housed in imposing new buildings uptown, while the Paper still operated from its ancient quarters near Park Row, with only the addition of a small, equally ancient building next door to accommodate its expanded operation. The only plausible explanation was that Sigmund must be a skinflint.

It was true that he valued frugality. He had worked too hard all his life to spend money for which he did not receive full worth. Fashion, show, the acquisition of possessions for their own sake, meant nothing to him. His house was as roomy and comfortable as it had ever been, and he enjoyed its familiarity as he did that of the building where he sat writing his editorial. Until hired carriages had become difficult to obtain when he needed one promptly, he had seen no need to own one. His household could not have run more smoothly, nor the meals been more to his taste, had there been half a dozen servants belowstairs instead of only Mary. He had no wish, nor need, to impress anyone, except through the pages of the Paper.

But even if he had been so inclined, he could not have spent as lavishly as others supposed. Much of the money that the Paper earned went back into it. If there were new methods for insuring faster and smoother press work or better printing, if superior matrices and stereotype plates were available, Sigmund paid whatever it cost to obtain them. The men who worked for him had no cause to think him niggardly. He had always paid the highest wages, luring good men away from other newspapers when he wanted them. Only Hearst, with his almost unlimited funds, had outdone him in this, but Sigmund would not have wanted men who would prostitute their talents to work for the *Journal*—men like that beau ideal Richard Harding Davis, who was probably happy to prance around the world for anyone who would pay his way handsomely enough, or Arthur Brisbane, antagonizing everybody who worked with him . . .

In any case, Sigmund's funds were not unlimited. He could not afford a serious loss in circulation. If war was indeed inevitable, it would have to come soon. Once it was a reality, and there was no purpose in opposing it, he had men who would cover it as brilliantly as any reporter of Hearst's or Pulitzer's, and with far more accuracy. Should this preliminary period drag on too long, however, he might never get his readers back. Still, he was not tempted to join those who were deliberately hastening the day.

When he had finished his piece, he sent for a copy boy. The boy, a scrawny fellow of about nineteen, with a pained, feverish look, came limping in. Sigmund made it a point to know the name and a little something about everyone who worked on the Paper. This small effort of memory often did as much for productivity as a few dollars more in salary.

"What's wrong with you, Jordan?" he asked the boy. "Are you ill, or in pain, or are you having trouble with your stepfather again?"

"It's only my feet, Mr. Herzog."

"Your feet?" Sigmund leaned across his desk to look down. Jordan had on a pair of stylish black shoes, narrow and sharply pointed, obviously new. They were blatantly out of keeping with his ready-to-wear suit. "What's the matter with your feet? They look elegant enough."

"They hurt, Mr. Herzog. It's the shoes. I'll get used to them, though."

"I certainly trust so. They must have cost you a week's salary."

Jordan winced a little, as though Sigmund's disapproval were a tangible blow. "Oh, they're not my shoes, Mr. Herzog. I'd never buy such expensive shoes. These are young Mr. Herzog's."

"You mean he gave them to you?"

"No, sir. I'm just breaking them in for him."

"Breaking them—?" Sigmund stopped, took a deep breath, and began again, softly. "I'd be obliged to you, Jordan, if you would explain to me exactly why."

The boy blushed. For an instant his eyes darted frantically, as though seeking some secret exit through which he could instantly disappear. Then he looked back at Sigmund and said, with some dignity, "He's paying me to do it, Mr. Herzog. He told me his feet are delicate. As far as I know, mine aren't."

"How much is he paying you?"

"Quite a lot, sir. Two dollars."

Sigmund reached into his pocket. "Take the shoes off and leave them with me. Here are your two dollars."

"Oh, no, sir, I couldn't accept your—"

"You will do as I say."

"Yes, Mr. Herzog." Jordan pocketed the money and began taking off the shoes. "I don't feel right, though, accepting money from you that I haven't earned."

"Then you shall earn it," Sigmund said. "I assume that like most copy boys you hope to write for the Paper someday?"

"Oh, yes, Mr. Herzog!"

Sigmund scribbled something on a scrap of paper. Though scribbled was scarcely the word. His briefest, most casual note was written in the same beautiful, clear, shaded script he had learned in school in Frankfurt.

"Take my copy to the composing room. Then take this note to Mr. MacRae. He'll give you an assignment. You'll be a reporter for the rest of the day. See that you earn the money well."

Jordan's eyes grew round. A smile fattened his face. "Oh, I will, Mr. Herzog. Thank you, sir."

The boy stood with the shoes in his hand, looking around the room; started to put them on the floor, straightened, and set them gently on the edge of Sigmund's desk; then he took the copy and the note and went out in his stocking feet.

Sigmund waited a moment before leaving his office with the shoes. In the newsroom outside his door, the late-afternoon tension of the deadline was almost palpable. Copy readers and reporters were hunched over their desks, scratching with pencils or drumming on typewriters. Telephones rang and were instantly snatched up. Copy boys moved in and out of the room, taking copy to the compositors, carrying proof back to the editors. No one looked up as Sigmund stood watching. It was the same each day, yet always as though he saw it for the first time. The smell was the same—a medley, pungent with printer's ink and perspiration. He loved that smell. It meant that men and machines were working to put out the Paper.

Samuel, in accordance with one of his duties as telegraph editor, was laying out a page. Sigmund set the shoes down on top of it.

"You are, I assume, planning to go home for supper this evening?"

Samuel stared first at the shoes and then at Sigmund. He had, since childhood, had a curious, blind way of looking into Sigmund's eyes that somehow seemed an impudence yet could not be clearly defined so.

"Mama invited Myra and me to eat with you. She said Hester is visiting."

"Good. Fine. We'll go uptown together at six. Wear your new shoes for the occasion. I've just bought them back for you."

Samuel murmured something that Sigmund did not catch. Sigmund was sure it was not, "Thank you, Papa," which was what Samuel repeated when asked, but there was no way of pinning down this suspected impudence either.

"Don't thank me, Samuel. I expect to be repaid. Six o'clock, then." Sigmund started away, and then paused to add over his shoulder, "It's such a beautiful day. We'll walk uptown."

Ada insisted that Sigmund soak his feet in hot water. She dried them herself and then massaged them and sprinkled them with her violet talcum powder.

"This is all nonsense," he grumbled. "I smell like a fancy woman."

"It feels good, doesn't it?" She shook her head. "I don't understand why you did such a thing. A man your age, walking all that way. It was too much even for Samuel. He has a blister as big as an onion."

Sigmund smiled. "I have no blisters." He waggled his long, straight, powdered toes. "There is nothing delicate about these feet. What did we walk? Five miles? For an old-time peddler, that's nothing."

"But it's years since you were a peddler, Sigmund, and Samuel never was one. He had on new shoes besides."

"Yes," Sigmund said. "Well, now they are well broken in."

Ada shrugged. It was her way of saying that she knew there was something more to this, but there was no use asking, because if Sigmund had wanted her to know he would have told her.

She sat down at the dressing table to brush her hair. He glanced at her as he put on his socks and shoes, and the thought touched his mind that she was a more attractive old woman than she had been a young one. The thought surprised him. He was not even sure what he meant by it. He peered into the mirror at her round, soft face, watching her twist her fine hair, almost as white as his, into its neat, taut knot, but all he saw was Ada. He could not remember that she had ever looked any different.

"Sigmund," she asked him, "why is Hester here? Is she having trouble with Walter?"

"Did you ask Hester?"

"Sometimes there's a difference between what Hester says and what she means."

"Are you suggesting she lies?"

Ada had finished with her hair, but instead of turning around she went on talking to Sigmund's reflection. "I don't think she always tells the exact truth."

"She was certainly taught to in this household. It's unfortunate if other influences have turned her from it."

"Sigmund." Ada spoke so softly he could barely hear her. "Hester was never strictly truthful, even as a child."

He did not want this said.

"You are confusing untruth with imagination, Ada. Hester has always been highly imaginative. She has the kind of mind that, properly disciplined, would be valuable to the Paper. If she were a man."

"That's why she said she came—to try to persuade you to let her work on the Paper."

"Why should you think that isn't so?"

Ada continued sitting with her back to him, looking at his reflected face. She sat perfectly still. Stillness was one of her qualities. When she spoke, only her mouth moved, yet the effect was not of impassivity but of calm. She had no mannerisms that he could bring to mind. As a young woman she had wept a great deal, but he had not seen her in tears for decades, not even when Ida ran off insanely to join a pagan cult. Her face was scarcely more lined than were the faces of her daughters, yet she looked her age. It came to him that he did not know the source of her stillness, and the thought struck him as even more curious than the one he had had earlier about her attractiveness. He was not ordinarily given to fancies, especially not about his wife of more than forty years.

"I don't say it isn't so," she said. "Hester has always wanted to work on the Paper. But why does she come now, all the way from Washington? She must know you would disapprove even more now, when she is a married woman with other responsibilities. If all she wanted was to feel you out once more, why didn't she write to you?

That's what she always used to do when she wanted to persuade you of anything, and then she lived right here in the house."

He wondered how she knew about the notes Hester had written him when she was growing up. He had never showed them to her, and she would not have searched them out and read them without his consent. Had Hester told her? He did not wish to think so.

"Perhaps it was an excuse for a little holiday," he said. "Quite understandable, I think. She isn't accustomed as yet to the life in Washington. Walter's work keeps him away from home a good deal, and Hester has had trouble finding friends. Most of the people they meet are gentiles. It's natural that she should be somewhat lonely for her own kind."

He was giving her the explanation Hester had given him. If he had only suspected at the time that it was spurious, he knew it now. This young lady who wanted Hester to accompany her to Germany was a friend ("the best of friends," according to Walter) and her name was Phelps—Susanna Phelps, his still-sharp memory supplied—which was not a Jewish name.

It annoyed him that Ada, who seldom questioned what he told her, did not accept this any more readily than he had. At the same time, it eased his conscience that she did not.

"Hester would never be lonely," she said. "That isn't what she needs people for. And if she told you it matters to her whether or not they're her own kind, I'm sure it's only because she thinks it matters to you."

"You're sure," he said irritably. "It seems to me you're sure of a great many things this evening."

She smiled, without disturbing the impression of stillness. "A mother's sureness, Sigmund, that's all."

"Yes," he said. "Of course."

He was moved to go to her and kiss the top of her head. She smelled of violets. For an instant his loins stirred. It was years since he had exercised his marital rights. She had been a good wife in this regard, as in all others: sweetly submissive; but he knew she was relieved when it was no longer required of her. There was a time when he had been visited by thoughts of women as active participants in his pleasures, women who were not ladies. He had never succumbed to these imaginings of his baser nature. Instead he had plunged himself with even greater concentration into the Paper. He might well have said that the Paper had always been and was still his only mistress.

Now, identifying the violet fragrance as from the same source as that sprinkled on his toes, his brief concupiscence subsided, but a residue of tenderness lingered in his voice when he went on speaking.

"It's true that Hester has always tried, perhaps a little too hard at times, to please me." He moved away from her to take a fresh collar from the chiffonier drawer and fasten it to his shirt. "I think perhaps she needs a little holiday before she settles down. I should have realized before she married Walter that she has too much curiosity and spirit to flutter happily, like other girls, from the home nest directly to a husband's."

"She would have liked to go to college," Ada murmured.

"Yes, and fritter away her time on studies of no possible use to a woman, except to give her pretensions to knowledge beyond her capacities." He refrained from adding the next line—that college was a defeminizer of woman; Ada knew his views on the subject well enough. "I should have arranged a voyage for her, given her the opportunity to see something of other lands, become acquainted with her own cultural heritage . . ." He was inventing this idea as he went along, testing out its validity on himself, rather than on Ada, who looked bemused by it. "Fortunately, it isn't too late. Walter tells me she has been invited by a very fine family to accompany them to Germany for a month."

"A Jewish family?"

It was the natural, the perennial question. It was always asked when a child mentioned a new acquaintance namelessly, or with an ambiguous name. *You don't know? Well, please find out. That way, no one will be hurt later on.*

But Sigmund answered testily, "No, no. Their name is Phelps. Mr. Phelps is with the State Department. An important man. Their daughter and Hester are the best of friends." He was further irked to realize that he had used Walter's phrase. "In political circles these matters are not emphasized so much."

"That's nice," Ada said. She was leaning a little sideways now to keep his reflection in view. "But is Walter willing to let Hester do this? Leave him all alone for a month to become acquainted with her—her cultural heritage?"

"Quite willing." Not only willing, Sigmund thought but did not

84

say. Eager. "He seems to be most understanding of Hester's need for a holiday."

Ada gave a small, very soft sigh. "Perhaps it's only a need to get away from Walter. I can understand that myself."

"Walter is a brilliant, cultivated man," Sigmund said severely. "He is accepted everywhere."

"I know. Perhaps it's only me. I always feel he's filling the room with his—with himself, his voice—squeezing me into a smaller and smaller space, until . . ." She stopped, gently blinking the somewhat heavy-lidded eyes that she had bequeathed to all her daughters and to her granddaughter. "Hester, of course, is different. She wouldn't let herself be squeezed."

"Hester and Walter are very well suited to each other." The collar button sprang out of Sigmund's hand and rolled to the floor. He left it for Mary to find when she cleaned, and took another. "When Hester returns from this voyage, she'll be ready for her responsibilities as his wife and the mother of his children."

Ada straightened, no longer seeking his reflected face. She said, "Yes," in customary acceptance of his judgment.

He had no more doubts about the wisdom of the voyage. It began to seem to him, in fact, that he had proposed it and that Walter had merely contributed the *modus operandi*. Why Walter had seized on it with such apparent eagerness, Sigmund did not know, unless Hester's restlessness had grown so trying that he would be glad of a short separation. There was no denying that Hester could be difficult. No one with spirit was easy to live with. In any case, this was the obvious solution and it would please Sigmund to make it possible for her. She had wanted so much of him that he had been unable to give her because God had willed to make her a daughter instead of a son! He had thought of that the day of her wedding— looked at her under the *huppah* with Walter, and thought that now it would be Walter's responsibility to give her what she wanted. But Walter could not afford to give her this voyage.

"I forgot to tell you," Ada said. "Hannah and Arthur are coming for supper too."

"Is that so? To what do we owe the honor?"

They seldom saw their second daughter and her husband, except at the yearly *Seder* and on an occasional *Shabbes* evening. The Baers lived across town, on Fifth Avenue, and went to a different synagogue. Hannah sometimes exchanged visits with Ada and Elsa, and now and then left Robert to spend a weekend or holiday with his grandparents, aunt, and cousins, but Sigmund sometimes forgot he had this other daughter. He could not think of Arthur at all as a member of his family. Once, when someone had said to him that he understood Arthur Baer, the banker, was his son-in-law, Sigmund had replied, "No, not my son-in-law," and then had to cover the lapse with some insincere foolishness about thinking of Arthur more as a son.

"I was surprised too. They're always so busy," Ada said. "But I thought I'd ask, because Hannah and Hester haven't seen each other for such a long time. Hannah said she would ask Arthur and let me know. When she telephoned back, she said Arthur wanted to talk to you about something anyway and this would be a good chance."

Sigmund could not imagine what Arthur could have to say to him. It was difficult to converse with Arthur on any subject unrelated to banking, in which Sigmund's interest was only political and historical, which Arthur's was not. If Sigmund mentioned the Paper, Arthur's face took on a look of apparent bewilderment, as though he were not altogether sure what the Paper was. But he assumed the same look if Sigmund spoke of Hannah or Robert. He was a short, pudgy, all but hairless man, much older than Hannah, with a cast in one of his protuberant eyes. It might have been the cast that gave the impression of bewilderment.

"I hope he doesn't expect to keep me after supper," Sigmund said. "I hope he remembers that I have a newspaper to get out."

Mary knocked on the door at that moment to tell them Hannah and Arthur had arrived.

"You can eat as soon as you're ready," she shouted, as though she were a block away instead of on the other side of the door. Her brogue was as thick as on the day she had come to them, but her shyness had evaporated long since. "I'm going to ring the bell for the others now."

Ada had taught her how to cook and clean, and to keep the *milchig* and *fleischig* dishes separate, and to wear a clean uniform and apron and take care of her hair so it did not fall into the food, but she had been unable to turn Mary into the kind of servant her mother had had, and that Hannah had. When, infrequently, there were guests other than family, Mary could remember not to ring the bell, but instead come into the parlor and announce the meal. She could not, however, remember what she was supposed to say. Usually she thought it prudent to give a few minutes' warning and, taking her cue from one of their customs, stood at the door and called out in a voice that had none of the softness generally associated with Irish voices:

"Wash your hands!"

With members of the family, she was so comradely that if it had not been for the uniform and the brogue, a stranger might have thought she was one of them.

"You didn't eat half your soup. That's why you're so skinny," she said to Hannah as she cleared away the first course. "Wouldn't you rather she had more meat on her bones?" she asked Arthur, and then answered herself. "Men don't like a skinny woman."

"All right, Mary, that's enough," Ada said mildly.

"Och, I'm talking too much again." Mary's rosy moonface was cheerful. "It's true, though. She ought to eat more."

"I really don't know how you put up with her, Mama," Hannah said when Mary had left the dining room. "She gets worse all the time."

"She's a good cook and she knows our ways. We're used to her. Anyhow," Ada said, "we aren't so fancy."

"She's a character," Hester said. "I've told a dozen good stories about her in Washington."

Samuel, who had come to the table in bedroom slippers that Myra had brought him from home, looked at her pleasantly and said, "None of them necessarily true, I'm sure."

From her place next to him, Hester glanced at him sideways. She had always done that, from the time they were children. They had always, unless separated for misbehavior, sat next to each other. "Would they be more amusing for being true?"

Samuel made one of his inaudible remarks. Before he could be asked to repeat it, he said to Hannah, "Mary's right, though, you know. Many men do prefer plump women. Not all, but many."

"That isn't kind, Samuel." Myra laid one hand on his arm. It was as difficult to see the rings embedded in her fingers as to mentally carve out from the pillow of flesh the tiny, slender girl who had married him. "Hannah can't help being too thin," she said.

Arthur looked around the table in his bewildered way, as though wondering whether anything was expected of him. Then, evidently deciding that something was, he said loudly, "She suits me. That's the important thing, isn't it? She suits me just fine."

Hannah said nothing. Elsa, at the other end of the table, was apparently arbitrating a dispute between David and Robert. Her voice drifted back: ". . . only nine years old, David. You ought to know better, a boy of fourteen . . ." Rebecca sat erect in her chair, her eyes moving from one speaker's face to the other's, her expression changing in tune to the words.

Mary began bringing in the main course. Boiled beef, made from "Papa's Meat," horse-radish sauce, mashed potatoes, string beans cooked with a fatty end of the meat. It was Sigmund's favorite meal, but he took only a little of everything. He had several hours of work ahead of him still, and could not afford to dull his brain with too much food.

"Did you know, Arthur, that the men who work on morning newspapers ordinarily refer to this meal as 'lunch'?"

"They do? Why is that?"

He did not seem to Sigmund to be interested, but it might have been his eye that made him look as though his attention was wandering.

"Because what is the supper hour for others occurs in about the middle of our working day. Samuel and I will return to the office shortly after this and stay there until the first edition goes to press, at about one o'clock. Nathan, on the other hand, ate before he left the house at five—I suppose he could properly call it 'breakfast'—and will be at his desk until three. A peculiar calling in many ways, Arthur, but an adventurous one."

Sigmund had started this as a courteous way of letting Arthur know that he had a limited time to listen to whatever it was Arthur wanted to talk about. Somehow it had turned into a recitation of chronology. There were some people who deadened one's conversation simply by being on hand to hear it.

"I hope you'll have time," Arthur said, "to listen to a proposition."

Sigmund spread open his hands in a gesture of helplessness. "As I've said—"

"It's important, Mr. Herzog." Arthur, thank heaven, had never dreamed of calling him *Papa*. "Important to the Paper."

Sigmund picked up his knife and fork. "Well, let's concentrate on our meal now. We must not spoil good food by talking so we don't know what we're eating."

Obediently, they all fell silent and began filling their mouths. Sigmund ate contentedly, taking small forkfuls and chewing each one until he had abstracted all possible flavor. He took great pleasure in his food, as long as it was within a somewhat limited range of dishes and prepared exactly to his liking. He enjoyed eating with his family around him, even when he was too preoccupied to know what they were saying. He enjoyed, this evening, the awareness that they were all at the long, laden table between him at the head and Ada at the foot. All, that is, except Ida, who did not count any more, and Nathan. Sigmund had done his duty by Nathan, giving him a home for his family and a job on the Paper. It was enough, without the irritation of having him around all the time. Fortunately he was such a satisfactory copy reader that Sigmund could, in conscience, keep him in a job whose hours coincided minimally with Sigmund's own.

"I wonder—" Hannah began, and stopped when her father glanced up sharply from his plate. He had never, of course, enforced absolute silence while they ate—he was no tyrant—but they had formed the habit of reserving conversation for the moments between courses and after the meal, while they sat digesting it. Hannah had been too long gone, too seldom here, to observe their customs as a matter of course.

Hannah, like Elsa, had married, at eighteen, a man old enough to be her father. Sigmund did not take to Arthur, but at least he was an excellent provider. Sigmund did not know why it surprised him that Hannah had made the more sensible choice. He had no clear recollection of her as she had been when she lived at home. When he thought he remembered, he was not certain whether the memory was of her, or of Elsa or Ida. They had all been quiet, well-behaved children and young girls, who gave him no trouble. They had all more or less resembled Ada, and each other. Hester had the same sallow skin, dark eyes, and plump prettiness, but it was not possible to confuse Hester with anyone else.

Hannah no longer resembled the others. She did not look like a member of the family. As Mary had pointed out, she was thin. The bones in her cheeks showed. Even the color of her hair had changed, grown prematurely white. There was an air of strangeness about her that came only fractionally from her modish clothes. Hester was also stylishly gowned, but she was still Hester Herzog—Hester Herzog Lowenthal. Hannah was an elegant stranger. She did not even seem Jewish.

Sigmund attempted, when he was eating, to keep his mind on

pleasant, or at least neutral, topics; it was better for the digestion. This evening, however, at the same time that he was enjoying his supper and the sense of his family around the table, he was prodded by concern about the Paper's decreasing circulation. He knew there must be a solution, even if war continued to be imminent without becoming actual. His whole life attested to the possibility of solutions when none seemed possible. In this case he had not yet thought of one, and it came to him, depressingly, that it was perhaps due to the slowing up of age, though he had never felt more vigorous.

What, he wondered, could Arthur Baer have to say to him that could be of any conceivable importance to the Paper? As Sigmund had been thinking earlier, Arthur appeared scarcely to know what the Paper was. Certainly neither he nor Hannah showed any evidence of interest in its existence. It was one of the things that made them seem so alien.

"Wait till you taste the pie!" Mary, coming in to clear the table, shouted. "It's the best apple pie I ever made, if I do say so myself. If you want, Miss Hannah, I'll give you the recipe for your cook."

"Isn't it your recipe, Mama?" Hannah asked when Mary had gone out.

"Not exactly. She improves on my recipes. I think she uses more butter in the crust. But she won't give it to you right. She'll change the quantities or leave something out, so you'll think your cook isn't her equal."

Mary came in for another load of dishes, and left again. Clearing the table was a long process, involving several trips to and from the kitchen in the basement.

"You ought to have a chambermaid-waitress, Mama," Hannah said. "This is too much work for one girl."

"Mary doesn't mind. She wouldn't want another girl around, interfering. Anyway, Elsa and I help her. Rebecca too, when she has time from school."

Arthur seemed to take an excessive interest in this woman talk, to which Sigmund scarcely listened. Even his eye seemed more stable than usual, fixing itself more accurately on the faces of the speakers. At one point he nodded, as though in agreement, though with what, Sigmund could not imagine.

"I have an announcement to make," Sigmund said. "It concerns only one of us here, but I am sure everyone will enjoy sharing the news."

They all looked at him except Ada, Elsa, and Samuel, who looked at Hester. Ada, of course, had been told, but why did the others assume they knew the person concerned?

"I won't go into all the ramifications, all the whys and wherefores," he said. "The point of interest is that Hester, with Walter's full approval and encouragement, will soon embark on a voyage to Germany, where she will remain for one month, imbiding the culture of her ancestors."

"Oh, Papa!" Hester sprang up from the table and ran to throw her arms around him, like a child. "Oh, Papa!"

"All right, all right," he said. "You needn't suffocate me."

"Did you know, Hester?" Hannah asked.

Hester shook her head. "It was just a wild dream. Oh, Papa!"

"Is she going alone?" Rebecca inquired from the other end of the table, her green eyes even larger, more luminous, than usual.

"Of course not. Ladies don't travel alone," Sigmund said. "Your Aunt Hester has had the good fortune to become acquainted with a young lady whose father will soon be stationed in Germany with the United States Consular Service, and your aunt has been invited to accompany them when they go. Which of you children knows what the Consular Service is?"

"Is it part of the Army?" Robert suggested.

"No, stupid," David said. "It's where Americans go if they get lost or something in a foreign country, isn't that right, Grandpa?"

" 'Lost or something' is not an answer that I would consider notable for its precision. And you are inaccurate as well as rude, David, in calling Robert stupid. A question to determine a fact is rarely stupid. However, you are roughly correct. Assisting Americans abroad is one of the functions of the Consular Service."

Mary brought in three pies. She placed two on the table for Sigmund to serve, and left the third on the sideboard for second helpings.

"Incidentally, also for the benefit of the children," Sigmund said as he cut into the first pie, "I should point out that we do not, of course, normally permit the wearing of bedroom slippers to the supper table. Uncle Samuel is wearing them because his feet are sore."

"From what?" Robert asked.

Sigmund slid the pie server under the portion he had cut, and transferred the wedge of pie to a plate. "From vanity, Robert," he answered. "As it says in Ecclesiastes, *all is vanity and vexation of spirit.*"

One of the rooms on the ground floor had been designed originally as a second parlor for the family, with the larger room to be kept pristine and unused except when there were callers. This larger room had always served as the Herzogs' only parlor. It still showed the scars of childhood barbarisms: a jagged irregularity in a doorpost that Samuel had cut his teeth on, a discoloration of a rug where Hannah or Ida had had an accident. Sigmund had turned the smaller room into a library that originally had contained only enough books to fill two shelves and now accommodated a fraction of the volumes that overflowed packing cases in the attic. He used it as a home office as well.

Had Arthur never been in the room before? Sigmund could not remember, but he behaved as though he had not.

"So many books," he said, looking around with his air of bewilderment. "They—well—press in on you, don't they?"

"I don't find it so. A love of books is traditional in our family—in most Jewish families, I should imagine."

Arthur nodded, the way he had nodded in the dining room at the women's discussion of servants. "I'm a practical man, myself," he said. "A banker hasn't much time for books."

"The Rothschilds seem to have had the time."

"Oh, the Rothschilds!"

Sigmund found it impossible to tell whether he spoke with awe or with contempt. The man was an enigma. Could he possibly be the fool he often appeared, and at the same time the financial wizard he was said to be, and evidently, from his wealth, was? Perhaps so. Business skill was frequently not coupled with intellectual power.

"That girl you have," he said. "That Mary. You're lucky to hold on to her. You'd have to get at least two in her place if she left."

"Yes, well, she seems to have no intention of leaving. She's been here since she came off the boat, and she's devoted to all of us." Sigmund took his watch from his vest pocket and snapped it open, holding it without looking at it. "I wish I had the time to chat with you, Arthur, but as I explained—"

Arthur nodded again. "I know. You have to get to work." He made it sound as though Sigmund were a night watchman whose wages might be docked. "But my proposition is very much to your interest. In fact, I'm surprised you haven't come to me, Mr. Herzog, in view of everything." He looked around the room with an expression that Sigmund could only interpret as pity. Because of the books that "pressed in"? "After all, I'm your son-in-law."

"Come to you for what, Arthur?"

Now the unstable eye gave Arthur a look of evasiveness. "Well," he said, "a loan. After all, that's my business."

"A loan?" Sigmund repeated in astonishment. "I have no need of a loan."

"You shouldn't let pride enter into it. Loans are a part of everyday business, international dealings, everything. Luckily for me." He gave a sudden, whinnying laugh. "But anyway, my proposition is something else." He paused, and then added with an air of someone promising a treat to a child, "Something better."

Sigmund looked at his watch. "I hope you can disclose it in no more than fifteen minutes."

"In no more than five. Though I think you'll be glad to stay longer when you hear it." All at once Arthur changed, grew brisk. "I happen to know your newspaper isn't doing well. It's pretty obvious you're personally hard-pressed. I've studied the problem very thoroughly, and I've come to the conclusion that with enough capital and proper management, it could be turned into a very successful newspaper. My—"

"Turned into?" Sigmund interrupted softly. "I'm afraid I don't know what you mean by *turned into*. Mine is one of the most influential, respected, and widely read newspapers in New York."

Arthur shook his head. "I'm talking about financial success. The kind the *Journal* and the *World* have achieved. They're the influential, widely read ones now. The *Journal* makes half again as much money charging one cent, as your newspaper makes charging two cents."

"Go on."

"What?"

"I suggested that you continue."

"Oh. Yes. Well, as I say, I've come to the conclusion that the Paper, properly run, has very good possibilities and would make an excellent investment." Something—perhaps some reaction he saw in Sigmund's face—made him lose the thread. When he picked it up again, he seemed to have skipped a section. "You would naturally stay on as publisher, with a substantial interest in the business, but I'd of course have the controlling interest. I'd want to put my own man in as business manager, and I'd have to have—"

Sigmund snapped his watch case shut and stood up. "Thank you, Arthur, for your concern," he said, "but it's useless to waste any more of your time or mine. You've evidently been misinformed, both about the state of my finances and the health of the Paper. I have no need of a loan, as I've said, and I am quite satisfied with the way the Paper is being run. In the last analysis, it is I who am running it, and I who shall continue to run it as long as I live, according to the same principles and policies that have made it, whatever your erroneous impression to the contrary, a great newspaper. I appreciate your offer, which I'm certain is well meant, but I need neither your help nor your interference."

Arthur remained seated, his eye swiveling wildly. "Please calm down, Mr. Herzog. Don't get on your high horse." His voice rose several decibels above Sigmund's. "It looks as if you don't know a good proposition when you hear one, but you must know your newspaper's in trouble, and there's no use trying to tell me it isn't. One reason I'm as successful as I am is because I have such an efficient information service. You're being swamped by the *Journal* and the *World*. I certainly thought you'd be relieved and happy that I'm ready to pull you out."

"I'm sorry to disappoint you, Arthur. Perhaps it will soften the blow if I tell you that even if all your hypotheses were correct, which they are not, I would be indifferent to your proposition. For one thing, no one but I, and after me a member of my family, will ever have a controlling interest in the Paper."

"You talk as if I'm not a member of your family."

"Yes, that's true," Sigmund said. "I do, don't I?" He took Arthur's hand from where it rested on the arm of his chair and clasped it in his own. "Good night, Arthur. I assure you I appreciate what you've said. More than you know."

He did not immediately leave after Arthur had gone out of the room. For some moments he sat at his desk writing figures on a scrap of paper. He began to smile. One never knew from what unlikely source an important idea might come.

When he proposed the idea to his editors and business manager the following day, they thought Sigmund's acute journalistic judgment was eroding. It was one thing to pursue a potentially ruinous editorial policy as a matter of principle, quite another to make an arbitrary, apparently whimsical business decision that could well be fatal.

"We're losing money now," Sheldon, the business manager, said. "Cut the price in half, and we'll be losing twice as much."

"If we become another penny journal, we lose our distinction," MacRae said. "We've already lost popularity but never dignity. With that gone too—"

"Gentlemen, gentlemen, all this talk of loss!" Sigmund shook his head. "Your lack of confidence grieves me. If anything is lost, it will not be by us." He sat erect in his chair. "I repeat: Beginning with Monday's edition, the price of the Paper will be reduced from two cents to one penny."

In January, the U.S.S. *Maine* had been sent to Havana to protect American nationals and property in Cuba. In February, the *Maine* exploded mysteriously in Havana harbor, killing 260 men. Sigmund wrote an editorial suggesting there was no proof whatever that the ship had been deliberately blown up by the Spanish. The editorial was read not only by those who agreed with his pacifist views but by many who were willing to spend a penny to see what this infuriating newspaper had to say now. In April, President McKinley yielded to the belligerence of the press and the public and reluctantly asked Congress to authorize forcible intervention in Cuba. Shortly after Congress passed a resolution to that effect, Spain declared war on the United States.

The *Journal* and the *World* had expected to raise their prices to two cents to help defray the enormous expenses they had incurred in covering events in Cuba, even long before the war began. When Sigmund lowered his price to a penny, and other publishers followed, Hearst and Pulitzer had to keep their prices the same. They continued to send boats filled with reporters, artists, and specialists of all kinds to cover the war in flamboyant style. Hearst chartered a steamer, fitted it out with a printing press and composing room, and sailed to Cuba himself with a staff of printers, compositors, reporters, and photographers. Sigmund relied on the Associated Press and a handful of his own first-class correspondents.

The *Journal* and the *World* were read for excitement. The Paper was often exciting too, because the events were. The Paper was also

reasonable, impartial, literate, and remarkably accurate. By the end
of that year, its circulation had more than doubled.

5

Years afterward, Elsa would recall that evening when Hester came
from Washington and they all had supper together. Things began
then that no one had any inkling of at the time. Even Hester, with
all her manipulating, could not have envisioned how her part would
turn out.

"I don't wait for life to happen to me," Hester was fond of saying.
"I make it happen."

Hester thought she could leave God out of it, and it was a long
time before she knew otherwise. If she ever did know, or admit she
knew.

She told everyone it was because of her that William had come
that evening. She made a good story of it. Hester could make a good
story of anything. Some of it was certainly talent—all the Herzogs
were clever with words—but some was because she cared so little for
the truth, or for anyone's sensibilities.

According to Hester, William—"poor William," as she put it—
had fallen hopelessly in love with her when he was fourteen and
Walter had brought her home for the first time to meet his family.
At the wedding, she said he had gazed with such bewitchment at his
brother's bride that he had literally had to be shaken, as though from
sound sleep, before he produced the ring. Naturally no one in the
synagogue had noticed. Who, at a wedding, looks at the best man?

"When I telephoned that evening to say hello to Mama and Papa
Lowenthal, and William knew I'd arrived from Washington, he was
at the front door almost before I'd hung up the receiver. He was still
standing in the hall with that calf-eyed, lovesick look on his face
when Rebecca came by. All he did was transfer the look to her.
That's all. If William was aware of the changeover himself, it didn't
show. It was like the time Walter started eating a dish of ice cream
when I'd meant him to have a piece of cake for dessert. I just substituted the cake and he went right on eating—and, of course, talking;
you know Walter—and didn't notice, as far as I could tell, that the
ice cream had changed into cake . . ."

Hester made it sound as though William had never seen Rebecca
before, and never would have seen her if he had not come that eve-

ning because of Hester's phone call. Later, of course, she stopped telling the story at all, but in the meanwhile it varied according to the audience, and grew. But Hester was always the heroine, even when she professed modesty—"One look at Rebecca, and poor William seemed hardly to recall who I was"—and William was always the fool. Poor William.

Poor William, yes, in the end. Poor everyone, for that matter. But a fool, William was not. Elsa had never thought he was right for Rebecca, but she had liked him from the first and still did.

"He'll never amount to anything," Nathan had grumbled. "If she has to pick a Lowenthal, why doesn't she pick Ernest?"

Elsa did not say that Walter's older brother was too old for Rebecca, because there was less difference in their ages than between hers and Nathan's. She did not say that Ernest was a woman chaser, because Nathan would not like to think she knew about such things.

"He's too much like Walter," she said. Nathan detested Walter.

"At least he has money. William hasn't a nickel and never will have. He's too much of a *nebbish*."

Nathan saw no irony in this pronouncement. To himself, Nathan was an able and successful man, temporarily sidetracked. Elsa had allowed him to doubt it only once, when he had brought home a sealskin coat for her and she had made him take it back because they were in no position to have luxuries. She should have kept it, or said, even though it would have been a lie, that she felt too warm in furs. That lesson she learned when she woke in the night and saw him lying with his eyes open and tears on his face, and she did not forget it.

"William will probably work for his father," Elsa said. "There's nothing wrong with the jewelry business."

"There will be, once a *nebbish* like William gets into it. What ability does he have?"

Elsa did not know what ability William had, but she knew he had brains. He was not brilliant, like Walter. He was nothing like Walter at all, not as big or as large-featured. Fairer, softer-voiced, less energetic, less obtrusive. Not brilliant, but intelligent, with a nice, quiet sense of humor. He was not the husband for Rebecca, but Elsa liked him. Later, when he behaved in a manner of which Elsa disapproved, she thought he would have behaved otherwise if he had been married to a different woman. Men had to be handled gently, so that

97

they did not know they were being handled at all, or in one way or another they erupted.

"I never noticed how handsome William is," Rebecca had said that evening. "Blond, blue-eyed boys are the nicest."

"Are you including your brother? He's blond and blue-eyed."

"Oh, Mama, how can you compare David to William? David's a brat. William is lovely. I'm going to marry him."

"Don't talk such foolishness, Rebecca. You're still a child, William is only a boy, and you scarcely know each other. You'll meet a great many young men in the next few years before you decide on a husband."

"Oh, I'll meet them. I'll go to the theater and to balls and I'll have a lovely time. And then I'll marry William. Think of it, Mama! Aunt Hester will be my aunt and my sister-in-law, both!"

"Is that why you want to marry him? Or is it because you think he's handsome?"

Rebecca had outgrown the habit of flinging herself down and drumming her hands and fists on the floor, but she still, on occasion, threw things; she still, when less severely provoked, as now, stamped her foot.

"I *hate* it when you're sarcastic, Mama. It's *horrid*. I'm going to marry William because I love him. Didn't you see the way he looked at me? It was the way Vassia looked at Wanda."

She could not believe that Elsa had no idea who Vassia and Wanda were.

"Don't you read *anything*, Mama? They're characters in a book by Ouida. He's a Russian serf who pretends to be a nobleman, and she's the Countess von Szalras, but he loves her for herself alone, the way I know William loves me."

"What else, Rebecca, would anyone love you for?"

"Mama, many young men would be very glad to marry the granddaughter of the man who owns one of the greatest newspapers in New York, whether they loved her or not."

"Is that what Grandpa told you?"

"Well, it's true, but it isn't true of William. He'd love me even if I was nobody at all."

"You are nobody at all, Rebecca. Your grandfather can't make you somebody. The only one who can do that is you yourself."

"Oh, Mama, you're always preaching. You don't understand anything romantic or—or *anything*."

She had run out of the room in a fury of tears and, as Elsa learned later, bumped into Hester in the hall. Hester had evidently proved a more satisfactory listener. Most of Rebecca's encounters with Elsa ended the same way, with Rebecca furious or weeping or both. Elsa had never known how to deal with her. She seemed to have no skill with children. Even David, who had once been tractable enough, scarcely listened to her any more. Elsa could see him gradually escaping the mold she had tried to set for him, and assuming the shape of his father. Rebecca refused anyone's shape but her own.

"She's very much like me," Hester had said that evening. But it wasn't true.

"You've always been hardheaded, Hester. Did you ever moon over anybody in a book—or in life, for that matter? And if you ever shed tears or flew into a rage, you must have done it where no one could see. Rebecca needs an audience."

"She knows what she wants, and she'll get it. That's like me."

Elsa said nothing, and Hester did not, for the moment, pursue it. She ambled around the room as though she had never been there before, stopping at the bureau to pick up and examine a Dresden figure that Hannah had brought Elsa from Europe; peering at Nathan's silver-backed hairbrushes on the chiffonier; running her hand over the carved footboard of the massive mahogany bed.

"People don't have furniture like this any more," she said. "In the fine homes in Washington, everything's French." She sat down on the bed. Elsa stiffened. Nobody in the Herzog household sat on beds. "Is this what you do every evening while Nathan's at the Paper? Sit in this room? How do you stand it, Elsa?"

"I have a good deal to keep me occupied. Mending, reading, writing letters to friends in Baltimore. Once in a while, if we're not too tired—there's a lot of work in this house with only one servant— Mama and I play backgammon."

"I'd go crazy."

"You forget I'm nearly fifteen years older than you. I'll be forty in a few years; hardly an age to go gallivanting around."

Elsa did not say that this was the time she looked forward to all day. This time alone in the quiet house, the children busy with their schoolwork in their own rooms, Papa and Nathan at the Paper. This was her time. She did not mind sharing it with Mama now and then, but she preferred to be by herself. As glad as she was to see Hester, she would not try to detain her sister when she was ready to leave. If it was not too late, she might work for a while on her history of the Jews after their return from the Babylonian exile. She had begun it a long time before as a simplified version, for her children, of this period when the Hebrew and Hellenic cultures had met and Judaism had emerged as a great religious and historic force. Rebecca and David had never been interested, but Elsa went on with it even though it no longer had a purpose and no one except herself would ever see it, or know it existed. Sometimes she felt guilty about wasting time on it, but not guilty enough to stop.

"Elsa," Hester asked out of the blue, "have you kept up with your German?" She was not looking at Elsa, but watching her own finger make a design on the bedspread. "I remember you used to read me Grimm's Fairy Tales in the original."

"How can you remember that? You couldn't have been more than three."

"I don't know how I remember, but I do. Of course I didn't understand a word—probably I wouldn't have understood it in English either, at three—but the sounds fascinated me. Have you kept up with it?"

Elsa had learned German as a tiny child in the home of Papa's parents in Frankfurt, when Papa and Mama had taken her there during the Civil War. For a while afterward, Papa had spoken it to her, but when he had begun publishing the Paper, he had stopped. He had no idea—no one did—that she had continued with it on her own. It was as useless as the Jewish history she was writing.

"After a fashion," she told Hester, which may have skirted the exact truth but was certainly not a lie.

"Will you teach me?"

"Teach you? What on earth for? When?"

Hester looked up at her and laughed. "Elsa, you look just like Mama, only prettier. At least you *would* be prettier, if you wore something fashionable and dressed your hair softly instead of like an old lady, and didn't purse your mouth that way." She leaned forward and took Elsa's hand. Elsa, feeling her touch, wondered whether Hester had a fever. "You will teach me, won't you? Just enough to get me started, so when I get to Germany I'll be able to say and understand a few simple things?"

"But, Hester, you're going home tomorrow. You can't learn even a few simple things in one evening."

"Don't be silly, Elsa. I'm not leaving tomorrow. I'll be here until the boat sails a week from Monday. We have almost two weeks. I'll come here to your room every night after supper, and you can give me a lesson."

"Papa said you were leaving tomorrow."

"Papa thinks it's his duty to send me home to Walter. He'll be delighted when I wake up feeling a little too delicate to make the trip. Nothing at all alarming, of course; only a female complaint that won't be cured until it's too late to bother going all the way back to Washington and returning for the sailing." She laughed again. "Don't look so shocked. Where's the harm to anyone? Papa's conscience will be salved, and I'll have a nice visit with my family and at the same time learn a little German."

Elsa thought of saying she was too busy to give Hester German lessons in the evening, but she could not satisfy herself that it was true. Nor could she refuse to give up her own pleasures for two weeks. Hester was her sister.

"How can you stay until you sail? You've only brought one small valise."

"My trunk is on the way. I sent it last week."

Elsa was silent for a moment. "Then you've known all along that you were going on this voyage; that Papa would send you. How could you know?"

"I know Papa. He hates to refuse me anything. If he thinks he has to, he isn't happy until he can make up for it some other way." Hester leaned back on her elbows on the bed, her skirt pulling up above her calves. She looked hoydenish, despite the elegance of her gown. "I knew if I begged him again to let me work on the Paper, he'd give me this voyage."

Her face was so flushed that Elsa wondered once more whether she had a fever. But she looked happy, not ill. Happy and pleased with herself. If there had not been such an unmistakable physical resemblance between them, Elsa would have thought that one of them —she or Hester—must have been a foundling.

"How can you be so devious?" she said. "Do you mean to say you've just pretended to want to work on the Paper in order to get other things out of Papa?"

"I haven't pretended at all. There's never been anything I've wanted more than that." She let her elbows slip down until she was lying flat on her back gazing up at the ceiling. "I'm going to get it, too."

"Papa will never—"

"Wait and see. Just you wait and see."

There was a silence.

"Hester, what about Walter?" Elsa asked then. "Does he really approve of your going off like this, as Papa said?"

"Walter?" Hester giggled. "Oh, he approves. As a matter of fact, it was partly his idea. Walter has a lot of ideas, you know. He has a theory now that there's something sinister about the Kaiser and the German Empire, and he wants to write a series of articles about it. There was no chance Papa would send him over there to get material, but if he'd send me—" She stopped and sat up abruptly. "Don't you dare tell this to anyone!"

"To whom would I tell it, Hester? I'm not even sure I know what you're talking about. Germany sinister?"

"Oh, that's Walter's notion. I don't know whether he's right or not. Either way, it suits my purposes." She slid to the edge of the bed and clasped her hands in her lap like a good, eager little girl. "Can we start tonight, Elsa? Now? *Ja, nein, mutter, vater, bitte, danke.* There's my vocabulary. What's next?"

Elsa laughed. She felt as though she were laughing at some clowning of Rebecca's or David's that should be frowned on instead, but she couldn't help it. No matter how outrageous Hester was, it was impossible to stay angry with her.

"Of course we can't start tonight, Hester. I'll have to make some sort of orderly plan, find some books." Elsa was surprised to realize that she was mildly excited at the prospect. "I'll try to have something ready for tomorrow night."

"All right." Hester got up. Elsa thought she was preparing to leave, but instead she sat down in Nathan's high-backed armchair. "I'd rather chat anyhow. I've been away from here so long I don't really know what's going on. People don't say anything in letters except the surface facts, and I'm not sure Mama sees even those the way they are. She always writes that Samuel's doing so well on the Paper, for instance."

"Maybe he is."

Hester shook her head. "He always hated the Paper. He always said he'd get away from it the first chance he had. I thought that was why he married Myra. With all her money, he wouldn't have to work for Papa."

"Myra doesn't hate the Paper, though. She talks about it as though it were the Bible, and Papa one of the prophets."

"Oh," Hester said. "So that's it. Yes, I noticed tonight the way she puts her hand on Samuel's arm. I could almost see the reins. Gee, haw. Poor Samuel."

She said *poor Samuel* differently from the way, later, she said *poor William*. Hester cared about Samuel. As much, Elsa thought, as she cared about anyone. They had always been close, brimming with shared secrets and undisclosed mischief. Even Papa had not succeeded in breaching their bond.

"She didn't give me a minute to talk to him alone tonight," Hester went on. "Maybe the Paper is the only place he can get away from her. What a pig she's turned into!"

"That's unkind."

"Oh, unkind! She can't hear me, can she? Maybe it would be better if she could. She might stop stuffing herself before she bursts out of her skin. Poor Samuel," Hester said again. "He always lets life push him into things. So do you, Elsa, and it's no way to get what you want. You have to push back."

"I'm different from you, Hester. I'm easily contented."

Hester ignored this. "I suppose a person must be born with the gumption to do it. Push back, I mean. Like me. Like Rebecca." She had returned, finally, to her encounter with her furiously weeping niece. "You made a mistake, you know, opposing William. A girl like Rebecca thrives on opposition."

"I didn't oppose him. I didn't endorse him. They're just children. I don't think they've exchanged a dozen sentences." Elsa sighed. "Hester, I hope you didn't encourage Rebecca's romantic nonsense by taking it seriously."

"Of course I took it seriously. One must always take children seriously. It's because you didn't that she ran away from you in tears, and because I did that she confided in me." Hester got up from Nathan's chair and sat on the edge of the bed again. Had she always been like this, unable to alight anywhere for more than a few minutes? "I told her that with her looks she could have anybody. That seemed to surprise her, as if she didn't know what a beauty she is."

"We haven't made a point of bringing it to her attention."

"She has a mirror, hasn't she? Anyway, it makes no difference. She wants William."

"She's too young to know what she wants."

"You're wrong, Elsa. She knows exactly what she wants, and exactly how to get it, just as I've always known. She has the same feeling I've always had about the Paper. Not wanting to write for it, because that's not her bent, but wanting to be part of it, wanting a share in its power and influence."

Elsa moved in her chair for the first time, drawing her shoulders together as though she were cold. Hester must be embroidering, as she so often did. Probably Rebecca had made some childish comment, such as she had made to Elsa about being the granddaughter of the man who owned one of the greatest newspapers in New York, and Hester had turned it into a flaming ambition. Rebecca had never given Elsa any evidence of such an ambition. Elsa may not have been her daughter's confidante, but there was nothing secretive about the girl. What she thought or felt might be sobbed out in anguish or screamed out in fury, but it was not kept to herself. This was all some fancy of Hester's. No child of Elsa's would ride that Juggernaut wagon.

"What has any of that to do with William?" she asked Hester.

"It has everything to do with William. One way or another, women have to get what they want through men."

"I don't know what you're talking about."

Hester smiled. "Of course you don't. That's why you're sitting in this room and I'll soon be on my way to Germany. And Rebecca will marry William and have a part in the Paper."

"William, apparently, is to have no say."

"None whatever. That's one reason for choosing William. Your daughter isn't as blindly romantic as you think. She'll wear him on her little finger like a length of string."

For a time, that conversation with Hester had troubled Elsa, but then she had put it out of her mind. William had not come to the house again, nor had Rebecca mentioned him. She did not tease, as Hester had done at her age, to be allowed to put her hair up and go out with boys. Her moods were as violent as ever, but she seemed contented enough with her romantic novels and her giggling friends, and in no particular hurry to grow up. If Hester had made her conscious of her looks, Elsa had seen signs of it only once, when Rebecca had been on her way to school and Elsa had stopped her because her face was so flushed.

"Do you feel all right, Rebecca?"

"I feel fine. Why?"

"I think you may be feverish. Let me see." Elsa had gone closer to lay the back of her hand against Rebecca's cheek. It was cool, but the flush was an alarming shade of crimson, and blotchy. "What on earth have you put on your face, Rebecca?"

"Nothing," Rebecca said, jerking her head away. "Leave me alone, Mama. I feel fine."

"Don't say 'nothing.' We tell the truth in this family."

"Oh, Mama, leave me alone! You're always picking on me and preaching. You're always—"

"Stop it, Rebecca. Never mind what I always do. Tell me what you have on your face."

"I'll be late for school."

"If you are, it will be your own fault and you'll have to take the consequences. And there's no use stamping your foot. You're staying right here until you tell me."

"Oh, my goodness, you'd think I was a—a robber or a murderer or something. It's only—I wet some red crepe paper and rubbed a little on, that's all. You'd think I'd done something criminal."

"In other words, you painted your cheeks." Elsa pulled her into the bathroom and began scrubbing her face with a soapy washrag. "Aside from the fact that you could get blood poisoning, don't you know that no respectable young lady paints her cheeks?"

"Aunt Hester's respectable, and she does. She uses something called rouge that comes in a little box with a puff. I only wanted to see how I'd look— Oh, Mama, you're getting soap in my eyes!"

"Aunt Hester is a great deal older than you are. Besides, what Aunt Hester does has nothing to do with you. If Papa or Grandpa knew about this, you'd be severely punished. I'll take into consideration the fact that you've told me the truth. No dessert for two days."

"Will you tell Grandpa why?"

"It's only important that you know why."

Rebecca had had her luncheon desserts both days. Nathan had taken them up to her room when Elsa was not around, but Rebecca had left the dishes on her bureau for her mother to find. She had not, however, painted her face again.

Soon Elsa scarcely remembered William's existence. Even when other things happened that Hester had predicted that night, she did not think of William.

Hester stayed abroad almost two months. She was entranced with

Germany, and the Germans apparently were entranced with her. She wrote that at the end of her stay with the Phelps family, she would spend several weeks in the home of a German family she had met. She wrote to Elsa in German, which she had picked up as readily as a child, describing such marvels as the *Romantische Strasse* and the castles on the Rhine. She wrote to Mama about the excellence of German housewifery and cooking. She wrote to Papa about everything from the *Gemütlichkeit* of German family life to the disinclination of the German Government to enter the Boer War. They all read their letters aloud at the supper table.

"She writes so well," Mama said. "It's like a serial story. I can hardly wait for the next installment."

A few days later, Papa brought home a fresh edition of the Paper, folded to an inside page, and passed it around the table.

IMPRESSIONS OF GERMANY
First in a series by H. H. Lowenthal, a traveler

"Who is H. H. Lowenthal?" David asked. "It's not Uncle Walter. That would be W. Lowenthal."

"What a dunce you are!" Rebecca said. "Any dunce knows H. H. Lowenthal can't be Uncle Walter. Aunt Hester is who it is. Hester Herzog Lowenthal. Is she working on the Paper now, Grandpa?"

"If I were as impolite as you are, Rebecca, I might say that you're the one who deserves the dunce cap. You know as well as anyone at this table my view on employing ladies on the Paper."

"But you've printed in the Paper what she wrote from Germany, just the way you print what Uncle Walter writes from Washington."

Elsa had to bite the inside of her cheek, the way she had sometimes done as a child to keep from giggling. She had been a great giggler in primary school, but she had outgrown it early. Still, she thought she might, appallingly, giggle now. Rebecca did poorly in her studies—poorly by Herzog standards, at any rate—but she was as sharp as a tack. Papa looked as if she had turned into one and he had sat on it. The inside of Elsa's cheek began to bleed a little.

"There is a vast difference, Rebecca, which I shall proceed to explain to you," Papa said softly. "Uncle Walter is a political expert, a paid correspondent on the staff of the Paper's Washington office, who reports regularly on events and people in government. Aunt Hester is not on the staff, either in Germany or elsewhere. She is not paid. She was not sent by the Paper to report on anything. Do you understand these distinctions?"

"Yes, Grandpa, but just the same you've printed in the Paper what Aunt Hester—"

"If you please, Rebecca, I haven't finished." He looked around at the others. "I sometimes wonder whether I've been too lax in allowing the children to enter into the general conversation at this table. I've done so to give them practice in expressing themselves, but I may instead have encouraged an unbecoming argumentativeness. Perhaps I'd have done better to insist on the old precept that children should be seen and not heard." He turned back to Rebecca, who looked about to burst with the need to speak but, for a wonder, kept quiet. "Because they are well written and of homely interest to the many readers of the Paper who have never traveled abroad, I have printed excerpts from Aunt Hester's letters to her family about life in Germany. If they are well received, I will print three or four more. By that time, Aunt Hester will be home with Uncle Walter in Washington, a housewife like your mother and your grandmother, and that will be the end of it."

Hester did go back to Washington. She had a baby, a son who, contrary to Jewish custom, was called Walter, Jr. But that was not the end of it. Readers liked her comments from Germany so much that when they stopped there was a flood of letters requesting "more from the pen of H. H. Lowenthal."

"As I told Papa," Hester wrote to Elsa, "most readers of the Paper don't know any more about Washington life than they do about German life. Walter tells the men what's going on in the Congress and at the White House and all that, but I can tell the ladies what Admiral Dewey's new wife is like, what she wears, and the impact she is making on social circles here. There's no reason why the Paper shouldn't have many more women readers than it does."

From then on, nothing stilled the pen of H. H. Lowenthal. Elsa imagined her propped up on one elbow, in bed, writing between labor pains; then using Walter, Jr., to lean her writing pad on while she nursed him. Her letters rarely mentioned him, except in reply to some question of Mama's. It was Walter who sent a picture of him when he was six months old. The photographer had done what he could, but there was no concealing Walter's jutting nose in the small, pugnaciously glaring face.

"I suppose he'll look better with hair," Hester wrote in one of her private letters to Elsa, and then immediately went on to a triumphant report of Papa's agreement to pay her for her writing. "Of course I had to give him an excuse. I told him I never can put anything aside out of the household money for little special purchases, and if he paid me it would be like the egg money farm women earn. He pretends it's going to come out of his own pocket, but I don't care. I know I'll be working on the Paper and getting a salary, just like any other member of the staff. I won't always be limited to social gossip either. You asked me what happened to Walter's notion about the 'sinister' Kaiser," she continued, not troubling to start a new paragraph. "Nothing happened to it. The whole idea was silly, as I told him when I arrived in Germany. He was annoyed, of course, that I couldn't send him any material to support his theory, but there was none to send. The Germans are the jolliest, simplest, warmest, most home-loving people imaginable, and the Kaiser wants only what's best for them and their beautiful country."

That was in 1900. Rebecca wrote a poem about the new century and sent it to Hester. Elsa never saw the poem, but she saw Hester's reply, because Rebecca flung it into her lap in one of her tearful furies, as though Elsa were to blame.

"The ideas are good," Hester wrote, "but I told you long ago you have no flair for writing and must turn your talents in other directions. You may think I'm cruel to tell you it's a terrible poem, but believe me, Rebecca, I'm being kind. If you want to get anywhere, you can't fool yourself. You have to know what you can't do, as well as what you can. How is William?"

That letter of Hester's went through Elsa's mind six years later, at the wedding. That, and many other things. She could not, for some reason, concentrate on what was going on under the *huppah*. Everyone looked bewitched by Rebecca's beauty, but her daughter's face kept sliding out of Elsa's focus. So did William's. At one moment she was noticing for the first time that he did have the Lowenthal nose, though on a modified scale, and was certainly not the handsome blond god that Rebecca imagined—not even blond, for that matter, but sandy-haired. A moment later, she did not see him at all. The whole occasion, her only daughter's wedding, a landmark, a rite of passage, seemed to slip away from her, like a dream about something that dissolves into a dream about something else.

She was thinking of Hannah, who was not at the wedding.

"You understand, Elsa. I couldn't bear it. All that happiness. Arthur and I would cast a pall over it."

"What does she mean, she couldn't bear it?" Papa said. "People bear what they have to. Anyway, it's been nearly two years. It's time she stopped wallowing in grief. Her trouble is, she has nothing else to do."

For once, Elsa had to agree with Papa. She had always been closer to Hannah than to the others. Hester and Samuel were so much younger, almost like her children; she had, in fact, helped Mama bring them up. Ida, though the nearest to her in age, had been a little odd from the beginning, as if she lived somewhere else, in a place for which Elsa had no map.

Hannah had been the only one who thought and felt as Elsa did. They had understood each other without many words.

Or so it had seemed to Elsa, until several months after Hannah's engagement to Arthur Baer. Hannah had never told her why she was marrying Arthur, but Elsa thought she knew. In one respect, he had less to offer than Nathan. He was not an attractive man. But he was evidently kind and generous and would always be able to take care of Hannah handsomely, away from Papa's house.

Elsa had come to New York to see Mama, who was recuperating from bronchitis. Sometime during the night, in the room she was sharing with Hannah, she was awakened by pillow-muffled sobs. During all the years of their growing up in this room, Elsa could not remember ever before hearing Hannah weep in the night. They were not weepers, she and Hannah.

"What is it? . . . What's the matter? . . . Are you in pain? . . . Please tell me, Hannah."

It took Hannah some time to stop sobbing and reply. What she said, the way she said it, sounded like somebody else, some stranger Elsa had never met before.

"You'll hate me."

"Don't be ridiculous."

"You will. You've never done anything dreadful."

Done? No. What dreadful thing had there ever been to do, even if Elsa had been so inclined? But she had had dreadful thoughts. In her mind and her heart, she had broken a commandment. "I'm no saint, Hannah. Far from it. You needn't be afraid of horrifying me, whatever it is."

But she was horrified. She had imagined some misstep within the bounds of her own temptations—a lie, a broken promise; even, at the outer limits, a coin found on the floor and silently pocketed.

"Arthur isn't abroad looking out for his European interests," Hannah said. "The reason he hasn't come calling is because he has broken our engagement."

"Why?"

"Oh, Elsa!"

Elsa did not know what time it was, but it must have been very late, because the lamplighter had turned off the gas in the street lamp near the house. The room was so dark that Elsa could barely make out Hannah's outline in the other bed. She thought of getting in with her, but she could not bring herself to do it. That piteous voice seemed not to belong to anyone she knew.

"Don't you want to tell me why?"

"You'll hate me."

"Stop saying that. Of course I won't hate you, Hannah. You're my sister. Is it because of this—whatever it is you've done—that Arthur has broken the engagement?"

Elsa could barely hear her say, "Yes," but then Hannah's voice strengthened and she sounded more like herself. "It isn't fair, either. After all, he did it too."

"*What* did he do? Hannah, you're talking in riddles."

"Of course I know it's not the same," Hannah went on as though she didn't hear. "He's a man. It's like Mama told me before I was engaged," she said sadly. "Why should a man run after a streetcar once he's in it?"

Elsa did not immediately know what this meant. Mama had never told it, or anything like it, to her before she was engaged.

"You see," Hannah said. "You're too shocked to speak."

"It isn't that. I don't— Do you mean—?" Elsa stopped, and started again. "Are you saying that you allowed Arthur . . . liberties?"

"Oh, Elsa, I'm so ashamed." Hannah began speaking rapidly now, the words gushing out. "He was sick in bed and he asked me to come and see him. Mama wasn't home, but I thought it would be all right to go; my duty, even, as his fiancée. I didn't know he'd be all alone in the house except for the servants. When he called to me to come up to his room, I thought surely he had other visitors, but he didn't. He said it wasn't wrong for me to be there because, after all, we'd be married soon, so I sat near him on a chair, and I don't even remember how I came to move from there and sit on the bed—"

"No!" The word erupted as though of itself. "I don't want to hear any more."

Hannah burst into tears. Elsa lay still on her back, rigid, until the crying stopped.

"Elsa?"

"Yes?"

"Elsa, what am I going to do?"

Elsa took a deep breath. "I don't see that there's anything you can do. You can't force him to marry you." She paused. "I think you're better off without him, if this is how he is. A man who takes advantage of a girl's innocence and then turns against her. Of course you shouldn't have gone up to his room under any circumstances, but he shouldn't have asked you to. He's at least partly to blame."

"He says he was testing me."

"Pooh!"

There was a silence.

"Elsa?"

"Yes?"

"I'm not better off without him. If he doesn't marry me, I'll have to—I don't know. Kill myself, probably."

"Don't talk such nonsense. He's not the only man in the world."

"He might as well be. No one else will marry me."

"That's not so. You'll find someone who cares enough about you to be forgiving." Elsa was not sure she believed this, but she thought Hannah needed it said. "There are such men."

"Not that forgiving. Not forgiving enough to . . . to—"

"To what?"

Hannah whispered it into the darkness. "Raise another man's child."

Even now, more than twenty years later, Elsa could feel the repugnance that had risen in her like a wave of nausea. She heard one of the wedding guests murmur in her ear, "Are you all right?" and she nodded and smiled without ever knowing who it was.

Nathan had wanted to have the wedding at the Waldorf-Astoria. Nothing but the best for his only daughter. Elsa, carefully avoiding mention of expense or inappropriateness, had convinced him of the dignity, good taste, and convenience of a small, quiet neighborhood hotel. Papa thought a wedding should be in the synagogue. Elsa would have preferred the synagogue herself, but she did not say so to Nathan. There was always a point on which Nathan would stand as though he were glued to it, and she had learned unerringly to recognize where it was.

The room had seemed airy to begin with, before all the guests had arrived, but it was close now. Elsa could see the perspiration glistening on the men's foreheads. One of William's friends had pushed his white *yarmulka* so far back on his head that it threatened to fall off. She thought she could tell which of the men she didn't know were gentiles, by the unnatural way they looked in *yarmulkas*, but it probably was not so. William, up there under the *huppah* with Rebecca, looked no more natural in his, in spite of his Lowenthal nose. *Because* of that, perhaps, since it resembled a Roman nose more than it did a Jewish one.

It might have been the warmth of the room that was making her giddy, frivolous with thoughts of noses on the solemn occasion of her daughter's wedding. She had always had a sense of occasion. She and Hannah had been the ones who most loved the festivals and the ceremonies. But her mind kept wandering away from this one. And Hannah was not there.

She had fallen asleep that night before Elsa did, and was still sleeping the next morning when Elsa left the house. Mama had been up, of course, but Mama had not asked her where she was going, and Hester, who would have asked, was in school.

Everything about that morning was as clear to Elsa as though it had happened the day before. She remembered coming down the steps from the front stoop and standing outside the house in the soft May sunshine to get her bearings. It was five years since she had lived in New York, and even then she had never gone anywhere alone, or by public conveyance.

The street was deserted. All the men were at work, and all the older children at school. The little ones were indoors with their mothers, who were doing their housework or supervising their servants. Across from Papa's house, bedclothes aired at one of the open windows. Mama had told Elsa the neighborhood was not what it had been.

Elsa began to walk. It was only a few blocks to where the horsecar stopped, but she could not go quickly. In order to keep the fresh binding she had just sewed to the hem of her skirt from becoming immediately torn and bedraggled, she had to walk carefully. When she saw no one around, she even lifted the skirt a little above the street.

In the surface car, people looked at her curiously. She was the only solitary lady in the car. But Elsa didn't care. None of them knew her. She did not even live in New York any more. She turned her face away from them and looked out at the avenue, watching the carriages and the delivery wagons, listening to the clop of horses' hoofs. When it was time to get out, she kept her eyes straight ahead.

The bank was on the corner. She walked in exactly as she had rehearsed it in her mind, as though she were another Hetty Green, accustomed to entering banks and being attended to at once. She held herself like such a person without difficulty. It was her customary posture—hers and all the Herzogs'. Papa had always made them stand erect. When Samuel had kept slumping, Papa had forced him to wear a shoulder brace until he stopped.

"I wish to see Mr. Arthur Baer," she said.

She must have succeeded in sounding imperious, because she was quickly ushered into his office, where she was momentarily intimidated. It was a larger office than Papa's, with a larger desk. Arthur, short, homely as he was, looked impressive in his dark frock coat and wing collar, the rich silk of his ascot tucked into a pearl-gray waistcoat. She had never seen a man at work dressed so elegantly.

"Good morning, Mrs. Herzog," he said, rising to greet her. "This is an honor and a pleasure." He did not look as though it were. His bad eye veered evasively away from her. "What brings you all the way down here? Have you decided Baltimore banks are not to be trusted, ha-ha, and you'd prefer to deposit your pin money with us?"

Elsa's courage revived. She took the chair he offered her and removed her gloves, taking her time before she spoke.

"I've come on a personal matter, Mr. Baer."

"A personal matter?" His eyelids flickered. "I'm delighted, of course, but I'm afraid I haven't much time." He gestured with a pudgy hand at the pile of papers on his desk, the telephone. "I am—as you see, Mrs. Herzog—a very busy man."

"I assure you this won't take long."

He sat down with a sigh and what he must have supposed was an air of polite resignation, but the same pudgy hand kept clenching and unclenching on the arm of his chair. "Well, of course, in that case—"

Elsa's eyes moved from his face to the window, through which she could glimpse Broadway; moved to the farmhouse pictured on the wall beyond his head; returned to his now slightly perspiring face. "Shall I come directly to the point?"

He answered by raising his eyebrows, thrusting out his lips, and turning his hands palms up.

"It's in reference to my sister Hannah," she said. "I understand there's some question about breaking the engagement."

Arthur Baer's neck seemed to swell and struggle against the stiff collar. It took him several seconds to manage a smile that satisfied him. "My dear lady, I hardly think—this really isn't anything I want —I should—discuss with you—"

"Nor is it anything I want to discuss with you, Mr. Baer. I'd have preferred to leave it to my husband or my father or my brother. But since I felt it would be in the best interests of everybody concerned not to let it reach their ears, I decided to speak to you myself." Arthur tried to say something, but Elsa went on while she had the momentum. "Hannah told you, of course, that she is going to bear your child?" Elsa looked directly at him, watching with interest as the color rose all the way up to his receding hairline.

"Really—I don't know—a lady, to walk into my office and say— I've never heard—" He gripped the arms of his chair as though to hold himself upright. "I really must refuse to discuss this with you, Mrs. Herzog."

"I think you'd better. It would be much more unpleasant with a male member of the family, I assure you." She gave him a serene smile. "Why not simply pretend, for the moment, that I *am* a male member, and explain to me how you can consider breaking your engagement when Hannah is carrying your child?"

Elsa had thought, planning it in bed the night before, after Hannah had fallen asleep, that this might be the most embarrassing part. She had never before in her life mentioned the subject of pregnancy to a man not her husband or a doctor. But she was not embarrassed at all. It was only later that she realized with dismay that she had been enjoying Arthur Baer's discomfiture too much.

"All right," he said. "All right, I'll answer you. But just remember, you insisted on it. He blinked furiously. Was he trying to blink his errant eye back into focus? "The fact is—I'm very sorry to say this to you, Mrs. Herzog—but I have no assurance, no assurance whatever, that this child is mine."

Elsa had already heard this from Hannah. It made her even

angrier to hear it directly from him. She could feel the anger shaking her, tossing her heart around in her chest like a ball. She sat very still and spoke very softly. "You know that isn't true, Arthur Baer. You know Hannah was just an innocent young girl whom you—"

"Innocent?" he broke in. "If she was so innocent, she'd never have come near my room, with me in bed. She knew exactly what she was doing." He shook his head. "I'm sorry. You don't know how sorry I am. I had a deep affection for your sister. She seemed to have all the right qualities. She's pretty and amiable and she comes from a good, substantial family. I'd never have thought her chastity was in doubt. I thought she'd kill herself rather than submit to a man before marriage. But I was wrong. She failed the test. It was a severe blow to me, I can tell you."

"I don't believe you were testing her. I think you simply gave way to your—your animal—passions." Elsa got the last word out with difficulty. "But in any case, how could you *dare*? Hannah trusted you, as her fiancé, not to ask her to do anything wrong, to protect her. It's you who deprived her of her chastity."

The slackness of Arthur Baer's jowls appeared to have tightened. He spoke coldly. "You have it wrong, Mrs. Herzog. The woman is responsible for keeping the man in check. If she doesn't do it—well, there's only one conclusion, because a good pure woman *would* do it." He was sitting back in his chair now, his hands relaxed on his knees. "I refuse to wonder the rest of my life whether the child I'm raising is really mine. I refuse to marry a girl I have doubts about. I've waited a long time to find the right wife. My standards are high, and fortunately I can afford to insist on them."

Elsa had to struggle to maintain the purity of her anger. It was horrible of him to suggest that Hannah was a loose woman, that the child might be some other man's. She concentrated on this hatefulness, tried to fill herself with it, to blame him utterly. The difficulty was that she agreed the woman was responsible for keeping the man in check. She looked at this smug, fat little man with his fluctuating eye, and could not, *could* not, imagine why Hannah had not done it. She found it impossible to believe that her sister had been overcome by—well, passion. Decent, well-brought-up girls did not have such feelings. Certainly not for Arthur Baer. It must be that Hannah—poor, foolish, innocent Hannah—had only wanted to please her future husband.

"Mr. Baer," Elsa said, "you cannot afford to insist on breaking your engagement to my sister. Believe me, you cannot."

He stared at her. Then he laughed. "Are you threatening me, my dear lady? Do you plan to horsewhip me?"

"If I had the strength, and a taste for violence, it would be a pleasure."

Arthur Baer shook his head, still laughing. "I admire you, Mrs. Herzog. I really do admire you. Your sister is lucky to have such a champion. I only wish, for all our sakes, that this had turned out differently. To tell the truth, I'm still fond of your sister, in spite of everything. But I can't marry her. I must do what I think is right."

"You will marry her, however," Elsa leaned toward him a little, trying to hold his wandering eye. "You will tell her at once that you must have been out of your head when you broke the engagement and that you are eager to marry her as soon as possible. You will find that you must leave this month to look after your . . . your banking in Europe, and you want to advance the date of the wedding so that you can take Hannah with you. Hannah is—"

"Just a minute, Mrs. Herzog—"

Elsa went on speaking her lines. "Hannah is never to know that I spoke to you, or that you didn't act entirely of your own accord. And you are never, as long as you live, to say one word to her about that day in your bedroom, or ever, by word or action, let her feel you have any less regard for her because of it. I'll know. Hannah and I are very close."

He had risen at one point in her speech, stood with his hands on the desk, bent toward her; both of them bending toward each other, so that their faces were almost close enough to touch. Now he had sat down again, lowering himself slowly into his chair.

"What?" he asked in a choked, stunned voice. He swallowed, but then could only manage the one word again. "What?"

"If you refuse," Elsa said, "I will tell my father, and he will use the power of the Paper to ruin you." She had thought of these words during the night, added to them, then subtracted again. The effect seemed even more chilling to her now than it had in the silence of her mind. "I'm sure I needn't be explicit."

She could not have been explicit had the need arisen. She had no idea what the Paper could do to him, but she believed in its awful power to do anything that might be required of it. The Juggernaut of her nightmares could crush Arthur Baer under the wagon wheels like a fly.

He sat without speaking, his mouth a little open. She thought he had turned pale.

"It isn't a hard choice," Elsa said. "You've told me you still care for Hannah. She'll make you a devoted wife and be a fine mother to your children. She's a good girl. I'm sure you know that in your heart."

Arthur had stopped looking at her. He began searching through the papers on his desk, reading a few pages, then putting them down and going through another pile. He got up and for some time stared at the picture on the wall, as if he might be counting the apple blossoms on the tree near the farmhouse. Now he was at his desk again, writing on a pad, screwing up one corner of his mouth like a man wrestling with figures.

It came to Elsa that he was not going to speak to her, that he had gone back to his work, intentionally ignoring her and everything she had said. She began drawing on her gloves, smoothing them slowly over her fingers. The anger, the purpose, that had sustained her drained away like blood, leaving her so weak she was afraid she could not stand. She had been driven to behave as she had never behaved in her life. It was as though someone else had moved in her flesh, spoken through her, using unwomanly and despicable methods, wielding the Paper as a bludgeon—the Paper she detested. And it had all been for nothing. She had only, in her ignorance, made a fool of herself.

Suddenly, loudly, Arthur Baer sighed. "Yes," he said, as though answering some question Elsa had just asked him. "A man can be stubborn. He can do something he really doesn't want to do, or not do something he'd rather do, out of plain stubbornness." Elsa could not see his face. He was holding a pad in front of his eyes, seeming to read from it. "Now, this is a funny coincidence. You mentioned Europe. It happens that I have interests in London and Paris that I want to look out for personally just at this time. I'll have to be gone for several months. It will make a very nice honeymoon."

Elsa never took to Arthur Baer, but at that moment she felt a great tenderness for him. "Yes, indeed it will," she said. "I wish I could see Hannah's face when you tell her you're taking her to London and Paris. It must be wonderful to have the power to make somebody else so happy."

That wedding, Elsa remembered better than she thought she would remember this one. All through the ceremony, Arthur had looked at Hannah with a sort of adoring wonderment. Had he assumed it for Elsa's benefit, out of fear of some reprisal that she had only hazily imagined but that to him had a specific reality? Or had Hannah acquired a mysterious, new worth to him?

Whatever, their marriage seemed satisfactory. If it was not, Hannah had never said so to Elsa. She had come back from Europe, her honeymoon, changed; slimmer, stylish, almost foreign-looking, with a cool poise that made her seem years older. Elsa had had a letter from her, mentioning casually that she had been in the family way, as though Elsa knew nothing of it, but had fallen getting out of a carriage in London and lost the baby. She never spoke of it again.

Even when Elsa moved back to New York, to Papa's house, she and Hannah saw each other only occasionally, and seldom alone. Once in a while, Hannah invited Mama and her to come to tea. She would send the carriage for them, and they would drive through the park to the imposing white house on Fifth Avenue. The butler would show them into the parlor—no, drawing room it was called now—and Hannah would pour the tea gracefully, offer them little fancy cakes to go with it, and inquire after the family.

"I always feel as if I'm calling on some lady I don't know very well," Mama confided to Elsa once, on the way home. "Some lady being gracious to someone who hasn't had her advantages."

Once a year, on Mama's birthday, Hannah came to lunch. She insisted on bringing the birthday cake, much to the annoyance of Mary, who considered it a reflection on her own baking. She also brought expensive presents in large boxes, most of which Mama put carefully away in their pristine state.

"Who knows?" she said to Elsa. "Someday I might want to lie on the sofa in a fur-trimmed negligee and eat Sherry's chocolates all day."

Hannah and Arthur came to dinner several times a year, on holidays, but they seemed more like guests than members of the family. When Robert was old enough, they brought him along, and now and then left him for a few days. "To get acquainted with this way of life," Hannah had said once, as though she were exposing him to the customs of some exotic tribe. But Robert had seemed more like one of them than Hannah did.

Now Robert was dead. He had died two years before, at the age of fifteen, of a burst appendix.

"Why?" Hannah had asked over and over. "Why? Why? Why?"

She had gone a little crazy, looking in the Paper every day for announcements of a child's death, and then attending the funeral to see how the mother was taking it. She went to the cemetery at least once during the week, and made Arthur take her again every Sunday.

"Papa," she said, "Robert always wanted to work on the Paper."

"He never said so to me. No one ever said so to me."

"Yes. Arthur even tried to buy an interest in the Paper for him once, but you wouldn't sell. He was your own grandson, but you wouldn't let him have an interest in the Paper."

Papa did not answer. Later, at the table, he said to Mama, "She's out of her head with grief. Robert wanted to be a banker like his father. Arthur never tried to buy an interest in the Paper for him. He tried to buy it for himself. Not because he cared about the Paper, but because he thought it would be a good investment. Like a railroad."

Was that it? Elsa wondered. Or was it the power Arthur had tried to buy?

"Did you ever stop to think? We all lose our first-born sons," Hannah said. "But Mama's and Elsa's were infants, and mine was a big boy. A big, beautiful, wonderful boy." Hannah, who had become less and less Jewish as the years went by, seemed, in her sorrow, more Jewish than any of them had ever been. "It's like a curse of God. Why should God curse me?"

Papa quoted from Job. "*Where were you when he laid the foundations of the earth? Declare, if you have understanding.* There are no answers, Hannah. Bear it as best you can and go on living. Take care of your house and your husband. One day soon you'll awaken and notice the sun is shining."

But Hannah had not noticed it yet. She was still too grieved to endure the happiness of a wedding. She still asked why such a terrible thing should have happened to her. Elsa wondered whether she really had no idea.

The sound of breaking glass was loud in the close, quiet room. Under the *huppah*, William ground the goblet with his heel, while Rebecca looked on admiringly, as though he were slaying a dragon.

"*Mazel tov!*"

They were married. Rabbi Schoenfeld was beaming as if he had created them. How many couples he must have married, the old rabbi who looked like Abraham in "Old Testament Stories for Children," and still a wedding made him beam like that. William was beaming too, nodding and beaming at everybody. Rebecca was crying.

"Oh, Mama, I'm a married woman!" She threw her arms dramatically around Elsa. "I'm Mrs. William Lowenthal!"

"It shouldn't come as a surprise to you," Elsa said. "You've been expecting it for six years."

"For goodness' sake, Mama, don't be sarcastic on my wedding day."

"No. I'm only trying to be a tempering breeze." She kissed Rebecca's hot, wet cheek. "But that's not my function any more, is it? Now it's up to William."

She watched Rebecca go off to greet her guests, managing the long train of her wedding gown as though she wore the clothes of a fairy-tale princess every day. William followed her around, still nodding and beaming, never quite catching up with her.

"Well, she got him," Hester's voice said in Elsa's ear, "just as I told you she would."

Hester was, as always, dressed in the latest fashion. Her gown, embroidered from collar to hem, had elbow-length sleeves and a voluminous skirt. She wore long white gloves and a wide-brimmed hat entirely covered with ostrich plumes. It was her contention that she cared nothing for clothes and dressed modishly only because Walter insisted his position demanded it, but she had such a flair for style that Elsa wondered.

"I don't think he was very difficult to get," Elsa said.

"No, but you didn't believe it would happen. Six years is a long time to keep a young man dangling."

The fact was that Elsa had not thought about William at all, one way or the other. From the time she was old enough, Rebecca had lived in a world of theaters and concerts and cotillions. Even after she passed the age when most girls married, men were attracted to her like ants to a lump of sugar, so thickly that Elsa had difficulty telling one from another in the swarm. She did not remember, until William reappeared and the others gradually fell away, that this was exactly as Rebecca had said it would be, all those years before. How Rebecca had managed to preserve William like a jar of plums until she was ready for him, Elsa never knew.

"It's a beautiful wedding," Hester said. "Hannah's missing something."

Elsa was glutted with memories of Hannah. She did not want to talk about her with Hester. She did not want to think about Robert, dead at fifteen.

"How is Walter, Jr.?"

"Walt?" Hester shrugged. "Healthy. Homely as ever. Even his new nurse, who adores him, calls him 'Beakie.' Odd, isn't it? He looks exactly like Walter, but Walter isn't homely. People say he's distinguished-looking."

Elsa laughed. "Hester, you don't expect a four-year-old child to look distinguished?"

But Hester had lost interest in the subject and did not answer. Her eyes roved around the room into which they had moved for the wedding supper. Wherever she was, she seemed to be searching for someplace, someone, else. She was married to an important man, had a son, lived in an elegant Washington town house, wrote a popular column for the Paper . . . What could she be looking for?

"Here comes Ida," she was saying in a lowered voice. "Did you ever? When I first saw her, I didn't recognize her."

Elsa had of course sent Ida an invitation to the wedding, but she had not expected her to come. Until recently, no one had known exactly where she lived. She had written rarely, strange little notes—often no more than "I am well and happy. Love, Ida"—addressed to "The Herzog Family," but omitting her own address. Perhaps she had been afraid that Papa, if he knew where she was, would go there and drag her home by the hair. But the last note, written five months before, had given a street number in Wilmette, Illinois.

"I shall come," Ida had written in answer to the invitation. "I will not stay at the house, but at the home of a friend in the Faith. Love, Ida."

She had not been heard from again until she arrived at the hotel for the wedding. Elsa had scarcely recognized her either. She had abandoned her struggle with her hair, which had always been too soft and fine to stay up properly, and let it hang loose to her shoulders, like a child. She wore a shapeless blue garment with wide sleeves and a braided, tasseled silk rope around the waist. Her face was almost unlined, though she was thirty-nine years old, and as peaceful as a baby's. Only the vague, dreamy, slightly protuberant eyes were wholly familiar.

"Lovely," she murmured now. "A lovely wedding. Primitive, of course. I must speak to the rabbi." She looked away from them, craning her long neck. Hester rolled her eyes at Elsa. "He's still with Papa. Papa spoke to me very politely. He's quite wrinkled, isn't he?"

"Not when you consider he's over eighty," Hester said. "For eighty, he has very few wrinkles."

"I never thought of him as eighty."

"No. People don't. He still goes down to the Paper every day and works seven or eight hours and sometimes more."

"The Paper," Ida said. "Yes."

Elsa had a feeling Ida might be going into a trance. "Wilmette, Illinois. That's a long way off, isn't it?" she said hurriedly. "What made you go there?"

Ida turned and looked at her. "Why, that's where the great house of worship is."

"Oh, yes, that religion of yours," Hester said. "What's the name of it? Bahai?"

"Not *Bahay*. Some pronounce it *Bahi*, but *Ba-ha-e* is preferred. And it isn't my religion, but everyone's—the universal religion."

"Oh? Well, anyway it isn't Judaism. You always wanted to get away from that. Those holy pictures you loved. She even had one of Jesus," Hester said to Elsa. "Can you imagine Papa, if he'd ever known about it? But I never told." She giggled. "I was saving it, in case I ever had to use it. What a nasty child I was!"

"You don't seem to have improved very much," Ida said with unexpected asperity. "It isn't kind to mock another person's religion." She turned to Elsa. "I must see the rabbi before I go. Will you come with me, Elsa? I'd like you to be there."

"Ida, I can't. I must stay with the guests. A supper will be served in a little—"

"Oh, I don't mean now. After the supper, of course. I'm not leaving before the supper." Elsa had the sudden impression that Ida was hungry, that perhaps she did not get enough to eat in Wilmette, Illinois. "I'll go and arrange it with the rabbi and let you know later . . ."

She was moving away as she said the last words, gliding around the knots of people in a curiously graceful manner. A young woman Elsa did not know approached her, said something to her, then joined her as she walked along.

"She's really quite mad," Hester said. "That costume. Everybody's looking at her."

"I don't think she cares. She seems happy. She never seemed happy at home. Absent, but not happy."

"Oh, well, who was happy at home?"

"Weren't you?"

"I? I just knew how to get what I wanted. The trouble is, by the time I got it—" Her eyes went roaming again, searching the crowded room. "You know Proteus? Well." She patted Elsa's arm as though consoling her for something, and went off, following her eyes.

The next few hours were a blur, against which certain moments remained discrete, pictorial.

Walter, encircled by a rapt audience, talking in his booming voice, talking, talking, yet seeming never to tire others as he tired the family. Distinguished. Yes, he was even graying a little; and his height, with the slight stoop as though leaning graciously to the level of ordinary men; and the imposing nose . . . "Taft. William Howard Taft. A man to keep your eye on. You'll remember I said so . . ."

Mama, the lavender dress so becoming to her soft face, her white hair, worrying because Hester said William would be useful to Rebecca.

"Useful. What does she mean, useful? Rebecca loves him, doesn't she?"

"I think so, Mama." How could Elsa know? Rebecca's sudden, feverish, protracted enthusiasm for William—Mama's anxious reverence for Papa—Hannah, going heedlessly, or willingly, to Arthur's bedroom . . . It was all alien to Elsa.

At her own wedding Elsa's pleasure had been pierced by dread of the mysterious ordeal that lay ahead of her. She had determined to prepare Rebecca better than Mama had prepared her, but when it came to it, Rebecca would not listen.

"Oh, Mama, never *mind*. Everything will be all right. I'm not a child."

Rebecca, holding court in her bridal gown, breathless with power, absently keeping William's hand in hers—beaming, nodding William, who so recently had been a slayer of dragons . . .

A glimpse of Samuel irritably shaking off Myra's clinging arm to confer with a man Elsa did not know . . . Samuel laughing, holding out his hand for something from the man's pocket—bills?—returning jauntily to Myra, composing his face into a mask of contriteness . . .

123

Papa, talking to Rabbi Schoenfeld, who was two years younger and looked ten years older, and then Papa moving away and Ida approaching the rabbi . . . Papa crossing the room to Elsa, erect, looming, the whiteness of his luxuriant hair and beard like illumination . . . *Mr. Sigmund Herzog, owner and publisher of one of the most influential newspapers in New York City, as indomitable at eighty* . . .

"As I was just saying to the rabbi, Elsa, we're establishing a dangerous precedent when we begin to secularize religious ceremonies by taking them out of the synagogue. If a wedding can be held in a hotel, why not a funeral, or the solemnization of a bar mitzvah? Before long, we'll question the necessity of a house of worship and relegate God to banquet rooms."

"I agree with you, Papa."

"Yes, I know. This was Nathan's preference. In matters of observance, Elsa, a wife may gently persuade her husband."

"Yes, Papa."

"Rebecca is a lovely bride. I don't, however, approve of everyone's telling her how beautiful she is. I hope you will remind her, Elsa, that beauty is only skin-deep."

"I doubt that she'd hear me."

"No, she probably wouldn't hear you. Your voice has never been emphatic enough, if I may say so, Elsa. Womanly gentleness is admirable, but it need not be coupled with weakness."

"No, Papa."

"No. For example, I think it was unwise to let Ida prevail upon you to have her here. She is only making a spectacle of herself."

He did not know then, nor did Elsa, what a spectacle of herself Ida was going to make.

"Papa—"

"Yes?"

"This is my daughter's wedding, Papa. Supposedly a happy occasion."

"I'm quite aware of that. Well?"

"Would you care to mention something about it—one thing, however inconsequential, Papa—of which you approve?"

But she had not said that to him, not aloud. It was too late for that. He was eighty years old. If she had wanted to discard the guise that protected her from him, she should have done it long before.

The wedding supper. Sliced cardboard with minced flannel—a

flaming dessert, marched around the tables by perspiring waiters (Who had ordered the flames? Nathan, explaining to the rabbi's wife that all the alcohol in the brandy was burning off?). Rebecca and William cutting the towering wedding cake, Rebecca's hand over his, guiding the knife . . .

HESTER: Can you make out the flavor of the frosting?

SAMUEL: Certainly. Shaving soap.

A five-piece orchestra ("Not nine, Nathan—not for only seventy people; it would look ostentatious"), William waltzing Elsa solemnly around the floor . . .

"You're very light on your feet, Mrs. Herzog."

"Don't you think you should call me something a little less formal, William, now that you're a member of the family?"

"Yes, I suppose I should." Turning red and knowing it. "I'm blushing. You must think I'm a fool, Mrs.—uh. A man twenty-seven years old blushing like a schoolgirl."

"You can't help it, William. It's your fair coloring. Now, what would you feel at home with? Mother Herzog? Mama Herzog? I wouldn't mind plain Mama myself, but you probably want to reserve that for your own mother."

"Why?" His smile, made somehow more appealing by two crooked lower teeth. The unexpected humor. "Can't I have two Mamas, Mama?"

Finally, again, Ida. The Ida to end all Idas.

"Rabbi Schoenfeld will see me now, Elsa. I've had chairs set up in an anteroom, where we'll be undisturbed. This is Miss Anna Wolff." Ida indicated the young woman who had approached and followed her earlier and who had apparently not left her side since. "This is my sister, Mrs. Herzog. She's joining us for our discussion with the rabbi."

Elsa was bewildered: by Ida, who had suddenly shed her vague dreaminess and become almost commanding; by Ida's projected discussion with the rabbi, on what subject Elsa could not imagine; by Miss Wolff, who was thickset, with bright black eyes and a great deal of dark hair on her face, and said, by way of explaining her presence at the wedding, that she knew Hester.

"Ida, I really can't go off and leave the guests. Why do you—?"

"Of course you can. No one will miss you. It isn't as if you were the bride." Ida had her hand on Elsa's arm, shepherding her toward the door as she spoke. Miss Wolff trotted silently behind them.

"This is very important to me, Elsa. It's why I came. Oh, the wedding, of course, but I wouldn't have made the long trip just for—I'd hoped others would join us, yet I knew it would be difficult. You were always the one who listened, Elsa, opened your mind. Miss Wolff—" She turned her head to give the young woman a misty smile. "Miss Wolff is an unexpected dividend."

Elsa did not know whether she went along because otherwise she would have had to tear herself rudely from her sister's grasp, or out of curiosity, or to humor Ida, who would soon be gone again and might never return, or simply because she was, as Papa had said, weak.

"Ida, I won't go another step," she said on the heels of this last thought, "until you tell me what it's all about."

Ida urged her on, tugging a little, as if Elsa were an obstinate child. "But I can't tell you in a minute, standing here. It's a whole beautiful message. You and Miss Wolff will hear it when I give it to the rabbi."

Miss Wolff had not opened her mouth except to acknowledge her introduction to Elsa. When Elsa stopped to make her protest, Miss Wolff stood patiently waiting until the sisters moved on again, then followed behind them.

"Did you say you were a friend of the Lowenthal family's?" Elsa called back to her.

"I don't think I said that." Her voice was almost as deep as a man's. "Did I?"

"She knows Hester," Ida explained, adding nothing to Elsa's information. "I didn't ask Hester to join us. She'd only have made one of her derisive remarks. But perhaps it was wrong of me not to try."

What Ida had called an anteroom was not much larger than a closet, with a telephone, a desk, a desk chair, and two miscellaneous chairs that were jammed against the wall. A printed card in an easel on the desk said: FLOOR MANAGER. Ida, for some inexplicable reason, placed this with the printing face down.

Rabbi Schoenfeld's patriarchal face appeared around the edge of the doorframe. "Ah!" he said, and came all the way in.

"Yes, this is right, rabbi," Ida trilled. Elsa had forgotten Ida's habit of singing commonplaces. "You found us."

He had shrunk with the years, but still he dwarfed the room with his height and his massive frame. Because he resembled the picture of Abraham preparing to plunge a knife into Isaac, Elsa had, as a child, been terrified of him. But he was a gentle, soft-spoken, scholarly man with a benign face, intelligent eyes that had turned watery, and skin that had come to resemble crumpled beige tissue paper.

"Ah!" he said again. "Elsa." He bent over her chair to take her hand between both of his. "The young couple has just slipped away. I pray for *hesed*."

"What's that, rabbi?" Miss Wolff inquired.

The rabbi looked startled, as though he had not noticed a third person in the room. He let go of Elsa's hand and turned around to her.

"There are differences of opinion," he said. "The translation I like is *steadfastness*, Miss . . ."

"Wolff," Ida said. "Miss Anna Wolff, a friend of mine who is interested in the message I have for you."

The friend of Hester's was now a friend of Ida's. But who *was* she?

"A message," the rabbi repeated. "You have a message for me? I understood you to say you had something urgent to speak to me about. I thought—a problem, an urgent problem." He smiled, and the tissue paper crumpled into a hundred new creases. "What else does anyone want to speak to a rabbi urgently about?"

"No, no, Rabbi Schoenfeld, no problem," Ida sang. "Won't you please sit down? There at the desk? In the seat of honor?"

He looked around the little room with an air of puzzlement that Elsa wholly shared. Miss Wolff, on the other hand, seemed not at all puzzled, only interested and expectant. Perhaps she, unlike Elsa or the rabbi, knew why she was there.

"But if I sit there, Ida," the rabbi said, "where will you—?"

"Oh, I shall stand," Ida warbled. "I shall stand and give you my message."

There were moments, in later years, when Elsa could look back on it objectively and be amused. More often, she felt exactly what she had felt at the time, listening to Ida and beginning to understand her purpose; exactly the same hot squirm of embarrassment, as painful as though she were hearing Ida's voice again and seeing the look on Rabbi Schoenfeld's face.

"Judaism is so narrow, you see. God manifests himself to man at various stages of human progress, in various ways. He has manifested himself to all our prophets: Abraham, Moses, David, Jesus, Mohammed, the Bab, and Baha Ullah. But the Jews recognize only the first three of these, rabbi. They cling to their own kind, their

127

own little circumscribed body of beliefs, and blind themselves to the wisdom of all the noble and enlightened prophets of other faiths."

She stood in the center of the tiny room in her shapeless robe, addressing herself to the rabbi, now and then stretching out her arms within an inch of his nose. Rabbi Schoenfeld appeared stunned to stone. Miss Wolff seemed to be taking notes.

"That's why Bahaism is so beautiful, rabbi. We believe in the unity of all religions. We believe in the simple life, service to the suffering, and peace among men. Could anything be more beautiful, rabbi?"

Ida paused, her large, somewhat bulging eyes fixed on him as though waiting for an answer, but when he had licked his lips and managed to begin, in a hoarse stammer: "Yes . . . service . . . peace . . . all religions—" she rode over the words with her own. Her voice rose and fell in a cadence that reminded Elsa of the chanting of Hebrew prayers, mesmeric, the meaning lost in the rhythm.

Finally Ida paused again, this time approaching the desk where Rabbi Schoenfeld sat and stretching out her arms to him.

"Cast off the shackles of Judaism, rabbi! Come into this beautiful, all-encompassing fold! Come into the fold, and bring your people with you!"

Her voice stopped. She stood as she was, her arms outstretched to the stone figure of the rabbi. Elsa, longing to escape, was paralyzed, shriveled in her seat, unable to tear her unwilling eyes from the old rabbi's face. There was no sound but the scratching of Miss Wolff's pencil. Years passed.

Rabbi Schoenfeld got up slowly from behind the desk, supporting his weight with his hands on the flat surface. He opened his mouth and moved his lips, but it was a moment before any sound emerged.

"Cast off—" His voice sounded clogged with phlegm. He tried, with only partial success, to clear it. "Cast off—!" and then gave it up. "You'll have to excuse me," he said hoarsely.

His exit was the blind rush of a seasick man to the rail.

"What's the matter with Ida?" Hester asked Elsa. "She came through here a while ago looking tragic, and floated out the door without a word to anyone."

"She'll be all right. She's going back to Wilmette, Illinois." Elsa did not want to talk about Ida. She looked around the room, where only the family and a few lingering guests remained. "There was a young woman here—I don't see her now—who said she knew you. I have no idea who invited her. A Miss Wolff? Hannah—no, Anna, I think—"

"Anna Wolff?" Hester shook her head. "She may know me, but I don't know—oh, yes! I met her in Washington, when I was covering the Roosevelt-Longworth wedding. I think she's a lesbian."

"A what?"

Hester laughed. "Nothing. A person from a Greek island called Lesbos. She looks Greek, doesn't she?"

"Greek? Wolff?"

"No, I suppose not." Hester laughed again, and Elsa wondered whether she had drunk a little too much wine. "It was just a notion," she said.

"But who *is* Anna Wolff, Hester? How did she get here?"

"I imagine she got here the same way she got to Alice Longworth's wedding. By walking in. She's a reporter for the *Journal*."

Elsa had not seen Papa in such a rage since she was two years old and he threw the sofa pillow at Mama. He must have contained his fury all day at the Paper, until it boiled over as he burst into the house. Elsa had seldom heard him raise his voice; in anger, he customarily spoke with chilling softness. But now his roar penetrated the thick, closed door of her room.

He had not calmed down by suppertime. As though for fear he might, he kept the newspaper propped against his water goblet, folded with the headline a foot from his eyes. Periodically, he snatched it up and read some part of the story aloud again, with comments. Once he even began while Mary was in the room, and was not stopped by Mama's urgent throat-clearing, which he seemed not to hear, but by Mary's coming to look companionably over his shoulder. When she had cleared away the dishes, he spread it all out again on the table.

CLERGYMAN URGED TO RENOUNCE FAITH
Daughter of Publisher Tries to Convert Rabbi
"Cast Off the Shackles of Judaism!"

Miss Ida Herzog, daughter of Sigmund Herzog, the noted publisher, yesterday urged Rabbi Mordecai Schoenfeld, religious leader of Temple Beth Torah for forty-two years, to "cast off the shackles of Judaism" and convert to the Bahai faith. The attempted conversion took place during the celebration of the marriage of Mr. Herzog's granddaughter, Miss Rebecca Herzog, to Mr. William Lowenthal, at which Rabbi Schoenfeld officiated.

(Wedding story, p. 9).

Miss Ida Herzog, who converted to Bahaism and left home twelve years ago . . .

"Only Hearst's filthy yellow rag would print a story like that," Papa shouted. "That isn't news. He printed it to make me a laughingstock."

"Now, Papa—" Mama said.

"'*Cast off the shackles of Judaism!*' I didn't believe it. I thought Hearst made it up to embarrass me. But it's true. I telephoned the rabbi, and he confirmed it. How can I ever show my face in the synagogue again?"

"That's foolish, Sigmund. You didn't do it. Rabbi Schoenfeld has known you, our whole family, for so many years. He knows—"

"He knows Ida is mad, because I told him. I apologized for her. But how even a madwoman could drag the rabbi away during her niece's wedding and try to convert him—convert a *rabbi!* . . . No wonder the *Journal* splashed it all over the front page. It's bizarre, that's what it is. Bizarre. I've been made a laughingstock by my apostate daughter."

Elsa sat in silence, scarcely able to eat, waiting. It did not come until nearly the end of the meal.

"How did Hearst get this story? Did that madwoman tell a reporter what she planned to do? Have you any idea, Ada?"

"I? Of course not, Sigmund."

"Do you know anything about it, Elsa?"

She took a deep breath. "Yes," she said, "I do. It doesn't say so in the story, but I was there."

"*There?* Where?"

"In the room with Ida and the rabbi and the reporter."

He looked at her in silence, trying to make her drop her eyes. That was one battle he had always lost, and he lost it now.

"Do you mean to tell me," he said, not shouting now, but softly, very softly, "that you actually participated in this insanity of your sister's?"

"No, Papa, I didn't participate in it."

130

"Ah, I see. You were there, but you didn't participate. Will you kindly explain this to me?"

"I was there because Ida asked me to be there. She said—"

"I see. She asked you to be there while she tried to convert the rabbi. You considered it a reasonable request, so you went along."

"I didn't know—"

"Perhaps I have the wrong word? Perhaps the word should be encourage, rather than participate?"

"I didn't encourage her, Papa. I had no idea—"

"You don't concede that by your willingness, by your presence—"

"Now, Papa," Ada said, and surprisingly did not leave it at that. "Why don't you give Elsa a chance to tell you what happened?"

He frowned at her across the table. "Ada, kindly keep out of this," he said, and then to Elsa, "I'm waiting for your explanation."

"It's not difficult to explain, Papa. Ida told me she had something to say to the rabbi that she wanted me to hear. She wouldn't tell me what it was. By the time I understood her purpose, it was too late to stop her."

"You mean you had no inkling before you went with her? Why did you think she had a reporter along?"

"I didn't know the young woman was a reporter. I don't know whether or not Ida knew. She introduced her to Rabbi Schoenfeld as a friend. But even if I had known, I couldn't possibly have guessed what Ida had in mind."

Papa was silent, pitting his gaze against hers again. "Well, I'm sure that's true," he said then. "I've never known you to lie. What I find it difficult to understand, however, is why Ida wanted you to be there, to witness her madness."

"She tried to convert me, too, Papa."

Elsa was a light sleeper. Nathan invariably woke her when he came home from the Paper. Usually she kept her eyes closed, trying to cling to the remnants of sleep as the closet door squeaked, drawers opened and shut, and shoes dropped. But tonight she was waiting for him.

"Oh, you're awake." He sounded pleased. He took off his jacket and sat on a chair next to the bed in his shirt sleeves. "I had a terrible night, Elsa. Sigmund came down to the Paper after supper and went on a rampage. I don't know what was the matter with him. Nothing was right. He looked at a piece of copy I was editing and tore it up, said it was time I knew the difference between news and rubbish, and if I didn't I ought to be working for Mr. Hearst . . ."

He went on for some time, while she stroked his hand and made soothing sounds. She scarcely listened to what he was saying. There was no need; she knew the plot by heart. Only the details, and occasionally the characters, varied. Sometimes it was a younger man on the staff who did not show him the proper respect. Occasionally it was Mr. MacRae, the managing editor, who thought Nathan could have made a story more concise when he had already cut it to the bone. Usually the persecutor was Papa.

"Papa was in a state before he left the house," she murmured. "It had nothing to do with you . . . he knows you're the best copy editor in the business . . . why do you think he won't let you do anything else? . . . he could never replace you . . ."

His hand felt cold and dry, like paper. In the morning, asleep, when his face seemed less deeply grooved and his color was better, she could see that he was still a handsome man. Now his eyes were dull and his skin was gray from weariness and bad digestion, and she could not remember his good looks. When he got into bed beside her, she could feel the sharpness of his bones.

"On any other newspaper, I'd have been managing editor long ago," he said into the darkness. "Sigmund never wanted to recognize my executive talents. I managed one of the biggest department stores in Baltimore, but he ignored that as though it had never happened."

"You're a brilliant copy editor, Nathan. Papa's afraid the Paper would suffer if he had to give the position to someone else."

"Well, it would, of course. Some of the men under me—their lack of knowledge—it's pathetic, Elsa."

She knew that no matter how tired he was, he would be wide awake for a while. Often, when he thought she was asleep, he sat at the window for as long as an hour before coming to bed. She did not try to imagine what went through his mind as he sat there in the darkness, but she hoped it was nothing of consequence. He was not the man to be alone with grave thoughts.

"Nathan—"

"Yes, my dear?" That was good. He only called her that when his self-esteem was restored.

"Nathan, now that Rebecca is married and David is so seldom home ("A traveling salesman!" Papa said. "He's going backwards. That's what I was when I came to this country in 1848, except that I

132

traveled on foot. Did he need a college education to be a high-class peddler?"), there's no reason for us to live here. We could have a place of our own, something small, an apartment, where we'd be—"

"Elsa, you're not starting that again?"

"I haven't mentioned it for years. I knew you were contented, and I could see that there might be some advantages for the children, but now—" His elbow was digging into her. She shifted away from it. "Nathan, I'm forty-six years old. It's time I was the mistress of my own home instead of being a child in my father's house."

"What are you talking about, a child? I pay for our room and board." At Elsa's urging, and over Papa's objections, he made a monthly payment that might have maintained one person in a second-class boarding house.

"I know you do, Nathan. It isn't a question of paying. Paying can't make me a grown woman in this house."

"I don't understand what you're talking about. You and Mama run everything together. You're as much the woman of the house as she is."

"Oh, no, Nathan. I only do as much work."

"Well, it can't be very arduous, with Mary doing most of it." He got up on his elbows and tried to peer into her face. "Elsa, we have every comfort here. We wouldn't like an apartment. You wouldn't like it. Besides, you're used to your family around you. You'd be lonely."

"No. I wouldn't be lonely."

"And it would be expensive. We'd have to buy furniture. You've always been so concerned about spending—do you remember when you insisted I return the sealskin coat?—and now you want to squander sums we can't afford on an apartment and furniture we don't need."

She had more than enough money to buy furniture. It was wonderful how money grew, fifty cents or a dollar at a time, untouched for twenty years. But she did not mention it to Nathan. She knew it would make no difference.

"There are furnished apartments. Or hotels. Many of the finest people are living in hotels now."

He sighed and lay down again. "Elsa, I'm getting old. I'm not as well as I might be. You know that. How can you ask me, at my age, to give up the home, the comforts, I'm accustomed to and move into some cramped apartment or shabby hotel? I'm surprised at your selfishness."

"Yes." Elsa closed her eyes. "Yes, I suppose it was selfish of me."

"All right. I'm willing to forget it." She heard him roll over on his side. "But I want you to promise me never to mention the subject again."

"I promise," she said.

6

"Is that you, Hester?"

"Yes, Papa."

"Would you be good enough to let a little sunlight into this room? It will be dark enough in the grave."

She crossed to the windows and raised the green shades. There was no sun. The gray light seemed wintry, though it was not yet October, and it did not reach the far corners of the room. Where it did touch, its pale rays defined, without brightening, the heavy mahogany chiffonier with the scars of years faithfully polished over, the mattress-striped Morris chair, the faded "Turkish" rug that Mama had bought in Atlantic City ("I don't know what came over me—Elsa tried to stop me—but he was such a nice man, and he cut the price in half because it was his last rug and he wanted me to have it"). Beyond, in semidarkness, stood the huge bed, and the bedside table with its array of bottles on a tray.

"That's better," Papa said, without opening his eyes. "Are you still there, Hester?"

"Of course, Papa."

"Well, I couldn't be sure," he said irritably. "Elsa slips in and out like a ghost. Often I've been speaking to her for several minutes before I realize she has gone again, without a word."

"I've brought you a book I think you'll like. *The Correspondence of Theodore Roosevelt and Henry Cabot Lodge*. Shall I read a little of it now?"

"You shall not. You know I hate to be read to. Bring a chair and sit over here near me." He opened his eyes and looked at her for the first time. "I wish you could stay. You're the only one who doesn't come out of a sense of duty. Not that I have any quarrel with a sense of duty. There's little enough of it these days."

"I'll stay until you're tired, Papa, and I'll come again every day."

134

"Fine. That is, if Walter can spare you."

Hester was startled. He had seemed so lucid. "Oh, Walter can spare me," she said.

"And the baby is well taken care of?"

"Walt is in excellent hands."

That was true enough. There was no better military school in the country—none better that accepted Jews, at any rate. It would do Papa no good to let him know he was lost in time, and it might remind him, if he had forgotten, that he had not spoken to her in more than two years.

"Does that mean he's forgiven me?" she had asked Elsa on the phone.

"I don't know. He's—changeable. All I know is he said he wanted you here. You'll see when you come."

It was strange to be in this room, sitting next to the bed with Papa in it. She must of course have been here before. She recognized the furniture, if not the smell of medicine and bedclothes and something she could not separate into its parts but thought of as old age. But she had no memory of herself in the room. She had slipped notes to Papa under this door, but never disturbed him here. Mama had always talked to her in the kitchen or the sewing room or the room Hester had shared with Ida. Whenever she thought of Papa in this house, she saw him at the head of the table. She had never before seen him in bed.

"Perhaps he'll take over the Paper someday," Papa said. "With his inheritance—your talent and Walter's—it's a distinct possibility. But in the meantime, I don't know. It worries me." He began moving his head from side to side on the pillow. "I don't mind telling you, it worries me."

"Don't think about it now, Papa."

He stopped tossing his head and looked at her coldly. No, she could not actually see his look in the half-light. She was remembering it, lost in time herself.

"If I don't think about it, who will?" he demanded.

He spoke softly, but he had nearly always spoken softly. There was no tremor in his voice. She did not have to raise hers to make him hear. Except for that momentary agitation of his head, he lay quietly, as though resting before his evening session at the Paper.

"The mistake I made," he said, "was in telling you not to marry William. No one was going to tell *you* whom to marry or not marry." He gave an almost soundless chuckle. "I should have insisted on William. Then you might have picked the kind of man I hoped for, a man capable of succeeding me on the Paper. What is William? A good advertising man when he wants to be, when he works at it. He's nothing more. He will never be anything more." The soft voice grew softer still. "He isn't even much of a husband, is he, Rebecca?"

Hester gave an indeterminate murmur. It was possible that the rust of age had completely eroded their estrangement from his memory. If not, she wanted to say nothing that might recall it to him. In the role of Rebecca, she was at least temporarily safe.

"God acts in mysterious ways. I must believe he has some purpose in decreeing that all the males in my line be flawed with weakness and that all the females choose similarly flawed men."

Was he still addressing Rebecca? There was no way of knowing. His eyes seemed to be open, but they were not turned toward Hester. The whiteness of his hair and beard blended with the whiteness of the sheets, so that his profile appeared discrete, an unframed etching.

"Not one of them has a feel for the beauty of a well-dressed page. Not one of them has that instinct for a story that sets off a humming in a real newspaperman's head: *This is truth, not rumor. This is big* . . . Evidently you came to the conclusion, Samuel, that the Coast Guard telegrapher must be either a madman or a prankster. Is your imagination so limited that it seemed to you beyond the realm of possibility that the Wright Brothers actually had managed to lift a flying machine from the sand dunes of North Carolina? Do you know what your misplaced skepticism has cost us? . . . Don't mutter to me, Samuel, about other newspapers that were skeptical. If you had not been, we could have scooped those other newspapers . . ."

His voice trailed off. She thought he had gone to sleep, and got up from her chair, intending to slip out.

"Sit down, Hester," he said. "I won't have you sneaking away as Elsa does. If you must leave, say so."

"I thought you were tired, Papa."

"How can I be tired, when all I do is lie here? I may not talk incessantly. Only a fool does so. A fool—" He gave the near-soundless chuckle again "—or Walter. The ordinary intelligent man occasionally pauses to think. Of course if you find my pauses intolerably wearying, by all means leave."

"Papa, you are probably the least wearying man I know."

136

"Including Samuel?" He did not wait for an answer. "You've always been in league, you two. It's strange. You're the cleverest of them all, and he—they said I was too old to go to the Paper every day. Even Mama. 'Why don't you go to the park, Sigmund, and sit in the sun?' Sit in the sun with a lot of doddering old men! Fortunately, I paid no attention—"

She thought he was wandering again, off on another tangent, but he wound back to Samuel.

"Fortunately I was there when Samuel got the AP story. I believe if he had been responsible, it would not even have appeared on the front page."

He stopped. She was too curious to resist prodding him. Immediately, she wished she hadn't. She had prodded him to within two years of his quarrel with her.

"What story, Papa?"

"What story? Haven't you been listening? The assassination at Sarajevo. Granted, none of us on the newspapers understood its international significance, but Samuel considered it a little Balkan disturbance that could not possibly interest Americans. As though the assassination of an archduke and his wife were not high drama in itself. The Serbian youth lurking in the doorway of the barber shop—the automobile approaching the spot—and the old emperor's grief—the ill-fated Hapsburgs . . ." His voice faded, and then suddenly strengthened again. "Samuel saw none of it. None of it. I've always thought it strange that you find him so congenial."

Was he jealous of Samuel? What could she tell him? Not that their alliance was grounded in mockery, Samuel's bitter and impotent and narrowly defined; her own gleeful, effective, directed not at Papa, never at Papa himself, but at the absurdities he cherished and at absurdities beyond him.

"He's the closest to me in age," she murmured. "The only one who didn't grow up while I was still a child."

She could not tell whether he was listening. When he spoke again, he had traveled into the present.

"Ludendorff has lost his nerve, you know. It's only a matter of months before this terrible war will end. The Huns must never be allowed to arm again. I intend to write an editorial to that effect. It would be disastrous to suppose that defeat alone can diminish their thirst for world imperialism."

The retort came swiftly to her lips, very nearly passed them. "Do you suppose victory will diminish England's?" She did not think he would have forgiven her again—or forgotten again—whichever it was. To her relief, he wandered back to the past.

"But this is no conversation for a young lady. Mama always tells me I only know how to talk to newspapermen." He turned his head toward her for a moment. If he saw a lady who was no longer young, the message did not get through. "I hope you're managing to accustom yourself to Washington at last."

"I am. It's a very interesting city."

"Hester, I may not be well, but I am not an idiotic old man to whom it is necessary to mouth soothing platitudes."

She laughed. "All right. I detest Washington. I loathe it. I'll never become accustomed to it. At the very first opportunity, I'm coming back to New York, where I belong."

The door at the other side of the bed opened noiselessly. Elsa beckoned from the doorway.

"Where are you going?" Papa asked, the instant Hester moved.

"I'll be back in a minute, Papa, I promise."

"Your promises aren't good for much," he muttered as she joined Elsa in the hall.

Elsa looked worn. For a time she had appeared to be reversing the natural processes, to be growing younger month by month. Now the reversal had ceased. It was not that she looked her age. The Herzogs all carried their years easily. Except for the sagging neck, partially concealed by the black band she wore around it, Elsa did not have the aspect of an aging woman but, rather, of one in the middle years who had been ill, or struck by tragedy.

"I thought you were supposed to be taking a nap," Hester said to her.

"I did. I dozed a little. You ought to go soon, I think. The doctor doesn't want him to get tired."

She had been the prettiest of the four of them. There were still traces, visible in spite of her frumpy black dress and severe hair style. Mama's gentleness was in her face, but without the soft, blurred outlines. Gentleness was a trap. That was one, at least, into which Hester would never fall.

"Every time I try to leave, he stops me," Hester said. "Does it really matter, anyway? He's going to have a long rest."

Elsa sighed. "We mustn't hurry it." She went on quickly, as though she had said something untoward. "Sometimes he seems reasonably content. Occasionally, when he's reliving some triumph, I think he's even happy. He isn't in pain, and I keep him quite comfortable."

"You shouldn't have to. I've told you that before. He ought to have a nurse. God knows, he can afford one."

"He'd hate having a nurse, and he doesn't need one. I manage very well."

Hester leaned against the wall. Sitting at a typewriter did not condition one to standing unsupported. She was dying for a cigarette, but Papa might smell the smoke and think she was a fallen woman. Elsa would probably think so too, though Elsa's disapproval would not stop her.

"You're too good," Hester said. "You won't get any thanks for giving up your own life to come here."

"Goodness has nothing to do with it. Absolutely nothing. And I'm not looking for thanks. You'd better go back in now for a little while, before he wakes up and calls you."

"What makes you think he's asleep?"

"He'd have rung his bell before this if he weren't. Papa was never, you may remember, a patient man. He hasn't changed."

"No. It's curious. In some ways, he scarcely seems changed at all. If you grant his basic assumption that it's 1903, or 1914, or that I'm Rebecca, or Samuel, everything he says is as logical and lucid as it ever was. The really strange thing to me is to see him in bed. He doesn't even seem very sick."

"I said that to the doctor. I asked him what was the matter with Papa. He told me if I wanted to put a medical name to it, arteriosclerosis would do, but what was actually the matter was that he's ninety-two." She put her ear to the door without opening it. Hester had heard nothing. "He's awake. Go on in. I'll come with his broth when I think you should leave."

The light in the room had changed, so that the figure on the bed was even more in shadow. Hester had not yet seen his face, only its lineaments, and it was just as well. Once, in Cairo, she had looked at the mummy of Ramses II, whose splendid, sixty-seven-year reign had brought such magnificence to Egypt, and seen with distaste and disenchantment a little brown face shriveled into insignificance.

"Hester?"

"I'm here, Papa."

"Come and sit down. You kept me waiting long enough."

139

"I was gone only a minute or two. Elsa wanted to make sure I wasn't tiring you."

"Yes. No doubt she thinks you might because she knows she does. Elsa is a good, dutiful girl, and she has never caused me a moment's trouble, but I must confess she wearies me. There are scarcely ten minutes in the day when she isn't hovering over me with a spoon or a tray or a question. 'Are you warm enough, Papa . . . Are you cool enough, Papa? . . . Should I straighten your pillows, Papa? . . . Do you want an alcohol rub, Papa?' I suppose you think I'm ungrateful."

"Of course you're ungrateful."

"No. I simply find the necessity for gratitude tiresome. I'm not accustomed to it." He had been lying so still all the while that she had begun to wonder whether only his head was capable of motion, but now he raised his knees a little, making a small hill of the covers. Instantly she got the impression that he had shrunk, like Ramses' mummy. "Now that I think of it, it isn't true she never caused me trouble. She married Nathan. That was trouble enough. I got rid of him, finally, after his fiasco in Baltimore, and she fished him back."

"He was harmless enough, as far as I could tell, and he was the best copy editor you ever had."

"A nincompoop is never harmless." Hester must have imagined that he shot her a sidelong glance; she could not have seen it. "Why are you defending Nathan, anyhow? You despise him."

She supposed it was for the sake of argument. Papa had always liked to argue with her, even when he pretended she was impudent to question his opinion.

"I despise most people," she answered.

He was not listening. After a moment, he said: "Nathan hasn't once come to see me. I'll not forget it. The fact that I'm relieved by his absence has no bearing whatever on his neglect. I shall tell that young man—"

Hester interrupted him. Why, at that moment? When she was little, Papa had punished her by locking her in her room. She had not minded. She had always been able to amuse herself. But once when he had left her she had pounded on the door with her small fists, not stopping when she bruised them. Why that time?

"Papa," she said. "Nathan has been dead for six years."

He did not speak. That other time he had unlocked the door, come into the room and stood silently looking down at her. What she felt now might have been the child's apprehension, perceived from the past like a star's light.

He said finally: "Now and then I doze off, lying here. There's nothing else to do." His voice was calm, conversational. "I dream. Pleasant dreams, sometimes. I dream about the Paper, so vividly I can smell the ink. I'm in my office, holding a news conference, the smoke from MacRae's pipe blowing in my face. I'm in the composing room, putting a head directly into type. Not many men can do that, you know. I'm listening to the ticking of the AP machine, or seizing a ringing phone because I know a big story is breaking and the man at the desk is slow—" He paused. "Mama is dead too, isn't she?"

"Yes, Papa."

"That's wrong. No, God decreed it, so it can't be wrong. But I expected always to have Mama with me. She was seven years younger. It should be Mama who comes with spoons and trays, not Elsa. Mama never wearied me." He paused again. "Shall I tell you something in confidence, Hester? What I have really cared for in my life are the Paper, Mama, you, and—and—" He moved his head to the side away from her. "Someone else."

"Rebecca?"

The head came back. He spoke testily. "That's what I said: the Paper, Mama, you, and Rebecca."

In that order? It made no difference to Hester. There were not so many people who cared for her that she could afford to be choosy about rank.

"When must you go back to Washington?" he asked her.

"I don't know. I'll stay as long as I can."

She could not bring him out of this dream. She could not tell him that she no longer lived in Washington, but in a hotel a few blocks away. This reality was too close to realities she did not want exhumed.

"I know you'd rather live in New York than in Washington," he said. "New York is my city too. All the while I lived in Baltimore, I longed for New York. But you'll become accustomed to it, Hester. A woman must, of course, go where her husband's work is."

She might have asked him why a man should not go where his wife's work was, shocking him into one of the discourses he savored. But, again, the reminder of her work might be a reminder of too much else.

"I've never ceased to marvel that it was Samuel who first brought Walter to the house," he said. "What could they possibly have had in common? I recognized Walter's brilliance at once, of course. Do you know how early he understood Germany's threat to the rest of the world? Fourteen years before the invasion of Belgium, when the Kaiser sent his troops to China during the Boxer Rebellion. 'Conduct yourselves like Huns,' he told them, 'that for a thousand years no Chinaman will dare look askance at a German.' We reported that directive to *Schrecklichkeit* in the Paper, discussed its implications, but no one listened. Hearst called the Paper 'that journalistic prophet of doom.' He'd have discounted it, of course, even if he knew. In his eyes, Germany could do no wrong . . ."

"Papa—" Hester began, but she did not have to divert him. At that moment Elsa came in with his broth.

"Hester and I are talking, Elsa. Why do you interrupt us?"

Elsa pushed aside the tray of medicines on the bedside table and set down a smaller tray. She lit the bed lamp. "It's time for your broth, Papa."

"Broth! I'd as soon drink dishwater."

"This is good and *kraftig*. Mary simmered a piece of Papa's Meat along with the bones. I've brought you a slice of rye bread to dunk in it."

"Why didn't you bring me the meat?"

"You know you can't have such rich meat, Papa." Elsa slipped one arm under him, and with the other raised his pillows; then eased him back against them so that he was partially upright. "Stop grumbling, now, and take this while it's hot."

She tied a napkin around his neck and held the tray close to his chest while he sipped from the cup and ate the broth-dipped bread. Hester kept her eyes on his hands, which were any old man's hands, fragile brown-flecked claws, like pale chicken feet, but less unsteady than she had expected.

"Elsa would love it if she could feed me," he said. "She tried, but I wouldn't let her."

"It might be a good deal easier for her to feed you than to balance a heavy tray until you've finished eating."

"Don't you encourage her, Hester. She'd love to think I was helpless."

"Drink the rest of your broth, Papa," Elsa said calmly. "It's getting cold."

"I have to go now, Papa," Hester said. She got up and kissed the top of his head with her eyes closed. He smelled clean but stale, like an old pocket that no amount of washing can rid of its past accumulations. "I'll be back."

"I wish you could stay." She had never heard him sound like that. Forlorn. "Come back as soon as you can. I'll be waiting."

When Elsa came downstairs with the empty tray, Hester was looking at herself in the vestibule mirror, which was framed by a wide mahogany hatrack. Her skin was still firm, and there was no sign of gray in her soft, thick hair. She no more looked forty-three than Elsa looked fifty-eight. The pince-nez she wore gave her an air of distinction rather than age, and the lenses diffused her eyes, falsely mellowing their expression.

"I thought you'd gone," Elsa said.

"I've been admiring myself. It's quite amazing what a sense of style and a little make-up will do." She knew without turning around that Elsa was pulling in her lips. "I'm better-looking now than I was at eighteen."

"Much good it's done you."

Hester laughed. "Oh, I don't know. I'd rather have something attractive facing me in the mirror every day. It's reassuring." She followed Elsa into the dining room. "What would you say to my staying here?"

"Staying here?" Elsa put the tray down on the table. "Staying here when? I don't know what you mean."

Hester went to the sideboard, picked up the silver cream pitcher, and put it back again with the rest of the coffee service. "All this stuff from the year one," she said, opening the china closet and peering in at the heavily decorated pieces. "It's like a museum. Didn't it ever occur to them to buy anything new?" She turned around to Elsa. "I was thinking of moving in for a while. God knows there's enough room."

Elsa stared at her. "Why should you want to?"

"I don't know. I must be out of my mind." Her eyes darted around the room. "Look, Elsa, have you a—? No, of course you haven't. Just a minute."

Hester went out to the hall table, where she had left her handbag. When she returned she had a cigarette in her mouth. Elsa seemed not to have moved.

"Hester—"

"Please spare me your outrage. It's no longer considered sinful for women to smoke, and I wouldn't care if it were."

Elsa waved her hand. "Smoke if you want to. What business is it of mine? I wasn't going to say anything about that." Her dry voice had a way of rising to another level, acquiring melody. "I wanted to apologize for telling you your looks hadn't done you much good. It was mean of me." She sighed. "It's easy to become mean in this house. If you have any sense, you'll stay where you are."

"You didn't stay where you were."

"I had my reasons."

"Well, I suppose I have mine, though I couldn't tell you at the moment what they are." Hester pulled a chair away from the table and sat down, flicking ashes into her cupped left hand. "I don't think I feel as you do about the house. God knows, it's an awful old mausoleum in a way and they should have moved out of it years ago, but I was always glad they didn't. It was a place to come. Everything else changed, but here Papa sat at the head of the table and Mama at the foot, and no matter what happened to us or how old we grew, we were the children."

"Yes," Elsa said, "it's different. You were happy here."

"No. I was safe." Hester got up and took a cup garlanded with pink roses from the china closet, emptied into it the ashes from her hand, and brought it back with her to the table. "Papa thinks I'm still living in Washington with Walter. I'll tell him I'm staying here because Walter had to go to Europe on an assignment and Walt is with Walter's parents."

"He may remember later. He drifts in and out of reality."

"Yes, I know. He may remember other things too. I'll have to face that when it happens."

Elsa was still standing, a small, erect, top-heavy figure. She must never have discarded the armorlike corsets into which Hester too had once laced herself. Nothing else could give her that pouter-pigeon look.

"What will you do with your apartment at the Belleclaire?"

"Nothing. It will wait for me. I don't plan to stay here the rest of my life. All I have to bring are a few clothes and toilet articles and my typewriter."

The door from the kitchen burst open, and Mary came charging into the room.

"I *thought* I heard voices! I *thought* it was you, Miss Hester!" Her

144

brogue was as rich as ever. She clasped Hester in arms the size of telegraph poles and then held her off to examine her. "My, you're a sight for sore eyes, you are. You're looking elegant too. Like a regular *shiksa!*"

"The supreme accolade."

"What are you saying, Miss Hester?"

"I'm saying you look pretty fine yourself. You must be enjoying your own cooking."

"Och, I know. I'm a big, fat cow, but who cares? I'm enjoying myself." All at once she looked down in astonishment at the negligee she was wearing, its worn silk edges barely meeting over her ample stomach, its fur trimming ravaged by moths. "Look at me, will you? I was lying down on my bed when I heard you, and don't you think I forgot I had this on? It was your mama's, *selig*. It's lucky Miss Hannah isn't here, because it was Miss Hannah gave it to your mama, *selig*, but she never wore it and after a while she gave it to me."

"Mary, I really think—"

"Och, yes, I know, Miss Elsa, I'm talking too much again." Her large, red-cheeked face turned redder still. "And what am I doing, anyway, blathering on about enjoying myself and all, with your poor papa lying upstairs the way he is? It's seeing Miss Hester again, after so long, knocked all the sense from my head."

"I'm going to stay here for a while, Mary. I'm on my way now to get my things from the hotel."

Mary beamed and said that was lovely and it would be more like old times with Miss Hester in the house again. She took it for granted that Hester would share Elsa's room, but when Hester said she had become accustomed to having a room to herself and would prefer her old one, Mary accepted this, as she had always accepted the Herzog vagaries, with amused indulgence.

"I think she suspects she's a distant relative," Hester said, when Mary had gone clumping into the kitchen and up the back stairs. "One of the Irish Herzogs."

Elsa did not laugh. "I don't know what's going to become of her. It worries me. Do you know she's been with us nearly thirty years? On her day off, she goes shopping or to the movies or has a cup of tea with some cook or chambermaid who temporarily meets her standards of refinement. Usually she's back early, shouting, 'I'm home, everybody!' I don't know how she'll manage without us. She has no life of her own."

"I'm sure Papa has left her something in his will."

"It wasn't money I was thinking of, Hester."

Hester shrugged. "What else can you think of? You can't adopt her. If she hasn't made any life of her own all these years, it's nobody's fault but her own. As long as she's taken care of financially, she's not your responsibility."

"Whose responsibility do you suggest she is?"

"You sound like Papa," Hester said, knowing how little Elsa wanted to sound like Papa. "I suggest nobody's responsible for making a life for Mary except Mary. She's no different from the rest of us. When it comes to it, we all have to make our own lives."

Elsa picked up the tray that she had set down on the table. According to some complicated labor agreement that Hester did not understand, Mary, on her way to the kitchen, had ignored it.

"Are you absolutely sure you want to stay here, Hester?"

"No, but I intend to stay." She held the door to the kitchen open for Elsa with the tray. "Unless, of course, I'm not welcome."

"That's not for me to say. It isn't my house." Elsa took the tray to the kitchen sink and put the dishes in a dishpan. There she sighed and turned around to Hester again. "Of course you're welcome. You're very welcome." She hesitated. "Maybe you'd like to have Walt here with you for the weekend."

Hester shook her head. "He wouldn't want to come. He's happy at the academy."

That was probably not true, Hester thought as she left the house. When she had last talked to Walt on the phone, two weeks before, he had said the school was "endurable." But he had been there only ten days. He never found anything endurable for more than three weeks.

Hester wondered whether, with a different sort of child, she might have been more motherly. Probably not. She had had no particular desire for a baby. Nothing had stirred in her when she saw him. No doubt there was nothing to stir. But Walt would have tested the most resolute maternal instinct. He had been far and away the ugliest infant she had ever seen.

He was still homely at sixteen, a gangling caricature of Walter, the stoop accentuated, the bold nose exaggerated, the sharp eyes blurred and magnified by the thick glasses he had to wear. Periodically she felt sorry for him because he was so out of kilter with the rest of the world, and she would take him from whatever school he was in and let him come with her on one of her journalistic missions abroad. It made no difference how much school he missed—he was always years ahead of his classmates—and sometimes he was excellent company, witty, and almost as formidably well informed as his father.

But in the end it was never any use. He had been expelled from one school for cheating, though he had no conceivable need to cheat, and from another for deliberately causing an explosion that demolished all the equipment in a chemistry class and caused a gash in the teacher's cheek from flying glass. On his last visit home, she had taken him with her to see Rebecca and asked him to entertain Clara for a short time while Hester and Rebecca talked. When it was time to leave, Clara would not come out of her room to say good-by, but she was given to fits of shyness and no one thought it unusual.

Hester heard the ringing of the telephone while she and Walt were still outside the door of the hotel apartment. Rebecca, whose qualities all seemed to have been served to her in double portions, boiled over with maternal feeling. She was incoherent on the phone.

"—what kind of—? I don't know what to call him. I don't—I never— His *cousin*, Hester—a little six-year-old girl—I'm sorry, because of you, but never—I must ask you—never bring him here—"

"Calm down, Rebecca. I can't understand a word you're saying. What did Walt actually do?"

Rebecca was not capable of calming down. Picking among the tossed-out fragments of shock and outrage, Hester managed to piece together the fact that Walt had held Clara on his lap, hugged and kissed her ("a whole lot, and funny," in Clara's words, as reported by Rebecca) and told her he intended to marry her when she grew up.

Walt did not deny it. He never denied anything. "I didn't hurt her."

"You frightened her, which is just as bad. Anyway, why—"

"I didn't intend to frighten her. My purpose was experimental. I'd say scientific, except it wasn't sufficiently objective."

"Can I translate that to mean you wanted to find out how it felt?"

"That's a fair translation."

"But why Clara, Walt? She's only a baby. There must be girls your own age who—"

"No," he said, in the same unruffled, reasonable voice in which he

147

said everything. "There aren't. Not for me." He reflected a moment. "It was stupid not to realize she'd run tattling to her mother."

The military academy's literature claimed that it was "a molder of strong, upright, courageous men, equipped to take their place as leaders of society." Hester did not believe it could mold Walt, but she had no idea what else to do with him. She had no trouble getting Walter to pay the high fees. As long as he did not have to deal with Walt himself, and could blame Hester for the kind of boy he was, Walter gave her anything she wanted for him.

She walked down the front steps. The edges of several of them were crumbling. It was a wonder the whole house wasn't crumbling after all these years. Anyone who could afford it had moved from the neighborhood long before, farther uptown, into a brick-façade house with curving staircases and large, gracious rooms, or into one of the luxurious apartment houses or residential hotels, or across to the East Side. It was absurd for a man of Papa's means to live the way he did, on an outmoded block in an outmoded house, with one servant. He would not even own an automobile, claiming it was ostentatious to possess something one could readily hire when public transportation was inconvenient. But Papa's absurdities were what made him Papa.

At Seventy-third Street, Hester walked east to Broadway, where the turreted and spired Hotel Ansonia took up the block to Seventy-fourth. Elsa had moved in there a week after Nathan's death, rising like a phoenix to the seventeenth floor and one untastefully furnished room, cooking her meals on a forbidden hot plate that stood on a board placed across the rim of the bathtub. In due course she had left Papa's synagogue and joined a Reform temple, where she could argue with the rabbi about his sermons; she had been elected vice-president of Hadassah; she had rolled bandages for the Red Cross and stood up in a meeting of two hundred people, when the chapter president especially thanked the Jewish women for their devoted war work, to say in her high, clear voice that they had not worked as Jewish women but as American women. She had also learned to play bridge, and in evening games with other widows in the hotel usually was the big winner, often taking home over a dollar.

In her own way, Elsa had achieved gusto. Hester had thought the way ridiculous, while recognizing that Elsa's natural dignity precluded ridicule from anyone else. Hester had also envied her the simplicity of her needs. When, after five years, Mama died and Elsa gave up her room in the Ansonia to go back and keep house for Papa, Hester was astounded at the vehemence of her own vexation.

"Elsa, you're having the time of your life; you're blooming. For God's sake, don't give it all up and go back there. Visit him all you want to, but don't be his housekeeper. Let him hire one."

"No, he's an old man. He misses Mama. I can't let a stranger take her place."

"Do you think you can take her place?"

"Better than a stranger."

Foolishly, Hester had battered away at her, knowing all the time it was useless. At last, in an excess of exasperation, she had flung out, "It makes no sense. You're not even fond of him. You never have been."

And Elsa had looked at her with terrible eyes and said in a treble version of Papa's softest voice, "Don't you ever say that to me again as long as you live."

Hester walked the few blocks to the Belleclaire. She had told Papa she belonged in New York, and she did. Not in Washington, that beautifully dressed, well-mannered matron with perfect features and a cold smile. New York was a hoyden, untidy, loudmouthed and expansive. She loved everything about it. She loved Broadway, where she was walking now. The crowds, the stores; the islands in the middle of the street, where old people sat on benches between the uptown and downtown streams of traffic and watched other people; the trolley cars with their varnished straw seats and gassy smell . . .

Walter said she had never tried to fit into the Washington circle, and of course she hadn't. She had detested the eternal dinners and receptions, where the men shaped the world while the women festooned the salons, tittering and gossiping in their expensive gowns. She had despised the women for enjoying it, and not kept her scorn to herself. The men had sometimes been amused by her acidulous wit, but it had made them uncomfortable, as though a trick dog had exceeded its capacities and juggled billiard balls.

"You know I have political aspirations," Walter said. "Is it your purpose deliberately to scotch them?"

"Why, Walter, what an idea! How could I possibly? One frail woman affect the course of history? As well say that Cornelia could have scotched Caesar's conquest of Gaul. As well say that—what was Alexander's wife's name, anyway?"

"He had several. Presumably they all knew how to keep their mouths shut, or he'd have been beaten before he got to Susa."

"But it can't possibly matter whether I keep mine shut. Who can hear me while yours is open, as it almost perpetually is? You'll talk yourself to Susa, wherever that is, drowning me out all the way."

They had baited each other for years, and both found it more entertaining than not. During those years, Walter had gone into a dozen different ventures. He was always hearing of things, in both newspaper and political circles, that were certain to make his fortune. Some of them had, but he had always lost it again the next time. Between fortunes, he was constantly in debt. At one family dinner in New York, he had announced proudly that he had paid off almost everything, and that all he owed in the world was a hundred thousand dollars. Through it all, Hester had jeered, whether their luck was up or down, but she had stayed on her end of the seesaw.

And Walter had, indeed, talked himself to Susa. It was only afterward that Hester found out how. He liked to tell the story that William Howard Taft, whose rise he had long predicted, had granted him an interview while sitting in the bathtub and soaping his huge expanse of skin. Hester thought it was probably not true, but it was effective. No one was flabbergasted when Taft, upon becoming President of the United States, appointed a man who had seen him in his tub as an Assistant Secretary of State.

"What did you do?" Hester inquired. "Threaten to phone him every morning unless he gave you the job?"

At the time, there was a witticism going around to the effect that anyone Walter got on the telephone might as well abandon all thought of work for the rest of the day. It was good-humored, because Walter was popular, but the suggestion that his eloquence could be an intrusion displeased him. When Hester twitted him with it, however, he was too elated for riposte.

"Of course Taft has no use for newspapermen as a class," he said, "but he has always liked me personally. For the past year or so, he has never missed reading my column, which he calls a capsule education. My grasp of politics and world affairs he finds impressive enough to override any lack of actual experience in the field, and he—"

" 'Let us now praise famous men.' "

"What?"

"Nothing. Go on with your paean to the Assistant Secretary of State. I know you will anyway. Incidentally, how many are there?"

"How many what?"

"Assistant Secretaries of State."

"What possible difference does that make?"

It had made no difference at all. Hester had cared nothing for the distinction that was so important to Walter. He could have been hired as a bodyguard as far as she was concerned, if it had meant a chance to get away from Washington, even from time to time. Those years had been the best of their marriage. They had traveled all over the world, often setting out with only a few days' notice, and she had loved it. She had scarcely cared where they went, as long as they were going, except for Germany, which was a special delight. Walter said one's first foreign country was like one's first love, but Walter's epigrams often would not stand close scrutiny, as she was careful to tell him. In fact, she had always felt more at home in Germany than in any country in the world. New York was only an oasis in an alien land.

It was during those years, when they never knew from month to month where they would be, that they began sending Walt away to school. Walter had approved at the time, but later he insisted Hester had misled him into believing a reliable housekeeper was too hard to find, when her real motive had been to rid herself of all responsibility for her son. She could not remember exactly when the piquant sorties had become deadly assaults, and it had been a long while before she understood why.

Their travels had not interfered with Hester's work on the Paper. Papa had finally given her a little cubicle next to his office, sealed off from the rest of the staff, but she could write her column anywhere. Walter, of course, had had to leave the staff of the Paper, though he had written an occasional article for it. At first Papa had been furious at what he called Walter's defection. To Papa's mind, no one ought to want to leave the Paper, even to become President. But Walter convinced him he had done it to gain experience that would be uniquely valuable to the Paper when he returned to the staff. Walter certainly had had no intention then of ever returning, and when the time came that he wanted to, Papa would not have him.

The clerk behind the desk at the Belleclaire greeted Hester warmly. Hotel clerks always liked her. So did waiters and chambermaids. She had that in common with Rebecca, but for a different reason. Rebecca badgered them with a bantering, highhanded charm, half *grande dame*, half commoner. Even those she intimidated were enthralled by Rebecca. They liked Hester simply because she was undemanding. She had grown too indifferent to small comforts and niceties to notice when they were missing.

Hester had two rooms to Elsa's erstwhile one in the Ansonia, but they were not more imaginatively furnished. Unlike Elsa, she had had things of her own that she might have brought along to add a semblance of individuality. Except for books, she had not bothered. She was not in the apartment much. She did not work there, unless an idea came to her that would not wait, and she was not tempted, like Elsa, to defy the hotel's regulations against cooking. She even took her morning coffee in a restaurant.

Her office was larger and airier now. It had her name on the door: H. H. LOWENTHAL. In private life, she had resumed her maiden name, prefixed by "Mrs." to account for Walt. No one who had not known her before knew she was the journalist whose column, featuring the drama in the lives of ordinary women throughout the world, was syndicated all over the country. If she could have adopted a disguising pen name for her column as well, she would have done it, but H. H. Lowenthal had become a commodity in itself. It was a valuable part of what Mr. Hearst had bought when he hired her.

Since she could pack in less than an hour to circle the globe, it took her only a few minutes to put what she needed for her stay at Papa's house into a small valise. At one time she had thought of selling or giving away some of her clothes. She had far too many and they were much too elegant for the life she lived now. But she had kept them all. In the beginning she had actually thought—she, Hester, the realist—that everything that had happened might magically dissolve and she and Walter would be together again. Now she knew that would never happen, but her closets were still stuffed with clothes. She liked herself in them.

"Why do you miss him?" Walt had asked her once.

She had no idea how Walt had sensed it. Sometimes she suspected that his brain was at a different stage of evolution from the ordinary person's, and that this was his trouble. She had answered him truthfully. "I don't know."

She and Walter had used and drained each other, and when she discovered he had been deceiving her for years with another woman, she had rid herself of him with disgust and what she thought was relief. But then she had begun missing him.

When she had finished packing, she sent for a bellboy to take her valise and her portable typewriter and get her a taxi.

"Don't work too hard now, Mrs. Herzog," the desk clerk said. "Come back to us soon."

He was under the impression that she worked as a secretary and that her employer was taking her on a business trip. She felt that if it had not been for her clothes, and her pince-nez, he might not have been certain she was a lady. As it was, he apparently took her for a gently born widow whose husband had not left her well off.

"Good-by, Mrs. Herzog," the doorman said. "Take care of yourself."

Yes. What choice did she have?

At least one of them came to see Papa every day, Elsa had said. "One of the children," was the way she had put it, and it was only when she added, "And of course Rebecca and David come often too," that Hester realized the children were Hannah and Samuel.

Papa's children. It was as though Papa's God had taken care of that for him, arranged it so he would have them for his last days, unencumbered, alone, as when he had sat at the head of the table with all of them around him, waiting, gauging his mood.

Only Ida, who Papa felt had gone mad, was beyond his aura. Hannah had been widowed for years and living in a suite at the Hotel Majestic, near Central Park West, among the paintings and tapestries and bronze animals from the Fifth Avenue house, attended by a personal maid and driven in her Pierce-Arrow by a colored chauffeur whose defects of character and incompetence at the wheel she discussed in a carrying voice, as though he were an oyster. Samuel's wife had dropped dead after her evening meal three years before. She had left her money to Samuel in trust, but he was not disappointed.

"I never expected it outright. She thought I'd gamble it away," he told Hester. "What I was afraid of was that she'd make my staying on the Paper a condition for getting any of it. After all, it was the Paper she married."

As soon as the will was probated, Samuel had left the Paper and retired from all useful work, though he was only forty-three. He had tried staying on in the apartment but found he couldn't stand his own company. Now he lived in an exclusive East Side residential club for Jewish gentlemen. No men of Russian or Polish extraction were accepted. He continued to dress elegantly, and kept a series of mistresses, usually stunning showgirls, as he had throughout his married life. He had always been a gambler, not only playing cards for high stakes but betting large sums on anything for which he could get a taker. From the day Myra died, he gave it all up, except for gentlemanly bridge games at his club, in which it was difficult to lose more than twenty-five dollars.

"There's no point any more, you see," he said. "I have all the chips."

Hester had understood everything except his monumental inactivity. "But what in heaven's name do you *do* all day?"

He had given her the unblinking Samuel stare. "Gloat."

Hester, paying the taxi driver outside Papa's house, wondered whether it was this or filial duty that brought Samuel here to see Papa so often. Perhaps Samuel knew no more why he came than she knew why she had elected to move in.

"Dinner's ready, but you'd better go and talk to Papa first," said Elsa. "He's been asking for you ever since you left."

Hester returned to the sickroom. The heavy curtains were drawn now and a brass floor lamp lit. She could see the face on the pillow better than before, but either the lamplight was too soft to reveal reality or he had not changed as much as she had expected.

"It's about time you got here," he said. "Where have you been?"

"I've been busy, Papa. I can't live in this room, you know."

"Don't be impudent." He said it as he always had, more as a ritual than in anger. "Elsa tells me you're staying with us."

"Yes, for a while." She sat down on the chair near the bed. "As long as Walter is away, and—"

He stopped her. "Walter? What are you talking about? You're no longer living with Walter."

She did not know what to say. How was it possible to thread her way through this shifting maze of memory?

"I meant Walt. He's away at school."

"Walt," Papa repeated, without expression. She was not sure the name had any significance to him. For a moment, when he said, "That blackguard!" she thought it had. But then it became clear he was referring to Walter. "He knew the Paper would endorse Taft. He knew my views on Bryan and his free-silver idiocy, but he pretended to Taft that I expected to endorse Bryan. For his own ambition, Walter made it seem I could be pressured into supporting a man for President of the United States against my convictions. He impugned the integrity of the Paper. *What will you give me, and I will deliver him unto you?* And Taft, that good, simple man, believed I could be delivered."

Papa had said all this so often that Hester could have repeated it word for word. She found it soothing now, like a child listening to the reading of the bedtime story she heard every night. "Taft was a disaster," she said, beginning their old argument.

"He was not. He was unfortunate in following a man of incredible vigor. He was simply too placid for his time."

"You're saying he was wrong for his time, whatever the reason. Yet the Paper supported him again in 1912, and lost the confidence of thousands of readers in consequence."

"I had no choice. Would you have had me support that grinning jingoist Teddy Roosevelt, once I saw him in his true colors?"

"There was always Wilson."

"Wilson?" Papa sounded as incredulous as when he had heard of Ida's attempted conversion of Rabbi Schoenfeld. "That *Democrat?*"

Elsa opened the door in her soundless way and poked her head in. "You'd better come now, Hester," she said. "Mary can't keep dinner any longer. It's calves' liver."

"Calves' liver? I had a lamb chop. Two bites and it was gone."

"You couldn't even finish it," Elsa said.

Papa ignored her. "Go ahead and have your supper," he said to Hester with unexpected amiability. He still called it *supper*. "Overcooked calves' liver tastes like rubber."

"David's here, Papa," Elsa told him. "He can keep you company while we eat."

"No. I'll nap. I'm in no mood for little children."

Elsa and Hester left the room. The house could not always have smelled musty, and yet that smell, mingled with the aroma of liver sizzling gently in chicken fat, was an evocation of Hester's girlhood. She was suddenly, for the first time in a long while, hungry.

"We were talking about Taft and Roosevelt," Hester said as they went downstairs. "He was as keen as a knife blade. It's a little unsettling to hear him go fuzzy like that, from one minute to the next."

"I'm not sure it isn't sometimes deliberate. Papa has no great affection for David."

David was waiting in the dining room, apparently staring at a painting that had hung over the sideboard since before he had come as a small boy to live there with his parents and sister. It was an oil painting of a bowl of fruit on a table, every apple and pear glossy and unblemished, a banana of unmistakable edibility arranged carefully across the top. Hester knew it was bad art, but she had learned that from Walter, not in Papa's house. The only art she had learned here was the art of language.

David turned around as though reluctant to interrupt his contemplation of the painting. He greeted Hester unsmilingly. "I heard you were here. Staying here." Almost everything he said sounded unpleasant. He had the blond good looks of the Herzog males, with none of their charm. Nathan, for all his failings, had had a likable enthusiasm and warmth, but Hester could find little in David to compensate for similar failings. He recognized his limitations no more than his father had. His career as a salesman had been foredoomed by his ineptness with people, but while he was in the midst of it he had blamed the product and the territory, and afterward he forgot he had not been a success and spoke of himself as a star salesman who had given up a lucrative calling to help out on the Paper.

"Yes, I'm staying for a while," Hester told him.

"I thought Grandpa never wanted to see you again."

"He seems to have forgotten that. He sent for me."

"Wait till he remembers." The thought seemed to put David in good humor. "I'll run up to see him now. I have some news he'll be glad to hear."

"You'll have to wait a little while. He's napping," Elsa said. "Are you sure you don't want to eat with us in the meantime?"

"Mama, I told you Ruth is expecting me." He looked with exaggerated impatience at his watch. "Go ahead with your dinner. I'll stay around another fifteen or twenty minutes, and if he isn't awake by then I'll have to go."

Elsa and Hester sat down at the table. David sat on one of the side chairs against the wall.

"I have to sit in Papa's place because of the bell," Elsa explained to Hester. She slid down in her chair and began searching the floor with her foot. "I never can find the darn thing. There!" She sat up straight and looked at Hester as though Hester had challenged her. "Oh, yes, I learned to swear when I was living alone. I find it very relaxing."

Mary, perspiring from her climb up the stairs, came in with a platter of liver and onions and a bowl of mashed potatoes on a tray.

"There's vegetable soup, but you'll have to have it after this if you want it, or tomorrow. I'm not going to have my good liver spoiled." She glanced at David. "Don't you want to stay, David? There's no more liver, but I can—"

"No, thank you, Mary," he broke in. "And I'm really getting tired of reminding you to call me Mr. Herzog or, if you must, Mr. David."

Mary gave him a brilliant Irish smile. "Then why should you bother?" she asked him. "I'll never remember. How can I, when the first time I saw you, all you were was a little *Fratz* six years old who smelled bad from throwing up?" She went out before anyone could comment.

David was furious. "It's as much your fault as hers, Mama," he said. "You don't teach her respect for her betters, and then you laugh at her lack of it."

"She can't hear us laughing," Elsa said, wiping her eyes. "And it's not my place to teach her anything, David. If you want to complain about Mary, Grandpa's the one to talk to."

"Grandpa! When did he ever listen to anybody?"

A little later David said he would have to leave. His news would have to wait until the next time he came. It would definitely not be tomorrow; he had other plans for tomorrow. Maybe the next day.

"Why make your grandfather wait, if it's good news?" Hester suggested. "Your mother or I can relay it to him, if you'll tell it to us."

David stared at her. The penetrating Herzog eyes had a hard blue glaze. "It's an exclusive to the Paper," he said. "I'm not going to hand it to the *Journal*."

"David!" Elsa spoke in a soft, shocked voice. "How do you dare suggest—?"

Hester stopped her. "Never mind Elsa. He's right. No good newspaperman would do anything else."

"I can't accept that. You're a member of the family. It's monstrous to imply that you'd try to—to steal a march for the benefit of another newspaper."

"What's monstrous about it?" David was on his feet. His face had gone white. "She works for another newspaper, doesn't she? Where do you think her loyalty lies? Not to the Paper, certainly. She proved that two years ago."

"I only wrote what I believed," Hester said, but she might as well have been talking to Papa.

"And now she's back, taking advantage of Grandpa's condition to stay here as though nothing had ever happened, fawning on him—"

"David, that will do!"

But David was gone before Elsa had finished the sentence, the front door slamming behind him.

Elsa pushed the remains of her food around on her plate with a fork. "I'm sorry, Hester. He hasn't listened to me since he was a little boy."

"It's all right. I don't blame him. He cares about the Paper and he thinks I don't. Yet Papa welcomes me to his room and takes a nap when David comes. Nothing is more frustrating than injustice."

"Perhaps not, but everyone gets a taste of it. If he were more of a man, he'd know how to swallow it without lashing out at you."

"The way you do, Elsa?"

Elsa did not answer that. "You know, don't you," she said, "that he's going to succeed Papa on the Paper?"

"Yes, I assumed so. There isn't anyone else."

"It worries me. He may be all right while Mr. MacRae is there to guide him. If he'll listen. But Mr. MacRae is over sixty, and when he's gone, I don't know. It worries me," she said again. "David isn't the man for it." She sighed. "Not half the man."

Hester looked at her curiously. She wanted to ask what Elsa had felt when she saw David, her newborn son, for the first time, but the question was so absurd that she laughed.

"I wasn't aware I had said anything humorous," Elsa said.

"No, of course not. I was thinking of something else." Hester paused. "Tell me, is it David you're worried about, or the Paper?"

"Both."

"But you've never had any interest in the Paper."

Elsa pushed her plate away and sat erect, her hands folded in her lap. "I've always hated it," she said clearly. "It's like some nightmare creature that thrives on disaster and devours our lives. I remember Nathan, a few months before he died, trembling with excitement in our bedroom because the Titanic had sunk and he was in the newsroom when word came over the wires. Nathan, who couldn't bear to see anyone so much as flick a horse's rump with a whip—" She broke off, and did not immediately begin again. "But it was Papa's life, and I don't want David to destroy it. If he does, he'll do it in spite of himself, because you're right, he cares about the Paper, and if he doesn't make a go of it, I think it would be the finish of him."

They both sat in silence. Mary came and took away their plates and brought apple dumplings and coffee. She looked at them and, for a wonder, said nothing except that the dumplings were hot and they should be careful not to burn their tongues.

When she had left the room again, Hester said, "I don't believe it's possible for one man to destroy the Paper," although she did believe it was possible. "In any case, there's nothing you can do. Someone I know used to say that if it would help a situation to worry about it, he'd worry; otherwise it was a waste of energy." Why hadn't she said the "someone" was Walter? There had been a time when she had not wanted to mention him, but that time was over. None of it mattered any more.

"I'd feel better if you were there again," Elsa said. "On the Paper. You could keep it from getting out of control." She took a forkful of dumpling, blew on it delicately to cool it, and then sat holding it. "After Papa—isn't here any more, why don't you go back?"

Hester looked at her in wonder. "Elsa, how can you think I could go back if I wanted to? They wouldn't have me. Not MacRae, not anyone who was there two years ago."

"But once the war is over, and Germany is no longer the enemy—"

"Germany will be the enemy for years to come. After all, her soldiers dismembered babies, didn't they?"

Elsa shook her head. "I've never believed that. I think they've done appalling things in this war, but they're human beings. Only an animal would slaughter babies."

"Thousands of people do believe it, however. Think what happened because I wrote what you're saying now. That they're human beings. Warm-hearted, genial human beings who love their homes and their children and their beautiful country, and want only what every nation must have for survival—*Lebensraum*." Hester paused to take off her pince-nez and wipe them with her napkin. She had not meant to get into this. She had finished with fervor long before. But she could not seem to stop. "Because I wrote that, the Paper was denounced everywhere for being pro-German. This country hadn't yet entered the war, but I was called a traitor. After Papa fired me, no newspaper would have me. Do you think I chose to go to Papa's archenemy? I could have gone to him first. I knew his sympathies were the same as mine. But he was a last resort." She lit a cigarette, frowning with annoyance at the wavering match, and waited before she went on. Elsa also waited. "He pays me well and treats me well. I wouldn't leave him now if I could."

"Suppose Papa asked you to come back—"

Hester smiled, as much because she felt in control of herself again as at what Elsa had said. "That's a pipe dream. You know it's too late for Papa. Even if it weren't, he'd never take me back. What I wrote was the least of it. He thought I took advantage of his not being completely in touch any more, and of MacRae's illness. Well, I did, of course. I believed what I had to say should be said, and I took my chance to say it. But the really unforgivable thing was that I went to work for Hearst."

There was a silence. Then Elsa said: "After David, there are no more males to take over the Paper. Whatever happens, it will have to pass out of the control of the family." She paused. "We'll all be free then."

"I don't—"

"Papa's bell is ringing." Elsa pushed back her chair and stood up. "I'll go and see what he wants."

Hester's hearing was excellent, but she had not heard the bell. Evidently Elsa was as attuned to it as a mother to a baby's cry in the night.

"Why don't I go? One reason I came was to give you a little rest." As she went up the stairs, Hester wondered whether there was any truth in that at all. Had she really thought of relieving Elsa? She was no more sure about that than about any other reason for her being here.

"How was the liver?" Papa greeted her.

"Delicious." She took her chair next to the bed. Already it seemed as though she had been coming to this room, sitting in this chair, for weeks or months. "Did you have a good nap?"

He snorted. "If I napped at this hour, I wouldn't sleep all night."

He still lay as he had when she first arrived, on his back, with his profile to her. Except for turning his head a few times and once raising his knees, he had scarcely moved. She wondered whether it hurt him to move, or whether he was too feeble. She could not think of him as feeble. His voice was as it had always been.

"Has David gone?" he asked her.

"Why, you old faker!"

"Don't be impudent. I asked you a question."

"Yes, he's gone. He had some news for you. Good news. But he insisted on telling it to you himself, so now you're going to have to wait until he comes again."

"I know his news."

160

"How can you?"

"Miles MacRae dropped in before the noon news conference to tell it to me. Graf von Hertling and his fellow ministers have resigned. The Paper has it on good authority that Prince Max of Baden will be named chancellor and foreign minister and that he'll immediately accept Wilson's Fourteen Points."

Hester said nothing. She should have pretended enthusiasm and could not. Papa might be reminded by her silence, but it was beyond her power to cheer for the devastation and shattered hopes of a country and people she loved.

"Forgive me, Hester," Papa said. "I forget I'm talking to a young lady. How are you to understand the significance of all that? What it means is the almost immediate end of the war, not in months, as we'd at best hoped, but probably in weeks."

She could cheer that. War was an evil necessity, and she would be glad when the killing was finally over, after four long years.

"That is good news, Papa."

Did he really not remember how much she knew and understood? There was no way of telling. Whether he forgot involuntarily or by design, he was in power, as he had always been.

"Wilson is an impractical idealist," he said. "Men will never sit down together and agree on peace while one nation has the means to wage war. But at least with Germany's fangs drawn, there will be no major wars in your lifetime or Rebecca's or her child's." He was silent for a moment. "Rebecca does have a child, does she not?"

"Yes, a little girl. Clara."

"That's good. We do better with girls." He turned his head from side to side as he had done earlier, as though in torment, and then lay like stone again. "David will succeed me on the Paper. I try to pretend there is some other possibility, but I know there isn't." For the first time, his voice sounded tired. "I'll confess to you, Hester, that I don't like him. If it's a sin to dislike one's own grandson, I can't help it. Who but God gave me the feeling I have toward him? On the other hand, he may be more capable than I believe. I'm not always charitable in my estimate of those I dislike."

"He's devoted to the Paper, Papa."

"Perhaps. And he can write. All the Herzogs can write. But he's weak and stubborn. He makes me afraid for the Paper." There was another silence, a long one. "Promise me something, Hester. Don't let David write my obituary."

"I promise."

"Your promises aren't worth much," he said, as he had said earlier that day. "But this one you'll keep."

When he spoke again, there was another change in his voice. It was as though he were talking from a long way off, yet every word was clear.

"The rabbi was here yesterday. Rabbi Schoenfeld? No, he's gone, isn't he? *Gone.* That was this young rabbi's word. 'I suppose many of your friends are gone,' he said. 'Do you mean dead?' I asked him. He blushed, as though I had said something shameful. When I told him I'd never had much time for friends, he didn't understand. How could he?"

The voice stopped.

Hester was not sure Papa knew any longer that she was there. Then he went on again, still as though far away, but calling her name.

"Hester—"

"Yes, Papa?"

"Hester, I never needed friends. There was such glory sometimes. The Paper exposed corruption and broke evil men; reminded great men to be humble; made presidents . . . Hester—"

"Yes, Papa?"

"I want to lay tefillin. Get me the boxes, please. They're in the top drawer of the chiffonier."

She got out the leather boxes containing the scriptures and helped him fasten them to his head and arm with the leather straps.

"You can leave now," he said. "This is between God and me."

From her seat in the front row, Hester looked back. Except for the aisles, there was no space not packed solid with people. She recognized Miles MacRae and the foreman of the composing room and Adolph Ochs of the *Times* and the mayor of New York, before Elsa nudged her to turn around.

They were all standing. Elsa was on her left side, Samuel on her right. She could not see the others. Elsa had her eyes closed, and her lips were moving. Hester looked at Samuel. For once he seemed unaware of it and did not look at her, but straight ahead at the rabbi.

"Yiskadal v'Yiskadas—" The rabbi was reading the Kaddish.

Papa, Hester said to herself. *Papa.*

"Oh, Papa," Samuel whispered.

BOOK II
1928–42

1

David worked on his editorial while he waited for William. Clymer had expected to write the editorial himself. He had been furious when David took it out of his hands.

"Don't you consider the endorsement of a presidential candidate within the province of the editor of the editorial page, Mr. Herzog?" Clymer had asked the question mildly enough, but his face gave him away. He had a cold, white, schoolteacher face, on which emotion showed up like a gouge in marble.

"Not when the publisher decides to take care of it, Clymer." David spoke softly. He had seen newsmen turn pale when Grandpa spoke that way. "Now it's within my province."

Clymer could not turn pale, because he was never anything else. He said something no one would have said to Grandpa. "Well, I hope it's safe."

He had left the office with his stiff-legged stride before David could answer. Grandpa would have called him back, maybe fired him on the spot, but there was no use doing that. Clymer was a good editor, and the men on his board seemed to work well with him. The Paper could not afford to lose him.

"Then why the devil did you provoke him?" Miles MacRae had said. "If you thought you had to write the editorial, why didn't you ask him whether he had any objection? That way you'd have mollified him."

MacRae had retired as managing editor a few years back, but he did not seem to care much for his peaceful life in Larchmont. He kept coming in to the city and hanging around the Paper, looking over everybody's shoulder. Because David, as a green young publisher, had needed his assistance, he considered himself David's mentor still, ten years later.

"I'm sorry, Miles, but I can't see asking a man on my staff if he objects to my writing an editorial for my own newspaper."

"I suppose you can't, and that's the pity of it."

David had not encouraged MacRae by asking what he was talking about. He was annoyed with himself for starting the thing, laying himself open to one of the old man's homilies. Habit. Once, MacRae would have handled Clymer, straightened him out without offending him. He had been good at that. Some thought he had been an even greater managing editor than the great Van Anda of the *Times*—more human. Maybe. But he was just a has-been now, a character, to be tolerated for old times' sake.

One way or another, though, Clymer should have it forcibly brought to his attention that the head of the Paper was entitled to deference.

"Forcibly, how?" Becky had said. "Fifty lashes?"

David should not have mentioned it to Becky either. She had never been sympathetic to him, never taken his part, from the time they were children. He did not know how he could have let her inveigle him into giving her a job on the Paper. He would get no thanks for it, no respect. Grandpa was the only man Becky had ever respected.

Ordinarily he did leave the editorials to Clymer and his board of editorial-page editors. It was not the way it had been in Grandpa's day, when the publisher was frequently the editor as well and might even write a news report from time to time. All the big newspapers had specialists now, special departments. But David enjoyed writing editorials, and occasionally, when he felt an issue was important, he liked to keep his hand in. He liked the chance to express his views as strongly and forthrightly as he pleased. It was one of the prerogatives of the head man. They could all shake their heads and make snide comments, but no one had the power to stop him from writing what he believed. The thing they really resented, of course—Clymer and the rest—was that he was so good at it. He had the Herzog gift with words. People might not like what he said, but they paid attention.

He went on with the editorial he was writing now, endorsing Herbert Hoover for the presidency. Hoover was a solid candidate, but not a man to stir public passion. David devoted his eloquence to Al Smith. He asked his readers to envision this uncouth product of loathsome Tammany Hall in the White House, at the head of the greatest nation on earth. He implied that New York, under Smith's governorship, had been riddled with graft and corruption. When he had finished, he had two paragraphs extolling Hoover to four denouncing Smith, but it was a powerful editorial. He had always been at his best on attack.

William came in as he was finishing. He came in smiling. It was hard to remember what William looked like without a smile. He always reminded David of a panhandler he had known when he was a reporter: a puffy-eyed wino with a gentle, ingratiating voice and a gentle, ingratiating smile who had sidled up to him whenever he went down to the Bowery. William was not a drinker, nor a cadger—he had other vices—but the resemblance was there. He had the smile and the voice, the bags under his eyes, the air of seediness in spite of a fresh shave and good clothes.

"Am I late?" he asked anxiously.

"No." He was. William was always late. But it was difficult not to reassure him. "Sit down."

He sat with his hands on his knees, looking expectant, as though David had sent for him instead of his asking to see David. In his time, William had sold more newspaper advertising than any single salesman of his era. Now he was an outstanding advertising manager with a staff of salesmen under him. In his self-effacing presence, with its emanations of pathos, his accomplishments seemed illusory.

"Well, William," David said in a hearty voice that did not sound like his own. He felt himself beaming. William evoked such falsities. "What's on your mind?"

William shifted in his seat. "It's a little difficult—I don't know—I suppose I might as well come straight to the point," he said, and then digressed into questions about Ruth and the girls, in none of whom, David knew, he had the faintest interest. He even got Marcia's name wrong, referring to her as Martha, though he had once been her uncle. "You're fortunate to have a family, David. Daughters. Do you realize I haven't seen my daughter since she was three years old? Living right here in the same city?"

"Well, whose fault is that?"

William looked hurt. He was still smiling, but he blinked his eyes as though he might cry. Since he had normally watery eyes, it was difficult to be sure, at any moment, that he was not crying.

"You know Rebecca never wanted me to see her." No one but William of her own generation called Becky Rebecca. "She thought it would be too upsetting, too confusing for a little child. I suppose she was right. Still—"

He let that die away and gave David the alert attention of a small boy waiting to catch a beanbag. David did not want to listen to William's sudden paternal sentimentality. He wanted to know what William had come for, so he could get back to work. But he could not leave such absurdity unchallenged.

"Clara's not a little child any more. She's—" David calculated rapidly "—almost sixteen. It's not likely you'd confuse or upset her now."

"Sixteen! It doesn't seem possible." William mused on this phenomenon for an appropriate moment, and then used it to plunge into what he had come to say. David had the uncomfortable feeling he often had with William that he had been maneuvered into providing the springboard. "That's it, you see. Rebecca makes—well, difficulties. She's a fine woman. I've always admired her, even though our marriage wasn't a success. But she does make difficulties. For me, at any rate. Maybe it's my fault, but there it is." He blinked so hard this time that some of the fluid was squeezed out of the corners of his eyes. "It's really impossible for me to go on working here, with Rebecca in the same office. I know you'll understand."

David could not speak at once, except to himself. The louse! The fourflusher! All that bunk, leading up to this cheap squeeze play! Fire Becky or I'll quit.

"No, I don't understand," he said aloud, in the soft, Grandpa voice. "In the first place, we discussed it before I gave Becky the job, and you said if she didn't mind, you certainly didn't. In the second place, you and she are not in the same office. She never has any occasion to go near your floor, and you have very little reason to go anywhere she's likely to be. Since she's only here three or four hours a day anyway, the chances of bumping into each other more than occasionally, are small. So I don't understand at all."

"You're angry," William said sadly. "It seemed to me that if I put it on this basis, you wouldn't be."

"You must take me for a fool. Did you really expect me to believe you had any motive but malice? Get rid of Becky or else. Threatening me. I ought to tell you to—"

William was making urgent attempts to interrupt. David, feeling himself getting in too deep, let him. The Paper needed William even more than it needed Clymer. Whatever MacRae might say, no one knew the value of the men on his staff better than David.

"No, no." William was speaking just above a whisper. "No, no, David, I don't want you to get rid of Rebecca. How can you think that? You know I'm not malicious." He had stopped smiling for a moment, but now the smile was there again. "I'm a good many reprehensible things, of course, but not that. Not malicious."

"Then what the hell do you want?"

William lifted his hands, and let them fall again as though they were too heavy to hold up. "Just—what I told you. To leave."

"I see. Just to leave. But if I decided to let Becky go—not because you're malicious and want her out, of course; simply my own decision—then naturally you'd stay."

"No, David, I wouldn't." William looked out at the sky, drew his lip in under yellowing teeth, released the lip and sighed. "I don't care whether Rebecca goes or stays. I thought that would be an easier way—" He turned from the window and went on in what sounded to David like a borrowed voice. "Sam Froelich can take over my job. I've been grooming him for it. He's a good man. Three weeks, I thought. Yes. Three weeks will be about enough for me to take care of things I want to wind up myself."

He started to rise. David reached across the desk, took his arm and pressed him back. "Wait a minute. You can't just walk out. We've got to talk about this. You've been here—how long? Twenty years?"

"Twenty-two."

"You can't come in here after twenty-two years and say you're leaving in three weeks and then just get up and go out of here, like that. I want to know what it's all about. What's bothering you? Money? Or what?"

"I'm sorry, David. There's nothing to work out. I'm—I have another job, starting the first of next month."

"Another job? How can you take another job without telling me, asking me— Is it for more money? Is that it?" David was half out of his chair now, leaning toward William, the soft Grandpa voice forgotten. "Why didn't you ask me for more money? Did you think I couldn't get it for you? Did you forget I'm the head of this newspaper?"

William drew back a little, as if from a whiff of bad breath. "I didn't want to make you angry. If you had just let me go," he said, sounding more like himself for a moment, and the next moment, not. "Yes, I will be getting more money, but that's not why I'm leaving. I know you'd have managed to give me a raise if I'd asked for it. Not for long, though."

"What does that mean?"

"I'm afraid there's no long future on the Paper any more, David."

"No *future!* What the hell are you—?"

"I said 'no *long* future.' Maybe it will be longer than I think. Or shorter." He sighed. The smile had gone, as though it had never been part of his arsenal. Without it, he looked less like a Bowery panhandler and more like a sad, clever, ravaged advertising man. "I can't wait around to find out. I'm almost fifty years old. If I were younger, maybe I could go down with the ship, and then surface and swim to one that's afloat. Now I can't. I'd drown."

"Well! Why didn't you ever tell me you could roll out metaphors like that? I'd have put you to work writing editorials. Or maybe human-interest stories."

"Don't, David. What's the good of it? Why can't we keep things pleasant?"

"Pleasant! When you tell me the Paper has no future? When you walk in here, without warning, and tell me—"

"I wanted to leave without saying anything. You wouldn't let me."

"Well, I'm letting you now." The pitch got away from him, slid up an octave. "Get out! Get the hell out!" He let William scuttle as far as the door, and then could not stop himself from asking, "Who is it? Who's pirating you?"

William was half in and half out of the room, his hand on the doorknob. As soon as he answered, he slipped out and shut the door. "I'll be working for Hearst. He didn't pirate me. I went to him."

David, alone in his office, gripped the arms of his swivel chair and shut his eyes. He had not witnessed Grandpa's rage when Hester had gone over to Hearst, only heard about it, but he felt he was reliving it now. "The son of a bitch!" he said out loud. "The dirty, sneaking, lying son of a bitch!"

After a time, he got up and went to the window. The view always soothed him. A commanding view. He could see the traffic crawling up and down Broadway, and he imagined he could reach down and pick up one of the miniature automobiles with its tiny occupants and hold it in his hand. To the south, at Twenty-third Street, the Flatiron Building reared its idiosyncratic silhouette against the sky. To the north, the Times Building, at Forty-third, reminded him of his realized dream, though it was not that building that had set it in motion.

David had passed by the Times Tower Building, on Forty-second

Street, with Grandpa in 1910, six years after Mr. Ochs had removed his newspaper there from Park Row.

Grandpa had said: "Look at it. An Italian bell tower to house a newspaper. Do you know Mr. Ochs had to borrow nearly three million dollars to finish it? *Vanity of vanities, saith the Preacher, vanity of vanities.*"

But David had said to himself at that moment that if he ever owned the Paper, the first thing he would do would be to abandon those terrible, decaying old buildings of Grandpa's and move uptown. He too would put up a structure that could stand as a monument to a great newspaper. Something as imposing as the Tower. More imposing.

He had done it. He had hired a progressive architect who had understood exactly what he wanted. A commanding building. A commanding view. Hester was the only one who had opposed it, but she had had no power to stop him. Grandpa had wisely left David a 40 per cent interest in the family corporation that owned the Paper.

"Not out of love or admiration, sonny. For the sole reason that you're male. Of all poor Papa's blind spots, that one was the most unfortunate."

Hester had never liked David, but there were other reasons for her venom. After her pro-German shenanigans, Grandpa had kicked her off the Paper, and when she went over to Hearst, he refused to speak to her for two years. When he was dying and sent for her, he had become senile and no longer remembered what she had done, but his will told another story. He had left her, of all of them, the smallest interest in the Paper. That was how much love and admiration he had had for her.

Even when her column for Hearst had been at the height of its popularity, syndicated all over the country, David knew she would have given her eyeteeth to be back on the Paper. She had just been marking time until Grandpa died, believing then she could wangle her way in again.

"You'll need all the help you can get," she had said, "and I have time. I work quickly. If you want—"

"I want nothing from you, Hester. You forfeited your right to work on the Paper." David had sounded to himself so much like Grandpa that he seemed to feel his face change into Grandpa's face. "You'll never work there again as long as you live."

Her defense had been to laugh at him, to say: "Come out from behind the wolf's clothing, sonny. I know you. Anyway, you misunderstood me. The help I offered was not for you personally. If you could fail at your job without dragging the Paper down with you, it would probably be a good thing, but that's a doubtful possibility. So what I had in mind was a little undercover assistance from an old hand. Just between you and me, and nobody the wiser. Because I have no intention of walking out on Mr. Hearst, and even if I had, MacRae wouldn't let me come near the Paper."

"I wouldn't let you come near it. If I wanted you, MacRae would have nothing to say about it. But we'll have to survive without your assistance. Even your undercover assistance. Because one thing leads to another, doesn't it?" He had let her absorb that for a minute, let her realize she was not fooling him with her deviousness. "And incidentally, from now on you're to stop calling me 'sonny.' You may find it amusing. I don't."

She had laughed again. "You don't find many things amusing, do you? It's too bad. You'd be surprised at the uses of a sense of humor. Sometimes it can even make one bearable to oneself."

But the last laugh was his. She still worked out of the Hearst office, but none of the New York newspapers carried her by-line any more, and the others were dropping her column as soon as their contracts ran out. She had geared the column to a simpler, more sentimental age, and now, for all her reputed wit and caustic tongue, she evidently could not change her Victorian style of writing. It was only a question of time before Hearst would let her go altogether.

William would get his comeuppance too. How or when, there was no way of knowing, but he would get it. The mills of God ground slowly, but—

He moved away from the window, feeling better, and went outside his door for a moment. The original plans for the building had called for a private wing for the publisher on a higher floor. David was to have had a large, luxurious office with an adjoining lavatory, a library that would double as a conference room, and another, small office for his private secretary. A chance remark of MacRae's had changed his mind.

"Do you know what I thought, the first time I ever saw your grandfather? He was sitting at his desk in that plain old office, right at the heart of the Paper, without a thing except himself to show who or what he was. And I thought, 'There's a man who knows his own worth.'"

David had had the plans revised to provide for a large but simple office on the same floor as the newsroom, with an adjoining room for his secretary. He had decided it would be more democratic to eliminate the private lavatory, and had simply had a special lock installed on one of the men's-room booths and kept the only keys. If all the wash basins were in use when he appeared, it was of course understood that one was to be made available to him. Recently he had overheard some of the reporters poking fun at these arrangements with a ribald parody on a new popular song, "One Alone to Be My Own . . ." but he had said nothing about it. Reporters were like children.

Now he stood silently outside his door, as he remembered Grandpa doing, surveying the newsroom. It was twice the size of Grandpa's, and employed twice as many people. He could see only some of them from where he stood.

Directly in front of the room, the city editor sat at his desk, with his rewrite men at desks on either side. In Grandpa's day, if the city editor wanted a man to go out on a story, he shouted for him. Now he barked into a loudspeaker. The men who waited for his assignments or banged out stories on their typewriters sat in the first few rows of desks if they were top reporters, farther back if they were newer or lesser, with the news assistants and clerks behind them. At one side of the room, under a window near the rear, David could just glimpse the bull pen, several desks arranged in a hollow square, presided over by the senior editors, who selected the news stories to be printed and their location in the Paper. There were many more beyond the range of his inspection, including all those behind the closed doors leading to the various departments such as Sports and Drama. He did not know a quarter of them by name.

No future, that son of a bitch had said. "No long future." If he closed his eyes, he could hear, feel, the clatter and throb, like the pulse of a living thing. The strong pulse. That son of a bitch, going over to Hearst for money after twenty-two years, sniping at the Paper to justify himself . . .

David went back inside his office. He picked up the editorial he had written and read it over, standing up, to make sure it was all right before he sent it down to the composing room. It pleased him to see how vigorous it was, yet how smoothly it flowed. He tried reading it aloud, and liked it even better.

In the midst of his reading, the door opened so suddenly that he

173

dropped the editorial on the desk. Becky never entered a room. She exploded into it. "Who were you talking to?" She looked around as though she thought someone might be skulking in a corner or hiding behind the draperies. "I heard you declaiming to somebody as I came in."

"I was talking on the phone. And I wish you'd learn to knock, Becky, before you burst in here. After all, this is a private office."

"Ah, come on, Davy Jones, don't be so self-important. It's only me, Becky."

He was always being accused of saying things that antagonized people, but Becky said whatever she liked and everyone thought she was fascinating.

It was only because of her looks, of course, and the style she affected. She had been one of the first to bob her hair after Irene Castle started the fashion, but she had her own way of wearing it, slicked straight back from her forehead and over her ears like a black cap. All her clothes were black, and she never went anywhere without a three-strand necklace of fake pearls around her neck, pearls that everyone assumed were real because she wore them. She wore no other jewelry except a narrow platinum wedding band that set off her long fingers better than the gold rings she had acquired from her two husbands. She had developed a way of walking into a strange room and standing still for a moment until people noticed her and asked each other who she was. Then she would pretend not to see the turned heads as she passed by.

No man could posture that way, creating an aura that made it not only possible but somehow endearing to be outrageous. A man had to stand on his own.

"I hardly think it's self-important," he said to her now, "to insist on the privacy of my own office."

"You're absolutely right, Davy Jones." She took a box of matches from his desk and lit a cigarette that he realized with astonishment she had been carrying behind one ear, like a grocery clerk's pencil. "The trouble is, I can't get over thinking of you as my little brother."

"Well, if you want to continue working on the Paper, you'd better get over it, Becky. Here I'm your employer, and you're an employee like any other. Grandpa always insisted on that kind of relationship with Papa and Samuel. Do you know he even required Samuel to call him Mr. Herzog in the office? I won't go that far—these are more informal times—but I do expect you to address me properly, not by that absurd childhood nickname, and to knock before you burst into my office." He waved away the smoke that had drifted toward him from her cigarette. "Also, please put out your cigarette. The rule against women's smoking in the office applies to you exactly the same as to anyone else."

"It's a silly rule, you know. Old-fashioned." She kept the cigarette in the corner of her mouth and talked around it. Any other woman would have looked common, but part of Becky's pose was to look like a lady no matter what she did. "Nobody pays any attention to it unless you're around. Why don't you rescind it? Even the colleges are legalizing smoking for women now."

"The colleges can do as they like. To my mind, it's disgusting to see a woman with a cigarette in her mouth, and I won't have it on my premises."

"How engagingly you put it! The premises are 20 per cent mine, you know, but I won't make an issue of that at the moment. I didn't come in here to argue about smoking."

David had never understood why Grandpa had left a larger share in the Paper to Rebecca than to Mama, who had nursed him all through his last illness. Ten per cent each to Hannah and Samuel was just. Hannah was rich without it, and Samuel had not been sufficiently devoted to the Paper. The 5 per cent to Hester was the slap she deserved. But the bequest to Rebecca seemed utterly capricious. It was not like Grandpa to leave her that large an interest in the Paper simply because he was fond of her.

Not that it gave her any real voice. For all her talk, she understood that. She was stubbing out her cigarette now. He opened the window to let out the fumes and took a few deep breaths of fresh, October air. If he could have done it without causing a revolution, he would have abolished all smoking in the building. He hated the smell of it.

"You can't print this," Becky said behind him.

"What are you talking about? What have you got there?" He strode over to her and tried to take the sheets of paper out of her hand, but she turned her back to him and went on reading. "How dare you pick something up from my desk and look at it without my permission! Give it to me immediately."

"All I need to take me back thirty years or so, is for you to stamp your foot," she said without looking up. "If this is private venom, I apologize. I took it for granted you wrote it for publication."

"Whatever I wrote it for, it's no affair of yours, Becky. You're here on sufferance, remember that. A—what should I call you?—glorified copy girl, I suppose, on sufferance." He heard his voice rising, and turned it soft and deliberate. "Your right to take from my desk and criticize anything I've written is about on a par with that of the woman who comes in here to scrub the floor."

She dropped the editorial on the desk and turned around. "You can't print it," she repeated, as if she had not heard a word he had said. "It's all lies."

"It is not your affair, I tell you. You don't know what you're talking about. You've been here seven months. What do you know about the newspaper business? You're—"

"Stop it. Don't shout at me, David. I can shout louder." She picked up the editorial again and waved it under his nose. "The Paper's readers won't stand for your lies. Supporting Hoover is one thing, but blaming Smith for graft and corruption is something else. Why don't you lay it at the right door? Why don't you go after Jimmy Walker if you want to blast somebody?" She tore the editorial into pieces and dropped them in the wastebasket. He stood there and watched her as though he were paralyzed. "That's what Grandpa would have done. Gone after the Honorable James Walker. Made a crusade of it."

It was too much. He had just calmed down from his encounter with that son of a bitch William, and now this—this— It was beyond words. He would have hit her if he could, but his upbringing shackled him. The only time in his life Papa had ever laid a hand on him was when he had punched Becky for teasing him. Gentlemen, even when they were five years old, did not punch females.

"Ah, Davy, come on. Don't look like that." Now she was smiling, cajoling, coming close to him and taking his face between her hands. "Don't be so furious. You're too smart not to know I'm right."

He took her by the wrists and pulled her hands down, hoping he was hurting her, knowing she would not give him the satisfaction of showing it. "Do you want two weeks' notice, or do you want to leave at once, with two weeks' pay?"

"Oh, for heaven's sake, stop it! Sit down and listen to me . . . All right, don't sit down. Stand there if you want to. I'll sit down." She took the chair William had recently vacated, hitched it around, and talked looking up at him. "I shouldn't have torn up your editorial, but you know me. I got carried away. Just as you got carried away when you were writing it. You'd probably have torn it up yourself after you thought about it. You know wild accusations like that are for Hearst and the tabloids, not for the Paper. We'd lose readers who depend on the Paper for the truth, and God knows we can't afford to lose any more readers. I don't have to tell you that."

He still stood on the spot from which he had watched her destroy the editorial. His legs felt numb, as though, if he tried to move, they would crumple under him. "You don't have to, but you're telling me," he said. "You're the expert, after seven months on the Paper. You're the expert on everything. Editorial policy, circulation, even politics. Walker. What do you know about Jimmy Walker? He's the most popular mayor New York ever had."

"That's right. Because people don't know what he's been up to. The Paper could—"

"Oh, but *you* know. You're the expert on this, too."

"Ah, Davy, stop it. Let's not get off the subject. I'm no expert on anything. I listen, that's all. People talk to me. They always have. They tell me things, and I listen." She felt behind her ear, made a funny little grimace, and dropped her hand back in her lap. "In any case, it doesn't take an expert to know the Paper's in trouble. Even the stenographers know it."

"Nonsense. You don't understand the difference between fact and scuttlebutt. We're having a few problems at the moment because of rising production costs and the competition of the tabloids, but so are all the other newspapers. It's nothing serious or lasting. We're certainly not 'in trouble.'"

She stared up at him. "Is that for public consumption, or do you really believe it? I suppose maybe you do. You never did like to face an unpleasant truth. Maybe that's why it didn't frighten you to get rid of probably the best advertising manager in the business."

"There! There you have it! There's your *truth*, your *facts!* Get rid of—"

"Oh, Davy, stop shouting. Sit down. You make me nervous standing there waving your arms around. Sit down and talk to me like a normal human being. William is what I came to discuss with you in the first place." She reached out and gave him a little shove. "Sit down."

He moved mechanically to his chair behind the desk, as though her touch had released the right button. Now that she had given him that gross distortion, he felt quieter, in command again. "There's nothing to discuss, Becky, except your misstatement of the facts. I didn't get rid of William. He came in here—" David broke off. "Listen, he couldn't have left this office more than half an hour before you showed up. What did he do? Go out and start spreading it all around that I fired him?"

"I don't think William spread anything around. That's not his style. He's—" She made a small sound, an abbreviated chuckle. "He's too ethical, I was going to say. That's funny, isn't it? Because, you know, it's true. He really is ethical about certain things. He'll use any lie or trick to get out of paying me a month's support for Clara, but he would never repeat a confidence or—" She gave one of her elaborate shrugs. "I don't know why I'm analyzing William. I gave that up as useless years ago. You were saying you didn't fire him, weren't you?"

"If it wasn't William that said I did, who was it?"

"The grapevine. Who knows how it started? How does any rumor start? If you want it corrected, tell me what happened and I'll see the true story gets out."

"I'll tell you what happened, all right. He came in here and told me he was quitting. Just like that. Hearst offered him more money, so after twenty years he's walking out. No discussion. No feelers to see if he could get more money from me. Nothing. Grandpa gave him his start, made him into something. What would he have been without Grandpa? A jeweler, working for his father, because he wasn't fitted for anything else. Grandpa and I made him into one of the best advertising men in the newspaper game, and after twenty-two years he gives me three weeks' notice and walks out."

Becky sighed. "You talk too much, Davy."

"You're perfectly free to go. It wasn't my idea, in the first place, to discuss—"

"Never mind. We all talk too much. It's a Herzog failing. We fall in love with our own words. The only one I know who outdoes us is Walter." She looked at him in her unblinking way, practicing on him her trick of widening her eyes to give the full impact of their green brilliance. "Did William really say he was leaving because of the money?"

"What he said, and the actual circumstances, are two different things. He admitted Hearst was paying him more."

"What didn't he admit?"

"That Hearst made him the offer. He tried to pretend he approached Hearst."

"Because he wanted more money? That makes no sense. If it was only money, he'd have asked for it here, before going to Hearst."

"Oh, he tried to pretend the money had nothing to do with it. He said he had no future on the Paper, and talked about getting old and needing more security, or some such hogwash. He had to say something. Probably he promised Hearst not to let it be known that he was pirated."

"Why should Hearst suddenly want to keep such a thing a secret? He's been openly hiring men away from other newspapers for years." She watched her finger making patterns on the polished surface of his desk. "I think William told you the truth, and you don't want to believe it. I think he's leaving because he's afraid the Paper may go under." She looked up into his face again. "I'm afraid of it too, David. Unless something drastic is done—"

"*You're* afraid of it! Who do you think you are?" He started to get up from his chair, and then felt that strangeness in his legs again and remained seated. After a moment, he found the icy, soft voice. "I've had about enough of you, Becky. I've let you talk and I've listened to you courteously, let you question me, even answered you as I would somebody who had a right to call me to account, but now I've had enough. You think you know all about the newspaper business because you've been here for a few months poking your nose into things, vamping some of the chiefs into letting you try your hand at this and that, listening to rumors and gossip. The fact is, you know next to nothing. It takes years to understand the functioning of a newspaper. You sit there with a lot of distorted notions in your head and try to tell me—"

Becky interrupted him. "I know," she said. "It was a mistake. Nobody can tell you anything you don't want to hear." She got up and went to the door, and then turned around again. "I do have a right to call you to account, though, Davy. After all, I'm a stockholder."

When she had gone, David lay down on the leather couch that stood against the wall opposite his desk. Two scenes like that, one after the other, were more than a man could stand. His heart was pumping so hard he thought he might be getting some kind of attack. Probably he ought to go home, but there would be no peace there either.

A young man expected to fight the world. He was fit for it. But by the time he was forty-four years old, some of the battles should have been won, finished. For him, none of them ever seemed to come to an end. He had thought when Grandpa died and the Paper was his, the building he had dreamed of built, that that contest, at least, was over. Instead, it had been the start of a ten-year struggle against outside forces and willful or unreasonable or vicious people, and it still continued. Clymer, William, Becky. That pirate Hearst. The tabloids, pandering to the lowest tastes, luring readers away from legitimate newspapers with lascivious pictures and obscene stories. Clymer, with no respect for his employer. That son of a bitch William, going over to Hearst for money after twenty-two years. Becky, telling *him*, warning *him*, as though *he* were the know-nothing with seven months' experience. "After all, I'm a stockholder." Next Hester would come around with her 5 per cent interest to tell him how to run the Paper . . .

It was almost time for the news conference. In Grandpa's day, the conference had been held in the publisher's office at noon, and Grandpa had presided. David would have liked to continue it that way when he became publisher, but he had been too green, too afraid of making a fool of himself. He would wait until he had learned a little more. In the meanwhile he would not lose face by letting MacRae preside at the daily conferences. It was the usual thing for managing editors on other newspapers. When David was ready, he would take over.

But he never had taken over. MacRae had persuaded him that he had too many other responsibilities, that the Paper was much too complex an operation now for the publisher to have a hand in everything. By the time David realized how he had been maneuvered by a man who was jealous of his power as managing editor, it was too late. The news editors had become accustomed to filing into MacRae's office, reporting to MacRae, accepting David as an ex-officio observer, while secretly—and sometimes openly—resenting his right to be much more. The news conference in the managing editor's office just before the afternoon deadline had become a tradition, and nothing was harder to change than a newspaper's traditions. MacRae had been able to do it after Grandpa's death—he had even altered the time of the conference—because that was a period of change and upheaval anyway. But now the custom was entrenched.

David thought he would not go to the conference today. He did not feel up to it, and he knew of no special news that might make it interesting. On ordinary days, he often found it a bore to listen to the editors outlining the routine local or foreign or feature stories their reporters had gathered for the next day's paper. Aside from perhaps commenting that it did not sound to him like much of an edition, there was nothing for him to say, no real reason for him to be there except to demonstrate that he was everywhere, that he had his finger on the Paper's pulse.

The only thing that tempted him to attend, as sick as he felt, was that Rick Schuman would be pleased if he failed to show up. Schuman was the Paper's second managing editor since MacRae had retired. The first, Bradford Jones, who had been MacRae's assistant, had gone over to the *Post* after two years, implying that he thought morning newspapers were on the way out. He was supposed to have said privately that he had chosen the *Post* because its publisher, Cyrus Curtis, was too busy with his various newspapers and magazines to interfere with any one managing editor. The trouble with Jones had been that MacRae had favored him too much, given him his head, so that he had come to consider the slightest criticism of his work, interference.

But David would have traded him back for Schuman any day. Jones had been difficult to work with, but Schuman was impossible. He was David's cross, and there was no way to jettison him, because he, even more than Clymer, was invaluable to the Paper. David had expected him to be easy to handle. He looked like what he had been, the editor of a successful country newspaper, with a long, loose body, a lazy walk, and a keen, amiable, big-featured face. But under that façade was a steely, hard-driving man who demanded, and very nearly got, perfection, and acknowledged no authority in his domain other than his own. Jones had resented what he called interference, but Schuman simply refused it.

"We've had enough in the Paper for a while about the shenanigans of bootleggers," David had said to him once, in the first months of his tenure. "The public is tired of it."

"You're mistaken, Mr. Herzog," Schuman had answered in his deceptive polite drawl.

"I don't think I am mistaken. In any case, you will please instruct your editors to leave the subject alone for the time being."

"I can't do that, Mr. Herzog."

"What do you mean, you can't do it? It's an order."

"I don't take orders, Mr. Herzog."

There was no way to deal with him except to get rid of him, but David could not let him go. He knew one of the other newspapers would snap him up the next day, exult over getting him away from the Paper. Schuman knew it too. David could see the knowledge in his face whenever they had a disagreement. Sometimes he thought he had never hated anybody as he hated Schuman.

He looked at his watch as he lay on the sofa, holding his wrist as far from his eyes as possible. When he could no longer see it at that distance, he would have to give in and get glasses, but he did not like the idea. Ruth had once told him he looked like Wallace Reid, the movie actor. That had been a long time since, of course—it was not the kind of thing she said to him any more—but he thought he had not changed much. All the Herzogs, especially the men, aged slowly. He had only a few lines around his eyes, that was all, and not a sign of gray in his hair. Grandpa had not gone completely white until he was well past eighty. But eyeglasses were distorting. Once he had to wear them, he would no longer look like Wallace Reid.

Five minutes to three. He sat up to see how he felt, whether he could face Rick Schuman in five minutes. His head throbbed a little, but—

The phone on his desk rang. He got up to answer it, noting that the peculiar sensation in his legs had gone and his heartbeat, even on his feet, no longer felt abnormal.

"This is Mock, Mr. Herzog." Charlie Mock was the head compositor. "We're holding the editorial page for you."

Oh, my God, the editorial! That bitch Becky had torn it up and then started all that other tommyrot and made him forget all about the editorial. The mild throbbing in his head turned into the drilling of a jackhammer.

"Well, hold it a little longer," he barked into the telephone. "You'll get my piece when it's ready."

There was no question, now, of attending the news conference, or resting, or leaving the office. He began searching frantically through the papers on his desk, looking for the carbon copy he knew must be there. He had to find it. There was no time to write the piece over again.

He wasted almost ten valuable minutes before he came across it, badly crumpled by his frenzied search. Then he had to retype it himself. If he let his secretary do it, she would have it all over the newsroom that the boss had been late with his copy. As he typed, he made changes. None of it sounded right to him now. He had not said enough about Hoover, and what had earlier seemed a powerful and righteous attack on Smith now struck him as bombastic and much too wordy. He cut the whole graft and corruption paragraph, but when he tried to think of something to substitute, some strengthening of his material on Hoover, his mind was suddenly empty. He sat there with his hands rigid on the keys and time running out. Then the phone rang once more. He let it ring, certain that it was another call from Charlie Mock, so furious at Mock's daring to nag him that his panic subsided and his brain began to work again. Easiest, quickest, would be to let the candidate speak for himself. In his file on Hoover he found a quotation of about the right length. It had been printed in the news section at the time of the statement, but there was no reason not to repeat it in an editorial.

He banged it out in his rapid, four-fingered style. One long, involved sentence—but Hoover's, not David's—and a short, reasonably effective closing one.

". . . While I do not, and will not myself, seek the nomination, if it is felt that the issues necessitate it and it is demanded of me, I cannot refuse service."

David added a line of his own, tore the paper out of the machine, and took it downstairs, not waiting for the elevator, walking calmly until he was out of sight of the newsroom and then running until he was in view of the printers and linotype operators in the composing room.

Like a copy boy, he said to himself on the way back. Like some goddam dilatory copy boy, panting into the composing room, terrified he would miss the deadline and be chewed out or fired for dawdling. Nobody could chew him out. Nobody could fire him. He should have taken his time, made Charlie Mock wait until he was goddam good and ready. Nobody could tell him he had to meet a deadline. He could have pushed the deadline back, stopped the presses, suspended the whole edition if he had felt like it. No wonder the men in the composing room had stared at him. The big boss, bringing his own copy down, rushing in with it because Charlie Mock said he was waiting. He must have been crazy. All the harassment he had been through had put him in such a state he hardly knew what he was doing . . .

"Here's your editorial, Mock. If you had used your head, instead of the phone, you'd have realized a publisher wasn't likely to miss his own deadline and there had to be a reason for the delay."

At least he had managed to salvage that much dignity. Mock had not liked it, of course. They were all little czars in their own realms, these department chiefs and editors. Every once in a while they had to be reminded that their authority was not unlimited, that they were all, finally, answerable to him.

He took the elevator upstairs, but when he got back to his office he still felt hot and breathless, as though he had not stopped running, and it seemed to him that if he did not get out of there right away, he might be prostrated. It had happened to him once in a college track meet on an unseasonably hot day. He had expected to win, but on the last lap the heat and the shouting of the spectators had begun swelling inside his head, exploding. He had been running a poor third until then, but he would have won if he had not collapsed. He knew he would have won.

"I'm going home, Miss Washburn," he said, opening the door into his secretary's adjoining room. "I'm not feeling well. If anything comes up—"

"Miss Kane," she said. "I'm Miss Kane, Mr. Herzog."

Yes, of course. Miss Washburn was the last one. He could not keep up with them. They left to get married or to have babies or because the hours did not suit them or because they thought somebody had insulted them. They never worked very hard or made any particular effort to please. In these boom times there was always another job.

"All right, Miss Kane. Did you hear what I said? I'm leaving for the day. If it's important, I can be reached at home."

It did not occur to her to say she hoped he would feel better. All she said was, "Yes, Mr. Herzog," and turned back to her typewriter before he had closed the door.

She had been talkative enough when he hired her. She had seemed so pleased to have the job that he had thought she might turn out better than the others.

"You can't imagine how glad I am to be working for a Jewish firm, Mr. Herzog. It's really dreadful. One job I applied for, the woman at the agency said they'd specified they didn't want a Jewish girl, but she called them anyway. If I'd wanted to lie about it, she told them, no one would know I was Jewish from my looks or my manner or anything. But they wouldn't even see me. Well, after

184

that, I *did* lie about it, and I had no more trouble getting any job I wanted. But you really can't imagine what a relief it is to be where I don't have to—well, sail under false colors, so to speak—"

He had let her finish, but he had wanted to make it clear that she could not come blabbing cozily to him whenever she felt loquacious. "This is a very busy office, Miss Kane, so I suggest you get right to work," he had told her. "We are not, incidentally, a Jewish firm. In the first place, we are not a firm but a newspaper. Nor are we a Jewish newspaper. The publisher of the Paper happens to be Jewish. Most of the people who work on the Paper happen not to be."

He had finished by telling her quite kindly that it was best for her to understand these things at the outset, that it would save her embarrassment, but he had seen at once that she was not taking it well. They were all alike. The smallest suggestion, the slightest criticism, turned them sullen. It was one more thing he had to contend with. Grandpa had been a terror to work for, a martinet, and still he had had them all falling over themselves to please him, hoping for nothing better than to stay with him and the Paper forever. But these were different times. People had no respect any more, no loyalty, no interest in one place of employment over another. It was too easy to change jobs for some trivial reason, some supposed benefit. Everything was too easy for them.

He went down in the elevator and out to the street. It was strange to be going home at this hour, with no crowds coming out of the buildings and so little traffic on Broadway. He would be able to ride comfortably uptown in a taxicab. Usually he took a series of streetcars, up to Forty-second Street, cross-town to Lexington, up to Eighty-eighth, and then walked over to Park. It was no quicker than by taxi, probably slower, but it kept him moving instead of sitting in one place the whole time, trying to urge the taxi through the traffic with body English.

The air made him feel better. He did not really want to go home. If Ruth was there, she would drive him crazy with questions, and nothing he answered would satisfy her. She would not believe he was sick or, if she did believe it, she would send for the doctor and meanwhile carry on as though he were dying. If the doctor said he was not dying, she would accuse him of deliberately trying to upset her. If he tried to tell her about William and Becky, she would listen only enough to hear that they had done something unpleasant to him, and then she would say that it was his own fault, that she had always told him what they were like.

An empty taxicab slowed down at the curb, but he waved it on and began walking uptown, not heading anywhere, just walking. If he had been like Samuel, with a little chorus girl or manicurist tucked away somewhere, he would have known where to go. That kind of thing was not for him. He had had a few experiences before he was married and working on the Paper, when he was a salesman out on the road, but he had never really enjoyed it. The women had revolted him with their imitation, paid love. One or two to whom neither money nor love was a requirement had revolted him even more. With Ruth, it had all seemed different.

Mama and Papa had not wanted him to marry Ruth. They said it was because she came from a different background with different standards, had not had his cultural advantages, would not fit in with his friends or his family. What they meant was that not only her grandparents but her parents as well had been born in Poland instead of in America or Germany or Spain or Portugal, where the only acceptable Jews came from.

He had told Mama and Papa they were old-fashioned and narrow-minded, but the truth was, he had never felt comfortable with Ruth's parents. Their accent and their manners had embarrassed him. There had been a smell about them and their stuffy little apartment on West 158th Street that he never got used to—a kind of spicy, foreign smell. Whenever he called on Ruth, he hustled her out as quickly as possible. As soon as he got her away, he could forget she had ever belonged there.

One of the other salesmen had introduced him to her. She was his cousin, and he said she was beautiful, a beautiful dark girl for a handsome blond man. David had been disappointed when he first saw her. She had seemed rather plain to him, small and sallow with big, staring eyes and thick ankles. But she had grown on him. She had fallen so instantly and helplessly in love with him, gazing at him as if she could not believe he was real, touching him to make sure. No one had ever loved him like that.

He had never before been certain that anyone loved him at all. Girls were attracted to him, but in the end what they cared about was not him but his adulation of them, and for that he had neither talent nor inclination. Papa? He supposed Papa would have had more affection for him if he could have admired, or pretended to admire, Papa. But David had known the truth about Papa from the time he was ten years old. It was impossible to think highly of a nonentity, a man who could not even provide a home for his own family, and David had never been good at pretense. As for Mama, he did not know. He wondered if anyone knew about Mama. She treated everyone in the same kind, firm, gentle way. He could not remember that she had ever kissed him, or anyone, spontaneously— only the ritual kisses of greeting or congratulation or good-by. Even her anger seemed considered, without passion. Yet she always appeared delighted when he called her on the phone or paid her a visit.

He stopped at the curb and hailed a taxi. "Hotel Ansonia, please." That was what he would do now. He would visit Mama. He was so busy that he had not been to see her for a long while, and he could not remember the last time she had come to the apartment. Ruth made such a fuss about having her that he shrank from mentioning it.

"Oh, yes, I know I have to have her. She's your mother and she's an old lady, and I'm certainly not a vindictive person, but it's hard, seeing how she hates me."

"Don't be ridiculous, Ruth. Mama doesn't hate you. She doesn't hate anybody."

"That's a nice thing to tell your wife, that she's ridiculous. There's nothing ridiculous about it. Don't you think I know the way she tried to keep you from marrying me? Don't you think I see the way she watches me and looks around the apartment criticizing everything?"

"I've never heard her say a critical word."

"No, she just looks. It would be better if she did say something. I'd think a lot more of her if she came right out and said what she was thinking, instead of only looking."

David settled back in the taxi and stared out the window. They were passing Forty-fourth Street, the Hotel Astor, where he had splurged and taken Ruth to dinner to celebrate their engagement. For one instant, as they started to eat, he had seen her through what he imagined to be Mama's eyes. The too-red dress, the way she held her fork in her fist instead of between her fingers. Then the image had disappeared into a cache of memory, and he had thought how lively and sparkling she looked, and that other men must be envying him her obvious adoration.

"My prince," she had called him.

Because she had had no idea that the things she said were sentimental or silly, he had found them moving. He had felt like a prince. All during their engagement, and for the first months of their marriage, he had been so happy that he wondered if he had ever been happy at all before.

Then it ended. When he thought about it, he pictured himself going through a door one morning and finding everything different. Back in the other room, where he had been the night before and could never go again, was the old Ruth and her prince. Here was the Ruth for the rest of his life, too absorbed in the fluttering movements inside her swollen belly to look up when he came in; absorbed in bottles and dresses and parties and weddings and a perpetual martyrdom, with the prince changed into a toad to which she fed all her grievances against life.

He scarcely knew his daughters. While they were small, his hours on the Paper had usually brought him home only when they were asleep. Later it was they who were busy with school and boys and seldom home. He heard of their doings almost altogether by way of Ruth's complaints and worries. Once or twice he had tried to make suggestions, but he had given it up.

"What do you know about girls? All you know about is the Paper, the Paper, the Paper, until it comes out of my ears."

There was no use saying that he had long ago stopped discussing the Paper with her. There was no use reminding her that everything she had, her clothes, her jewelry, the apartment on Park Avenue, the private school for the girls, came from the Paper. She would not hear him.

"I know something about girls. I have a sister."

"A sister? Becky? God forbid Marcia and Harriet should turn out like Becky! Besides, that's got nothing to do with this generation. What do you know about the way young people act today? The temptations nice girls are exposed to? Drinking, wild parties, carrying on in the back of automobiles. I'm the one who paces the floor at night waiting for them to come home, not you. How can you tell me what to do? You don't know the first thing about it."

As though he were a monk, cut off from the world, instead of the publisher of a New York newspaper. The Paper had printed a series of feature articles on the excesses of what one writer called Flaming Youth, but he did not think Ruth ever looked at the Paper. He was not sure she read anything. The only sources she mentioned were other women, storekeepers, and the radio.

Now she blamed him for the way the girls had turned out. Harriet had married a gentile and gone with him to Alaska, where he had something to do with mining. Since they seldom heard from her, and then only sketchily, Ruth was free to imagine any horrors that came into her head. She seemed to believe Alaska was a massive, uncivilized ice floe and to resent any effort to set her straight. But Marcia's manner of life was even more of a torment to her. Harriet was at least married, if only to a gentile. Marcia had left college in her sophomore year and rented a studio in Greenwich Village, where she lived with an artist and wrote poetry. For all they saw of her or heard from her, she might have been living in Alaska too. David sent her a monthly check, which she never bothered to acknowledge. The check was the only way he affected either of his daughters' lives.

"If I had had a little help in bringing them up," Ruth said. "If I had ever been able to turn to you for the slightest bit of help or advice—"

The taxicab was approaching Seventy-third Street. David had grown up in this part of town, but he had no feeling for it. Becky had made him walk over to West End Avenue with her one day, after they had been to see Mama on her birthday, and cried because Grandpa's house had been torn down, but it had meant nothing to him. He had hated his life in that house, with six people telling him what to do—five, after Hester got married—and nobody under him, not even a goldfish. He had always wanted a goldfish, but Grandpa had not believed in keeping anything in a bowl or a cage. If it had been one of the others, instead of Grandpa, who had not believed in it, he could not have had a goldfish either. What he had believed in had had no influence on anybody.

"What entrance you want, mister?" the taxi driver asked him.

"Seventy-fourth."

"I once took Irish Meusel here," the driver said as David was paying him. "He useta live here, y'know. The whole team useta live here. That was a while back, though."

David went into the hotel and took the elevator to the seventeenth floor. It was a walk to Mama's apartment, down one corridor, around a corner, and down another. The carpeting had a slightly musty, not unpleasant odor. As he neared Mama's door, it became mingled with the smell of her lilac toilet water. She had used lilac toilet water, the same brand, as long as he could remember.

It was only after he had rung the bell that it occurred to him she might not be home. Ruth always spoke of her as an old woman, but she went out more and had many more interests than Ruth. He had come all the way up here, the good son leaving work early to visit his mother, and it would be for nothing. He would not get credit for coming without first making sure she was there. She would think he had had something to do in the neighborhood, that his visit was incidental.

But now he heard footsteps, and in a second the door opened. It was not Mama who stood in the dim hall, but a young girl. He could not imagine what a young girl was doing in Mama's apartment.

"Good afternoon," he said. "Is Mrs. Herzog home?"

The girl giggled. "Yes, she's home. Don't you—?"

"Who is it, Clara?" Mama's voice called from inside.

"It's Uncle David." She giggled again. "You didn't recognize me, did you?"

He was annoyed at her whispering, as though she thought he had been stupid and would not want Mama to know. "I can hardly see you. Why don't you tell your grandmother to have a decent-sized bulb put in here before somebody breaks his neck?" He went past her to the room at the end of the hall. "Hello, Mama, how are you?" He bent and kissed her cool, lilac-scented cheek. "I was going to call, but then I thought I'd just take a chance and come up and surprise you. I suppose that was foolish. You might not have been here."

"I'm always here on Thursdays." She smiled at Clara, who had followed him in and was leaning against the mantel. "Thursday is Clara's day."

"Clara's day?"

"I come to see Grandma every Thursday after school."

Curiously, though she resembled Becky, she was plain, an awkward girl, too tall, with muscular legs that seemed to go on endlessly from the hem of her short skirt before they reached her big feet. She had William's fair hair and skin, the brilliance of Becky's green eyes muted by an admixture of William's mild blue, fringed with short, pale lashes. At her age, David's girls had been too pretty and popular to have a free minute after school. "That's very nice of you, Clara," he said. "I'm sure Grandma appreciates it."

"I don't come because it's nice." She was looking at Mama instead of at him. They were exchanging a look. He had never seen that expression on Mama's face before. "I come because I want to," Clara said.

She was still leaning against the mantel. On one end of the shelf behind her head stood an old, faded, gold-framed photograph of Papa as a young man, before Mama had met him. A wedding picture of Becky, also in a gold frame but with the easel broken, leaned against the mirror at the other end. In the center stood the large, seven-branched brass Menorah that had stood on the mantel in Grandpa's house. During Hanukkah it was replaced by a smaller one, with nine branches.

Mama thought the mantel was decorative. She would not hear of having the useless fireplace walled in or even replacing the extinct gas logs with an artificial electric fire that would at least have looked cheerful, served some purpose. The entire place was old-fashioned and uncomfortable, only a little better than the one room she had lived in for a few years after Papa died. She had a small bedroom in addition to the living room, and instead of cooking in the bathroom she had converted a closet-lined alcove that angled off the hall into a sort of kitchenette, with a two-burner electric stove, shelves for utensils, and a little icebox for which she wheedled the restaurant in the hotel into selling her ice.

"Every time I come here, Mama," David said, "I wonder why you insist on staying in this place when you could have a nice, modern, housekeeping apartment."

"I'm used to it here. It suits me."

"I like it," Clara said. "I like it the way it's always been. A housekeeping apartment wouldn't be nearly as much fun as cooking when you're not supposed to." She and Mama exchanged that look again. "Grandma can make anything on her little stove. Sometimes I stay for supper, and she even makes sweet-and-sour fish for me, instead of having it Friday."

"Why don't you sit down, Clara?" he said. "You don't look very comfortable standing there." He leaned back to look up at her. "You must have grown a foot since I saw you last. No wonder I didn't recognize you at first."

She turned red. "I haven't grown, Uncle David." Her voice was like William's, so soft it was sometimes hard to hear her. "I was this tall when I was fourteen." She moved away from the mantel and picked up a bulging leather schoolbag from the desk. "I'd better go, Grandma. I have oodles of homework."

"All right, Little One. Take a few chocolate peppermints to sustain you on the way."

Clara giggled, gave her grandmother a kiss and a one-armed hug, and then put down the schoolbag to open the bottom drawer of the dresser. A strong aroma of chocolate emerged from the open drawer. "I guess two will sustain me for a block and a half. Does anybody else want any?"

"I don't eat candy," David said. "I try to keep in shape."

Mama said, "I'll have one. A chocolate peppermint or two can't change anybody's shape, and often does wonders for the disposition." She slipped it into her mouth and blew a kiss to the departing Clara. A small smear of chocolate on her upper lip gave her an incongruously rakish look, like a poster picture of a sedate, elderly woman on whom a mischievous boy had crayoned a mustache.

"I suppose that was directed at me," he said.

He was not sure she heard him. She denied that her hearing was failing, but she often did not answer when he spoke to her. Now she sat looking at him pleasantly, her eyes moving over his face. She was still, he thought, a pretty woman. Her skin was wrinkled but fresh, without the yellowing that disfigured some dark-complexioned women as they aged, and her soft eyes showed clear and bright through her glasses. The ribbon she wore around her neck, black or gray or lavender to match her dresses, seemed becomingly decorative rather than a means of concealing sagging flesh. "It's nice to see you, David. How have you been?"

"Fine, Mama. Fine."

"Ruth?"

"She's fine too. Busy with a dozen things. Clubs, charities, all that." Mama would like charities. "At night she's so tired she seldom feels up to doing anything. It's weeks since we've gone anywhere or had anyone in. Of course she loves it. She thrives on it," he added hastily, "and it suits me. After a day at the Paper, all I want is a quiet evening at home."

"What do you hear from the girls?"

"Oh, they're fine. Harriet loves Alaska. She says it's a very stimulating, exciting place to live, and it's growing so fast that Edwin's future is assured. Marcia's happy in Greenwich Village. She's making a great many interesting friends."

Mama asked whether Harriet was pregnant yet. He said no, though for all he knew, she might be, and would let them know after the baby arrived, perhaps send them a birth announcement with a few dutiful lines scribbled on it. Mama asked whether Marcia was interested in anybody. He said no, because the only kind of interest Mama meant had marriage at the end of it.

"Not just now. She's concentrating on her writing now. She's very serious about it," he said, though he could not think of anything Marcia had ever been serious about except having a good time. "I think she has the Herzog talent."

"So has Clara," Mama said with sudden animation. "As a matter of fact she brought me a poem today that I think is quite remarkable for a girl of sixteen." She got up and opened a drawer of her desk, where everything was arranged with almost mathematical precision. "I'd like to read it to you. To my mind it ought to be published. I think you may want to put it in the Paper."

"We don't use poetry, Mama."

She ignored this, or did not hear it. "It's called *The Tree*." She began reading in her clear, light voice:

> *She is long-limbed, tawny-skinned,*
> *The sun has dappled through upon her;*
> *Her hair is dark and moist with the kiss of clouds,*
> *And her eyes are cool and still like liquid onyx.*
> *She lifts her arms and the stars glide through her*
> *spread fingers;*
> *She dances a temple dance in solitary majesty,*
> *A sober slave-maid, proud and weary,*
> *Chained to the savagery of the elements.*
> *She bathes in moon-sifted waters, and yields*
> *Her glowing body to the eager sky.*

Mama put the sheet of paper down on the table next to her chair and folded her hands in her lap. "Well?" she said. "Don't you think it's worth printing?"

"I don't know, Mama. I don't know much about poetry. It seems pretty pretentious to me. And the last line—" He raised one eyebrow. "It isn't exactly what one expects of an innocent young girl, is it?"

"Oh, for heaven's sake, David, it's a poem; it's about a tree," she said sharply, sounding all at once like Becky. "I think you ought to print it."

193

"The Paper doesn't use poetry, I told you. Even if we did—"

"All right, I'll send it to the *Times*. They have a poem on the editorial page every day. I'm quite sure they'll want to encourage this sort of talent."

"Well, I hope she really does have talent, Mama. The poor girl will need it."

"What does that mean?"

"Just that with neither looks nor charm, a girl has a difficult time. Talent—" He shrugged. "I suppose if she has enough of it, she can feed on it."

Mama was staring at him with her lips pulled in between her teeth. As a child he had been frightened by that lipless look, had sometimes burst into tears before Mama had said a word. Now she stood up abruptly and returned Clara's poem to the desk drawer. "Clara is a lovely, intelligent, delightful child," she said mildly, her back to him. "You don't know her at all, of course."

The breath whistled out of his lungs as though he had been holding it. "Whatever you say, Mama. I didn't come here to talk about Clara. Tell me what you've been doing with yourself."

"I? Nothing momentous." She sat down again. "I keep busy. The women at temple wanted me to serve as president of the Sisterhood again, but I declined. It's time the younger women—" She broke off with a little smile that seemed not to be for him. "If I were younger myself, I think I'd do something in politics. Any kindly fool can take Thanksgiving baskets to the poor."

David laughed. "*Politics*, Mama? What do you imagine you could do in politics?"

"To begin with," she said serenely, "I'd campaign for Al Smith for President of the United States."

"Well," he said. "Well, if that's an example of your political wisdom, Mama, it's good you're taking baskets to the poor instead. I suggest you read my editorial in the Paper tomorrow if you want to know a little about Al Smith. There's a good deal more I had no space to say. The graft and corruption he's responsible for. The—"

"Nonsense. The graft and corruption are in New York City. Our dandified, do-nothing mayor is responsible for that, not Al Smith."

"Ah! Now I understand. You've been listening to my charming sister."

"I listen to many people, David. I also read a great deal. After that, I make up my own mind." She removed her pince-nez and rubbed the red marks on either side of her nose with her forefingers. Before clipping the glasses back on, she glanced up at him with a cold, naked face that did not seem to belong to Mama. "Have you and Rebecca been quarreling again?"

He shrugged. "It's impossible not to quarrel with Becky, Mama. She thinks she knows best about everything. She's always trying to run the show. You never got along with her yourself, even when she was a child. She was forever screaming and raging and getting in your way."

"When she was little, I used to kick her under the table like a puppy. Not hard, of course, just so I could move without falling over her." Mama laughed. "She certainly was a handful."

"She still is. Would you believe she stalked into my office this afternoon, tore up an editorial I had ready for the printer, and proceeded to tell me how to run the Paper? I was foolish enough to humor her when she begged me to give her a job. I let her putter around the place and think she was useful. Now, after seven months, she imagines she knows more than I do. She even accused me of bringing the Paper to the edge of ruin by firing William, which of course I didn't do. That—that scoundrel came to me, after twenty-two years . . ."

Mama was listening to him attentively, but with no particular indication of sympathy. It might have been thirty years earlier. No matter how justified his adolescent grievances; no matter how carefully he had prepared his complaint, sometimes even writing it out and memorizing it, she had listened with that same terrible impartiality. A juror, not a mother. Halfway through, he had always been sorry he had come to her. And had always come again. Hoping that once, just once, she would be outraged at what had been said or done to him. By now, he should have known better. "William did finally tell you he was leaving, then," she said. "I know he was dreading it."

"*You* know?" David rose out of his chair as though propelled by a hidden spring in the seat. "Do you mean William told *you* he was leaving?"

She looked up at him in surprise. "David," she said, "William and I are very old friends."

"Friends! How can you be friends with a lowlife like that? After what he did to your daughter. It's preposterous. He doesn't even care about his own child. Your wonderful Clara. He hasn't seen her since she was a baby. Becky has to get after him to support her. Is that the kind of person you consider a friend?"

She had turned her face away from him as he spoke. For a moment he thought she was not going to answer him, but then she did, still with her profile to him. "William is a weak man, yes. He's also kind, gentle, considerate, and generous, and those are not inconsequential virtues." She paused. When she went on, she seemed to be talking to herself. "The men around me have all been weak, all but one. My father was the exception." David had never before heard her refer to him as anything but Grandpa or Papa. "He was neither kind, gentle, considerate, nor generous," she said.

"I suppose I'm included. I suppose I'm one of your so-called weak men," David said. "You don't realize, Mama, that you know nothing about me. You've never really troubled."

He was not sure he had spoken loud enough for her to hear. She did not turn around. But there was no use repeating it. His head had begun to throb again, and he crossed to the window and pressed his forehead against the cold pane. The apartment faced on a court, because Mama was disturbed by street noises. Opposite, a dark-complexioned woman was pulling down her shade. "You ought to move out of here, Mama. The place is running down. Soon there won't be anybody living in the hotel but Puerto Ricans."

"At the moment, there are many more congenial women of my own age living here than there are Puerto Ricans. Besides, I have nothing against Puerto Ricans."

"Only against Polish Jews."

"Polish—? Oh." Behind him, he heard her sigh. "David, if you're trying to pick a quarrel with me, you aren't going to succeed. You know quite well that I don't care whether Ruth is Polish or Chinese or has green hair, as long as she's making you happy, and that's the end of that." Her chair creaked. "I'll make some coffee. I've got a few *Schnecken* from Reuben's to go with it. The latest copy of *The Nation* is there on the table, if you want to look at it. I'll only be a minute."

He did not move until he heard her come back with the tray. Then he heaved himself away from the window and slumped into the chair he had vacated.

"That looks good, Mama. Thanks. Maybe it will revive me." He took a sip of the hot, strong, clear brew that she made by boiling up the ground beans with a raw egg, and that he thought was better than any coffee he had ever tasted. "I've had a terrible day."

"Try not to think about it. Take some *Schnecken*. I heated them a little, the way you like them." She pushed the plate across the table to him. "On an asbestos mat with a pot over them. Necessity is the mother of ingenuity. No, don't say it. I know it isn't necessity, strictly speaking. I know I could afford an apartment with an oven. As Clara said, this is more fun." She bit into a bun, chewed and swallowed before she went on. "Besides, if I had a real kitchen I'd feel I had to cook all the time instead of when I'm in the mood. There are so many good restaurants in this—"

"Mama, you're talking to keep me fom telling you about the day I've had. You don't want to listen to my troubles. You never have wanted to."

She chewed and swallowed another bite. "Of course not. Who wants to listen to troubles? But I do it just the same. I was trying to distract you, to keep you from dwelling on— But that isn't what you want, is it? You didn't come to be distracted." She poured more coffee into his half-full cup. "Tell me what's wrong, then. It's not likely I'll be any help, but I'll certainly listen."

He wanted more *Schnecken*, but he pushed the plate away. "No, thanks, Mama, I won't bother you with it. As you say, you won't be able to help me, so why burden you?" His smile felt as he intended it, bright and careless. "It isn't serious, anyway. Not even, properly speaking, troubles. Annoyances would be a better word. Annoying people, exaggerating the facts in annoying ways." He looked at his watch. "I'd better leave. I have a few things to do—errands—before I go home."

Once again he thought she was not going to answer. It took her so long this time that he started to get up. He could not keep sitting there in the silence after he had said he had to leave. But just then she spoke, brushing the crumbs from the table into her cupped hand. "It's the Paper, isn't it? Things aren't going well—"

"Who told you that? William?"

"David, please don't shout. I find it very distasteful." She sat back with the crumbs clutched absently in her fist. "William must have given you his reasons for leaving. If he's wrong, I'm sure it's an honest mistake. He was happy on the Paper. He didn't want to go until he believed he had no choice. How can you be angry with him for that? And if he's right—if the Paper really is in serious difficulties—"

197

"Of course it isn't in serious difficulties, Mama," David said in a reasonable voice. "All the morning newspapers are experiencing certain problems now, but they'll straighten out. What is serious is the wild talk. Serious and vicious. Because if these rumors spread, you see, Mama—if, for example, our advertisers begin to believe that the Paper is in a precarious state—it could cause great harm."

"Yes," she said. "I see."

She sat in silence then, watching his face. He could have been anyone. A stranger, sharing her table at the Tiptoe Inn. He had met her there once for dinner and found her sitting with an old man whose napkin, tied around his neck like a bib, was a manifest menu of his meal. There had been no tables for two, she had explained to David after the old man had finished and shuffled away. No, she had not been repelled by the way he ate. She had not noticed it. He had been telling her about his escape from the Ukraine during the pogroms.

"I always talk to strangers when I'm alone," she had said to David. "You'd be surprised at some of the things they tell. It's an education."

That was the way she was looking at him now, as though she were waiting for him to go on educating her. But he had nothing more to say. He had been foolish to discuss it with her at all. She was not the wise, all-knowing figment of his childhood, only an elderly woman with limited schooling whose life was bounded by her hotel, her temple, her charities, her family, and her friends. "Mama, I hope you really will read my editorial carefully tomorrow," he said to her kindly. "It would be a great mistake to vote for Al Smith. I realize he's a much more colorful figure than Herbert Hoover, but he isn't—"

"I'm not going to vote for him because he's colorful," she said. "I like what he stands for. He's against prohibition, for instance."

David laughed. "Why, Mama, you never drank anything in your life except a little wine for the kiddush and Pesach. What do you care about prohibition?"

"That really doesn't deserve an answer." She started to gather the dishes together, looked with surprise at her still-clenched fist, and then opened it with a little laugh and released the crumbs into a coffee cup. "In any case, I don't think you have to worry about my one poor vote. The country won't elect a Catholic President." She made a small pile of the plates and cups and looked at David across them. "Was there anything else you wanted me to listen to? I'm at your disposal, you know."

"At my disposal. No," he said. "No, I really have to go." He got up and went into the hall for his coat and derby. Mama followed to see him out. "The nights are getting chilly. It will be winter before we know it." He stood for a moment with the coat over one arm and the derby in his hand. "Mama, exactly what did William say to you?"

She had to put her head back a little to see up into his face. He was not a tall man, but he had topped her since he was thirteen. At first that had pleased him, given him a sense of manhood, of power, but later it had bothered him. He had not wanted her diminished.

"I gave you the gist of it before," she said.

"It's not the gist I'm asking for. I want to know what he told you."

She shook her head. "You don't really, David."

"Mama," he said softly, "would I be asking you if I didn't want you to tell me?"

"Yes, I think so. I think in a way you've done that all your life."

"Mama, I don't know what you're talking about. I just asked you a simple question. Are you going to answer me or not?"

"Right here? Standing here in the hall, with you poised to leave? You had plenty of time before, if you really—"

"Mama," he said sharply. "Just tell me."

She hesitated still, but then she said, "Very well, but bring me the stool from the kitchenette, please. You can stand if you like, but I can't. Walking is easy—I can walk miles—but standing tires me."

She did her best to make the whole thing ridiculous. When he got her the stool, she sat on it with her hands in her lap and looked straight at the wall, like a dunce in an old-fashioned schoolroom. All she needed was the cone-shaped cap. "William said what I've already repeated to you, that it broke his heart to leave the Paper, but he felt he had to leave while he was still in demand, because if he waited too long—"

"Mama, I wish you'd look at me while you're talking, instead of giving a recitation to the wall."

"It hurts my neck to keep craning it up at you. I have a touch of arthritis in my neck. If you want to come back into the living room and sit down—"

"Never mind. Go on. You can skip all William's flowery hypocrisy. What I'm interested in is the lies he told you about the Paper."

"If they're lies, David, he believes them. He thinks the Paper hasn't long to live, as he put it. You've said false rumors will frighten off the advertisers, but according to William, he has been meeting resistance from advertisers for a long time, and it constantly gets worse. He says the Paper hasn't kept up with the rapid changes in the business, that you're still trying to run it the way Papa did, and—let me see—"

"What lying drivel! Grandpa wouldn't recognize—"

"There's no use interrupting me to rage at William. If it distresses you too much to hear what he said, I'll be only too glad to stop."

"Oh, Mama, go on!"

"He mentioned one change that was made, raising the price of the Paper to three cents three years ago, that he thought was a great mistake in the face of competing newspapers and tabloids at two cents. He said others agreed with him, but you felt it was a necessary step to combat rising costs." She paused again. "He also said that morale was low. He told me how many people have left in the past seven or eight years, but I don't remember the figures."

"Morale! There's no morale anywhere these days, no loyalty, no dedication. People change jobs the way they change their underwear. I'm not accountable for the times we live in, the irresponsibility—"

"No." She got off the stool and managed to look up at him, in spite of her arthritis. "No, you're certainly not accountable for that, David."

"Oh. But I'm accountable for everything else. Is that what you're saying?"

"How can I? I don't know. It's for you to say."

"Mama—"

"Not to me. You don't have to say anything to me, David. What happens to the Paper is of very little importance to me personally. What happens to you is something else."

He shrugged his coat on and bent to kiss her, holding the derby behind him. "Believe me, Mama, nothing is going to happen to me or to the Paper. What William told you is a lot of vicious drivel to justify his deserting the Paper and going over to Hearst. Put it out of your mind."

She said nothing until he was out in the corridor. Then she came a few steps after him. "David, maybe you shouldn't put it out of yours."

He walked away from her without answering. Not once, he thought. Not once in his life had she aligned herself with him against the others. Not once. He could still remember passing the principal's office in P.S. 9 one day— How old could he have been? No more than nine, because after fourth grade, P.S. 9 had been only for girls. Nine years old, but he still remembered the high-pitched voice coming clearly through the thick door:

Miss Feely must be lying. My boy would never do such a thing.

And he had felt like crying, without knowing exactly why. But he knew now. Never for him, that fierce lioness voice. Never once.

He went down in the elevator and out to Broadway, and then stood there in the middle of the block, unable to decide whether to take a taxi home or to walk or ride the streetcar to Seventy-ninth Street and take the cross-town bus. It was still a little early. He might walk in on one of Ruth's mah-jongg games and have to greet all those women whose names he was supposed to remember and always forgot, and the clatter of the tiles and the cawing of a dozen middle-aged females would follow him no matter where he went in the apartment.

"You could have been more gracious to my friends," Ruth would say.

Gracious was her latest word. A few months ago it had been *scintillating*. She used words like packages of gum, selecting one to chew on until the flavor had long disappeared before she finally discarded it and chewed another. He would find himself waiting for the current choice, tensing for it.

He began walking slowly up Broadway, thinking about not going home at all, ever again. It was not the first time he had thought about that. Once, he had even worked out in his mind a plan for Ruth's support and the monthly check to Marcia after he had disappeared. But he had known at the time that it would come to nothing, just as he knew now that he was on his way home. There was no place else to go.

On a Sunday evening in early November, the Honorable James J. Walker and a woman companion were sitting at a table in a Westchester inn listening to Vincent Lopez's band. A nearby table was occupied by several prominent underworld figures, one of whom came to the mayor's table and whispered to him that the notorious racketeer Arnold Rothstein had been shot. Walker paled and left the inn immediately. Rothstein's murder led to a series of investigations of corruption in Walker's government that ended in his resigning his office and leaving the country in temporary disgrace. Two days after that evening at the inn, however, Walker was elected to a second term as Mayor of New York City.

At the start of the new year, Terry Clymer wrote a pungent editorial entitled "Crime Is Big Business," a watered-down version of which appeared in the Paper under the title "Crime Cannot Pay." A few months later, a convention of underworld bosses held in Atlantic City adopted a plan to organize the rackets into cartels on a nationwide basis.

Sober newspapers reported these matters briefly and with dignity, reserving their more prominent space for the Pact of Paris or the inauguration of Herbert Hoover as thirty-first President of the United States. The pages of the tabloids were splashed with lurid pictures of such events as gangland murders and the fifty thousand dollar funerals of gangsters, for whose flamboyant exploits the public had a sneaking admiration.

It was not until the cataclysm of October 1929 shocked the country into a change of mood that morality regained popular approval. By that time, the Paper, still selling for three cents a copy, had lost more than one third of its circulation and was heavily in debt.

2

Becky arrived at the hospital after she was sure the others would all be there. She did not want to bump into any of them in the street or in the elevator. She did not want to sit with them in the large waiting room, where all the regulars now knew the family and asked sympathetic questions. At the other end of the hall, out of sight around a corner, she had discovered a smaller room, occupied principally by ambulatory patients rather than visitors. They were too intent on themselves to pay much attention to her. She could focus on the door of Room 304, which she could just glimpse from where she sat, and they would not be aware of or care what door she was staring at. She could slip into the lavatory opposite, and when she returned nobody would notice her red eyes.

"Of course I've been here. What do you think I am?" she would say to the others later. "I was too nervous to sit, that's all. I've been walking around."

Nobody at all was in the little room when she got there. No nurse or doctor was going in or out of Room 304. She could see the white placard under the number. She could not read it, but she knew what it said. NO VISITORS.

There was no use thinking about it. When she was with the others, there was no escape, but here alone, even with the door of 304 staring her in the face, she could switch it off for a time. Some people seemed to soak themselves in their misery as though it were a hot bath, but she longed only to emerge.

Somebody had left a newspaper on a chair across the room. She got up to get it. She did not have to keep staring at the door to know when it opened. It was just habit. If anything . . . well, happened, she would hear soon enough, even if she were somewhere else.

The newspaper was yesterday's, and she had of course read it. If she had not been so distraught, she would have thought to bring to-day's newspapers in with her to go over while she waited. Yesterday she had not even remembered to phone in to the Paper until she had left the hospital, though there was a public booth just down the hall.

ROOSEVELT LANDSLIDE PREDICTED, one of the head-lines screamed, as though it were startling news. The Paper had made the prediction weeks before. It took no seer. On her way to the hospital that morning she had seen three tattered women fighting over the contents of a garbage pail. They would have blamed Hoover. A new President might lead the country out of this fearful trough, succeed where Hoover had failed. Becky half believed this herself, though the paper was supporting Hoover.

The Paper had supported Hoover last time, too, of course. David's editorial. She did not want to think in that direction, but now it all began to unreel in her mind and she could not stop it.

He had left out the nonsense about Al Smith's part in New York's corruption—at least he had done that—but even without it the edito-rial had been terrible, full of misstatements and almost incoherent, an embarrassment. He had always imagined himself a powerful writer, like Grandpa, but when he had been a reporter, every story he wrote had had to be done over by a rewrite man. Grandpa had never known it. Miles MacRae had let Grandpa believe what he thought Grandpa wanted to believe. But she knew he had told David his writing was too undisciplined for a newspaper. More kindly, cer-tainly, than Hester had once told her she had no talent, because MacRae was a kind man. Becky had cried when Hester said she was not a writer, but in the end, of course, she had been grateful for the

203

truth. But David blamed unwelcome truths on the meannesses in others, and so kept his own concoctions impervious.

Terry Clymer had raged when he saw that editorial. He was a first-class writer himself and had excellent men on his board, and he had to have what he called "tripe like that" on his editorial page. He had threatened to quit, but she had managed to talk him out of it.

"Oh, come on, Terry, don't take it so seriously. One editorial."

"But a crucial one, and supposedly under my aegis," he said, but he blushed at her use of his first name, and she knew it was with pleasure. Like most men who were cold and formal, he enjoyed being treated as though he were not.

"I know, Terry. I understand how you feel. Only, it isn't worth quitting over, is it? And I don't see how the Paper could possibly do without you or replace you."

He said, "Well—" and then smiled the tight little smile that looked as though it hurt him. "I must say you make this a more agreeable place to work."

"I? I'm only a—a glorified copy girl."

"Hardly," he said. "Hardly."

But, some months later, when David had caught his editorial on crime in the composing room and "cut the heart out of it," as Clymer had put it, even diluting the title, nothing she had said could persuade him to stay.

"What were you doing in the composing room, anyway?" she had asked David afterward. "Lying in wait?"

She should have known better than to challenge him again. She did know better. But he had always, since childhood, had a way of triggering her temper. And of course she, his. What he had said, omitting the embellishments, was that he, like Grandpa, kept his eye on every aspect of the business, that it was fortunate he had happened to be in the composing room in time to catch that absurdly blown-up editorial, that Clymer's work was deteriorating anyway and he had had it in mind for some time to let him go, and that if Becky did not stop poking her nose into things she knew nothing about, she would also find herself out on her ear.

David's idea of keeping his eye on every aspect of the business seemed to be to stand around the newsroom or the composing room or some other department until he thought up something to find fault with. Usually it was something trivial that he made monumental. Once, he had fired a reporter for writing a play at his desk. Reporters were always writing plays or books while they waited for assignments, but either David was unaware of it or thought he could put a stop to it by making an example of one man. When he was not exaggerating some minor error or dereliction, he was, as in the case of Clymer's editorial, pouncing on a shortcoming that existed only in his own mind. The major flaws, he failed to recognize.

A woman patient came carefully along the hall, holding to the handrail along the wall, her slippers making small, whispering slides on the asphalt tiles. When she came to the end of the wall, she had a few unsupported steps to take into the little waiting room. She stood still for a moment and surveyed the chasm, a woman of about Becky's age, looking pitifully vulnerable in her quilted blue robe.

"Shall I help you?" Becky asked her.

"No, thanks." The woman had a rough, uncultivated voice. She tried to smile. "I'm supposed to be able to do it alone."

Becky waited, holding her breath, until the woman had tottered to a chair and cautiously lowered herself into it. Then she rushed into the lavatory as though she had had a hurry call, and sat on one of the seats and cried.

She was not crying so much for the woman as for everyone damaged, frightened, and vulnerable, including herself. Or maybe not so much for that as simply crying, which she did as others sighed or sneezed or yawned, for relief—a reflex. Clara maintained it was physiological, a hypersensitivity of the lachrymal glands. Clara had it too, and hated it.

The woman was waiting for Becky.

"It's my pelvis," she said, before Becky had reached her chair. "I fell down the cellar steps carrying the laundry."

She lived in a house in New Jersey. They had saved for it for fifteen years but they would probably lose it now because her husband had been laid off at the plant and he could not seem to find another job and now they had all this terrible expense of the hospital and doctors besides and she had been telling him for weeks to fix that top step but he always put everything off . . .

Becky hoped she had not told her husband the injured pelvis was his fault, but it was likely that she had, and Becky knew she herself would probably have done so too. Most husbands and wives were antagonists, usually unequal, and they had to employ whatever weapons came to hand. She was glad to be finished with all that.

"You're not a patient," the woman was saying in a suddenly accusing voice. "Those are real pearls, aren't they?" As though the two things were equally offensive.

"No, they're not real." Becky spoke confidentially. She would not admit this to just anyone. "Everybody thinks they are." It was perfectly natural to be fooled.

"They're a wonderful imitation, I must say," the woman said. "By the way, my name's Rich. Mrs. Rich. Only, I'm not."

Becky laughed obligingly. "I'm Mrs. Herzog." Only, I'm not.

Clara, who had had a French governess and six years of French in school, called it *legerdenom*.

It had, of course, been the only thing to do. She did not want Albert's name, and she could not resume William's. In any case, she had always felt like Becky Herzog. Mrs. William Lowenthal and Mrs. Albert Kahn were shams. Except for Clara, they might have been characters in a play. And Clara might almost have been a product of parthenogenesis, for all William had ever had to do with her.

"You have somebody sick here in the hospital, I suppose," Mrs. Rich said.

"Yes."

"A relative?"

"Yes, a relative."

Mrs. Rich looked offended, but Becky considered that she had done as much as could be expected of her for Mrs. Rich. Two other patients came in, a young girl on crutches with her leg in a cast and a sprightly old man who announced that he was going home in two hours and eighteen minutes. Becky, deciding they could all get along very well without her, assumed a distant, unapproachable expression —what Hester called her *grande-dame* look.

A nurse went into Room 304 and came right out again. Evidently she was taking temperatures and had gone in automatically, forgetting there was a private nurse. After three days of sitting and watching the door of the room, Becky recognized the significance of every going and coming.

The girl with her leg in a cast took a lipstick from the pocket of her robe and applied it without using a mirror. Becky thought she must need lipstick herself. She had a way of scraping it off with her teeth when she was nervous. It was, of course, in the very bottom of her handbag, under the sodden handkerchief and the get-well card "from Charlie Mock and the boys in the composing room."

Charlie had given her the card when she stopped in at the Paper on her way to the hospital. If she didn't mind, as long as she was going anyway, he said, and carefully removed the stamp.

Becky was fond of Charlie Mock. Even in his leather apron, his hands black with ink, he looked more like an ambassador than a compositor. He had a fine head of silver hair and strong, chiseled features. His accent was pure Brooklyn, but his voice was full and rich, and he had courtly, old-fashioned manners.

The first time she had ever appeared in the composing room, the printers and the men at the linotype machines had gaped at her as though she had come from the moon. But Charlie Mock's behavior suggested that women in black dresses and pearls and high-heeled shoes were commonplace visitors. "Good afternoon, Mrs. Herzog," he said. "Have you come to see us in action? Is there anything special I can show you?"

"Everything," she told him. "I want to see how everything works."

She had gone back again and again, and he had always been patient, demonstrating and explaining, making her feel he enjoyed it, even though she must often have been a nuisance to him. The day he told her he was leaving, and she finally, with the greatest difficulty, wormed the reason out of him, it was the one more thing she needed to make up her mind.

"I recognize every man's dignity," he said, "and I want no one to ignore mine. It's happened too many times, Mrs. Herzog. I would truly prefer to go hungry and to keep my pride."

"Will you wait, Charlie? I think I can promise you a change, and soon. Will you please not ask me anything, just take my word for it and wait?"

"Naturally I'll take your word, Mrs. Herzog. Certainly, since you ask me to, I'll wait."

His men had come to trust her too, by that time, and no longer regarded her as a curiosity. She had pointed this out to Clara, who had once suggested she embarrassed people by dressing for work as though she were going to a luncheon.

"No one is embarrassed, Clara, by a woman who knows her own style."

"You'd look all right in any style."

"All right isn't good enough. A woman should make herself as attractive as she can."

"Attractive to whom?"

"It doesn't matter to whom."

"Usually it does. Most women want to be attractive to men. But that's not it with you, is it?"

Clara had never questioned her this way until the past few years. She had never really questioned her at all, at least not openly. Becky had been both delighted with her compliance and impatient with it; afraid, sometimes, that she might have too much William in her. But there had always been contrary signs, small rebellions. As young as seven and a half, Clara had one day secretly equipped herself with stick, string, and bent pin, and eluded her governess in Riverside Park to trudge along the river front, asking vainly for bait at boathouses and yacht clubs, her shyness forgotten. Hauled back home to Becky, she had seemed more excited than frightened or repentant. Even her howls, when Becky spanked her with the back of her chased silver hairbrush, had sounded somehow triumphant.

"Most women need men," Becky answered. "The thing is to make yourself as attractive as you can so you can go anywhere with confidence. Buckingham Palace, if the occasion arrives, and face the king as if you belonged there. It's for yourself."

Mama had talked about Clara that day Becky went to her. Mama always talked about Clara, but this was different. "She's thinking of leaving Barnard, Becky, do you know that?"

"Yes, of course I know it, Mama. Clara tells me everything."

Mama looked as though she did not believe this. Nobody believed it. But that was the unique, the wonderful thing about their relationship. Clara had always told her everything, and now that she was old enough, Becky told Clara everything too.

"After only six months," Mama said. "To go to work on the Paper. Do you approve of her cutting short her education this way?"

"Mama, don't interfere."

"I never interfere. I'm simply asking whether you approve."

"At the same time making it perfectly clear you don't." But Becky did not want to quarrel with Mama. Not today. Not over Clara. "It's up to her, of course, but if she decides she doesn't want to stay in college, I won't try to persuade her. Actually, Mama, I think she may be wasting her time there. All she's ever wanted to do is write. She isn't interested in anything that doesn't relate to that."

"Everything relates to that."

"Yes, maybe, in a way. But she reads everything. Half the time, when she's supposed to be studying for some course, she's reading a book that has nothing to do with it, or writing a poem or a story. She's immensely talented, Mama. Why wouldn't she be, with her inheritance? Herzog *and* Lowenthal."

"I know all about her talent, Rebecca. It was I, remember, who sent her poem to the *Times*."

Becky said nothing. It should have occurred to her that the poem was good enough to be published, but she was no expert on poetry. She had thought only that it seemed very good for a girl of sixteen. Surprisingly, Clara had shown it to Mama first. She must have written it in school, and then Mama had happened to be the first person she saw afterward. "Yes, that's why I believe the Paper might be a better place for her than college," Becky said. "The Paper will teach her what she really wants to learn." And there it was, the smooth opening into the thing Becky had come there for, and she added, "That is, if there still is a Paper when she decides she's ready."

"Meaning?"

Becky sipped her coffee. Mama had made coffee for her and Postum for herself. Mama had decided recently that coffee was bad for her heart. As far as Becky knew, there was nothing wrong with Mama's heart, or with any of her other organs. But Becky suspected she thought it was a little indelicate for a woman over seventy, a lady, to claim robust health. "Meaning," Becky said, "that our dividends will be drastically cut again and the future of the Paper is very much in doubt."

"Yes. Well," Mama said calmly, "William told me two years ago the Paper was doomed. Nevertheless, it seems to survive."

"Barely, Mama. Just barely. It's like the one-horse shay. We keep patching it together, but any day it's going to fall to pieces."

"The one-*hoss* shay was never patched together. It had no weak spot, so it lasted until it all collapsed at once."

Mama and her erudition. Clara was always bringing home bits of it, like the chocolate peppermints Mama still kept for her in the bottom drawer of her dresser. *Do you know what Grandma told me today?* "Oh, Mama, what's the difference? I wasn't trying to make an exact analogy, just—" But then she saw a still more direct opening, and her annoyance faded. "Anyway, this one-horse shay does have a weak spot." She waited, but Mama, characteristically, did not ask what it was. "Its driver."

Mama, who rarely moved without purpose, stirred in her seat. She always sat in the largest chair in the room, a dreadful, dark red-plush wing chair in which she looked like pictures of Queen Victoria on her throne, only prettier. "The driver," she repeated. "I suppose you're referring to David."

Becky put down her cup. Sometimes, as now, she could feel a kind of force rising inside her—a tide. But it was too soon. To check it, she relit the stub of her cigarette that had gone out in the saucer, took a puff, and sat back. "There are things that could be done to save the Paper. David won't do them."

"I have no influence with David. If you're telling me because you think I can persuade him to—"

"No, Mama, that's not why I'm telling you. It's not only what he won't do, but what he can't. He can't treat the people who work for him with any sort of understanding. He can't accept advice or criticism. He can't see his own shortcomings. I've tried for a long time, and so have others, to reach him, to get him to change, but it's no use. He can't change."

"No," Mama said. She stirred her Postum, releasing its faint, peculiar odor of molasses and ripening grain. "I'm not sure anyone can."

"He's ruining the Paper. I know he doesn't want to, or mean to, but he's ruining it." Becky ground out the remains of her cigarette. "If he remains as publisher, we'll be finished in six months."

Mama's bland, waiting look changed a little. "*If* he remains? Certainly you don't believe anyone can persuade him to step down?"

"I know no one can." Becky paused. "He has to be made to leave, Mama."

"How? Do you propose to hire strong-arm men to take him out bodily?" She smiled distantly. "David has always been stubborn, you know. He'd be back the next day."

"What I propose is that the stockholders vote him out. For the good of the Paper."

"That's nonsense. You can't vote him out. Grandpa left him the controlling—" She stopped. "The largest interest," she finished in a fading voice.

"The largest individual interest," Becky said. "Grandpa knew exactly what he was doing. He couldn't bring himself to bypass his only possible male successor, but he hedged his bet." She leaned forward now, letting the tide rise, and she saw Mama shrink from it a little and then recover. "He left the rest of us the controlling interest, Mama, because he knew David. If David mismanaged the Paper, he wanted us to have the power to force him out. We should have done it long ago. The Paper has gone downhill almost from the day David took it over. God knows we gave him his chance. Thirteen years, Mama. But now we have no choice. We have to get him out to save the Paper."

Becky stayed as she was for a moment, her arm across the table. It surprised her to see her hand, which she had imagined clenched, lying open and relaxed. She withdrew it to light a cigarette. Mama still sat like Queen Victoria, cool and unmoving in the red plush wing chair.

"I don't give a hoot in hell about the Paper," Mama said. "Not a hoot in hell."

Oh, my God! Becky thought. *She's going to block me. She and David together are going to block me.*

Becky wanted to scream, but screaming only toughened Mama. Usually she could not help screaming anyway, because no one could be more infuriating. But she must not do it now.

"You don't mean that, Mama," she said quietly. "Grandpa's whole life went into the Paper. He made it more than a great newspaper. He built a dynasty on it, made it a powerful kingdom for his descendants to inherit. We can't let it be destroyed by the weakness of one man."

"You're very eloquent," Mama said dryly. "But you seem to forget that the one man is my son and, incidentally, your brother."

"If I'd forgotten that, I wouldn't have waited all this time to act. Don't you think it's painful for me? I love David too."

Clara had asked her not long before whether it was really possible to love David. "I don't know much about it, of course, not having any siblings, but can you love him no matter how unlovable he is? I mean, is it Uncle David you love, or the idea of him?"

It was not always easy for Becky to follow the subtleties of Clara's mind. "What do you mean, the *idea* of him?"

"Well . . . Brother, with a capital B."

There was no use thinking about that. "But it will do him no good," Becky went on to Mama, "if he stays as publisher until everything drops out from under him. If the Paper fails, it will be his failure. And there will be nothing left for any of us."

"If you mean money, that's of no concern to me. I can get along perfectly well in one room, just as I did after Papa died. My material needs are minimal."

"But Hester—"

"The rest of us can help Hester."

"You know she won't accept help."

"She will if she's starving. She's not that much of a fool. In any event, I don't intend to kick out my son to save my sister's pride."

"Oh, my God, Mama! It's not—"

"There's no need to take the Lord's name in vain."

Becky choked on the smoke from her cigarette. She got up and went into the bathroom, threw the stub into the toilet, and stood with her arms and head raised to the ceiling, trying to stop the cough. As it subsided, she caught a glimpse of herself in the mirror. She looked like a dark, short-haired, red-eyed Aimee Semple McPherson. The Lord's name in vain. *Dear God, please help me!*

In the living room Mama had not moved. "I tried a cigarette the other night at Mrs. Henlein's," she said. "Several of the women smoke, you know. Mrs. Henlein's grandson gave her an amber holder for her birthday. Anyway, I tried one, and almost choked to death, the way you did just now. The other women said I'd get used to it, but I can't imagine why anyone would want to get used to anything so thoroughly unpleasant."

Did she believe that the subject of the Paper was closed, or that she could fend it off with small talk? "Much more than our money will be involved if the Paper fails," Becky said. "Hundreds of employees will be thrown out of work to swell the bread lines and sell apples on street corners. Hannah won't suffer, certainly, and I suppose Samuel will get along. I can tighten my belt too, but—"

"If you had to, it would be good for you. You've certainly never known the value of money. It's none of my business, of course, how extravagant you are, but don't expect me to worry about the prospect of your having to tighten your belt."

"I don't expect you to do anything," Becky screamed. "Let the Paper go to rack and ruin! Let David be destroyed with it, knowing he was responsible! Let Grandpa's life become meaningless! Let my future go down the drain! And Clara's! Your granddaughter's! What for? What on earth for, Mama?" Without warning, she began to cry, the tears gushing out of her eyes and down her cheeks. "Oh, Clara wants it so much—so much—" Sniffling and sobbing, she rummaged for her handkerchief, tried to mop up the flow, tried to stop the whole uncomfortable, unattractive procedure, and could not. "The Paper would go to C-Clara some day, and she'd be wor-worthy of it. She'd make Grandpa pr-proud."

Mama waited until Becky had finished and was drying out. Then she went inside and returned with fresh coffee, poured a cup and put it into Becky's hands. "I used to think you were acting," she said. "I didn't see how anybody could be so theatrical naturally. You take after Grandpa, I suppose. He was more restrained, but he had a sense of drama too. A cruel sense sometimes. Do you remember the time he made Samuel walk all the way uptown in his new shoes, because he thought it outrageous that Samuel had paid a copy boy to break them in for him?" She patted Becky's arm. "Go on, drink your coffee while it's hot. You need it."

Becky nodded and drained her cup. She felt depleted of emotion, unable to care what happened. In a little while she would care again, but not now. Now she was back thirty years, drinking hot cocoa in Mama's room, recovering from a siege of weeping. A hot drink had always been Mama's way of coping with a temperament as foreign as a Zulu's to her own. "Thank you, Mama. I did need it. I feel better now."

"I'll just get these dirty cups out of the way. No, you sit still. Relax a little. I'll be back in a minute."

Becky lit a cigarette and rested her head against the back of the chair. When Mama returned, she would have to go on with it. There were other arguments, though at the moment she could not think of them. She was not sure any argument could stand up against Mama's illogic. Mama, who was so coolheaded, so sensible, saying she was willing to let the Paper go under because she cared nothing about it—did not "give a hoot in hell for it" (Queen Victoria, swearing)—and David was her son. How could any Herzog not give a hoot in hell for the Paper?

Mama came back. There was a water stain on her skirt. She had taken to wearing light colors in the daytime, light grays and tans and violets. They were cheerful, she said. It would be dark enough in the grave.

"Mama—" Becky began.

"Never mind." She settled herself in the red chair again. "I've decided what I must do."

Becky's numbness dissolved in a rush of anxiety. *Oh, please, God, don't let her—*

"I won't vote to oust my son," Mama said. "I can't do that."

"Then, it's the end of everything."

"What I will do," Mama said, ignoring her, "is abstain from voting at all. You don't need my vote. You, Hannah, Hester, and Samuel have 45 per cent of the stock among you. If you all agree that David must go, you can outvote him. I'll have no part in it."

Becky lowered her eyes. It was too soon to rejoice. She must never rejoice. David had brought his failure upon himself, but that made it no less sad. "If he's voted out as publisher, we'll give him another position, Mama. Create one for him, if necessary."

Mama was looking at something, or nothing, beyond Becky's head. "I believe Grandpa planned it this way," she said. "I believe he knew what to expect of each of us." Her mild, dark eyes returned to Becky's face. "Yes, you're right; he did know exactly what he was doing. Right or wrong, he always knew. Even, I think, at the end."

Becky thought she must have closed her eyes for a moment or two, because another patient had come into the little waiting room without her noticing. She stared in panic at the door of Room 304. Had she missed some crucial entrance or exit? But the door was so closed and silent still that she felt nothing could have changed in the room behind it.

Evidently she had forgotten to look unapproachable, because the man she had not noticed moved from across the room into the chair next to hers. He was not, she saw, a patient at all, but a man in a business suit. He was about her own age, a little paunchy but attractive in what Clara would have described as a well-worn way. Like an older Fitz. But Becky did not want to think of Clara and Fitz just now.

"A curious place, a hospital waiting room," the man said without preliminary. "All the slipped masks that otherwise hide our private agonies."

Becky raised one eyebrow. "Are you suggesting mine has slipped?"

The question was far too inviting, the quizzical hauteur of the raised eyebrow an insufficient restraint. But she could never resist

214

such encounters. She was intoxicated by her own powers, served by their simulation of sexuality.

"Of course it has," he said in an instantly lowered voice. "Surely you don't ordinarily look so haunted. You have a face for taking and giving happiness."

"A mask, you mean."

He hitched his chair a little closer. "Ours, sitting here, only slip for an interval and are hurriedly replaced. Put us behind one of those doors out there, and we tear them off and lie exposed and trembling in our high beds."

"Not everyone is without courage."

He looked annoyed. "I'm speaking of the average human. You or me." He took out a spotless handkerchief and very swiftly and deftly mopped his forehead and his upper lip. "Or my wife, who happens to be trembling in one of those high beds now." He did not wait for the encouraging question. "She had a breast removed. She's taking it very hard."

"That's understandable," Becky murmured.

He had no need to hear her. "She's afraid I'll be repelled, won't love her any more. I can't reassure her. No matter what I say, she thinks I'm only putting a good face on it. We've been married twenty-two years, and she thinks this will kill my love. A missing breast." He spread his hands apart and looked at them. They were unused hands, with clean, filed nails. "Such remarkable things are done with prosthetics these days."

But the husband always knows, Becky did not say to him or for him. "They certainly are," she agreed, and thought that this was one more man she was glad she was not married to, even with two natural—well, breasts. Bosom, Mama would say, if she had to mention it at all.

"It's a great deal easier to talk about such things with a stranger, somebody one never expects to see again," the man said. "I'm sure you've found that true."

Becky wanted him to go away now. "No." She smiled and batted her eyes at him. "No, I really can't say I have."

Whether or not he retreated at once, she did not know, because now the doctor was coming down the hall, entering Room 304, and she rushed out into the hall to wait. He was in there a long time, or it seemed a long time. Once, she went close to the door and tried to hear, but if there were voices or other sounds they did not reach her.

An endless time. Yet when the door at last swung noiselessly open, she felt unprepared. The doctor came out twirling his stethoscope. She supposed he had individual features that she would have recognized in the street, but just then he was a blank-faced, hurrying, antiseptic figure interchangeable with any other doctor. She could not even remember his name.

"Doctor—"

"Yes?" He paused with one foot forward, ready for flight. "Oh, yes. Mrs. Herzog. There's still no change."

"Is that good or bad?"

"It's—" He looked over her head and down the hall. "Let's say it isn't encouraging. Anything can happen, of course. Over a period of nearly thirty years in the practice of medicine, I've learned how often the most confident prediction is proved inaccurate."

"In other words, Doctor, you hold out little hope."

He turned back to her with a professional, inappropriate smile, patted her shoulder, and walked briskly away.

Becky had another session in the lavatory. Afterward, she stayed there bathing her face with cold water, until she looked normal again. She did not want the man who had talked to her about his wife to see her with swollen eyes. He would ask her nothing, she was sure. He was of the vast number who tell and tell and never ask. But her tears would give him an advantage. She did not intend to enter into conversation with him again, yet she would feel his condescension.

When she returned to the waiting room, he had gone. There was probably little purpose in staying there herself, now that she had seen the doctor. She had to leave eventually. But she sat down again. Anything can happen, the doctor had said.

She had said that to herself after she had left Mama's room that day. The rest should have been easy, but anything could happen. People behaved in unexpected ways. She had known she would have trouble with Mama at first, but she had been confident that when she explained exactly what was involved, Mama's good sense would prevail. Then she would have needed only Hannah or Samuel, and it was unimaginable that both of them would have some unknown reason for backing David. Now, because of Mama's refusal to vote at all—something that had never occurred to Becky as a possibility—she needed the two of them and Hester as well. With three Herzogs involved, anything could happen.

Hannah still lived in the Hotel Majestic, in the same apartment she had occupied for nearly twenty years, with the same paintings and tapestries and bronze animals. The same clothes, Becky sometimes thought. She had grown eccentric with the years and wore rusty, out-of-style black dresses, while dozens of expensive, newer things hung in her closets.

"Who cares what an old lady wears?" she had been saying since she was fifty. "I grab the first thing that comes to hand."

She was fond of Becky, who found her entertaining and visited her regularly. "I'd leave you all my money if I could," she had said once. "Unfortunately, most of it belonged to Arthur, and I feel conscience-bound to will it back to his family. You'll get anything of my own, though, if you keep on being nice to me."

"I'll never be nice to you for that, Hannah," Becky had told her. "Any time I don't like the way you behave, I'll raise the roof, and you know what you can do with your money."

Hannah had given a high-pitched cackle of delight. She had an old crone's laugh, an old crone's stringy body, but there was an air about her. Even in her shabby clothes, she looked like somebody. "I'm not surprised," she said when Becky told her what was happening to the Paper. "I told your mother years ago that David would never amount to anything. If Robert had lived, it would be a different story."

Becky followed her glance to the large photograph of Robert that hung on the wall. He looked the way she remembered him, thin, meek, and humorless.

"He was a brilliant boy, you know," Hannah said. "He'd have made something of the Paper. As it is, you ought to sell it, get rid of it. What do you want it for?"

"Get rid of it? Grandpa's whole life went into it. He meant it to be—"

"What's the difference? He had his fun. Now that he's dead, you can do as you please. He certainly won't know. Or maybe you think he will." She had hooded lids that partially obscured the large, Herzog eyes, giving them a sly, witch's look. "You've always been religious, haven't you?"

"Once in a while I go to temple with Mama on a Friday night or the High Holy Days. If that's being religious— Besides, we have no religious belief in an afterlife."

"We? Oh, you mean Jews. Well, personally, I have no religious belief in anything."

"You must have had once."

"Oh, well, yes. Once. All of us had once. Papa made us." She was looking at Robert's picture again. "It never did me any good that I know of."

Becky wanted a cigarette, but if she lit one Hannah would start coughing and refuse to stop until the cigarette was out again. "Grandpa may not know now what we do." In spite of anything, Becky could not help feeling that he might. "But while he was alive, he took care of whatever we were likely to do after he died. We can't sell the Paper. You know that as well as I. His will prohibits it."

Hannah shrugged. "Wills can be broken." She looked at Becky's face and gave her cackling laugh. "You're shocked, aren't you? My God, sometimes you're as self-righteous as your mother."

Lacking a cigarette, Becky jumped up from her chair, went to the window, and looked out at the pale green haze of budding trees in Central Park. It was surely a fiendish trick of fate that had put her into this family. Mama would say God was testing her, but Becky did not believe He was that childish. He would not goad her to see whether He could make her lose her temper.

"Oh, come and sit down," Hannah said, behind her. "Don't be so touchy. I don't give a damn whether you sell the Paper, or what you do with it. It was just a suggestion."

Mama didn't give a hoot in hell. Hannah didn't give a damn. Never mind, Grandpa. I'm here. Clara and I are here. She went back to her chair. "Even if I felt free to sell it, I wouldn't," she said. "I want it to continue, be a great newspaper again, Grandpa's heritage, for as long as there's a Herzog or a descendant of a Herzog to carry it on."

"Hip, hip, hooray!" Hannah said, leading the cheer with one scrawny arm. "That's all right as far as I'm concerned. What I thought you were saying was that David had made such a mess of it there was no hope of carrying it on."

"No hope while David is running it. If we can get him out as publisher, there's every hope. That's why I'm here. We need your vote as a member of the corporation."

"Oh. I thought you came to see me. I might have known it was because you wanted something."

"Hannah," Becky said calmly, "don't be such a damn fool."

Hannah grinned. She could, of course, have afforded the best dentist in the city, but her teeth looked as though she had picked them out of a mail-order catalogue. "Well, you do want something, don't you? Not that I'm not used to it. Nobody comes to see a rich old woman for her charm." She got up and opened the doors of a hideous, heavily carved oak cabinet, squatted down with the apparent limberness of a girl, and extracted a bottle from the back of the bottom shelf. "This is good stuff. A British steward I know brings it to me straight from the boat." She set the bottle down between them. "What are you looking at me that way for? Are you wondering if I'm a secret tippler? I've discovered that an afternoon nip passes the time and one before bed helps me sleep, and I'm only sorry I didn't have the idea a long while ago."

"What I was really wondering," Becky said, "was how you come to know a British steward."

"If you have enough money, you can come to know anybody." Hannah brought out two glasses, one of crystal, the other a jelly glass, poured the whisky, and gave the jelly glass to Becky. "You don't mind this, do you? It's all I have left. That *Schwarze* breaks everything. Soon, if I don't get rid of her, I won't have a dish to eat on. I don't know why I've kept her for seventeen years, do you? She's no damn good. No *Schwarze* is any damn good. Why don't you drink up?"

"I'm waiting for you. I thought we might drink to the future of the Paper."

"I'll drink to anything. *L'chaim!*"

"*Sholem!* But that's not the toast I proposed."

"All right, now we'll have that one. To the future of the Paper! If any."

"It's partly up to you."

"To me?" Hannah blinked at her. "What have I to do with it?"

Becky put down the thick glass with a clatter. The whisky felt hot in her throat. "Now, you listen to me, Hannah—"

Hannah cackled. "All right, all right. Can't I have a little fun? No reason everything should come to you so easily."

So easily. Oh, my God! Becky thought, and took too large a gulp of whisky, so that the tears came to her eyes.

"Stop that," Hannah said hastily. "Don't go off on one of your crying jags. You know I'll vote against David if you want me to. What do I care about David? He was a nasty child, and he's a nasty man."

Becky stopped in the kitchen on her way out. Flora was sitting at the white-porcelain-topped table reading the *Daily Mirror*. She was older than Hannah, but her brown face was as smooth as a chestnut.

"How's Ronald, Flora? Has he found a job yet?"

Flora had smiled widely at sight of Becky, and she did not stop smiling as she answered. "He ain't gonna find no job, Mrs. Herzog. Who's gonna hire an old colored man, when they's all those young white ones outa work?"

"Can the two of you get along on what my aunt pays you?"

Flora shrugged, still smiling. "We gotta get along, don't we? What we gonna do, cut our throats?"

"Maybe I can find something for him on the Paper. Cleaning the machines or—I don't know. Something. I can't promise, of course—"

Flora was shaking her head. "He can't get no job down there, Mrs. Herzog. Mr. Herzog won't hire no colored man."

"What makes you think that?"

"I know it, that's all."

There was no use probing further. "Well, we'll see. Things may change soon. Don't count on it, Flora, but we may very well find him a job on the Paper."

"I don't count on nothin', Mrs. Herzog."

Becky opened her handbag. "In the meantime, maybe this will help a little. Easter outfits for you and Ronald, or whatever you need."

Flora smoothed out the twenty-dollar bill that Becky had pressed into her hand and stared at it. She stopped smiling for the first time. "This is too much, Mrs. Herzog. I can't take all this money."

"Oh, don't be silly, Flora. I want to give it to you. Here." She grabbed the bill out of the brown hand and stuck it in the pocket of the woman's uniform. "That's that. Now. Tell me what to buy for my aunt's birthday next month. Glasses? She says she only has one left."

Flora was smiling again. "That ain't so, Mrs. Herzog. You know your aunt. She's got a good couple dozen packed away in a box. No sense getting her anything she can keep. Candy is best, or fruit. Strawberries. She do love strawberries."

"That's a wonderful idea. I'll send her a basket of fruit from Hicks with lots of strawberries. Thank you, Flora."

"Thank *you*, Mrs. Herzog. Thanks from Ronald, too. I still think it's not right for me to take all that money, but—"

"Shut up, Flora. You talk too much. All the Herzogs talk too much."

Flora giggled. "I guess I'm not a Herzog. I guess I'm a Baer."

"Don't you believe it. After seventeen years in this family, you're a Herzog. Mr. Baer was just passing through."

When Becky got down to the street, she realized she had no money for a taxi to take her to Samuel's club. He would pay the driver when she got there, but she did not want to put him to the expense. His income had dwindled so that only by watching his pennies, he had told her, could he go on living at the club.

It was a long walk to Fifty-ninth Street. By the time Becky got on the cross-town car, her feet, in the high-heeled shoes, felt twice their normal size. She thought of Samuel, forced to walk all the way up from Park Row. Grandpa had always been hard on Samuel. She could remember thinking, when she was no more than nine or ten, that she would never let anybody treat her that way. No one but Albert Kahn had ever tried. She often wondered how she could have lived with Albert all those years and not killed him. Or he, her. They had come close enough sometimes. How could she have thought that hell was better for Clara than a home without a man to act as father?

Samuel was waiting for her in the club lounge, sitting on one of several leather sofas. It was a man's room, expensively furnished but bare-looking. The tall windows were hung with dark green damask draperies, the walls with portraits of past presidents of the club, all of whom looked to Becky like either Andrew Jackson or George Arliss. An enormous rubber plant and a scattering of ashtrays on stands completed the décor.

"I'm sorry I'm late. I couldn't get a taxi," Becky said. "If I'd crawled across Fifty-ninth Street on my hands and knees, I'd have been here sooner than on that streetcar."

"You didn't inconvenience me. I simply played another rubber." He got up and kissed her. At any given time, his face was as smooth as a baby's and smelled of bay rum, as though he had shaved within the hour. "Do I detect the fragrance of whisky?"

"You do. I've been boozing with Hannah. Did you know she likes her little nip twice a day, and gets it from a steward on a British ship?"

"No!"

Samuel's blue eyes shone. He loved gossip. The tale of Hannah's little nips, carefully disguised and highly colored by Samuel's sense of story, would go the rounds of the club. It was incomprehensible to Becky that he could have used his gifts on the Paper but preferred to make his reputation as the raconteur and wit of a small club for Jewish gentlemen.

He chortled over the incident of the jelly glass. "She gave it to *you*, and had her own drink from the crystal? Marvelous. We have an old codger living here—in fact you can get a glimpse of him over there in the card room, the one with the cigar butt clamped in his teeth. He's as rich as cream, but apparently he conceals it from his family, or thinks he does. He has an old suit he saves to wear when they visit, and shoes with holes in the soles. 'I vant dey should luf me for myself,' he says." Samuel's voice thickened with German gutturals. He could reproduce any accent. "'A man vants people should luf him for himself.'" Samuel paused for a second before he looked at Becky. "That's right. Don't laugh. It's really a better story than Hannah and the jelly glass, because there's pathos in it."

"I'm not sure Hannah isn't pathetic."

"Oh, well, we all are, sooner or later, aren't we? Here I am, talking about old codgers when I'm one myself."

He moved in his chair to catch in the glass that protected the nearest club president the reflection of his lean, pink face. Unlike most of the Herzogs, he had grayed early, to a shade that was as close to silver as it was possible for hair to be. Becky had never seen a strand of it out of alignment. After her divorce from Albert, he had taken her on a month's trip to Europe, while Clara stayed with Mama. Every morning before breakfast and every evening after his five-to-seven nap, it had been her assignment to go to his room and brush the hair on the back of his head into place. She had thought it would be ungrateful to ask who did it when she was not there.

"What's the verdict?" she asked him.

He turned solemnly back to her. "Not bad at that, considering, wouldn't you say?"

"Privy is what I'd say," Becky answered from Samuel's store of idiotic family humor. According to Samuel, this had been Hester's early version of *pretty*. Nobody else remembered it, but it had become part of Herzog lore. "Very privy."

It was always good for a laugh. "Well, at least Joanne seems to find me passable," Samuel said. "I told her I couldn't afford to pay the rent on her apartment any more. I thought she might walk out, but no. It seems she lufs me for myself."

Joanne was the latest and longest-enduring of Samuel's long string of mistresses—a lively, good-humored divorcée in her late thirties, originally from New Orleans, who had once been a model and still looked like one. Becky had met her several times and thought her delightful. Mama, who refused to meet her, persisted in thinking she came from Texas, and called her Samuel's "Texas steer."

"She's not like the others, you know, Becky," Samuel said.

"Ah, Sammy, none of them was ever like the others." Only Becky was permitted to call him Sammy. At one period, because of a little dancer who had told him he looked like a Pete, not a Samuel, he had insisted that everyone call him Pete, and had signed himself S. Peter Herzog. The name and the dancer had passed into oblivion together.

"No, really, Becky, this is no illusion," he said. "We share many interests outside of the bedroom. We're companions. Now that I know it wasn't my money that kept her with me, I can readily envision her staying on into my old age."

"Why not marry her and make sure?"

"I don't want my ways disturbed to that extent. A life without responsibility suits me precisely." He signaled a passing steward and ordered coffee and the little moist, crustless sandwiches that were a speciality of the club. "Besides, Joanne is better off this way," he went on when the man had gone. "I'd be an insufferable husband. It's only because I'm not sure of keeping her that I don't indulge myself in Herzog temperament."

"Nonsense, Sammy. You haven't an atom of—"

"Only," he broke in, "because it has never been permitted to flower. Papa stamped it out. Myra bought it out. Poor Joanne, if I took away her only weapon, would be helpless."

Becky did not believe a word of it. She wondered whether he believed it himself. If Joanne had refused to marry him, this was exactly the kind of rigamarole he would invent, and eventually come to think of as true.

"But I'm talking about myself too much, as usual," he said. "You told me on the phone you had something to discuss with me. Before we get to it, I want to know about Clara, whom I haven't seen in months. I hope I'm still one of her favorite relatives."

"You always have been. She adores you, as you know. Nobody sees much of her these days. She's working very hard on the Paper, trying to learn everything she can as fast as she can, as though she were eighty instead of eighteen and time was running out."

"And when it actually is running out, we behave as though there's no end to it. What about men? Is there anyone?"

"No one special. An occasional date. I tell her she needn't be in love with a man to go out with him, but she claims not to be interested in going out for the sake of going out." Becky shrugged. "I suppose I should be glad, with what goes on today among the young, but I wouldn't worry about Clara in any case. She's not the sort to drink bathtub gin or neck in the rumble seat of a car. And I feel she's missing so much. At her age, I was wading in boys. I never sat home." Becky watched the steward approaching with their tray. "Of course, I had nothing else to do. Clara's hours are irregular, and she does often come home very tired."

"But enjoys it? Gets along all right with David?"

"She manages to keep out of his way."

"Which, I imagine, is more than most people do."

The steward was setting out the sandwiches and coffee. Over his head, Becky glanced at Samuel. He winked at her. "If I'm not mistaken," he said when the steward had gone, "something along those lines is what you want to speak to me about."

He was waiting for her to ask him how he knew, but she did not ask. They had talked about other things, and he had entertained her, as he always did, and she had been willing to put off coming to the point, because until she did, nothing was in danger. But now, all at once, she wanted only to come to it and get it over with. "I'd like your vote to get David out as publisher. It's the only way to save the Paper. I know you've never been particularly interested in the Paper," she said, "but if we could put it back on its feet, increase the dividends again, it would help you financially."

Samuel picked up a sandwich and bit into it. He was the only man she knew who looked elegant even while eating a sandwich. "That would be a happy turn of events, my present financial state being what it is. However, you're wrong when you say I've never been interested in the Paper. I never wanted to *work* on the Paper, but that was because of Papa. If he had been a different sort of father, I think

224

I might very well be in David's shoes now, and making a good job of it." He gazed down at the bitten crescent of sandwich in his fingers. "Or maybe not. Maybe I would never have been worth a damn anyway."

Becky said, "Sammy—" with no idea of what else she meant to say. But instantly he looked up again, smiling, the familiar Samuel, and spoke before she could go on.

"Be that as it may, of course you can count on my vote. David no more belongs where he is than the man in the moon."

"Sammy," she said, leaning over to kiss his cheek once more, "you're the only man I've ever really loved."

It was dark when Becky left the hospital. The taxi driver went through the transverse at Ninety-sixth Street, talking all the way. If he was to be believed, he had been associated in some way with every conceivable horror of the Depression. He had seen ruined financiers leap out of Wall Street windows, women fainting on bread lines, babies with bellies swollen from hunger. A man he knew had gone berserk with despair and killed his entire family. A relative had walked all the way to Washington with the Bonus Expeditionary Force and been burned out of his Hooverville shack and tear-gassed out of town by federal troops.

"Those soldiers, ma'am, they even chased veterans with no legs across the river. Hoover's orders. I ain't never been political or nothin', but I'm sure gonna vote this time, and I'm gonna make the missus vote, if I hafta drag her. We gotta get rid o' that bum."

Clara would have agreed with him. She thought it outrageous that the Paper was supporting Hoover. Was the slogan on its masthead— "Independent of any man or party"—simply hypocrisy? Would Great-Grandpa have wanted to see it become nothing but an organ of the Republican Party and a tool of advertisers?

Clara was too young to be practical. She preferred not to believe that the Paper could not always voice the independent views it had in Grandpa's day. Newspapers had become big business and had to operate accordingly, more often trying to preserve the status quo than attacking it. Where the public's welfare was clearly at issue, the Paper was quick to concern itself; to inform; to expose, if necessary, and sometimes to lose advertisers in the process. But in order to influence, it had, first of all, to survive. It could not offend too many advertisers. It could not brandish every new cudgel. Hoover had made mistakes, but the catastrophe was not of his making, and no other man in that office at that time would have been able to avert it. There was little reason to suppose that a new President would have some magical means of reversing the tide. But Clara was nearly twenty years old, and believed in the virtue of change.

The driver was still talking as he drew up to Becky's apartment house, but she had stopped listening. Away from the Paper, where disaster was only the stuff of which news was made, she did not know how to cope with the misery that pressed in upon her but did not belong to her. The doorman who came to help her out of the taxi, the elevator operator who took her up to the seventh floor, would be gone in weeks, supplanted by self-service, in an economy move that would add these workers to the millions of unemployed. She could give them everything she owned, as she had given Flora the last bill in her purse, and the millions would still be hungry. If she thought about it, the food she ate choked her and did not feed a single child. It was better to put it out of her mind.

She would not have chosen an apartment house in this neighborhood. She much preferred the East Side. But she had moved here to be near Mama, who would not leave the Ansonia. When Mama had had pneumonia and nearly died, and then taken a long time to recuperate, Becky had had her living with them for almost a year. Becky had been married to Albert at the time, and having Mama there had only added to the tensions. Mama had gotten along fine with Albert, as she always had with William, and although Becky knew she had never openly taken sides with him against her, he had claimed her as an ally. Mama must have been one of the few women in history who got along better with her sons-in-law than with her daughter. By the time she had fully recovered, she and Becky could not be in the same room without screaming at each other. Not that Mama had ever actually screamed, but she had started Becky off and then looked at Albert and Clara in martyred wonderment.

She and Becky could not live together, but after her near-fatal illness, Becky did not want her alone on the other side of town. Now it was just as well that Becky had moved, taken an apartment less than two blocks away from Mama for Clara and herself. They could not have afforded to stay in the Park Avenue apartment anyway, with times as they were and William's checks for Clara's support more irregular than ever. In another year, when Clara was twenty-one, the checks would stop altogether. But by then the Paper should be showing profits.

The apartment itself was attractive enough, three large, sunny rooms with a view of the river. Becky had furnished it with some of the best of the Park Avenue pieces, including an early-eighteenth-century gate-leg table on which she and Clara ate dinner when they were home, and a beautiful Chinese cabinet of black lacquer with a gold design. Becky had bought the cabinet at an outlandish price after a fight with Albert about money, and afterward had no recollection of what it looked like. But when it had arrived and replaced a conventional mahogany desk, it had made the Park Avenue living room. It made this one as well.

A note from Clara stood on the table, propped against a jade griffin.

Dear Mother:

Delilah was leaving as I arrived. She claimed she was "sickening for something, most likely the grippe." Knowing Delilah, I'd guess it's more likely some Samson she's sickening for. Anyway, she couldn't possibly do anything about dinner, but she'll be in tomorrow if she feels better. I'd turned down a dinner invitation because I thought she'd have everything ready, but now I might as well go, and you'll need only to rustle up something for yourself.

I hope everything is all right at the hospital. Whatever happens, remember it's idiotic to blame yourself. IT WAS AN ACCIDENT, pure and simple.

I won't be home late.

> *Love,*
> *Clara*

Becky read it over several times, and then threw it away. For years she had kept every note Clara wrote her, but the volume had grown to such proportions that she had had to become selective. Clara had started leaving her notes when she was six. That first one had been written on the back of a brown paper bag and stuck in Clara's door, where Becky would see it when she came for the ritual tucking-in and good-night kiss. In it Clara confessed that she had wet her pants because she had waited too long to go, and promised never to do it again. Between that one and this, thirteen years later, the notes had involved not only other confessions and apologies, other ordinary messages, but an array of arguments, explanations, essays, and appeals. All seemed to Becky to have a special quality, even when they disturbed her. All seemed worth keeping.

This one disturbed her because it did not say whose dinner invitation Clara was accepting. Clara always told her exactly where she was going and with whom. The omission must mean that she was going out with Fitz, in spite of all Becky's warnings. She had refused to promise to stop seeing him, but Becky had hoped she would think it over and realize what a mistake she was making. Becky was disturbed not only because seeing Fitz was so wrong, so impossible, but because it was driving a wedge between her and Clara. It was not that Clara had never before done anything against Becky's wishes. But other times they had battled it all out openly, with Clara occasionally driven to defiant shouting or to running out of the apartment, sometimes to Mama's for comfort, but always in the end rushing back into Becky's arms, and both of them drowning in tears. This time Clara had removed herself from the battle, shut Becky out with a cool secretiveness that was altogether unlike her. Becky considered speaking to Fitz, but to do so would be to accept the finality of her exclusion, and was unlikely to get results anyway.

There was no use fretting herself into a headache. She could feel one beginning behind her eyes. The thing to do was to talk to Clara when she came home, try again, and in the meantime stop thinking about it. She would not rush to the hospital in the morning either. She did no one any good sitting there hour after hour, watching the door of Room 304, periodically overwhelmed by tears. Tomorrow she would telephone, and if there was still no change she would go down to the Paper in the normal way and visit the hospital after she had done her work for the day. The nurse would let her know if there was any need for her to be there before that. "Don't wallow in emotion," Grandpa had told her once, during one of her orgies of weeping. "It's bad for the health."

She washed and changed into a pale green negligee that Clara had given her for her birthday to show her how well she looked in color. It was becoming enough, pretty to wear in the house, but it had no unique style. It was not Becky. Clara, who was so quick in other ways, seemed unable to learn about style. She wore whatever was current. Fresh and attractive as she was, people did not turn to look at her. When Becky entered a room she still stopped conversation, though she was long past youth. Youth and beauty had their limits. Style was the thing.

Becky sprayed scent behind her ears and in the hollow of her minimally sagging throat and freshened her lipstick before going to the kitchen. If Clara had been home, she would have prepared something interesting—she liked to cook, and was good at it—but scrambled eggs and coffee would do for a dinner alone. She was careful about her weight. In the days when nobody had worried about keeping slim, she had eaten like a horse. She and Albert had belonged to a Saturday-night poker game that was played in a different home every week. Each hostess tried to outdo the others in the lavishness of the spread she put on the table at midnight: cold turkey and tongue, potato salad, herring salad, salmon mousse, cheese, rye bread and pumpernickel, pickles and olives, two or three cakes, and of course beer, bottles and bottles of cold beer. They had all eaten hearty dinners at seven o'clock or thereabouts, but they all stuffed themselves again. Becky had once weighed almost one hundred eighty pounds. She was tall enough to have carried it reasonably well—no one had thought of her as fat—but now she weighed forty pounds less. She still had a figure, though. The girls these days tried to look like slats of wood, the flatter the better. They might as well have been boys. And older women copied them. Adults seemed suddenly to be taking their standards from the young, instead of setting standards for them, the way it always had been.

She scrambled the eggs and made the coffee, added a slice of dry toasted rye bread, and brought it into the living room, setting it on a doily on the gate-leg table. If Delilah had been there to prepare it for her, she could not have looked more untouched by the process, though she had not even worn an apron. She never wore an apron, and never got a spot on herself. Hester said nothing would dare to spot her. Fat that would spurt from a pan to spatter anyone else, Hester said, simply quivered and lay still when Becky looked at it.

Becky lit a cigarette to smoke with her coffee. Hester had been sitting across from her at this table, both of them smoking with their coffee, when she had said those things.

"You're a formidable woman, Becky. I suppose you know that," she had also said.

"Formidable? That's a harsh word."

"I don't mean it harshly. It's what I once was myself, or thought I

229

was, or meant to be. But it takes passion, and I ran out of passion. Maybe I never had enough to begin with."

She was only seven years older than Becky. They had always been more like sisters than aunt and niece. That night, looking at her across the table, it seemed to Becky that Hester had aged with the unnatural swiftness that sometimes resulted from grave disease, though she had not been ill. Her hair was still black and there were not many lines in her face, but she looked flattened out, empty, as though all her juices had drained away. The lively intelligence was still in her eyes, but Becky had the curious impression of a layer that if peeled away would leave an old woman's glazed indifference.

"Hester will go along, won't she?" Becky had asked Samuel that day at his club. "I can't think of any reason why she should back David, but you know her better than anyone else."

"Not any more. I scarcely see her. She won't let me come to her hotel—I suspect it's so sleazy she's embarrassed to have me see how she lives—and she claims she hasn't the clothes to come here. As though I'd care how she dressed," Samuel had said, though Becky knew he would care very much. "A few months ago she let me take her to Child's for lunch. *Child's.* Once I ran out of family news, we had nothing to say to each other. She lives in another world. If there's a way into it, I can't find it." He had turned away to blow his nose delicately and lengthily into his snowy handkerchief. "I'm afraid I no longer can predict what she would do."

Becky had thought it possible that Hester would resist seeing her at all. It was almost a year since they had met at Mama's, after several times when Hester had said she would come and had failed to show up. When she finally did come, she arrived almost an hour late. Becky had been furious, and said so. Instead of apologizing or snapping back or tossing it off as she once would have done, Hester had simply picked up her things and left, and Becky had not seen her since. But when Becky telephoned to ask her to come to the apartment for dinner, she accepted at once, even before Becky said she had something important to talk to her about.

Becky had arranged it for Delilah's day off and sent Clara to eat with Mama, so that she and Hester could talk without interruption. She had found a cut of beef approximating "Papa's Meat" and cooked it the way Mary had taught her when she was growing up in Grandpa's house. Hester had eaten as though she were famished. Becky had begun to wonder whether that was why she had come so readily—to get a square meal. It was terrible to think that they had all taken care of Mary until she died but they had not taken care of Hester. The fact that Hester would not let them made it no less terrible. Despite what Mama said, Becky was not sure Hester would not rather starve first.

"A long time ago, I told your mother you and I were alike," Hester said over coffee and cigarettes, "because we were both going to get what we wanted. That's what formidable women do." She was smoking her cigarette down to the very end, holding the little stub with her fingernails. "There's a fundamental difference I couldn't have been expected to recognize then. You go on believing, time after time, that what you want will stay forever desirable after you get it, as whole and shining as your dream of it. I stopped early on. I stopped wanting. It saves a great deal of trouble."

"For God's sake, Hester, take another cigarette before you broil your fingers," Becky said, pushing a full package across the table. "What are you telling me? That if I save the Paper from David, it will turn into a frog before my eyes?"

Hester lit a fresh cigarette. She took her time about answering. Becky had always been fond of Hester. Not loved her, as she loved Samuel, for all his absurdity; it was not easy to love Hester. Enjoyed her, though, and once greatly admired her. Now there was something frightening about her. Pitiable, too, of course. The dress she wore must have been twenty years old. The fabric was so expensive, so fine, that it had lasted all this time, but the style that then had made other women envy her chic, now made her ridiculous. Still, she was frightening. Becky was repelled by what she had said, and did not want to hear what she had yet to say. But until Hester promised to vote David out, which she had so far resisted doing, there was no choice but to listen to her.

"I'm thankful," is what she finally said, "that it isn't Samuel in there making a mess of things—as it very well might have been, give or take a circumstance—and I wanting the Paper for myself and mine. Samuel's a more harmless and engaging man than David, and kin to me in a way I'm sure David couldn't be to you, or to anyone. Even so, I'd have done to him what you propose to do to David. That's the trouble with wanting. That's one reason I've given it up."

Becky looked at Hester with narrowed eyes. She forgot she needed her good will. "How dare you suggest I'm doing something terrible to David so I can get hold of the Paper! I don't know about you.

Maybe you're cold-blooded enough to knife your own brother for your personal advantage, but don't put me in your class, Hester." Becky had started in a quiet voice, but she could never keep it quiet. Invariably the volume got away from her. "I want to save the Paper, yes! Because it was Grandpa's life, and his legacy to all the Herzogs. And yes, I want to take over as publisher! Because everyone else is incompetent or has abdicated or died, and I'm the only one left to do it. And yes, for both those reasons I want David out! But to save him too, not to knife him. If the Paper fails, the world will know it was David's failure, and that's something he could never bear. So don't you ever again in your life accuse me of stabbing my brother in the back to get something he has that I want, because if you do—"

Hester, who during all of Becky's outburst had sat back in her chair, an expression of polite interest on her face, puffing at her cigarette with evident pleasure, now interrupted. "There's no point in threatening a person who doesn't want anything, Becky. Anyway, you needn't. I have no intention of repeating myself on the subject."

"That isn't good enough. I want an apology."

"For what? All I said was that if I were in your shoes, I'd do as you're doing. It's you who gave it all that significance."

"I know what you meant. I'm not a fool," Becky said, but her anger was dissolving as quickly as it had surfaced.

Hester took off her glasses, cleaned them absently with her napkin, and put them back on. In the moment without them, her face looked younger, more familiar, though Becky could scarcely remember a time when she had not worn them. "Another of my new insights," she said, "is that it's well to look for harmless meanings in distasteful statements, and to take all other kinds at face value."

Becky wrinkled her nose. "That isn't new. It's called making the best of everything."

"But I'm not trying to make the best of everything. I'm trying to make nothing of everything."

"Oh, stop it! I can't stand listening to such nonsense. You talk like an idiot. Maybe if instead of burying yourself in that dump of a hotel, feeling sorry for yourself—"

"I don't feel in the least sorry for myself. That's for people who have stood helplessly by while fate mishandled them. I was never helpless. I did my own mishandling."

Becky looked away. They talked of other things. After a time,

Becky said, "I've been wanting to ask about Walt. It seems so callous not to, but Mama thinks you don't want him mentioned."

"It's Walter who doesn't want him mentioned. I suppose you know Walter and his new, young wife have had a son? Do you know they've called him Walter, Jr.? As though Walt never existed?" At Becky's horrified look, Hester gave a harsh little laugh. "That's another way of making nothing out of something. It doesn't really matter, of course. Walt will never know, and even if he did, it wouldn't touch him. I think he's probably less miserable now than he's ever been in his life. Very little is expected of him. He gets exactly the same treatment as everybody else. And he's protected against himself. They wanted to put him in charge of the library, but he refused. I think he doesn't want to be trusted."

"Have you seen him, Hester?"

"Three months ago. He asked me not to come again. It's better that way, for both of us."

"Have you any idea when he's likely to get out?"

"He won't get out. He'll die there."

"What are you talking about? They can't keep him there for life. The boy recovered."

"That's right. He'd be paroled in a few more years. But he'll die before that."

"How can you possibly know a thing like that?"

"I know because he told me."

It took Becky a moment to absorb this. "Oh, my God, Hester!" she said then. "But you reported it, didn't you? So they can take measures to—?"

"I didn't report it. No measures would stop Walt. He's too clever. Besides, I think it's wise." She put out her cigarette and reached across the table to grasp Becky's arm. "Now, listen, if you cry I'm going to leave. I won't sit here and be inundated by your tears. You asked me and I told you and that's the end of it. If I don't cry, why should you?"

Becky blinked and swallowed and pulled her arm away. "Do you want some more coffee? If not, I'm going to get rid of these dishes. No, don't help me. You know I can't stand anybody helping me. I have my own system and you'll only get in my way." She was clearing the table as she talked, stacking the plates, gathering up the silver, the movements of her hands as deft as a magician's and almost as hard to follow. "Come into the kitchen and sit down and talk to me while I wash these things. I could leave them for Delilah, but I can't stand dirty dishes in the sink overnight."

Hester sat on the kitchen chair, the skirt of her purple moire dress trailing the floor. "You're an incongruous *Hausfrau*, Becky. Anna Karenina in the kitchen." She paused for the rush of water from the faucet to subside. "I shouldn't have told you about Walt."

"You had to tell someone."

"Why? You didn't want to hear it. Why would anybody want to hear it? And I didn't really want to tell it. There's no relief in the telling. On the contrary, I've given it substance, where I'd rather it had none."

Becky, her rubber-gloved hands plunged into a snowstorm of soap-suds, shook her head. "That's too convoluted for me. It's the way Clara talks sometimes. I have a more unvarnished mind." She looked at Hester over her shoulder. "Right now it's a mind that brings me back from all this to our original subject, David and the Paper. What about it, Hester?"

Hester lit another cigarette. "Did you know David came to me once, years ago, to see if I could get him into the Columbia Club? He couldn't ask Papa, of course. Papa would have been appalled at his even thinking of joining a club where Jews weren't wanted. But David had an idea that with my connections I'd be able to manage it for him. I couldn't, of course. Nobody could have. But he was sure that if I'd really gone to the trouble, I'd have gotten him in. He's never forgiven me. It isn't the club's policy he blames. It's me."

Becky pulled off the gloves and turned around, but Hester stopped her before she could speak.

"Don't explode, Becky. That wasn't a change of subject. I told it to you so you'd know, if you don't already, that nothing you do or say—nothing that results from it, however beneficial, either to David or to the Paper—will have any effect on him. If he feels as he does because I couldn't get him into his college club—" She stopped. "I realize this won't change your decision. It may make a difference in your expectations. You'll have my vote, of course."

All Becky said was, "Good." It was only anger she could not contain, anger and tears. She finished the dishes and put them away, talking to Hester about Mama and Hannah and about Clara's talent, meanwhile thinking that now everything could begin: her real life. Her life and Clara's.

"Come back inside," she said to Hester when she had hung the dish towel to dry. "I have something else to discuss with you."

Hester sighed. "What have I let myself in for? I was perfectly comfortable until I left my little room. Now I'm so full of Herzog words, I'm getting mental indigestion. I don't think I can stand any more of them, either yours or my own."

She went into the living room, though, and sat down, lighting still another cigarette, gorging herself on them as she had on the food.

"I didn't put this to you beforehand, because you might have thought of it as bribery," Becky said, "when what it is actually is an appeal." She looked down at her hands, and then up into Hester's face. "I want you to come back to the Paper. I need you there."

It seemed to Becky that Hester had begun shaking her head even before Becky had come to the point. "That's out of the question."

Becky leaned toward her. "It isn't. It can't be. I tell you, I need you. I need your help and advice. What experience have I had, compared with yours?"

"There are a dozen people on the Paper to give you all the help and advice you want. Anything you want. All you have to do is crook your finger."

"Outsiders, Hester, not family. It isn't the same. They may be loyal, but they're not Herzogs. They can't care about the Paper the way we do."

"Not I, Becky. I've finished with caring."

"Don't talk like an idiot. Listen to me. I can't write. You know that. There has to be a Herzog on the Paper who can write. Someday it will be Clara, but she's not ready yet, and won't be for a long time. I need you."

"You seem to forget I lost my job with Hearst because I couldn't write. Not for today's readers."

"Don't be such a damn fool. That was only your column. It was meant for a different era, and there wasn't any writing, however brilliant, that could have transformed it. I don't want you to write a woman's column. I have much bigger plans for you, much—"

"No, Becky. No." Hester was shaking her head again, but not as she had before. Now she had pulled back from Becky, and her head was moving from side to side as though a hornet were following her. "Don't make plans for me. I won't be part of anyone's plans."

"Make your own, then. Tell me what you'd like to do, where you think you'd fit in best, and that's where the Paper will find a place for you."

"No. You can't badger me back into life. I don't want it. I've had enough of it." She stood up. "I'm going."

Becky saw her to the door. There was nothing else to do. "Think it over, Hester," she said. "Please, just think it over. The Paper needs you."

Becky did not really remember exactly what she had said to Hester to try to persuade her to come back to the Paper. Now, two years later, sitting in the same chair with her after-dinner cigarette, waiting for Clara to come home, she was not even sure whether she had decided from the beginning to ask Hester back if David was voted out, or whether the idea had struck her that evening. She knew she had been astonished by Hester's refusal, and determined not to let it go at that. How could any normal, healthy, intelligent human being give up on life? If one way of living went wrong, there were so many other choices. God knew, Becky had found that out. She had offered Hester another way as much to save her as because the Paper needed her. In fact, Becky had not been altogether certain of Hester's usefulness to a modern newspaper. It might have been not only her column that the times had outgrown, but Hester herself. Still, Becky was not going to let her rot in her shabby hotel room and her twenty-year-old clothes, even if that was what Hester thought she wanted to do.

The telephone rang twice before Becky finished her cigarette. Once, it was one of the bull-pen editors, Harper Green, calling from the Paper with some rambling complaint that Becky did not understand and would not have dealt with even if it had been clear. Green had been a copy reader under Papa and appeared to think this gave him special privileges with her. Becky was never sure, when he called her like this, whether he was drunk or growing senile. Ordinarily he seemed a typical member of the bull pen, quiet, erudite, content with his night hours, asking nothing better than to be among the first to read and appraise the news as it came in to the Paper.

"Harper, listen to me," she said when she could get a word in. "I'm sorry you're having trouble, but the one to handle it is Schuman. Why don't you speak to him before he leaves his office tomorrow?"

"I fail to see what this has to do with the managing editor," the

236

old man said, reverting to his customary dignity. "In your father's day, the bull pen always had direct access to the publisher."

"I know, Harper, but we're a much more complex operation now, and I believe it's essential to divide authority. In the newsroom, the authority is Rick Schuman. I'm not going to try to do his job or interfere with him." Becky was not sure whether Harper Green was in any condition to take this in, but she had to talk to him as if he were. "I realize I've made a lot of changes in a short time, and it's hard to get used to change, but I wish you'd try to go along with me. I don't want to see you discontented, Harper. You're too valuable to the Paper."

He mumbled something that she could not catch, but he did say, "Thank you." Becky heard that, and she thought it sounded like more than a formality. She hoped he would be all right, stay sober enough or lucid enough to go on doing his work. She had a horror of seeing anyone fired, instantly imagining him in rags, selling apples, or fighting for the discarded food in garbage pails, like the women she had passed on her way to the hospital that morning. The only economy she had refused to make on the Paper was to reduce the staff.

She had scarcely hung up after Harper Green's call when the phone rang again. This time it was a man she had met at a dinner party the week before. His name was Theodore Rosenthal—Ted Rosenthal, he announced himself—and he was related to a former Assistant Treasurer of the United States. To Becky's ears, he had the voice of a well-bred, wealthy Jew, though what she meant by that, she could not have said. As he talked, she tried to recall his face. He had sat next to her at dinner, but he had been called away soon afterward—was he a doctor?—and she had difficulty sorting him out from other men she had met the same evening. It had been a very large dinner party.

"If you care for the ballet, that is," he was saying. "I don't recall that we spoke of it, though I do know you mentioned a love of music."

"Did I?"

"You had been to hear Heifetz that afternoon, as I remember."

All at once she saw him clearly. She had told him about the Heifetz concert because she had been so astoundingly moved by it, though her knowledge of music was limited. She had told him she could understand why Heifetz was called "fiddler to the angels," and he had leaned toward her with his head a little cocked, as though he were hard of hearing, and said, "Yes. Yes, of course," in that cultivated voice. A somewhat beefy, fiftyish face, with very bright eyes—dark? light?—under heavy gray eyebrows, and a good, firm mouth. Yes, a doctor. A specialist. Heart, she thought, but it might have been something else. A widower. Or was he divorced? Not married, at any rate, so that was all right.

"I like the ballet very much indeed," she said, which was not true. All that gliding and leaping that was supposed to be telling her something and never did. "I'll be delighted to go."

She was smiling as she hung up, smiling and humming to herself as she cleared away her few dishes. It was no surprise to her that a man she had met at a dinner party wanted to see her again. Men had been wanting to see her again since as far back as she could remember. But it had never failed to please her, and now it amused her as well. After all, she was over fifty, far past the age of the dazzled stare and the hopeful phone call, but she still got both. She was more popular, still, than Clara had ever been, which was sad and painful, yet, in another way, objectively, invigorating.

When she had finished in the kitchen, she took off her mules and sat with her feet up on the sofa, reading and listening to the radio. She was reading *Dodsworth*, a novel by Sinclair Lewis that Clara had recommended. So far, Becky did not care much for it. The frivolous wife with her loose morals offended her, and she considered the husband a damn fool for putting up with such a woman. But Becky had begun to think about the hospital again, and there was no use letting herself do that, because it would not help. The book at least took her mind off it. As she read, she began to find Samuel Dodsworth less exasperating, and to become interested in his problems, so that she forgot the time.

Becky liked it when Clara was there, reading in a chair across from her or scribbling at her desk in the bedroom, but she did not really mind being alone. She considered an evening to herself a treat. Other unattached women of her age were regarded as encumbrances, difficult to fit into a guest list, invited out of pity for a time, and eventually dropped. Becky had been more in demand since her divorce from Albert than before. No one ever seemed to think of her as an extra woman, even when she was. And now that she had the added luster of her position on the Paper, she was asked out so constantly that she was sometimes, for all her energy, exhausted. She was always making up her mind to stay home more, but when it came to it, she found it impossible to refuse an invitation if she had nothing else to do. Who could tell whom she might meet, or what she might hear?

She was just coming to the end of the novel when she heard Clara's key in the door. She looked up, smiling, a little bemused by the story. Clara came quietly through the foyer and stopped at the entrance to the living room. Her cheeks were flushed and her eyes shone. Sometimes she seemed pallid, almost plain, but now she was quite pretty. The new, longer skirts became her, so that she even had a touch of style, conventional yet attractive.

"Hello, darling," Becky said. "You look as if you've had a good time."

"So do you. I didn't think you'd still be up."

"Oh, well, I wanted to finish this." She held the book out for Clara to see. "It's really very good, isn't it? I'm delighted Dodsworth found someone else and walked out on that dreadful wife. Turn off the radio, will you, baby." Becky sat up. "A man I met at the Strauses' a couple of weeks ago called to invite me to dinner and the ballet on the fourteenth. Ted Rosenthal. Dr. Rosenthal. He's a surgeon. Most attractive. Why are you fiddling with the radio? Just turn it off, and come and sit down. Tell me what you've been doing all evening. What time is it, anyway?" Becky lifted her arm and shook back the flowing sleeve of her negligee so she could see her wrist watch—the diamond watch Albert had given her for their fifteenth anniversary and paid for with stolen (well, misappropriated) money, though she had not known it at the time. She frowned. "It's almost one o'clock. I had no idea. You said you'd be early."

"I thought I would be." Clara left the radio and bent down to kiss her mother on the cheek. "I'm going to bed, if you don't mind. I haven't stopped since I got up this morning. I'm too tired even to talk."

Becky caught her by the wrist. "You've been drinking, haven't you?"

"Why do you say it like that? As if you didn't know I ever took a drink? I'm not drunk, Mother, if that's what you mean. We ate at Barney's, and I had two orange blossoms before dinner. You can't eat in a speak-easy without ordering cocktails."

"And of course you had to eat in a speak-easy."

"The food is cheap."

"You were with Fitz, I suppose."

"Mother, I told you I was tired. I really don't want to stand here answering questions." Clara had such a soft voice that as a child it had often coupled with her shyness to make her almost inaudible. Becky had found it irritating and tried to make her speak up, yet once she knew the softness did not derive from lack of spirit, she rather admired it. "We can talk about it tomorrow," Clara said.

Becky kept hold of her wrist. "I just want to ask you one thing first." She did not want to ask it at all. She did not want to know. But suddenly she had to know. "Look at me, baby."

Clara looked at her. Clara would tell her the truth. She never lied to Becky. From the time she had been old enough to understand, Becky had impressed upon her the importance of telling the truth, above all to her mother, until it had become as automatic for her as breathing. "Yes," she said. "What is it?"

"Look at me," Becky said again, although Clara's eyes had not left hers. "Have you gone to bed with Fitz?"

The color spread from Clara's cheeks to her hairline, and down her throat, where it disappeared into her dress. Even her nose turned red. "Mother!" Her voice was one shade louder than a whisper. "You can't ask me a question like that!"

"What do you mean, I can't ask it? I am asking it." Becky dropped Clara's wrist and stared at the opposite wall. "And I'm afraid you've answered it."

"No," Clara said. "I haven't answered it, and I won't. You want me to profess my innocence or confess my guilt, but I have no intention of doing either. You have no right to expect it. I'm not a child any more, Mother. My life is my own, not yours."

Becky's head snapped around to her again. "Don't you dare talk to me like that!" she said. "You're nothing but a little *Fratze* who would still be reciting lessons in school if I hadn't let you go to work on the Paper. If it hadn't been for me, you wouldn't know Fitz existed. I was fool enough to think you'd learn how to be a reporter from an old hand, but that isn't what he's been teaching you, is it? He ought to be ashamed. And you. I thought you had more sense, more decency. What do you think can ever come of it? Do you think he's going to divorce his wife and marry you? A Catholic? And even if he did, what kind of marriage would it be? A Jewish girl who has had all the advantages you've had, and a low-class Catholic mick. It would break Grandma's—"

"Oh, Mother, for heaven's sake don't bring Grandma into it," Clara broke in softly. "For heaven's sake, stop ranting."

"Ranting!" Becky screamed. "Now, you listen to me. As long as you're living under my roof—"

Clara interrupted again. "I'll move out any time you say. It would probably be a good thing. A girl my age shouldn't still be living with her mother."

"What are you talking about? You're only—"

This time it was the telephone that broke in, shrilling above Becky's voice. She put her hand to her throat. "Oh, God!"

Clara touched her arm. "Do you want me to answer it, Mother?"

Becky shook her head. She went to the phone and picked up the receiver. She was not conscious of saying anything, but she must have said, "Hello," because Samuel began to talk. She did not have to listen to know what he would tell her, because she had known the moment the phone rang. When she had hung up, she turned around to Clara and nodded.

"He's dead?" Clara whispered.

"Twenty minutes ago." Becky stood perfectly still in the middle of the room. She began to cry without changing her position or covering her face, letting the tears wash down her cheeks and her neck.

"Don't, Mother," Clara said.

Becky began moving her head from side to side. "I killed him. You know that, don't you? Just as surely as if I'd taken a gun and shot him."

"Now, stop that!" Clara took her by the shoulders and shook her a little. "That's just a lot of melodramatic nonsense."

"No. It's true. Ruth knows it's true. She said if he died it would be my fault."

"What does that prove? She was beside herself. She didn't know what she was saying. Or maybe she did. Maybe she said the worst thing she could think of out of resentment. She's never had any use for any of us." Clara was talking louder than usual to make herself heard over Becky's sobs. "Anyway, it's ridiculous, Mother. It was an accident. Nobody commits suicide by stepping in front of an automobile. It isn't sure enough." She put her arm around Becky now, and Becky let herself be led back to the sofa. "Besides, if Uncle David was going to kill himself because he wasn't the publisher of the Paper any more, why would he wait so long? He hasn't been the publisher for two years."

Becky cried a little longer, but the flow was ebbing. "That's true, isn't it?" she said finally. "Of course you're right. I don't know what's the matter with me. Listening to Ruth's vindictive spewing. Torturing myself. Of course it was an accident. Poor David." She reached into the pocket of her negligee for a wisp of lace-trimmed handkerchief with which she mopped her eyes and blew her nose, reducing it to a sodden rag. "Uncle Samuel said he never came out of the coma."

"Well, that's good, isn't it? Not to be aware of what was happening?"

Becky reached for her hand. "I don't know what I'd do without you, baby."

"Well, that's all right." Clara's voice shook a little, but she frowned and swallowed and went on more steadily. "I'm not going anywhere. Except to bed. And you'd better come too. Look at the time."

"Yes, I'm coming. We have a newspaper to get out tomorrow. The Paper doesn't stop, even for death."

3

All the windows in the newsroom were open, but the room seemed airless. The big ceiling fans did nothing but move the heat around. Shirts were glued to backs and fingers slipped wetly on typewriter keys. A listless poker game was going on in the back of the room, more out of habit than because anyone really felt like playing. Every little while someone sent a copy boy out for beer, which was warm by the time it arrived.

None of the office doors was closed. Some, like Rick Schuman's and Andy Mulvey's, were never closed anyway. Schuman wanted to keep his eye on things at all times, or at least to give that appearance to the men under him. Mulvey, the sports editor, worked best within sight and sound of human activity. On the other hand, Dan Wilbur, who headed the book-review department, was a fiend for quiet and was likely to glare at anyone who let in the noise from the newsroom by opening the door for no matter what purpose. Yet even Wilbur's door was not closed today.

Hester preferred quiet when she was working, but she had come in early and finished her regular feature article before the worst of the heat had begun. For the moment, she had nothing to do. She considered going upstairs to see if Becky needed her for anything, but it was too hot to make the effort. If Becky had taken over David's former office, she would have been right here, a few doors down, where Rick Schuman was installed now. Some typically complicated mixture of delicacy and shrewdness had decided her to remove herself to another floor.

"I'm not replacing your former publisher. I'm succeeding him," she had told the staff. Among Becky's gifts was a flair for suggesting subtle meaning where there was none. "Mr. Schuman will occupy the head office on the newsroom floor. I'm moving upstairs, out of his way."

They had applauded her after every few paragraphs, as though she were a performer or a political speaker, both of which, in a way, she was. She had made a grand entrance that first morning, sweeping into the newsroom (and later into all the other departments) in a new outfit, an elegant parody of a business suit—beautifully cut black jacket and skirt, collared white silk blouse, the pearls intricately twisted around her neck—creating the impression that she was someone they had never seen before. They had all stopped whatever they were doing to look at her as if she were, indeed, a strange woman, not yesterday's Becky Herzog, who had been around for several years, working at this and that, flattering, soothing, and stimulating where needed, while she learned the business. No one had ever ignored her—it was not possible to ignore Becky—but now they paid intense attention. Intense and wary. One reporter picked up the cards on his desk and shoved them into a drawer, though his desk was in the back of the room and partly hidden by a post, where Becky could not have seen it.

"I'm your new boss," she said. "This is not, I'm sure, a bombshell. If it's like everything else that goes on here, you heard of it while it was still an unformed thought. That's one of the things that makes this a great newspaper. Our people know about the news before it happens."

Becky made this sound cleverer than it was. She could always make more of anything she said than the words conveyed. The newsroom staff laughed noisily, but they were still wary.

"You also no doubt know that the reason I'm here in this capacity is that my brother, Mr. Herzog, was prevailed upon to lend his talents elsewhere. He is to be vice-president of the Manhattan National Bank, one of the largest in the city, as you know, with

243

branches throughout the country and the world. Because of his confidence in my ability to take over here, he felt free to accept this fine offer."

It was the best she could do. She did not say *a* vice-president (one of five). She used the prestige of the bank to create an impressive aura. Whatever they might have heard as rumor, none of them knew as fact that David had walked out of the building in a wild rage the moment Becky told him "for the good of the Paper" he was to be "executive manager" instead of publisher. He had never even sent back to his office for his personal belongings, and he had never again spoken to any member of the family.

"Exactly what are you going to tell him an executive manager is?" Hester had asked Becky beforehand.

"Oh, I'll say he has to pass on all administrative matters. Of course he won't, but I'll see to it he thinks he's doing it. I'll make it convincing."

She might have, but she had had no chance to try. David had stormed out without asking for a definition. Within an hour, Becky had had Hannah on the phone, badgering her as only Becky could badger, until Hannah promised to put pressure on the bank of which Arthur Baer had been president to offer the former publisher of the Paper a position. If David had wondered at this providential coincidence, he had evidently not let wonderment stand in his way. No one in the family knew how he had fared as a vice-president of the Manhattan National Bank. None of them had ever again seen him alive.

But, that first morning, Becky said: "Mr. Herzog has found an important and congenial new métier. Mine has always been the Paper. Long, long before I came to work here, I learned about it at my grandfather's knee, and knew that someday I would be part of it. That I would be its publisher, I of course never dreamed. A woman publisher? It was years before my grandfather would allow a woman into the place at all. But here I am."

She got the effect of flinging her arms wide without actually doing it. When the applause spattered out, she changed her tone with perfect timing to businesslike briskness, making the statement about succeeding David, not replacing him, and moving her office to another floor.

"This is one small change among many I intend to make, but it's significant. Every publisher has his own style. Mine will be primarily to delegate authority. Here in the newsroom, for example, each editor will not only be responsible to your managing editor, Mr. Schuman, but will be responsible only to him. And although he and I may consult on matters of general policy, I intend to leave him alone to manage his department and deal with his editors as he sees fit. This goes for every department of the Paper, from the composing room to the business office. As long as I have confidence in the man at the head, I won't interfere with him in any way. If I should lose that confidence, he will no longer be of value to the Paper."

She had been talking into the microphone on the city editor's desk. Now she left it and took a deliberate walk down the length of the room, looking into every face and glancing at each desk.

"You may be wondering how you, as individuals, will be affected by having a woman as your publisher," she said when she returned to the microphone. "I can assure you, not at all. As I strolled around the room just now, I noticed a peculiar, antiseptic atmosphere. An air of diligence and virtue." She paused a little longer than was comfortable. "You can take them all out of your desk drawers now, the cards and the bottles and the novels-in-progress." She paused again, unsmiling. "If your city editor and your managing editor need a bunch of drinking, gambling, swearing, novel-writing bums to help me get out a great newspaper, it's all right with me."

This time, the laughter and applause shook the walls. The young reporters in the back of the room cheered and stamped their feet. Becky smiled slightly, serenely.

"None of the changes I intend," she went on when it was possible to be heard, "are prompted by my sex. They spring from a need for increased efficiency and economy in these difficult times. But don't worry about losing your job in the interests of economy. A salary cut may, I'm afraid, be inevitable for all of us, from the top down, but no one who is pulling his weight will be fired."

It was masterful. Instead of grumbling about a cut in salary, she had them grateful for the security of their jobs. Then, immediately, she caught their attention with something else.

"You'll all be interested in one specific change that I believe will vastly increase our declining circulation and help to put us back on top again, where we belong. Effective with next Monday's first edition, the price of the Paper will be reduced to two cents. Now, I ask you, will anybody in his right mind read any other newspaper when he can read the Paper for the same price?"

They answered her. They actually chorused, "No!" Only Becky could have reduced a roomful of tough newspapermen and -women to such glowing idiocy. When she waved her hand at them before sweeping out again, Hester would not have been surprised if they had blown kisses to her.

Hester could see through her open door the city editor's desk, where Becky had stood that morning. She had brought Hester along, wearing her down, exhausting her with pleas for moral support, which Hester knew were fraudulent (no one ever needed moral support less than Becky) but could not keep on resisting. Or did not really want to resist? Hester would have denied that at the time, but she was no longer sure. Could she have been duped into believing she would go down to the Paper with Becky for just one day and that would be the end of it, unless she had wanted to be duped?

By evening she had known there was no return to the non-life she had thought she craved. The gabble of voices, the clatter of typewriter keys, the ringing of telephones, the clicking of the AP wires, the smell of tension, the smell of paper and of printer's ink, had dragged her back among the living.

"I know your work," Rick Schuman had said to her. She had not been fooled by his drawl, or his gangling, genial, farm-boy look. It had not surprised her when he went on to say, "Pabulum for a former generation's sentimental, housebound ladies. Can you do anything else, Mrs. Lowenthal?"

She might have said, "No," or "I don't know and I don't care," and still escaped, but what she said was, "Try me."

The name on the open door of her office was not the name Schuman had addressed her by that day. He had agreed it had outlived its usefulness. If it seemed that she was, after all, better alive, H. H. Lowenthal, at least, was better dead.

HESTER DUKE it said on her door. Duke was English for Herzog. They all got back to it one way or another, except Hannah, who had always been less of a Herzog than any of them. There was Ida, of course, who might no longer be a Herzog, for all anyone in the family knew. They never heard from Ida, scarcely remembered her except as a character in a Herzog anecdote. Ida, trying to convert the rabbi at Becky's wedding. That girl reporter, Anna Wolff, who had bamboozled her way into the middle of the scene and written it up for the *Journal* was writing lurid features for Hearst's *Mirror* now.

Principally sex scandals, for Lord's sake, at—what? Sixty? She could not have been much younger than Hester.

Hester's feature articles were almost as widely read, and certainly by a far more discriminating audience. She wrote about individuals in the news: generals, society women, labor leaders, financiers, candidates for governor. As an interviewer, she had developed a talent she had not known she had for leading people to reveal themselves. She wrote with natural gusto and wit, as she had never done as H. H. Lowenthal, and managed to tell the truth without enraging more than a handful of her subjects—just enough of them to inspire a little lively correspondence on the editorial page.

"If you want me to retire next year, you'd better remind me, because I may not think of it," she had said to Rick Schuman a few months back. "I'm having too much fun." Which was, considering everything, preposterous, but almost true.

"Keep writing, Hester," Schuman had answered. "Just keep writing. Talk to me again about retirement when you're around eighty, and we'll make some long-range plans for it."

Periodically, Becky reminded her that it was all her doing. "If it hadn't been for me, you'd still be rotting in that dreadful hotel room." She said it with pride, not malice. There was no malice in Becky, only fast-burning fury. She was not looking for gratitude. All she wanted was credit, for which she had an unappeasable appetite. Hester did not deny it to her—it *was* Becky's doing—but Becky, who was as lavish with credit as with everything, and hoped for the same abandoned demonstration from others, no doubt found Hester's response disappointingly spare.

Hester shifted a little in her chair. She had to pull at her skirt, which was stuck to the seat. Out in the newsroom, almost directly on a line with her desk, a fly was buzzing around Joseph Fitzsimmons' head. Fitz waved it away absently, but when it came back, let it alone. He was poking at his typewriter with an apparent listlessness that had nothing to do with the weather. He always wrote that way, as though nothing could be more wearying, more unimportant, than the story he was working on. When he had finished, the story would be sharp and vital, no word superfluous, no word lacking. He had the desk directly in front of the city editor's desk, the number-one seat for the top reporter on the Paper. Sweat was running down the side of his face that Hester could see, finding the deep groove from the end of his nose to the edge of his mouth. He seemed not to notice it. She wondered what he was writing about with such concentration on this hot August day. No. September. The first of September. Could any mere local news be absorbing, when half the world was holding its breath in terror?

She had shared her fantasy about Germany with such as Hearst and Dreiser and Mencken. Still, it was incredible to her now that for so long after she had let other, more private illusions slip quietly away, she had been mesmerized by her youthful vision of that fairytale land. Perhaps she had confused her love for the man she had met there (or what had passed for love in her silly young body) with love for his country. After more than forty years, she could still remember the poetry he had written to her, and the brutal violence with which he had made love. Walter, when she went home to him, had seemed tame in comparison. But she had been not much more of a fool than some others—than Clara, for instance, with her enduring Fitz fantasy—and she had paid for it most of her life.

A matter for regret, yes, but not for bitterness. Bitterness toward whom? As she had once told Becky, she had done her own mishandling. Curiously, Elsa, who believed God had punished her for her sins, whatever they were, by taking her only two sons while she still lived, thought Papa had done a terrible thing to Hester in his will. To Hester, her share seemed just, but Elsa accepted the death of her children as justice from God and considered Papa's retribution for Hester's perfidy vindictive. Well, Hester had lost her son too, and it might have been comforting to believe God, or Walter, had done it to her, but she had learned to live without comfort.

Something was changing out there in the newsroom now. The pall of lethargy was lifting. Somebody shouted words Hester could not hear. Fitz looked up sharply from his typewriter and then shoved his chair back and rushed out of her range of vision. Hester had just reached her door when Becky exploded from the elevator and disappeared into Schuman's office. A copy boy streaked by. Hester grabbed his arm. "What's happened?"

He shook off her hand, answering over his shoulder as he ran. "Germany has invaded Poland. It just came over the AP wire."

Hester stood still, staring after him. For some reason she could not have fathomed, she spoke to herself in German.

"Jetzt geht's los!"

248

What might have looked like bedlam to an outsider, was only the frenetic but more or less orderly process of getting out a newspaper in the light of cataclysmic news. Reports from the Associated Press and the Paper's foreign correspondents came ticking steadily over the wires. Copy boys rushed the flimsies to the bull pen, where Morris Fishman, chief editor, was writing the banner headlines. Later he would go down to the composing room to make sure the front-page matrix was to his liking before it was rolled into the printing press. Rick Schuman, whose calm was not often noticeably ruffled, came out of his office to hover over the bull-pen editors as they sifted the reports. Becky hovered over everybody for a few minutes, and then went back upstairs to hold an emergency conference with her business and advertising staffs, to be joined after the Paper went to press by the managing editor, the bull-pen chief, and a number of others.

Becky sent for Hester the next day.

"I'd come down to you when I want to see you, of course," Becky had once explained, "but it wouldn't look right. Except when I attend a news conference in Rick's office, everyone comes up here to me. If you didn't, it would look like—well—"

"Nepotism?" Hester had suggested. Which had seemed mildly amusing to Hester, considering the origin of the word, but had produced an unsmiling nod from Becky.

"The outward forms can make a difference in your acceptance, and Clara's, by the staff. Grandpa believed that, didn't he? I know he wouldn't allow Samuel to call him 'Papa' in the office."

"That wasn't so the staff would accept Samuel."

When Becky was going full tilt, she did not hear comments that might deflect her. "Clara claims the best she can do is not call me anything. Peculiar things embarrass Clara. But I suppose names are the least of it these days. People are much more informal."

Anyone who had ever heard Becky dithering over nothing would have wondered how she could run a newspaper. After all, she could not run it on sheer personality, even though it sometimes seemed that she could and did.

But she was not dithering that day, after the invasion of Poland, when she called Hester to her office. "I've made some major decisions. Tentative decisions," she said. "As usual, some of my chiefs think I'm out of my mind and others approve. I want to know what you think."

Hester sat down in a chair upholstered in dark blue, a counterpart

249

of the one Becky sat in on the other side of the desk, except that Becky's swiveled. Matching blue draperies hung at the two corner windows. Blue was also the predominant color in the Persian rug, and in the still life, given to her by one of her male admirers, that hung over the gray settee. It was a small office, made smaller by cutting off part of one end for Becky's private lavatory, but it had elegance. Even when there was no breeze in this corner room, high above the city, it conveyed coolness.

The first time Becky had called Hester up there to ask her opinion of some proposal, Hester had not believed she really wanted to hear it. A sop, she had believed, Becky's way of making her feel more important to the Paper. Or she was to be used as a sounding board to reflect the resonance of Becky's voice. But whenever Hester thought she understood her niece's mind, she found she was wrong. Out of that welter of shrewdness and obtuseness, sentimentality and toughness, willfulness and sophistication, no one could accurately predict what would emerge.

"I talked to the Washington Bureau last night," she said now, "and to the Paris and London offices this morning. France and Great Britain will declare war on Germany tomorrow. They're going to need material aid from us. I think we ought to support Roosevelt's efforts to get the Neutrality Act repealed."

Hester stared at her. "We've never supported Roosevelt in anything."

"The picture has changed." Becky's tone was impatient. She fingered her necklace, the long, dark red, almond-shaped nails contrasting with the round whiteness of the pearls. "I'm suggesting we change with it."

"If we supply arms to Great Britain and France, we may be drawn into the war ourselves."

"Then we will be. I don't see how the Paper can advocate neutrality while that terrible little man goes on persecuting Jews all over Europe."

It was dangerous to bait Becky, but in this case Hester thought it had to be done. "Do you mean because it's a Jewish newspaper?"

Becky's composed expression instantly became a glare. "What are you talking about?" she said, working up to a scream. "A Jewish newspaper! You sound like one of those crank letters we get. Do you realize the only Jewish editor on the staff is Morris Fishman? Do you think *he* can make it a Jewish newspaper? When he's responsible to

Rick Schuman, and Schuman is a German? Well, of German descent, anyway. I don't even know what a Jewish newspaper *is*. Except one that's printed in Yiddish for Jews who can't read English. You might as well say Macy's is a Jewish department store. You might as well—"

"All right, Becky, you believe that. But if the Paper advocates abandoning neutrality now, when the Jews of Europe are in danger, a good many readers, advertisers, Roosevelt-haters, and Jew-haters are going to believe otherwise. Or say otherwise, which amounts to the same thing."

"Well, then, to hell with them! Thank God, we can afford to say that now. To hell with them!" Her voice subsided. "Which brings me to my next decision. Tentative decision," she added again. "I've been thinking about this for a long time, in the event war broke out in Europe. I've been talking to people; reading . . ."

Becky liked to imply that she was a profound and analytical reader, but Hester had no reason to think it was so. What she did accept was that Becky did, indeed, talk to people—to shrewdly chosen people—and that she listened to everybody, and that she could thoroughly milk anyone's brain with such skill and charm that its owner did not know it was happening.

"This war won't be like the last one," she was saying. "Before we got into that one, it was a remote event to the masses of people here, something that was happening to a lot of foreigners on the other side of the world. Today everyone knows that what happens over there affects us, is vital to us. Suppose Hitler overruns Europe—I've heard it said he has the military power to do it—and suppose our guns aren't enough to stop him without our men behind them. Suppose, suppose, suppose. There isn't any reasonably intelligent person in this country who won't be wondering and worrying and wanting to know."

Becky was leaning forward now, punctuating her words with little taps of the long, red nails on her desk. Her green eyes were brilliant with excitement. In the room's cool light, the aging of her face was softened and she looked extraordinarily beautiful. It struck Hester for the first time that the room had been designed for that.

"I propose to tell them," Becky went on. "I propose to cover this war as no war, no event in the news, has ever been covered before. I want to increase the staff, get hold of many more first-class people to go to Europe and report on every aspect of the war from the fighting on the battlefield to the panic on the border villages in France to the debates in Parliament. I want to print news, news, news, even if it has to be at the expense of advertising. I want to make everybody realize that whatever they want to know about the war, they can find out by reading the Paper." She stopped abruptly and leaned back. "What do you think?"

"If you want the product of the lengthy consideration you've allowed me, it's that it will cost a lot of money."

"Yes, of course it will. Too much, the business department tells me. But I'm convinced it's an investment. I believe we'll gain so tremendously in readership that whatever we spend now, or lose, will be returned to us many times over." She paused. "If the war lasts long enough, that is."

"Especially if this country gets into it?"

Becky studied the ceiling. "Needless to say, I hope that doesn't happen. But I'm a realist. I know it may. And if it does, I want the Paper to be ready." After a moment she looked at Hester again. "If you disagree, I wish you'd say so."

"I don't disagree. How can I? You took hold of a dying newspaper and brought it back to life. Wouldn't I be a fool to think you don't know what you're doing now?"

Becky looked pleased. "Well, some have doubts. The business department thinks I've gone crazy. Sam Froelich is worried about advertising space. But the editors are all enthusiastic. Well, all but Morris Fishman, who's afraid we won't have a balanced newspaper, but he's an old lady anyway. Balanced! It's not going to be a balanced world, is it, with that terrible little man on the loose?"

It was obvious that this time Becky had made her decision before she sent for Hester, that she might have been disappointed if Hester had disapproved but it certainly would not have changed her course. Something else was on her mind. Hester waited patiently while she meandered, talking about Clara, whom she had sent down to Washington for a while (to see how the Paper's bureau down there operated, she said; to get her away from Fitz, she did not say) and about Elsa, who had aged suddenly after David's death but now, at seventy-nine, seemed to be picking up again.

"I still tell her she ought to have someone there to look after her, but she won't hear of it. She insists she doesn't need anybody and couldn't stand having anybody around. It worries me. Last week I caught her cleaning the bathroom because the way the chambermaid had left it didn't suit her. Isn't that a Herzog for you?" Becky laughed and shook her head. "We're all wonders in our own way, aren't we? Look at you. Changing your style, your subject matter, and your name, and making a whole new reputation for yourself as an outstanding newspaperwoman in only seven years."

"And so?"

"What do you mean, and so?"

"I assume you're leading up to something."

Becky was not at all discomposed. "As a matter of fact, I am. I talked to Rick Schuman about it, and he agreed it was an excellent idea." She paused. "How would you like to go to London?"

"To *London?*" Hester knew she was gaping, but it seemed the only logical response. "I wouldn't like it at all. Why should I go to London?"

"I wish it could be Germany," Becky said calmly. "You'd be wonderful in Germany, with your knowledge of the country and the language, but it would be too dangerous. They probably wouldn't let you in anyway. We'll have to settle for London."

"Would you mind telling me what you're talking about?"

"What I've been talking about all along. Coverage of the war. I want you to do in London what you've been doing so brilliantly here. Interviewing the men and women who are shaping Great Britain's part in the war, or being shaped by it. Telling our readers what—"

"No, Becky. Absolutely not. It's ridiculous. I've never heard anything so ridiculous. I wouldn't think of going. I like New York. I'm comfortable here in my apartment and my office. I have no intention of pulling up stakes at my age and running off to London to help you cover a war."

Becky looked at her with narrowed eyes, as though trying to see her more clearly from a long distance away. "I thought you'd be thrilled," she said. "I'm offering you a chance to be at the center of history. Most people would jump at it."

"I'm too old to jump."

"Who's going to be interested in reading about people like John L. Lewis or Senator La Follette now? Our readers will want to know why Neville Chamberlain thought he could trust Hitler, what Winston Churchill has to say about the fulfillment of his prophecies, whether the man in the street still believes Great Britain is impregnable—"

"Becky—" Hester stopped, and started again. "Becky, if you're telling me I'd better go to London because I'm of no use here any more, you're wasting your time. I can't be threatened. It's been pleasant to work on the Paper, but I can live without it. That's what you've never been able to understand about me. There's nothing I can't live without."

"Oh, Hester, don't talk like such a damn fool! Who's threatening you? If I didn't need you for a much bigger job in London, I'd never let you leave here. I couldn't have done what I've done if it hadn't been for you. Not a day will pass that I won't miss you."

"You won't miss me unless you fire me. I'm not going anywhere."

"Fire you! Really, Hester, I don't know what you think I am." Becky gave an exaggerated sigh. "Of course I'm disappointed. This is going to be a big thing for the Paper, the biggest since the innovations I made when I became publisher. I did hope you'd be in on it. You'd have been wonderful in London. You'd have—"

"Stop it, Becky. Give it up. You wore me down seven years ago because, for one thing, I wasn't eating regularly. It's different now. I'm not in the least tempted. The war will have to get along without me. I intend to grow old in peace."

Hester took a taxi from Flushing Meadow to her apartment in Tudor City. She had gone to the World's Fair for the fifteen-minute armchair tour of Futurama, as background material for her piece on Norman Bel Geddes, who had designed the display for General Motors. Her fellow travelers on the conveyor belt that carried them over the America of 1960 in miniature had seemed enthralled by the vision of fourteen-lane superhighways, radio-controlled traffic, cities with fifteen-hundred-foot-high office buildings. Hester was thankful that she probably would not be alive to see any such reality, or, if she was, would be too old to be embroiled in it. Both the past and the future were unthinkable. Only in the present was it possible to survive.

She liked coming home to her apartment. The squalor from which Becky had rescued her seven years before had not actively bothered her, had scarcely impinged on her consciousness, but this place suited her current existence. She had one large room, sparsely but comfortably furnished with low-slung chairs; wide, square, short-legged tables; and a huge divan, covered with cushions, that served as both sofa and bed. Everything was black and white except the two paintings, one by Joan Miro and one by Jackson Pollock, both copies.

"It's so stark," Becky had said the first time she saw the room, and, "I'd rather have a genuine Any Artist than a fake Great Artist."

To the first of which comments Hester had answered, "I think starkness becomes me," and to the second, "I wouldn't."

She had a small kitchen, but she was no more interested in cooking than she had ever been. Unlike the rest of the family, she cared very little what she ate. If she did not feel like eating in a restaurant, she often brought in prepared food from Horn & Hardart's and reheated it. She was doing that now, after returning from the World of Tomorrow—waiting for baked macaroni and cheese to get hot in the oven while she took off her Chanel suit and put on an old wool bathrobe—when the doorbell rang.

Hester decided not to answer it. She always answered the telephone like any good newspaperwoman, but she often ignored the doorbell. The only significant inanimate object that would come by that route was a telegram, which would be slipped under the door if she seemed not to be home. Any animate presence would go away in a little while. Sometimes she was curious enough to risk opening the door, but this was not one of the times. The possibilities were limited to Becky and Samuel, who occasionally dropped in on their way somewhere else, one or two lonely old friends, or some stranger who had the wrong door or wanted to know where the right one was. She did not feel like contending with any of them, especially in her bathrobe.

The bell rang again. Then whoever it was tried knocking a few times. This was followed by a voice. Hester, interested by such persistence, tiptoed over to the door and put her ear to the crack.

"Aunt Hester, are you there? It's Clara."

Hester opened the door at once. "Clara! What are you doing here?" She kissed her grandniece's cheek. "I thought you were in Washington."

"I was. I just came in on the train."

"Well, take off your coat and sit down. Does your mother know—?"

"Mother thinks I'm still in Washington." Clara put down the overnight case she was carrying and shrugged out of her coat. She sat in one of the chairs, had trouble disposing of her long legs from its low seat, and changed to the divan. "I thought you were probably here, even when you didn't answer the bell."

Clara was often ill at ease until she got past the beginning of an encounter. It exasperated Becky, but Hester found it appealing. Most of the other Herzogs had surely emerged bumptious from their mother's wombs. Clara had been a shy, gentle child with a soft voice that one had to bend down to hear. Some of that quality remained to her now, in her late twenties. She looked like Becky, without being at all beautiful. Her skin and hair were fair, like William's, and she had the fresh, wholesome color of a country girl. All this was deceptive, giving small clue to the essential Clara. Hester was very fond of her. "Have you eaten? I'm heating macaroni and cheese. There's plenty for two."

"Fine."

"Do you want to stay for the night?"

"No, thanks," Clara said, to Hester's relief. It was a long while since she had shared, or wanted to share, a bed with anyone. "I'm going home later. I just wanted to talk to you about a few things first, and—well, you know Mother. She wouldn't understand my not rushing to her as soon as I got off the train. It'll be better if she thinks I did."

Clara took off her shoes and inched back against the cushions with her feet under her. She had been here several times before, usually at Hester's invitation, occasionally dropping in as she had this evening. Only once that Hester could remember had there been a discernible purpose to her visits, other than the pleasure they had in each other's company. That once, she had come the night after Hester had received word of Walt's death. Hester had not wanted to open the door then, either, but she had thought it might be someone about the arrangements.

"Mother said you didn't want to see anybody," Clara had said in the doorway. "I just thought I'd stop by and make sure. I won't come in if you'd rather I didn't."

She had stayed all night, sitting on the divan the way she was doing now, with Hester in a facing chair. They had drunk orange blossoms that Clara had brought along in a Nedick's carton of orange-ade to which she had added homemade gin, and smoked the room into a thick fog. Toward morning Hester had made the first mention of Walt. "He always said he meant to die there, you know. They told me it was pneumonia. I suppose they'd say something like that, or they'd be admitting negligence."

"Does it matter?"

It had seemed to Hester, after all those orange blossoms, a profoundly wise question. "Of course, I'm to blame," the orange blossoms had made Hester say.

"I don't see how you can know that. I don't see how anyone can know who's to blame for anything." Perhaps Clara had had fewer drinks. "It's all too complicated," she had said.

Later, when Hester had sobered up, she had still considered this a sensible way to look at it.

"Shall we have a drink before we eat?" Hester suggested now. "I'm afraid I can't offer you an orange blossom—no orange juice—but anything else—"

Clara shuddered. "How did we ever drink that stuff? I haven't been able to look at gin since repeal."

Hester made Manhattans. They each had two, and then ate the macaroni and cheese, which had cooked too long and was a little burnt on top, with a salad Clara concocted out of odds and ends Hester kept on hand to nibble when she got hungry late at night, and apples for dessert. They had their coffee after everything else was cleared away, Clara back on the divan and Hester in one of the low-slung chairs.

"I never cared for Washington myself," Hester said, in answer to a comment of Clara's. "During all the years Walter and I lived there, I never felt at home."

"Washington is all right. It's an attractive city. What I got fed up with was the dissension and dissatisfaction in our bureau there. They all seem to think the New York office hasn't enough respect for the Washington correspondents and gives too little prominence to their stories. There was even a rumor that I was there to spy on them and report back to Mother on their competence."

Hester lit a cigarette. She had offered one to Clara earlier, but Clara had given up smoking. It had come to her one night in Washington, when she had finished her last pack and was fuming because it was too late to buy another, that it was "crazy to let anything get such a hold over you," and she had not smoked since. What about Fitz? Hester had not said.

"It's been worse since the invasion of Poland," Clara was going on. "Now they feel whatever they send in, even reports from top political analysts, is pushed to the back of the Paper, or not used at all, while anything from the most insignificant foreign correspondent makes the front page. Jack Wilson wrote an anti-Roosevelt piece while I was there. He claimed no one told him the Paper was pro-Roosevelt now."

Clara had slid down among the cushions and was gazing up at the ceiling as she talked, the calf-length skirt of her dark red jersey dress fanned out on the white divan. Becky always said Clara's style was too conventional. "You and I have always made our own style, Hester." But Hester thought what Clara did was to make conventional style her own. Nothing she wore was striking, but whatever she had on seemed so precisely suitable that it was impossible to imagine her in anything else.

"I'm glad we've come out for Roosevelt, of course. You know how I feel about him," Clara said. "But it seems so—well, expedient. That, and what I saw and heard at the Washington Bureau." There was a long pause. "Sometimes I wonder if I'm not in the wrong business."

"Everybody wonders that sometimes."

Clara did not appear to hear. "Grandma once said the Paper is a destroyer. At the time, I thought—" She sat up abruptly and pushed back her thick, short hair with both hands. "I'm just thinking aloud, and not making much sense. What I really came to ask you was whether you'd consider subletting me this apartment when you go to London."

Hester looked at her in silence. Then she watched herself grind her cigarette out slowly in an onyx ashtray. "What makes you think I'm going to London?"

"Oh, dear, wasn't it supposed to get out? But you know newspapers, Aunt Hester. It's all over Washington."

"What," Hester asked, "is all over Washington?"

Clara frowned. "That Mother is sending you to London to do features on the British in wartime. What's the matter? Isn't it true?"

"Your mother asked me to go. I said I wouldn't. Evidently—"

"You said you wouldn't? Why?" When Becky was astounded she narrowed her eyes. Clara opened hers so wide that white showed all around the green irises. "I should think it would be the most marvelous, exciting opportunity to be in the thick of—"

"Don't *you* start, Clara. I have no intention of going. I'm not in search of excitement. Or of anything else, for that matter. The whole idea is preposterous. I'm an old woman, for God's sake!"

"What's age got to do with it? You'd be doing over there what you're doing here, except that over there is where everything's happening now. I don't see how any newspaperwoman—I've always thought of you as the, well, quintessential newspaperwoman, Aunt Hester, and I just don't see how you can resist it."

"You must want this apartment very badly."

Clara looked down at her skirt, smoothed it needlessly over her legs. "That's a horrid thing to say. You know I'm not that kind of manipulator."

Still, Hester thought, Clara managed, like all of them, to get what she thought she wanted.

"The trouble with you is, you don't know how good you are, so you suspect you're being maneuvered for something other than your merit. You should have heard the talk in Washington. Do you think anybody said, 'Oh, that old woman! We don't have to worry about her'? All the columnists are afraid your stuff from London will push them right out of the Paper. And that's the truth. I do want the apartment, but I wouldn't try to flatter you into going to London just so I could have it. If I thought you'd be unhappy there, or incompetent—" Her voice sank to the inaudibility of her childhood. Hester had to lean forward in her chair to catch the words. "You can't believe I'd do that to you for the sake of an apartment."

"No, I know you wouldn't, Clara." Hester lit another cigarette. Somewhere the conversation had veered off the track, away from her, become a matter of the quintessential newspaperwoman and the rivalry of her peers and Clara's tender sensibilities. "The point is," she said, trying to bring it back, "I'm comfortable here, and I simply don't want to leave." But she was no longer sure that was the point.

"Then there's nothing more to be said." Clara sank back against the cushions again. "There are other apartments to be had, of course. This would just have been easier to explain to Mother. I'd be looking after it while you were away, taking care of your things. It would sound temporary. By the time you came back, she'd be used to it. It wouldn't be such a shock when I rented a place of my own. I hate to upset her."

Hester asked a question that had been in her mind a long time. "Hate to, or are afraid to?"

She was prepared for indignation, but Clara said, "A little of both,

I suppose. I hate the scenes. I hate them so much I'm afraid to bring them on, though sometimes I do it anyway. Beyond that, I can't stand hurting her. I suppose that can be a kind of cowardice too. You can't always spare the people you love. Not unless you're willing to count for nothing."

"She might not be as hurt as you think. After all, if you got married you'd move away from her, and as far as I know she's never been opposed to your marrying."

"That's different. If I married someone suitable, that is. A nice, cultivated Jew of German or Sephardic descent, preferably well off." She got up on her elbows. "It's such absolute nonsense. I don't believe Mother remembers she's Jewish except the few times she goes to temple with Grandma, but when it comes to marriage, she thinks like some old orthodox woman in a *sheitel*."

"If she doesn't remember she's Jewish," Hester said, "she must have forgotten being turned away from the Laurel-in-the-Pines in Lakewood, for all her charm and the fact she was the granddaughter of the publisher of the Paper. She must have forgotten her brother couldn't get into the Columbia Club, even though—"

"That's all changing, with the spread of education. In fifty years, maybe sooner, people will no more band together and shut others out because of their religion or the color of their skin than because their eyes are blue or brown. Mother thinks I've turned against Judaism. What I've turned against is parochialism. The world is full of all kinds of people. I refuse to be limited to what I was brought up to believe was my kind. My kind is the human race."

Had this come to her spontaneously, Hester wondered, or as a rationalization for Fitz which had been transfused into a truth? Perhaps all revelation was only the aftermath of inspired self-justification.

"End of speech," Clara said. She had a good smile, one that engaged her entire face. "What I really wanted to say wasn't that at all. It's the rage to get me married that's the prime puzzlement. Why? Not to get rid of me. Not on account of Fitz, because it started before Fitz." She was still up on her elbows, looking at Hester with the concentration one often saw in a child's unmindful stare. "Can you tell me why Mother, or any Herzog except, maybe, Aunt Hannah or Uncle Samuel, who at least got money out of it, should promote marriage?"

Hester stirred in her seat. She reached for another cigarette, and then decided she had smoked enough for a while. If it had been anyone but Clara, she would have found a way of ending the evening. She did not want to become involved in what Clara was going to involve her in, nor remember what Clara was going to make her remember. But that night with the orange blossoms in the Nedick's carton gave her no choice. That, and her fondness for this girl whom she now and then wished had been hers. Perhaps she would have enjoyed Clara's childhood, not dropped her like a hot cinder whenever she chose to gallivant over the face of the world with Walter. Or perhaps she would have dropped her just the same, and with Clara it would have made no difference. "There's no recommendable alternative," she said. "That's not to say there aren't alternatives, or that they don't work for some women. But I know of none a mother could conscientiously recommend to her daughter. Or an aunt to her niece."

"Marriage, though, is recommendable? By Grandma, who was never happy until after her husband died? By Mother, who was miserable with two men? By you, whose husband left her for another—?" She broke off. "I'm sorry. Maybe I shouldn't have said that. But it isn't still painful, is it?" she asked anxiously. "After all these years?"

"No, of course not." No, not painful. Calloused over. "But none of that is relevant. Your name is Clara."

"Clara *Herzog*."

"Yes, well, a penchant for failing at marriage isn't, as far as I know, carried in the blood. Your grandmother failed only herself, I think. Maybe your mother couldn't have been a successful wife to any man, but you're the product of the attempt. I—" Hester paused. "I'll tell you this now, but it is never to be referred to again between us. My marriage—I don't know what it would have looked like to anyone else, but Walter and I were at home in it. I could have held him. He loved me. Instead, I drove him away. There's scarcely a day of my life that I haven't regretted it. I needed him to complete myself, but until he was gone I thought love was something else. So don't sneer at marriage to me." She spoke coldly, willing the ready tears in Clara's eyes to remain unshed. "Not to me."

Clara looked away. "I have to sneer," she said in the soft voice. "What else am I going to do?"

Hester said nothing. There was nothing to say that Becky had not surely said, over and over.

"Mother tries to be understanding," Clara went on, after a long pause. "She tries. I think this hurts her more than anything, that it's closed off from her and she can never find the way in." There was another long pause. "The way she looks—the way she is—all that temperament and fire. I'm sure people think— But the excitement she generates in others, in men—I don't believe she knows what it feels like. That's why she has such power. She's free."

"In one sense, maybe. But no one is free. She loves you."

"Yes, and the Paper. Still, she's not controlled by either." Clara sat up. "I've talked too much. I have things to sort out, but I didn't intend to do it aloud and make you listen. Thanks for bearing with me. I'll go home now."

Hester saw her to the door, closed it behind her, and then called her back. "Don't look for another apartment yet. This one may be available after all. I'll let you know in a few days."

Hester closed the door again and lit the cigarette she had denied herself before. She got out her notes on Futurama and Norman Bel Geddes and read them over, but she could not recapture the interest she had felt at the time of her interview with the designer. For seven years she had relished meeting the molders of American taste, society, and politics, peeling off their protective coating with skillful questions, etching them in carefully measured acid for readers of the Paper. She did not know whether the flatness she felt now had begun as she rode home in the taxi from Flushing Meadow—whether it had been there in her mind, like stale beer, all during Clara's visit, prodding her toward what she had reopened the door to say—or whether it was a result of the things Clara had agitated with that soft voice.

She had felt it before, and with this same suddenness. One day, as she had sat down to write her syndicated column for the Hearst newspapers, all the sprightliness that had made H. H. Lowenthal famous had abruptly fizzled out. Hearst had kept her on for some time, hoping she would recover from the slump, but it had been no use. Her trouble had been neither a slump nor, as was popularly supposed, an inability to update her style. She had simply looked at her material the way someone might suddenly look at an outgrown marriage partner and wondered what she was doing writing such pap, and after that there had been no way to bring it back to life.

She put the notes aside and finished her cigarette. One thing she had considered satisfactory about aging was that nothing new would be expected of her any more. She could go on as she was, undisturbed, for as long as she cared to and was capable. The only changes would be endings. It was no part of this cozy picture to find her work turned meaningless again, and to realize it mattered.

She had been fooling herself into believing Becky still needed her around. During Becky's early years as publisher, she had made constant use of Hester's experience in areas where she thought it wiser not to appear uncertain to other members of the staff. She had tried out all her ideas on Hester first: Could she use more photographs on page one without having the Paper look like one of Hearst's yellow journals and sacrificing its dignity? What about a Woman's Page, with the by-line of some well-known society leader who would be willing to give her name (Hester would do the writing) in exchange for the distinction? Couldn't a couple of the less popular sections be cut from the Sunday edition with impunity? Would it be feasible to eliminate the Saturday edition altogether until the financial situation improved? Was there any reason why she shouldn't use her many contacts to solicit more advertising personally?

Becky had always teemed with ideas, and she had relied on Hester to weed out the absurd or overambitious from the acute before she presented them to her executives. On occasion she had felt that the publisher should express herself editorially, and had asked Hester to put what she wanted to say into readable prose. Once or twice she had lost her temper with an editor or department head who was, incredibly, impervious to her propitiatory charms, and depended on Hester to smooth things over, as Becky had so often smoothed them over for David.

It was like Becky to pretend that Hester was still indispensable to her, apart from the regular features she wrote, but of course she was not. Becky's enormous natural self-confidence had long since been fortified by experience. She knew a sound publishing idea from a foolish one without advice from Hester. When she wanted something said on the editorial page, she worked through the editorial-page board. Those she could not compel with the force of her personality she steered clear of, directing them through others. Hester had come to the Paper in the belief that her competence and good sense would be vital not only to buttress but to restrain a vain, shallow, strong-minded, intemperate, alluring woman with a heart of mush. She would have thought her own value a matter of indifference to her at the time, but perhaps she had, after all, underestimated Becky in order to enhance it.

She got up to go to the bathroom, and on the way out stopped to examine herself in the medicine-cabinet mirror. Even in the ancient bathrobe, with most of her make-up worn off, she did not look like an old woman. She had the strong, Herzog bones, with enough flesh on her face to plump out the lines. Her health was excellent. At her age Papa had been in his prime, and still vigorous at eighty.

When she returned to the living room she went to the window and looked out over the lights of the city to the East River. She and Walter had once stayed at a hotel where they could see the Thames from their room and tell the time on Big Ben. She did not remember its name, but she must have it somewhere. One day Walter had taken her to lunch in a hole-in-the-wall Chinese restaurant in Soho, where they had had their best meal in London and where Walter had astounded her by talking Chinese to the proprietor. When he had been busy with his diplomatic duties, she had wandered through the winding streets and shops of Chelsea, watching and listening to the ordinary people, filing them away, as she had filed everything away, for some possible eventual use in the Paper . . .

"German democracy is a sham. The people have no faith in it. They vastly prefer the idea of *Herrenvolk*, and someday they'll proclaim it with guns."

Was it in London that Walter had said that to her? Yes. They had walked the length of the Strand, arguing about it, Walter's voice booming out in anger, so that people turned to look at them. He had never convinced her. Now that it had happened, there were Americans still who mistook its implications. Or applauded them. Hearst was publishing a series of syndicated articles by Hermann Goering, Hitler's "marshal of the empire."

Through the eyes and ears of men and women threatened by the march of the German armies, the significance of those boots goose-stepping over the face of Europe could be made vividly plain to readers of the Paper.

It would be a kind of expiation to Papa. Except that an act of expiation properly involved pain, sacrifice. She wanted to go. Had wanted to, of course, from the beginning, and been afraid it was nonsensical. But Clara was right. What did age have to do with it? Papa had still been the quintessential newspaperman on his deathbed, at ninety-two.

As she brushed her teeth before going to bed, Hester thought how surprised Becky would be when she told her in the morning she had changed her mind. Then she revised this notion. That *Hexe* had probably known all along that in the end she would go.

4

Becky was aware that before the war many people, both inside the Paper and in the publishing world outside, had regarded her success as a publisher as a fluke, more the result of personal enchantment than of acumen. That she was no longer so regarded had been gratifyingly obvious to her for some time. She had just had another evidence of enhanced respect for her judgment in the meeting from which Sam Froelich, her advertising manager, was now leaving her office.

She and Sam had not always seen eye to eye. Becky suspected that in his resistance to some of her ideas Sam had been influenced by William, whose assistant he had been before William had left the Paper. It was unlikely that William's experience of her would have impressed him with her possibilities as a publisher. Or as anything much else. She had made his life miserable; more miserable, probably, than he had made hers, though it had not been her fault. No more than having black hair was her fault. It had taken another husband, another twelve years, to make her realize that. She had simply not been cut out for marriage. It had brought out the worst in her and the worst in the men she married.

William would not have said anything ugly about her to Sam—that was not his way—but what he failed to say could have been just as damaging. Sam had fought her on almost every proposal she made. He was one of the few men she had never found a way to get around. One of the few people, if it came to that.

But Sam had not fought her today, though she had been prepared for trouble with him. Paper, ink, and metal had been rationed, so that it was impossible to produce the big newspapers of the prewar years. Many publishers had decided to use a large part of their limited space for advertising, which was plentiful and highly profitable, and to cut down on news. Becky, in the meeting just concluded, had proposed the opposite. The Paper would accept ads from all regular advertisers, but restrict their space to a small percentage of what they had been buying. This would mean a loss of immediate, readily available income, but it was Becky's contention that in the long run it would pay off.

"As long as I can remember," she had told the advertising staff, "my grandfather, before he left for his office, would say to us, 'I've got to go and give New York the news for breakfast.' He built a great newspaper on the premise that this was what New York wanted to read. The news. The authentic news. All the news. I've always subscribed to that premise, and I do still. I think if we forgo easy profits now, and continue to print all the solid war news we can squeeze into our pages, we will attract readers away from newspapers that are concentrating on advertising, and they'll stay with us when the war is over. Since advertisers go where the readers are—well, gentlemen, I don't think I have to labor the point."

One of Sam's assistants had asked whether editorials and features were to be sacrificed, along with advertising.

"I'm not suggesting we sacrifice advertising," she had corrected him. "I propose that we cut down on the space we'll allow for it, and do it proportionately, so that none of our advertisers can complain of unequal treatment. That's the whole idea." She had glanced at Sam, but his square, stolid, cold-eyed face was not readable. Becky would have thought of it as a typical Nazi face, except that he was a Jew. "We'll also have to cut down on some kinds of editorial, and probably scrap certain features and columns for the duration. But anything that bears directly on the news, whether it's interpretative or investigative or whatever, I'd be opposed to eliminating." She had looked at Sam again, tried without success to will the pale blue eyes to leave their indifferent examination of the desk at which she sat and meet her gaze. "Of course I'll be glad, as always, to hear any contrary views."

Froelich had given a slight, fleeting smile, as though to suggest he knew she had no interest in contrary views. But he must have realized that was not so. She had never made David's mistake of refusing to listen to disagreement or advice. It was the only way to test the validity of her position.

"Sounds all right to me," Sam Froelich had said to the desk. It had taken him several seconds to add the rest of it. "Some argued against all the emphasis on war coverage when it began three years ago. Now we've got the figures to prove it was a good move. Nobody can argue with circulation figures."

She thanked him warmly for his confidence, tried to smile at him, but he went out without further comment, without once looking at her directly. It was possible, she thought suddenly, that this big, pallid, unresponsive man was actually attracted to her, and tried to hide it with pretended antagonism. Yes, very possible. He was considerably younger than she was, but that had never made any difference. Some of the boys Clara had dated as a young girl had seemed as interested in her as in her daughter. Once, one of them had tried to kiss her while Clara was getting ready to go out with him. He must have been barely out of his teens, and Becky in her late forties. Whatever she had that appealed to men, it did not depend on age, either theirs or hers. It would explain her difficulties with Sam Froelich. He had not wanted to go along with her openly this time either, but her achievements gave him no choice. He could not, as he had said, argue with the circulation figures.

She had always been talked about and written about, but more because of her looks, her individuality, her personal behavior, and the comparative oddity of her position, than because of her accomplishments. It was different now. People no longer referred to her as an attractive and temperamental woman who, of all things, published a newspaper, but as an astute publisher, a capable successor to her distinguished grandfather.

Becky had expected to succeed at the job. She had thought of it as primarily a matter of handling people—wasn't everything primarily a matter of that?—and she had never had much trouble handling anyone, except husbands. When it had turned out to be considerably more complex than she had imagined, the sureness of her judgment had surprised her. She had, after all, no great intellect or learning, no particular knowledge of politics or business, no executive experience. Yet time after time she had known exactly what to do. Almost as if Grandpa had been there whispering in her ear.

She knew now that what she had was a talent for getting people to talk, and then listening—scarcely anyone seemed really to listen—and appraising what she heard. The idea of rationing advertising in order to concentrate on news had neither burst upon her with inspired brilliance nor been the result of original thought. She had questioned a businessman who told her he had found a small ad for his product in newspapers that concentrated on solid reporting more productive than a full-page ad in newspapers that featured columnists and accepted advertising at the expense of news. She had listened, simply listened and seen the significance for the Paper, and taken it the necessary step further.

Her decision three years before to give the war the widest possible coverage had been based on the same kind of selective drawing out and listening. Wherever Hitler's armies marched, the Paper's reporters were there ahead of them. No government was overthrown, no treaty made, no attack launched, but that a newsman from the Paper was on hand to wire the news to New York within minutes of its conclusion. Just once had a major event taken place in a vacuum of reporters, and Becky fretted about this still, after more than a year. The fact that no other newspaper had had a reporter stationed closer to Pearl Harbor than Honolulu either was only a minor solace. If she had known—if she could have heard a hint of the danger so many knew about and no one properly heeded—what a scoop it would have been for the Paper!

She looked at her watch. Ted Rosenthal would be here in less than an hour to pick her up for dinner. He much preferred coming to her apartment, but she was working too late today. "I could find my way blindfolded to your door," he often said. "The moment I get off the elevator, I can smell your perfume."

One of Ted's drawbacks was that he said things so often. He also had an old-fashioned distaste for the idea of a woman in a position of influence and control, disliked being reminded of her role by seeing her here, and at the same time pointed out his closeness to the publisher of the Paper wherever it might enhance his own prestige.

But he was a good old stand-by. He was always there if she needed a man as an escort or wanted an evening's companionship. She could appear with him anywhere. He looked impressive, a solid, erect man with thick white hair, bushy white eyebrows, and an air of assurance. One would have guessed him to be an ambassador, or the president of some prominent organization, or what he was, an eminent chest surgeon. He had beautiful manners and a fine, cultivated voice in which he could talk about anything, sometimes with more aplomb than knowledge.

Ted was attractive enough and rich enough to charm a much younger woman, but he was completely in thrall to Becky—which, considering her age, was heart-warming. He had asked her to marry him the third time she had gone out with him, and he repeated the offer periodically—more, probably, because he had that habit of saying over and over whatever had sounded good to him in the first place than because he still had hope. He did anything she asked of him, put up with anything; not meekly—she could not have endured perpetual meekness—but with enormous good humor. Once, when he had come to dinner in her apartment, she had become so infuriated with him over something she no longer remembered, that she had thrown in his face a full glass of the wine he had brought her.

"I'm so sorry the wine doesn't please you," he had said, calmly mopping himself with his napkin. "It's really a very good Pouilly Fumé, but I think now that I'd have preferred something drier myself."

She had had to laugh, of course, and she had been closer to marrying him at that moment than at any time before or since. Closer, but not really close. He tolerated her shenanigans now because he was afraid of losing her, but he would not be so accepting of a wife. It did not seem to occur to husbands and wives to be afraid of losing each other, even though so many of them so frequently did.

In any case, she had no wish to be married. She was never lonely. When Clara had first gone to live in Hester's apartment, Becky had missed her terribly, and been angry and hurt at her wanting to go, but she had gotten over that. Everyone thought it was natural for a young woman that age to want her own place, and Becky supposed it was. She wished she had been the one to suggest it. If she had been, Clara might not even have done it; at the least, she would have been touched by Becky's understanding. As it was, Becky had carried on like a fool, weeping and raging, accusing Clara of wanting to move out only so she would have a place to bring Fitz, calling her a whore. Clara had walked out then and there, though she had come back the next night for her things and they had made it up, both of them crying and saying how much they loved each other. It had all been very unpleasant and exhausting and had accomplished nothing, because Clara had gone to live in Hester's apartment anyway, and Becky knew she would never come back to live with her mother again.

"You've had her a great deal longer than most mothers have their daughters," Ted had said when she told him. She told Ted almost everything. Not because she felt so close to him, or because he was so comforting—she didn't and he wasn't; he never said anything she had not thought of herself—but because he was completely unshockable and nonjudgmental. She was sure that if she told him she, or someone she cared about, had gone downstairs and slit the doorman's throat, he would do no more than shake his head a little in sympathy with both killed and killer, and say he was sorry to hear it. Becky found this soothing.

"You still do have her, of course," he had said whenever the sub-

269

ject came up. "You see her every day at the—er—office." Stumbling over the word as though it were obscene. "She might have married and moved a continent away."

"She still might. I married late. If she did, I'd be happy. I've always been prepared for that."

Because marriage is a desirable state for a woman, she might have said but had not. Not to Ted, who was always urging it upon her. He would not understand why she considered herself an exception. She knew he thought he would make her happy, turn her into a successful wife. It was an illusion Becky intended to help him preserve.

She went into the lavatory to wash and change for dinner. She kept several wardrobe changes in her office closet for occasions such as this, when she was going out to dinner downtown after an especially long day and had no wish to taxi through traffic all the way up to her apartment to dress. She also had two or three bottles of perfume here, locked in her desk drawer against the cleaning woman, who had once doused herself so thoroughly with Chanel 5 that Becky had sniffed her out in the corridor days later; and an extra string of fake pearls, in case she broke the string she usually wore.

Her costume was new; black, of course, with a short jacket over an off-the-shoulder dress. She would wear the jacket to dinner at the Chambord and remove it in the theater, where they were going to see By Jupiter, a hit musical by Rodgers and Hart. Most women her age would not think of buying such a dress, but she still had good shoulders. Creamy, Albert had called them, and they had not changed.

Albert had once thought of her as a goddess. He had looked pained the first time he saw her come out of the bathroom with the toilet flushing behind her, as though it hurt him to realize she had been doing what everybody else did in there. For the first few years he had been an awful fool about her. Then, when he changed, he had shown himself for what he was. Except that he had loved and treated Clara as though she were his own, he had been a terrible man. Terrible. Maybe he would not have been if he had married someone else, but his marriage to her was all Becky had to go on, and in that he had been terrible. Of course, so had she.

Becky tilted her feathered John Frederics hat over her forehead, from which her short black hair, minimally streaked with gray, was brushed smoothly back in the same style she had worn for over twenty years. She was ready before the time for Ted's arrival. One of

270

Grandpa's dinner-table maxims had been that punctuality was the politeness of kings. "It was said by a king of France. I feel certain he intended to include queens."

While she waited, she sat down at her desk again and looked over some of the material for the next edition of the Paper. The Vichy government in France had established compulsory labor for men between the ages of eighteen and sixty-five and for unmarried women of twenty to thirty-five. Hester, who apparently found London dull since the heavy bombing raids had subsided, had somehow managed to get into France, interviewed several of these unwilling workers, and sent in a fascinating feature.

"M. Dupont" regards this not as a French regulation but as an enforcement of German demands for labor collaboration. "I can do nothing except submit. I am too old," said "M. Dupont," who is 63, "but there are others, Madame. We French will not lie down for long under the alien boot. Wait and see.

Hester's piece had already been cleared by the foreign desk. Clara, who was now an assistant to the foreign-news editor, had attached a note to it for Becky.

"Either Aunt H. had an interpreter whose interpretation she has liberally interpreted, or she had 'M. Dupont' told what to say, or she plain made it up. It's too good to be true. But it's good."

Clara was replacing a young man who had been drafted into the Army. She would have preferred an assignment overseas—a preference that had surprised Becky, since it would have meant separation from Fitz—but Becky would not let her go during wartime. One of the Paper's war correspondents had been killed by a land mine. Hester had barely left a London building for an air-raid shelter when a bomb razed it. Fitz was the one Becky would have liked to send over there, but Rick Schuman would not hear of it. He was not, he said, going to be stripped of all his best local men. Fitz had won a Pulitzer for his New York reporting—a series of articles exposing a Brooklyn crime ring—and so brought added distinction to the Paper as well as to himself. He belonged in New York.

That was the trouble. Fitz had always been too competent to get rid of. Besides, it might not have helped—distances mean little these days—and it would certainly have antagonized Clara.

Clara's relationship to Fitz was the only thing that had ever really come between them. Becky could not even be sure what the relationship was, or whether it was still grinding on after all these years, or was over or changed in some way since Clara was down there in Tudor City on her own. Clara, who had once told her everything—everything boys said to her on dates and whether they had tried to kiss her and whether she had let them—had never been willing to talk about Fitz. If Becky so much as mentioned his name, or referred indirectly to his effect on Clara's life, it was likely to end in screaming and tears and walking out. Whenever Becky thought about Fitz, she hated him. But she did not hate him in person. He was too good a newspaperman.

When Ted arrived, Becky was reading an item for the Paper that had come out of Germany, quoting Hitler as saying Franklin Roosevelt was a Jew whose name was really Rosenfeld. Hitler's particular antipathy was a point in favor of the President, about whom Becky did considerable private vacillating. The Paper had been one of the few newspapers that had supported him enthusiastically for a third term, but now there was speculation that he might seek a fourth, and she did not yet know what she thought about that. She had heard talk that he kept a list of people who opposed his policies, that he wire-tapped their phones, had them investigated by the FBI, and tried to discredit them by associating them with fascism. If she pursued this and, if it proved accurate, published the findings, the Paper would have to break with Roosevelt. Yet his conduct of the war was brilliant and might suffer if he lost wide support. There were times when a newspaper had to suppress the truth for some higher purpose. On the other hand, an exposure of this nature would guarantee a dramatic rise in readership . . .

"Good evening, my dear," Ted said. "You're looking lovely, as usual." He came around the desk to kiss her on her proffered cheek, having long since surrendered on the question of mouth-kissing, which she abhorred. All that interchange of saliva. "Though I cannot, for the life of me, get used to seeing you sitting at that desk surrounded with papers, like a busy executive."

"Can't you, really?" She patted his face. "But you see, Ted, I *am* a busy executive."

He smiled and kissed her fingertips. "In that charming new dress, Becky, my dear, and that most becoming hat, you are certainly an unlikely looking one—an extremely unlikely looking one indeed."

Clara thought he was an ass. In some ways, of course, he was, but he had uses that were impossible to explain to Clara.

"I suppose you and I will never understand each other's choice of beaux," Becky had said to her.

How many women of Becky's age had any beaux at all, much less a choice?

At the end of the evening, Ted suggested that they drive up to Riverdale on Sunday, while the weather was still pleasant, and have dinner at Arrowhead Inn. When she told him she had other plans, and did not elaborate, he looked uneasy.

"It's unlike you to be secretive." He tried to say it lightly, but he was not good at lightness. "It must be a man."

"Yes," she said, because it was literally true, if not true in the way he feared, and a little uneasiness was a necessary injection now and then. "Yes, it's a man. Why shouldn't it be?"

She thought about that on Sunday, on the train to Mamaroneck, smiling to herself at the instant proposal that had followed. It was too bad she had not kept a record of all the offers of marriage she had had in her life, beginning when she was fourteen and had looked almost as much older as she now looked younger than she was. Even without counting Ted's repetitions, she probably could have won some kind of contest. As far as she knew, no one had ever proposed to Clara. "Good book?"

Clara, on the aisle seat beside her, looked up, keeping her place with her finger. As a child, Clara had never heard anything when she was reading. Forcibly roused to come to a meal, she would wander in dazed, her fingers between the pages, as now, prop the book against her water glass, and go on reading until she was stopped. Sometimes, especially if Albert had objected, Becky had let her alone. A love of books was a Herzog trait, preparation for work on the Paper. "Yes, it's very good. *Wickford Point*, by Marquand," Clara said. "I've never read anything that slides back and forth in time so smoothly."

"That's not of much practical use to a newspaperwoman, is it? Sliding back and forth in time? Our concern is with now."

Becky knew at once that she had said the wrong thing. Clara, who was remarkably equable for a Herzog, had come along with considerable reluctance and was not in her sunniest mood. "Are you suggesting I shouldn't read anything that isn't useful to me in my work? That's one you haven't tried before. Controlling my—" Clara stopped and shook her head. "I made up my mind I wasn't going to get into an argument with you today, no matter what, and here I am, bringing one on myself, over nothing."

Becky looked out the window. "You talk as though all we do is argue."

"I didn't mean that, Mother. We get along better than any mother and grown daughter I know. We, at least, like each other. But when we do have an argument, you'll have to admit it's usually a lulu."

"*Like* each other?" Becky said, turning back to her. "*Like?*"

Clara's face reddened. She might have been still in her teens, though she was ten years out of them, her cheeks rounded and smooth and easily blushing, for all sorts of reasons at which Becky could only guess. "Love is a given. It's there unless it's rooted out," she said. "Liking is an external, individual thing."

"You're over my head again."

"I'm talking about mothers and daughters. The girls I know pay duty calls on their mothers. I'd seek you out even if we weren't related."

"Well, that's good," Becky said, and patted her hand. "Go on back to your book, if you want to. I'll try to figure out the best approach to take with Walter." She gave a little laugh. "Do you remember how you used to write down everything you wanted to say before you called anyone on the phone?"

Clara smiled. As a child, she had had dimples. Becky could not remember when they had disappeared. Otherwise her smile was as it had always been, open and full of pleasure. "It never did much good," she said. "The other person always threw me off by not speaking the right lines."

"That's what will happen to me today. Unless Walter has changed, he won't speak any lines I can imagine."

Clara stopped smiling and opened her book. Becky knew she was nervous about meeting Walter, and had come only because Becky had insisted she needed her for moral support.

Clara's peculiar shyness had always exasperated Becky. Fortunately it had not interfered with the child's work. As a reporter, Clara could talk easily to anyone about anything. This made her schoolgirl bumbling in other situations all the more absurd. Once she had grown up and developed a little charm and style to grace the keenness of her mind, Becky would have liked to show her off to William, but Clara did not want to meet him. Yes, she was mildly curious, but what was the use? They were strangers to each other, yet they would have to behave as though they were not. It would be awkward for both of them.

Becky had not thought of Walter at all, not in years, until the situation in the Washington Bureau, which had been gradually deteriorating, had gotten out of hand. Washington correspondents complained that their stories were being killed or relegated to obscure pages in the Paper for arbitrary reasons. Some blamed the national editor in the New York office. Some blamed the Washington Bureau chief. Others blamed both, suggesting that a more dynamic and influential chief in Washington would have the power to affect what happened in New York. Whatever the cause, the morale in Washington was so low, and the stories coming from the bureau so far below standard, that Becky had to take measures.

She held a conference in her office. She listened to those who thought making the Washington Bureau independent of supervision by the national desk would solve the problem, those who believed all the Paper's power should remain centered in the New York office, those who felt that a new, stronger bureau chief was the only change needed. Except for a few prodding questions, Becky said little. She listened.

"A man of real stature and proven ability," Rick Schuman said. "But who is there?"

"You know how I feel about centralized power," Becky said finally. "One of the first things I did after becoming publisher was to divide authority. In this case, I'd be in favor of independence for the Washington Bureau, with its stories bypassing the national desk and going directly to the bull pen and Rick. I'd suggest we bring Bill Norman home and assign him elsewhere. Maybe none of what has happened is his fault, but we need someone as bureau chief who can hold his men together under trying circumstances. I agree with Rick's estimate of the kind of man it should be. If we can't find him on the staff, we'll have to look for him outside."

She had already thought of Walter when she spoke, but she had told only Clara. She wanted to feel him out first. "I think he'll jump at it. From what I've heard, he's just moping about in some big, old mansion on Long Island Sound, writing his memoirs or something."

"Why should you think he has any interest in working on a newspaper again?" Clara had asked her. "Couldn't he have done it long ago if he'd wanted to?"

"Walter worked at a regular job only if it was exciting, or if he had to. When he married Laurette, he didn't have to. I forget how much her father was said to have settled on them, but it was substantial. By now, Walter must have run through most of it."

"That's just a guess, isn't it?"

"No. You know me. I have my sources."

Running through funds, Becky might have added, was a Lowenthal weakness. William had worked hard enough, earned good money, and promptly dropped most of it at the race track, where he had also taken up with a long string of doubtful characters, female as well as male. According to William, it was Walter who had introduced both him and Samuel to the fascination of easy money, but Becky's extravagance that had kept him trying for it long after the fascination had faded. Albert had blamed her too. Maybe she had been extravagant, but, for the most part, it had been to provide the right setting for Clara. Only weak men would have allowed it to push them into what those two had done.

Walter had at least gambled on a grand scale and not on cards or on horses but on the fertile seeds of his own lively mind. He had made and lost fortunes with what Hester had once called an awesome panache. The chance to return to the Paper's Washington Bureau after all these years and take over as chief would surely appeal to him as an adventure. And it would be a coup for the Paper to get him for the job—a former member of the cabinet and the State Department and a newspaperman with long experience in Washington.

In the cab from the Mamaroneck station, Clara stared silently out the window. Becky wished she had worn something a little smarter than her old Glen-plaid suit, though it was a good one and fit her well, and this was, after all, the country. She had had her hair and nails done, anyway, and her hat was cute, like an overblown derby. The general effect was attractive enough, and that was what Walter would notice and pass on to William. If only she didn't go silent and awkward, as she sometimes did!

"Don't worry, baby. Just relax and be yourself."

"I'm not worried. I don't relish the role of exhibit, that's all."

"What do you mean, 'exhibit'? I'm here to offer Walter a job, not to put you on exhibit."

"Unfortunately, the two aren't mutually exclusive," Clara said. "It's all right. I'll live through it." She turned away from the window. "I may even enjoy myself, once I'm there. He must be an unusual man."

The cab wheeled between stone pillars with a name plate that said THE DUNES, wound around a long driveway, and slid to a stop under the portico of a massive, turreted house on an overhang of rock. Directly below was a wide strip of beach leading to the sound, but no visible dunes.

" 'So twice five miles of fertile ground / With walls and towers were girdled round,' " Clara murmured.

Becky was paying the driver. "What?"

"Xanadu," Clara said.

"I don't know what you're—"

Becky broke off. A man was coming around from the back of the house. Or the front. At any rate, the side facing the sound. He wore baggy gray pants, a brown coat sweater of the type Becky always associated with the proprietors of stationery stores, and a soiled white cloth hat with a floppy brim. He was stoop-shouldered and had a peculiar gait, forward-thrusting yet sluggish, as though he was not sure he wanted to keep up with himself. As he approached Becky and Clara, he took off the hat, revealing a large, domed head, bald except for a fringe of yellowish-white hair. The prow of his nose emerged from a sea of wrinkles.

"Oh, God!" Becky whispered.

"Is *that*—?"

He was within earshot now. Unless he was deaf. He looked as though he might be deaf as well. But when Becky said, "Well, Walter, here we are," in what sounded to her like a reasonable imitation of her normal voice, he answered at once.

"Well," he said, "well, Rebecca. And this, of course, is Clara. Little Clara." He kissed them both. Becky tried to see whether Clara pulled back, but she could not tell. "Forgive my appearance, please. I meant to change before you arrived, but I was taking the last good sun of the year, and I'm afraid I dozed off. I work so hard during the week, you see, on all my projects, some of which I'll show you later, that I really must take Sundays as days of rest." He paused to smile at them, showing perfect upper teeth and an intermittent row of crooked lowers. "Rebecca, you are as beautiful as ever. You scarcely look a day older. Clara resembles you, doesn't she? And yet with something of William? The coloring, yes, but something else? Yes. The expression, I think. You haven't seen your father in a long time, have you, Clara? Pity! But what am I doing, keeping you standing here? Come in! Come in!" He put an arm around each of them and hauled them up the steps with surprising strength. "Laurette's at church, but she'll be back any minute. Anglican. You knew Laurette was Episcopalian, didn't you? It would please her if I converted. One can't, of course, now, with all the Nazi business, but I may after the war. It makes no difference to me one way or the other, and Laurette would be pleased." With his arms still around them, he began kicking at the bottom of the immense oak door. "Where is that butler? He's never on hand when he's needed. Clara, how do you like my modest little cot?"

"Xanadu," Clara said in a strangled voice.

"Right!" Walter shouted. "'Where Alph—' No, let's see . . . *Where Long Island Sound's clear waters ran, de-da-de-da-de-da-de-da, Down to a sunless—no—Out to a sunny sea*. Ring the bell, won't you, Clara? That man must be—"

The door opened suddenly inward, catching Walter off balance from his final kick. Somehow he managed to keep his own feet, as well as Becky's and Clara's, translating the momentum into a stumbling rush that carried them past the man at the door and into the hall.

"Well!" he said triumphantly, releasing them and turning to the butler. "Show the ladies into the salon, Mar. I'll go up and get into something more respectable. It won't take me a minute."

He negotiated the wide stone staircase that proceeded from the hall with that same uncertain pace, seeming to bound, yet making slow work of it.

"This way, please," the butler said in an undefinable accent. He was a small man in a white coat that needed pressing. His skin was the color of café au lait; his hair was black, smooth, and oily; his eyes were a liquid brown and faintly slanted. Everything about him was indeterminate: race, nationality, even the name by which Walter had called him, which could have been Oriental or short for Mario or for Martin.

"Look," Clara whispered as they followed him through the huge, dim hall. "I don't believe it."

She was indicating a suit of armor, propped on a stand in a corner of the hall, arranged to look as though it contained a knight with a lance in his mailed glove. Just beyond were open double doors, through which Mar waved them with a bow from the waist.

"The salong, ladies. Please be seated."

He left them in a room that Becky calculated to be about forty-five feet long and thirty wide, with a twenty-foot ceiling. As large as it was, it was so crammed with antique French and Italian furniture that it was difficult to walk around. Tall windows on one wall, heavily draped with gold damask, looked out over the water. The windows on another wall gave on a small, neglected garden. The draperies were worn and the upholstery of some of the chairs had come away from the frames. Above the oak mantel that ornamented a cavernous stone fireplace hung a sepia drawing of a seated nude that Clara said looked like an original Picasso. Walter later confirmed that it was.

"This place," Clara said, sinking into the soft cushions of the smallest of three sofas, "doesn't exist. The butler doesn't exist. Walter—is he a man or a talking-machine?—he certainly doesn't exist. It's all a fairy story you read me before I went to sleep, and now I'm dreaming it." She took off the cute, derby-like hat. Becky started to tell her not to, and then stopped. Clara put the hat down next to her on the sofa and loosened her hair with her fingers, which made her look younger but not as smart. "I always used to dream jumbles like this after you read to me. Gingerbread houses with our furniture in them. Albert's face on the *Schneider* who cut off Konrad's thumb because he sucked it—"

"I never read you a story about anybody cutting off anybody's thumb."

"No, I guess not. I guess it was Fräulein."

"Walter was always the same," Becky said. "My grandmother used to run to her room when she knew he was coming, because she couldn't stand all the talk. But he was very much sought after. He's a brilliant man, and he knows something about almost everything." Becky paused. "He looked so different to me at first that I thought — But I don't think he's really changed at all."

"How old is he, Mother?"

"I don't know exactly," Becky said, although she did. She had thought of his age for the first time when she saw him coming toward them from the other side of the house and realized that she had somehow expected to find him intact, preserved like a butterfly in a glass cube, in that moment, seventeen years before, when she had seen him last. "Is that a telephone next to you, Clara? There's one at the other end of the room too. I wonder why anyone would need two telephones in one—"

"I have twenty-six in the house," Walter said as he appeared in the doorway. "Two here and one in each of the other rooms in current use, including bathrooms and the kitchen. In addition to the social function, I do a great deal of business on the telephone and find it a convenience to have one at hand wherever I am." He shot back his sleeve to look at a nonexistent wrist watch. "I wonder what can be keeping Laurette. Well. Why don't I show you over the house while we're waiting?"

He moved ahead of them through the rooms, upstairs and down, a tireless guide in a beautifully tailored dark sack suit with shiny elbows and a seat worn so thin that once, when he bent to point out the carving on a chest, Becky could see the white of his underwear through it. He took them into the hotel-size kitchen, all in monel metal, with two stoves, two ovens, two double sinks, and dozens of cooking utensils, of every size and description, that hung from a ceiling rack. At Walter's request, the butler, Mar, who seemed to be making no preparations for lunch, demonstrated the lowering and raising of the rack by means of an electric button on the wall.

"My own invention," Walter said. "My concept, that is. I know nothing whatever about electricity, but I know anything man's imagination can conceive, man's ingenuity can create. 'The imagination may be compared to Adam's dream—he awoke and found it truth,' as Keats said."

"Keats? I thought I knew all Keats's work," Clara said.

"That's from one of his letters, not a poem. You ought to read his letters. Come into the library and I'll see if I can find the volume to lend you."

In the library, a large, square room with a desk in the center and shelves of books on every wall from floor to ceiling, he forgot to look for Keats's letters. Instead he called their attention to a pile of long yellow pads on the desk, the top one covered with penciled writing in a sprawling hand.

"My autobiography," he said. "In one sense, a history of the world in the past fifty years, with details known only to me. It's a monumental task, of course, but a necessary one. 'History is the witness that testifies to the passing of time; it illumines reality, vitalizes memory, provides guidance in daily life, and brings us tidings of antiquity.' You should know that one, Clara."

"Yes, I think— Cicero?"

"Good girl! I see you've got her educated, Rebecca. I approve of that. The purely decorative woman is a thing of the past, intended for a time when men hunted or warred or worked sixteen hours a day in the company of other men, and returned home tired out, glutted with companionship, needing nothing from their women but a bowl of soup, a pretty smile, and a warm bed."

"How far along are you in the autobiography?" Clara asked him.

"Oh, not far. About a quarter of the way through the first volume, I should say. I've been working on it for about a year, but it goes slowly. I write in longhand—unfortunately I can't think on the typewriter—and then, also, I have so many other things to do. I must show you—"

He drove them out of the library and down the hall to another room. On the way Clara asked him how many volumes he thought his autobiography would require. About ten, he said. Becky figured that at that rate he would be approximately 109 years old when it was finished.

The room he took them into was small, and empty of all furniture except a metal table on which stood a piece of unidentifiable machinery and several vials filled with liquid. Cartons of bottles were piled all around the floor. Walter loped to the table, unstoppered one of the vials, and put a dab of the liquid on Becky's wrist and on the sleeve of Clara's jacket.

"Smell it!" he ordered.

"Yes," Becky said. "What is it? Toilet water? I can't identify the scent."

"Carnation?" Clara suggested.

"Toilet water! Carnation!" Walter roared, more in grieved astonishment than anger. "It's perfume, the finest perfume, a subtle blend of floral essences and spices." He moved closer to them and lowered his voice to just above a whisper. "Since the war, no one in this country has been able to obtain the essential oils used in making perfume. I foresaw this and managed, through sources of my own, to get hold of a substantial quantity. All I need now is a means of manufacturing and distributing the perfume on a large scale, and I'll make my fortune. There will be millions in it. Millions." He gave them each one of the bottles on the table. "This blend, I've made myself. Only you and Laurette will have it now, of all the women in the world. Use it, enjoy it, make a note of the comments of your friends, but don't breathe a word of where you got it. If it were known that I've cornered the market on these oils—well—"

He left the result to their imagination and led them back to the "salong," where Walter's wife now waited for them and Mar was setting up four small folding tables.

Laurette was a tiny woman in a pale blue dress, with blond hair that streamed loose over her shoulders, and a heavy gold cross on a chain around her neck. She had a child's small, blurred features in a thin, lined face, and a child's high-pitched voice.

"I'm so glad you could come," she said, and thereafter sat in silence, her gaze, glassy and blank as a doll's, fixed on Walter's face as he talked.

His voice went on and on. Becky drummed with her fingers on the arm of her chair, but he did not notice. For a time she listened to the extraordinary flow of language. Hester had once said that even when he discussed the weather with the elevator boy, he spoke as though he had rehearsed every choice word. But he was saying nothing of interest or use to Becky. She was bored by his talk about himself and the projects he would never live to finish, and she could not follow his metaphysical excursions or his literary references. She stopped listening, as his wife had surely done long before. Clara was not even looking at him. He had her trapped in a corner of the sofa. Every so often he would turn and talk directly to her, with his hand on the arm of the sofa and his arm across her, as though he feared she might escape. She kept her eyes steadily on the Picasso above his head and said nothing. He did not seem to mind. It probably made no difference to him whether anyone listened or not.

Suddenly he shouted, "Wait!" rousing Becky to attention. She had no notion what had gone before. "I must read it to you in the original. There's absolutely no other way to impart the full flavor. Wait! It will take me only a moment."

They all watched him go out with his dragging lope. As soon as he had disappeared, Laurette said, "The reason he walks like that is because he had a slight stroke last year. Nothing else was affected, just some of the muscles on the left side." She spoke carefully and distinctly, like someone not altogether at home in the language. "Clara is your only child," she said, almost in the same breath, looking at Becky with her vacant, blue doll's eyes.

"Yes," Becky answered, though it had not been a question.

"We have only one also. Walter, Jr. He's away at school, but he comes home every weekend. I do hope when he marries he'll have more than one child." She began speaking more quickly, as though racing against Walter's return. "Your family doesn't believe in large households, does it? Samuel has no children at all. Not that we aren't fond of Samuel, because we are. Tremendously. He comes up to see us once or twice a year, and we always look forward to it. Still, children—" She stopped and turned to Clara for the first time, speaking as to a small girl. "I'm sure you would have liked to have a little brother or sister, wouldn't you?"

Clara, who was often embarrassed without apparent cause, seemed not at all disconcerted by this absurdity. "No, not really," she said. "I always thought the advantages outweighed the supposed handicaps."

"You weren't lonely?"

Clara shook her head. "I don't think it's possible to be lonely for someone you've never had." She paused. "I'm sure your son would agree."

"My son would agree to what?" Walter inquired, coming in with a book in his hand. He did not wait for an answer, but seated himself next to Clara again, crowding her with his bulk, and began immediately to read.

> "*Nel mezzo del cammin di nostra vita*
> *Mi ritrovai per una selva oscura.*
> *Che la diritta via era smarrita—*"

"What on earth is that?" Becky broke in. "Italian?"

Walter frowned. "Yes, of course. Dante's *Inferno*."

"Well, I'm sure it's lovely, and I'm sure you have a fine accent, but since I haven't the faintest idea—"

"A fine accent? Of course I have a fine accent. There's little use in speaking a language fluently if one doesn't also speak it properly." He turned around to Clara, barring her with his arm. "You understand what I'm reading, don't you, my dear?"

Clara had to pull her head back to keep from talking into his mouth. "Well, *nostra vita*, because that's straight from the Latin, but not the rest of it."

"You don't know Italian? Pity. It's a beautiful language. You should learn it. However, it isn't altogether necessary to know what the words mean. Listen to the rhythm, the music."

He went on reading. Laurette's eyes remained fixed on his face. Clara stared at the Picasso. Becky got to her feet.

"Walter, listen to me," she said, standing directly in front of him. "Either you stop reading that gibberish, and stop talking long enough to give somebody else a chance to get a word in edgewise, or Clara and I are taking the next train back to the city, and you know what you can do with your lunch." He half rose, opened his mouth to say something, but sat back and closed it when she sailed on. "We've come up here to see you after seventeen years, and all you've done since we walked into the house—since before we walked into it —is talk about yourself and your own interests. You haven't asked what we've been doing or how we are. You haven't asked about a single member of our family. You haven't so much as mentioned the Paper. We could be blocks of wood or—or megaphones for you to shout into—shout about yourself—" As so often happened, she was working herself up past the point she had intended to go, her voice getting away from her. She could not stop. "Your poor wife," she said, and turned to glance at Laurette, whose doll eyes looked twice their former size, "your poor wife had to hurry to get a few sentences in while you were out of the room. And now—now—this really takes the cake—you have the gall to sit there reading Italian that nobody understands, so you can hear the sound of your own voice! After seventeen years!"

Walter sat perfectly still for a moment, watching her as though to make sure she had finished. Becky darted a quick look at Clara, who seemed to be trying to dissolve into the corner of the sofa. Her face was scarlet, but when she caught Becky's eyes, she gave a barely noticeable wink.

"Rebecca, you're perfectly right. She's perfectly right, you know, Laurette, my dear," Walter said to his wife as though she had disputed it. "I get carried away and talk too much. That's always been my failing. The fountain overflows. More abundantly, of course, after the twenty years of silence between us, and in the presence of this delightful daughter of yours who knows and understands and has read and loves so many things in common with me." He swung around to beam at Clara, who managed a presentable smile, and turned back to Becky. "I'm not, however, as uninterested and uncaring as you believe. The fact is that I've kept careful track of you and your family over the years, and have little need to make inquiries. Samuel visits us regularly, and I speak with him very frequently on the telephone. He tells me everything that's going on. I know you've made a remarkable success of the Paper, Rebecca, and that Clara is one of your star reporters—"

"Your news is a little stale," Becky said, but her anger was gone. She sat down again. "Clara hasn't been a reporter for several years. She's on the foreign desk now, assistant to the editor."

"Ah, yes, of course. Samuel did tell me. I'd forgotten for the moment." He slid hastily past this, as though afraid Becky might challenge it. "One bit of news that saddened me so I've frankly been avoiding mention of it is that of Elsa's—your mother's—illness. I understand her mind has been affected. It must be a sorrowful thing to witness in a woman of her former intelligence."

"There's nothing former about it," Clara said before Becky could speak. She had pushed herself forward, abreast of Walter. Her soft voice was firm. "Or particularly sorrowful. Grandma isn't always in the same world as we are, or with the same people, but within her own sphere she's as logical and contented as she ever was. She never forgets who I am. It's just that she sometimes thinks I'm younger, or that we still share a room. She can't remember the name of the woman who takes care of her, but she's invented her own name for her. She calls her 'Charming.'"

Walter chuckled, and Laurette spoke almost the only words she had uttered in her husband's presence. "Oh!" she piped in her child's voice. "Charming!" There was no way of knowing whether she was commenting on Mama's aberration or merely repeating the name.

If Becky could have done it without Walter's seeing, she would have stopped Clara with a look as soon as she started. Becky did not want Mama's condition discussed. She did not see how Clara could talk of it as she had. To Becky it was so horrifying that she tried to put it out of her mind whenever she was not actually with Mama. She went up to the Ansonia to see her almost every day, but she could scarcely bear it. Mama may never have forgotten who Clara was, but she did not always know Becky. Sometimes she thought she was Hester. Once she had mistaken her for Ida, and given her a lecture on apostasy—something about its being possible for other people, but not for Jews, who were different, *sui generis*. Becky had been too upset to listen closely, but the Latin phrase had stuck in her mind because it was so pitifully incongruous, a woman who could not even recognize her own daughter, speaking Latin. Afterward Becky had

had to go into the bathroom to cry. She had to do that almost every time she went there.

"Now, don't you fret. Your mama's doing fine," the companion-nurse would say to her without fail, in the same words, reminding Becky of Ted. She was a big, amiable, rather stupid woman, who was kind to Mama but certainly not charming. The first woman Becky had hired had been much less so—a German refugee who, instead of being grateful for her escape, had had a chip on her shoulder and considered the little she had to do for Mama beneath her.

"One time, Grandma asked me what I had learned in school that day," Clara was saying. "She used to ask me that every day when she was living with us, and I'd tell her in what I'm sure was the most boring detail, but she always listened with interest and asked intelligent questions. This time—"

"You'll have to forgive me for interrupting," Becky said, addressing herself to Laurette, "but I'm afraid I must trouble you for a cup of coffee or tea or whatever's easiest. I suddenly feel quite faint." She rested her head against the back of the chair and closed her eyes, hoping this was a reasonable approximation of a state she had never in her life experienced. "No, don't bother about me," she said to Laurette, who seemed to be hovering. "I'll be all right as soon as I have a little something. The trouble is I had no breakfast."

"No wonder! This is absurd," Walter shouted. "Do you know what time it is, Laurette? Don't bring tea or coffee. See that luncheon is served at once. Here, Clara. Give your mother some of this wine. One always thinks of brandy as being the revivifier, but I find this equally effective."

Becky heard him clump off to the other end of the room, talking all the while about the importance of breakfast. She felt the edge of a glass pressed against her lips and automatically opened her mouth. A little syrupy liquid got through before she closed it again and slitted her eyes to make sure the guiding hand was Clara's.

"Don't be an idiot. Pour it into a plant or somewhere," she whispered. "It tastes like Pesach wine."

"Faker!" Clara whispered back. "But thanks. I'm starved."

"How are you now? Better?" Walter inquired, returning from his journey across the room. "Yes, I can see you are. Your color has improved. Can you sit up and take notice? I have something to show you."

Becky sighed and slowly opened her eyes, resisting the impulse to

286

flutter the lids. Walter was holding a photograph under her nose. For a shocked instant, Becky thought it was of Walt as a young boy. The resemblance was less strong at second glance. This was a gentler face, without the sharp, hard ugliness, without the cold intelligence. There was something of Laurette in the eyes, a glazed blandness.

"Walter, Jr.," his father announced. "Taken last year on his birthday."

"He looks very much like you," Clara said, craning to see.

Becky wondered how much Clara remembered of the first Walter, Jr. Not too much, Becky hoped. Not that dreadful incident when she was only six years old and that monster of a boy had tried to molest her. Could that have had some effect on her? Something to do with her not marrying? Becky was dubious about all this psychoanalysis people were going in for, digging up things that were better forgotten. But what did she know? Maybe there was something to it.

"Yes, and we're remarkably close," Walter said. "One would think that impossible, considering the disparity in our ages, but we've bridged it, Junior and I. He's deeply interested in all my projects, particularly the memoirs. He looks forward to assisting me when he has finished his schooling. I could surely use an assistant. There's a tremendous amount of research to be done, and all the typing—" He bent close to Clara, the photograph held against his chest now. "You would be perfect for the job in the meanwhile, you know, Clara, my dear. I've become aware of that in just this brief time. You're in tune with the way my mind works. You've had the background to understand my references." He bent closer still, smiling within an inch of her face. "I wonder whether you would consider it."

"You must be out of your mind," Becky said before Clara could answer. "Do you really imagine Clara would leave the Paper to do your typing? Or to do anything else, for that matter? Have you forgotten she's a Herzog, and that someday the Paper will be hers? And you're actually suggesting that she—"

"As a matter of fact," Walter broke in, the smile left over on his face, "she's also a Lowenthal. Some very real accomplishments have been credited to that name. I hardly think it would demean Clara to be associated with it further. However, when I made the offer, I had quite frankly forgotten about the Paper for the moment."

Becky and Clara spoke at the same time.

"Thank you just the same, Uncle Walter. I appreciate—"

"*Forgotten—?*"

They were interrupted by the entrance of Laurette, followed by the man, Mar, wheeling a tea wagon.

"Lunch is served." She made one of her limp half gestures. "Won't you all please sit down? There's a little table for each of us."

"Yes, sit down! Sit down!" Walter boomed in the voice of a hand-rubbing host. "A little more wine, Becky? No? Clara? Well, help yourselves. We live simply here, as you see. No elaborate meals. No ceremony. Help yourselves."

Becky stared at the food on the tea wagon. It was all in cans, the top of each rolled back into a spiral around a key, revealing neat rows of oil-bathed sardines, anchovies, and sliced herring. A small plate of plain crackers completed the spread.

"We use paper plates and napkins, as you see," Walter said. "This is to spare Mar, since these days he is our only servant. It's incredibly difficult to get reliable people in wartime, you know, especially 'way out here in the sticks." All this was said in front of Mar, who pushed the tea wagon from person to person with no expression on his unidentifiable face. "Actually we prefer it this way, don't we, Laurette, my dear? We have so much more privacy than with a staff of servants milling about."

Becky ate a sardine on a cracker, chewing it slowly to make it last. She did not dare look at Clara. Sometimes they had only to glance at each other to burst into wild laughter, like uncontrolled schoolgirls. Not that this was altogether funny. It was not, really, funny at all. What was Walter doing in this mansion, with a wife like Laurette, an original Picasso on the wall, furniture that was falling apart, and canned sardines for a guest luncheon? *Walter Lowenthal?*

"What is Mar?" she heard Clara ask after the man had left. "What nationality?"

"Something of a mixture. Japanese enough, however, to have been in danger if he had stayed in California with his old parents."

"Then you don't believe they should be interned?" Clara asked him eagerly. "The Japanese-Americans?"

Walter moved his stooped shoulders. He looked at Laurette, who for once was not looking at him but was absorbed in retrieving and popping into her mouth a bit of oily fish that had dropped from her cracker to the rug. "Even if I would ordinarily believe it, which I would not," he said, "how could any Jew in these times believe that any innocent citizen anywhere should be interned?"

Becky did not know why Walter had looked at Laurette when he spoke, but she knew why Clara was looking at her. They had had a raging argument about this a week before, with Clara saying she was ashamed to be associated with such a policy and Becky telling her she had no intention of letting any traitorous pro-Japanese sentiment influence the Paper and if Clara was not careful Becky would fire her the way Grandpa had fired Hester for voicing pro-German sentiments. Clara knew Becky would never fire her, just as Becky knew Clara would never leave, no matter how ashamed she claimed to be. They had made it up the way they always did, though neither of them had changed their minds. Clara, for all her soft manner, could dig in her heels like any Herzog.

"Walter Lippmann believes it," Becky said. "He believes they're a menace to our safety, that many of them are enemy agents, communicating with the Japanese navy that's reconnoitering off the Pacific coast. He was one of the first to push for mass internment."

"I have a great deal of respect for Lippmann, as a journalist and as a man," Walter said, "but in this instance he is utterly misguided. The people he refers to are as patriotic as any other Americans. As well have interned Pa—your grandfather in the First War because he was born in Germany, or Samuel because he was his son." Again Walter looked at Laurette. She had finished eating now, and the glassy blue eyes were once more fixed on his face. "But let's change to a pleasanter subject, shall we? Laurette dislikes this sort of conversation, don't you, my dear? War, politics, man's inhumanity to man, anything ugly or controversial, distresses her. She has what Yeats called 'a gentle, sensitive mind.'"

Laurette lifted one hand from her paper plate, and dropped it back. "Oh, no," she piped. "Oh, no, you must talk about anything you like." She waited a moment in the silence that followed and then said she had better go and see about the coffee. "Unless anyone prefers tea?" She went out with the plate clutched in her two hands.

"Yes," Walter said, looking after her, "a gentle, sensitive mind. She makes me happy. She's precisely what a man of my dynamic, restless temperament requires. There is quite enough stimulation in here." He tapped the hairless summit of his domed head. "Quite enough for two ordinary men and two ordinary lifetimes."

Becky took a deep breath. She no longer wanted to say what she had come to say, but she could not leave without a word and remember him here with his thin trousers and canned fish. "I should think you'd need more scope for your energies," she said. "It's a wonder to me you've never gone back into newspaper work."

He looked at her with a peculiar little smile, and then looked away. He had only begun the smile with the last part of her remark, yet when he spoke he ignored that part. "Scope," he said. "Scope. My dear Rebecca, you have obviously not understood the dimensions of my work here. The autobiography alone is, as I've said, a monumental undertaking, a life's work. My foray into the perfume industry would wholly occupy the forces of any other man. There are further projects that I haven't even mentioned to you." His loud voice moderated a little. "I have all the scope I can use."

Laurette returned with the coffee, wheeling the tea wagon herself this time. Becky became impatient with her awkwardness in exchanging the soiled paper plates for the clean cups and saucers, and began doing it for her. In another hour, Becky and Clara were on the train back to New York.

"That woman's a moron," Becky said. "She can't even hand a person a cup of coffee without getting muddled. How on earth can Walter stand her?"

"It's hard to live with someone so—so towering, and not get muddled," Clara murmured in that barely audible voice she still reverted to at times.

"What?" Becky asked sharply, although she actually had heard, but Clara did not repeat it. Instead she said, "I think he finds in her exactly what he said he did. All that talk earlier about men coming home tired and glutted with companionship—that could apply to Walter himself, couldn't it? Coming home after the hunt, after Hester. Too old for it now, sick of it, glutted . . ."

"But he's still hunting," Becky said, pleased that for once she could follow one of Clara's labyrinthine concepts. "The memoirs and the perfume and whatever else he has in mind."

Clara had her book in her lap, a strip of paper between the pages to keep her place. She played with it as she talked, turning it on end, stroking the cover, opening and closing it. Becky longed to tell her to keep her hands still, but she could not say anything like that to Clara any more without starting something.

"I remember reading once about a primitive tribe," Clara said. "I don't remember much about it, whether it really existed or was fictional or what, but anyway, when the warriors were too old to fight, they still put on all their war gear and went out with the young men to the edge of the battlefield and shot their arrows or hurled their spears or whatever the weapons were—I forget—which of course fell far short, but it didn't matter. They did that as long as they had the strength for it, and then they lay down and died." To Becky's relief, she stopped fiddling with the book and folded her hands on top of it. "I'm glad you persuaded me to go. He's a strange, wild man—a little mad, maybe—but he's a giant. I'll never forget him."

"You can go again. I'm sure he'd be delighted."

Clara shook her head. "I won't go again."

"You made quite an impression on him. He'll tell your father, of course." Becky began to laugh. "I thought I'd die when he offered you a job. Wasn't that absurd? I went there to offer *him* a job, and there he was in his threadbare clothes and his shabby house, offering *you* one."

"Maybe it wasn't so absurd. Maybe he knew why you were there."

"What are you talking about?"

Clara only shrugged. "Anyhow, what happens now? We've still got the problem with the Washington Bureau."

"I know. I began thinking about it as soon as I saw Walter was on his last legs." She frowned. "It's a wonder Samuel never told me, not even that Walter had had a stroke."

"There was no reason for him to think you'd be interested."

"Of course there was. Samuel knows I'm interested in everything. I'd never have come all the way up here—well, no, I don't really regret that. At least Walter met you."

She imagined what Walter would tell William: *A brilliant girl . . . Attractive, too . . . Well brought up . . . One can tell at once she's had the finest governesses, been to the best schools . . . obviously first-class material for the Paper . . . yes, a foreign-news editor, and eventually, of course . . .*

"What we must do is keep Bill Norman on in Washington, at least for the time being, and make it appear it's through his influence that the bureau is given independence from New York. If his men believe he has that kind of power, they'll respect him. The only problem is to prevent those in the know from leaking the truth." Becky smiled a little. "I think I can manage that. They're all men."

Clara laughed. "Mother, you're a wonder!"

"Are you just finding that out?"

"Oh, no. I've always known it. Haven't you been telling it to me all my life?"

Becky jerked around in her seat, prepared to be angry, but then she saw from Clara's face that she was only teasing.

"Next stop, Grand Central!" the conductor intoned. "Grand Central, next stop!"

It was bitter cold at the graveside. The wind kept whipping the rabbi's words away. Not that it mattered. They were traditional words. Those who knew them did not have to hear. The others listened to their own words.

It began to snow a little into the open grave. Becky moved closer to Clara and tried to take her arm, but Clara shifted away. The letters blurred on the headstone over the grave next to the open one, which as yet had no headstone.

NATHAN HERZOG, the blurred letters said. 1840–1911.

She had lived thirty-one years without him, longer than the whole span of Clara's life. After all that time, it seemed like putting her next to a stranger who would not have recognized her if he had passed her in the street.

Becky walked ahead when it was over, mopping her eyes, but Clara caught up with her.

"That was a funny thing to do," Becky said. "Pulling away from me like that."

Clara's eyes were dry. She spoke in the voice that could scarcely be heard. "I'm sorry. I couldn't— It was between the two of us. Between Grandma and me."

"I don't know what you're talking about, baby," Becky said.

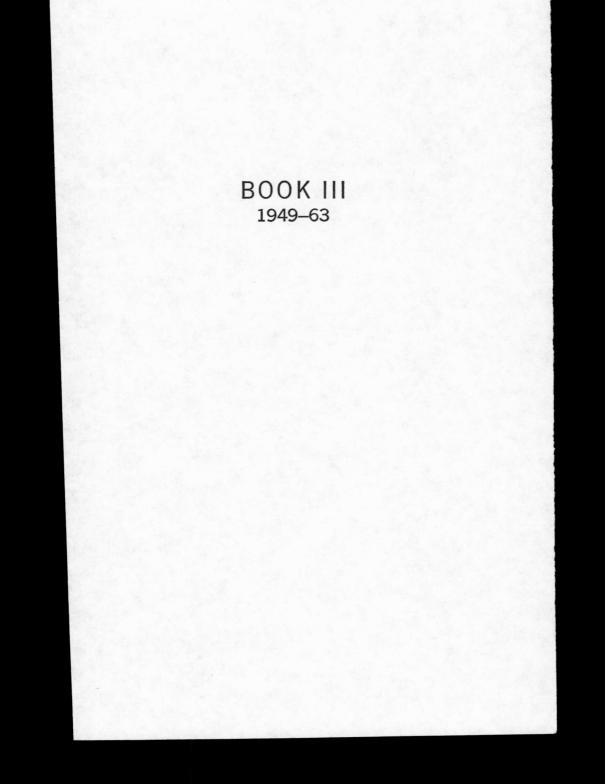

BOOK III
1949–63

1

Clara waited at their favorite table in the Café Cluny, the one in the front corner near the radiator. There was no need for the radiator now. It was September and still warm enough to sit in the open, without the protection of the glass enclosure that would soon go up between the terrace and the sidewalk. Then the radiator would be comforting. Now Clara sat there because it was where they always sat. The habitués all had their favorite tables. At the same hour in any café in the city, one was likely to see the same people at the same tables.

She was more than half an hour early, but she never minded waiting. She liked sitting with her cup of *express*, watching the people go by—dark-suited businessmen and diplomats carrying briefcases; housewives with their string bags, hurrying to the street markets before they closed for half the afternoon; students eating *frites* wrapped in paper as they walked along, making a lunch of the starchy morsels that stained the paper with grease from the frying but were tasty, filling, and cheap.

The coffee was scarcely worth ordering—two swallows and it was gone—but the cup gave her the right to the table as long as she wanted it. They would have wine later, and talk about what they had done and seen and thought since they had last been together. They always had so much to say to each other that they knew only dimly what was going on around them.

Now, though, before he came, the ambience absorbed her. She tasted the crisp coating of the students' potatoes change to mealiness on her own tongue. She gauged apprehensively the time required to reach the market before one o'clock. She followed the course of the sun that ran warm along the streets, emptying like another, freer-flowing river into the Seine at both ends of the Boulevard St. Germain and one end of the Boulevard St. Michel.

She remembered no such flooding September sun in New York, only a straggle of rays that nudged the long shadows of the giant buildings and spilled into batches of sizzling glare on the pavements. Here the sun took gently to the low roof tops, spreading its golden light without cruelty. Even in midsummer, 80° was ordinarily a torrid day for Paris.

At times she could not believe she had lived here for nearly three years. At other times it seemed impossible that she had ever lived anywhere else, that her images of a different place, a different life, were real and not an elaborately concocted or vividly dreamed world that existed nowhere but in memory.

Everything that had once been so unyieldingly strange to her was comfortably familiar now. Even the hours of her work, which kept her at her desk when most people were relaxing or sleeping, and left her free during many ordinary business hours, had become a normal pattern. Even the language—a language she had thought she could speak and understand until she had had to communicate on all the levels of encounter—now seemed as natural to her as her own. When she arrived at the office of the Paper in the evening and heard the chatter of American voices, it was no longer with grateful relief. Often she found herself speaking French when English would have done as well.

"It's wonderful that you've adjusted to everything so beautifully," Mother had written in one of her earlier letters. "I'm delighted. It will be a valuable experience for you, and the change you obviously needed. You'll come back refreshed, and prepared for the bigger job here that I have in mind for you . . ."

Mother had been holding that bait out to her ever since—that promise of an unnamed, prestigious job on the Paper when she returned to New York. Lately the tone and emphasis had shifted. The last few letters had grown more and more peremptory.

"It wasn't my idea to have you stay over there indefinitely. . . . It's time you thought about coming home. . . . Someone else can easily take your place there. I need you here for something far more important. . . ."

This morning's letter had been different still. Mother could of course order her home, stop her salary unless she complied, but Clara knew she would never do it. Never dare do it. There was as much sadness as satisfaction in the knowledge. Mother, who had always dared anything with anyone.

Clara was not yet ready to go back. She didn't know when she would be ready. Maybe never. She loved Paris. She had a life here now. As far as she knew, nothing had changed back there. Mother, who ignored whatever she could not override, did not suggest it had. She simply brushed all that aside, refused to recognize it as the cause of Clara's being here in the first place.

She had brushed it aside at the time. "Don't talk like an idiot. There's no question of your leaving the Paper. How can you possibly contemplate such a thing? You're going through a stage, that's all. You're stale. What you need—"

"Mother, I'm not stale and I'm not going through a stage. I want out. I've been trying to write a novel for years, and now I'm going to write it. I've been trying to do too many things for too many years, but the Paper always had to come first. Now I'm through with it."

"You're saying you're through with me."

"Of course I'm not saying that, Mother. I'm talking about the Paper. I know what it means to you, and that's fine. But for me it's been one grand illusion, and now it's over."

Mother had not heard her. What she had insisted on hearing was a rejection of herself, something more believable to her than a rejection of the Paper. She had carried on like a maniac. She had screamed the things she always screamed when she lost her temper, bringing in Grandma and Fitz and Clara's father in an irrelevant hodgepodge of recrimination and aspersion, and run down at last to a predictable finale of penitent tears. Clara had wept too, of course, melting with relief from tension, hating herself for it.

"Oh, baby, what an idiot I am! What idiots we both are!" Mother had dabbed at her face with one of her elegant little perfumed handkerchiefs. In ten minutes she would be beautiful again, but just then she had looked like a red-eyed, swollen-nosed, pitiable old woman. "Sit down a minute. I'll send for coffee and we can talk sensibly."

Clara had sat on the gray sofa in Mother's cool blue office and drunk coffee and promised herself not to be swerved by pity or love. But it was neither of these that Mother invoked in the end.

"You wanted to go to Europe a long time ago, and I wouldn't send you because of the war. How would you like to go now? Work out of our Paris Bureau? With your knowledge of French and your experience on the foreign desk here, you'll fit in very quickly. Anyway, it will be something different and exciting for you, and since you'll be working at night you'll have plenty of time to write your novel during the day." She had added what Clara should have known she did not mean and would forget as soon as it was said. "If you still feel the same way about quitting the Paper afterward, we'll say no more about it."

A shabby, middle-aged man was walking slowly up and down on the sidewalk in front of the café, eying the passers-by. At intervals he would select a certain woman or girl, or two girls walking together, and thrust under their noses as they passed a large, flexible, lifelike rubber rat. Whether this produced a shriek, a shrill giggle, a horrified backward leap or, from one dignified elderly lady, a perfectly self-contained wave of dismissal, the man's impassive face never changed. Each time, the audience in the café howled with laughter. At the precise moment when it began to pall, the man pocketed the rat and passed his bedraggled hat among the tables.

He would return tomorrow, and everybody would laugh all over again. Paris never changed, yet was always a fresh delight. But Clara had not written much of her novel. She worked in the bureau on Rue Caumartin from five or six in the evening until one or two in the morning, had something to eat, alone or in company, usually at one of the all-night restaurants in Montmartre, and staggered to bed in her apartment on Rue St. Lazare at three or four. Often she was out on assignments during at least part of the day. Sometimes she had to leave France for several days to cover an event or interview some notable in another country. She needed time for just living, too. For sitting in a café and laughing at a man scaring women with a rubber rat. For waiting. Loving.

She saw him now, crossing the Boul' Mich' with the skill of long practice, making the cars dodge him instead of the other way around. His black hair, as black as Mother kept hers still, was coarse and dry, but the sun gave it a sheen. He had the face of a pale Indian, sharp-boned and fierce and of no readily divined age. This last, since he was a year and a half younger than she, Clara considered a special advantage.

He came toward her without smiling. He was not an easy smiler. It had puzzled her at first. She had been accustomed to Fitz's Irish grin. He kissed her on both cheeks, in the French manner, and sat in the chair she had saved for him, his knees bumping hers under the little table. He was a big man, not much taller than she was but bulky, with heavy shoulders and large, hairy hands and large feet. When she wanted to tease him she told him he looked like an ape, but it was not true. He was striking, even handsome in an angry sort of way, and for all his visible hairiness, there was not much hair on his body.

"How did it go this morning?" She was usually the first to speak. He was like a stringed instrument that had to be plucked or bowed before it would resonate.

"Well, I think." Indoors, the sound of that bass-drum voice invariably made heads turn, but here in the open, amid the traffic of two boulevards, the deep rumble was dissipated. "I think I'm over the hump. If I can keep my American perspective instead of looking at De Gaulle as a Frenchman would, I'll be all right. The trouble is, I've been here so long, my American perspective keeps slipping away from me." He put one hand over hers and signaled a waiter with the other. "What's your mood today? Red wine or white? . . . Yes, mine too. . . . *Deux coups de rouge*," he said to the waiter, who had come at once. Waiters always came at once when he wanted them. Probably when they looked at him they were afraid not to. "What about you?" he asked her. "Did you have a good night?"

"Routine. The real action never seems to be where I am. When it was here, I was in New York. Now that I'm here, it's somewhere else. I'm thinking of asking for an assignment in Asia."

"Never mind that. I'll show you where the real action is."

She widened her eyes at him. "When?"

"Don't be in such an indecent hurry. We're civilized people."

"Civilized? You?"

"We're civilized people, and we're going to sit here quietly and have our wine. Later on, if I'm so inclined, I may suggest that you accompany me to my apartment, where we'll dispose of the question of real action. In the meantime—"

The waiter came with the wine. They did not resume their foolishness when he had gone. They talked for a long time with their heads close together, she murmuring and he rumbling. Finally they left, walked down the Boul' Mich' to the Seine, and crossed the bridge to the Ile St. Louis, where he lived.

She had met him at one of Hester's Sunday *soirées*.

Hester had not gone back to New York after the war. She had fallen in love with France and the French, as she had once fallen in love with Germany and the Germans.

"This time it's with my eyes open," she had told Clara. "I know all about the French watching indifferently while their neighbors were dragged away by the Nazis. I know plenty of them actively helped the Nazis, even substituted for them. Do you think it would be any different in America? But I know about the resistance fighters too, the young men shot down in the streets of Paris, and the peasants who hid Jews in their cellars—"

"Do you think that would be any different in America?" Clara had asked her.

"No. But there are other differences. There's something cool and proud and private in the French character that appeals to me. I feel at home in Paris as I've never felt anywhere, not even in New York. What New York daily newspaper would devote a front-page column to a discourse on language or the body of an author's work? *Le Figaro* does it in almost every issue. Such things are important here, and not only to a small, elite group. Yesterday when I went into the little *épicerie* where I buy my groceries, the proprietor urged me to see the Matisse exhibit at the Grand Palais. Can you imagine going into Reuben's for a sandwich and having Mr. Reuben tell you about an exhibit at the Metropolitan Museum? Besides, as long as I have a choice, why shouldn't I live in the world's most beautiful city?"

Hester had been as obstinate about not returning to New York as she had been originally about leaving it. This time, however, there was no one to maneuver her into changing her mind. Mother had gone through the motions, invited her to come back to the New York office, but Hester had known it was only a gesture. Fitz wrote an immensely popular column for the Paper now, called "East Side, West Side," that included some of the same kind of material with which Hester had dealt. There was no room for another such feature writer.

Hester had resigned from the Paper and moved out of the Hotel Scribe, which was so filled with Paris-based journalists that it was like a press club. She had bought an apartment on the Left Bank, just off Boulevard St. Germain, with a large living room, a tiny bedroom, and a tinier kitchen. Her income from the now prosperous Paper enabled her to live comfortably without a salary. When she felt like it, she worked on a collection of her feature articles, sorting, discarding, and adding new material for a New York publisher who had expressed interest in bringing it out as a book.

"I'll probably never finish it," she said to Clara one day. "You can, if you want to, after I die. Meanwhile it's something I can say I'm doing when people ask. That's ridiculous, isn't it? Why can't I just say I'm enjoying Paris? I don't have to be doing anything. I'm over seventy years old, for God's sake!"

She did not look it, of course, any more than any of them ever looked their ages. She had slimmed down during the war, but her face was still plump. Most of the lines were around her eyes, and these were partly hidden by her glasses. She wore beautiful clothes and she went to a good hairdresser, who kept her hair looking naturally dark. It was not vanity so much, she said, as affirmation. There had been a period when she had not cared about such things, because she had stopped living.

The Sunday soirées had begun with a few people she had met in the course of her work. Most of them were writers or artists or politicians. They dropped in because Hester's apartment was convenient and Hester was intelligent and witty and knowledgeable about what interested them. Some, discovering that she was indifferent to food and disliked bothering with it, started bringing along cheeses and patés, Paris ham, quiches from the charcuteries or their own kitchens, and that grew into a custom. Hester provided the wine. Word got around, and before long, people she did not know were coming. It was a well-established tradition by the time Clara got to Paris.

Clara had been there almost seven months before she went to the first one. She was concerned about the unexpected inadequacy of her French, and she did not care much for crowds of people. Hester did not press her. Clara finally pressed herself, because she knew all that was holding her back was the shyness that had always plagued her, and she was not going to let herself give in to it. Shyness in a woman her age was an absurdity.

The man who came to the door was a thin, gray-haired Frenchman who looked like an ambassador. He spoke English to her before she had opened her mouth. They could always tell. "I am desolated," he said, "but I cannot let you in. You have not been here before, have you? There is not, you see, a limitless capacity, and so Madame Duke has made a rule. After thirty-five have come, no one else may be admitted, not even one more. Usually there are not so many, but one can never be sure. The habitués know to be here early. Now you know also, and next week you will arrive among the first, n'est-ce pas?" He made her a little bow. "I shall look forward to meeting you."

He had not given her a chance to say a word. He had not asked her name. He was perfectly courteous, regretful, but it was as though she had, as the thirty-sixth arrival, no real existence.

"Does it make any difference that I'm Madame Duke's grand-niece?"

Clara could not tell from his expression whether he suspected her of lying to get in or was dubious about the correct procedure in a case without precedent. In either event, he was disconcerted into a flurry of such rapid-fire French that Clara caught not one word. He disappeared, leaving the door open, and she slipped inside.

"He's an idiot," Hester said, leading Clara into the bedroom to take off her coat. "Not that he isn't charming, and probably the foremost art critic in Paris, but an idiot just the same. Whenever he's here, which is most Sundays, he constitutes himself my doorman and bouncer. The thirty-five-people limit is his idea, not mine. There are never that many, but as soon as he decides it's getting crowded he begins turning people away."

Clara's coat topped a mountain of coats on the bed. She combed her hair, which was getting too dark to qualify as blond any more, even with a rinse. Mother had been after her to bleach it, but she could not be bothered running to the hairdresser every time the roots started showing.

"Is he in love with you, and this is his way of being protective?"

Hester laughed into the mirror. "In *love* with me? At my age?"

"Why not?" Clara asked, freshening her lipstick. "Mother's not that much younger, and she still—"

"Your mother is a phenomenon. Don't try to compare anyone to her. Don't try to compare yourself to her. She's *sui generis*."

"*Sui generis.* Grandma used to like to say that."

"Come on," Hester said. "You look fine. Stop stalling."

Hester took her arm and drew her into the other room. People were crammed together on the sofa and the chairs. Those left over were sitting on the floor or standing. The smoke was so thick that it was hard to see anyone at the opposite end of the room. There seemed to be three separate groups, each engaged in its own discussion. Every so often someone would shift from one group to another. Hester introduced Clara to a few people near the door and then left her, to take a chair in the approximate center of the room. Immediately, all the groups converged on this central chair. No one, after the initial "*Enchanté*" paid any attention to Clara. She began to feel suffocated from the smoke and the French that swirled around her head.

"*Je crois que vous ne vous sentez pas bien, Mademoiselle.*"

The voice was deep and booming and, despite a good accent, unmistakably American. Clara smiled with relief, ready to like whoever it was, to be at ease with him before she saw him.

He had a dark, fierce face that did not change expression when she turned toward him. She thought he must have been watching her from across the room before he came around behind her. She thought he looked as he did because he was angry that no one was bothering about her. He was young and she could understand what he said. In this company of people who spoke gibberish and didn't care whether she lived or died, he was an instant friend.

"No, I don't feel very well," she said in English. "It's awfully close in here, and when they all jabber away at one time in French it gives me a headache."

It surprised her that he was still too angry to return her smile. "You'll get used to it. Exposure's the only way. In a month or two you'll begin hearing words, and then phrases, and finally meanings. Would you like a glass of wine?" He started off for it without waiting for her answer, then turned back. "Would you rather get some fresh air? A walk around the block?"

"Well, I don't know. I just came—" There was no question that she wanted to get out of there, go with him. She was thinking of Hester. Not that Hester had thought much about her, leaving her to shift for herself in this mob of foreign strangers. "Just a minute."

A very young man was talking earnestly to Hester, bending over her chair. When she saw Clara, she simply pushed him out of the way with her forearm. It was the kind of thing Mother might have done. Or even Grandma. Once, when Clara was a child and Grandma was recovering from pneumonia and walking with a cane, they had been together in an elevator where a man was endlessly adjusting his tie in the mirror. Grandma had watched him with growing exasperation and finally rapped him on the shoulder with her cane.

"You've been admiring yourself long enough, young man," she had said. "I'd like to rest against that corner now."

Clara had almost died of embarrassment. At the same time, she had thought it was marvelous to be able to do such a thing, and wondered whether she would have the courage too, when she was older.

"Hester, I'm a little headachy," she said now, taking the place of the man Hester had pushed aside. "I thought I'd go out for a breath of air. I'll be back."

"There's no need to come back, unless you really want to." Hester was looking past her to where she had been standing with the fierce-faced man. "I don't think many of the people here tonight would interest you particularly. Go on and enjoy yourself, and don't worry about coming back."

Clara knew then that Hester had told the man to come and look after her. Maybe the anger in his face was because he had not wanted to and now he was stuck with her. It reminded her of a terrible thing that had happened to her when she was fifteen, a big *klotz* of a girl, taller than most of the boys. The son of a friend of Mother's, a college boy, had invited her to a fraternity dance—been made to, certainly—and had had to dance and dance with her, dragging her clumsy, embarrassment-frozen body around the floor, because none of the other boys cut in. Finally one did, but not before Clara had seen in the mirror that her partner was holding a dollar bill behind her back.

"As soon as I've had some air, I think I'll go straight home," she said to the angry man when they were out in the street. "Why don't you just walk me as far as the Métro and then go back to Hester's?"

"I'm not going back to Hester's. There are too many people there tonight. Wouldn't you like a drink of something before you go home? A tisane? The French think they have medicinal value. Maybe they're good for headaches." He took her arm companionably. "You can try one, anyway. It's a nice walk to my café."

It never occurred to him that she might have been trying to get rid of him; why should it have occurred to her that he was with her because Hester had forced him? Only the memory of humiliation related her to that poor *klotz* of a girl with her adolescent skin, her paralyzed tongue, her overweight and unloved body.

He still wore what she had thought was an expression of anger, but she saw now that it was not really an expression; rather, the way his heavy black eyebrows grew, slanting down toward his nose, and the hard, sharp boniness of his face, the straight line of his mouth. His eyes were so dark that the pupils were almost invisible. That heightened the effect. That, and the fact that he seemed never to smile.

It was a mild night. The Boulevard St. Germain near Hester's apartment was almost deserted, but as they approached the Latin Quarter they came upon more and more people, mostly students, strolling, spreading across the pavement and not making way until the last possible moment, sitting in the glassed-in cafés with their wine and beer and Gauloises cigarettes.

"My name is Clara, by the way. Clara Lowenthal. I'm Hester's grandniece."

"Yes, I know. Hester told me. You work for a newspaper."

He said nothing more, asked nothing. What had Hester told him? He still held her arm in the crook of his. The sleeve of his jacket—he wore no topcoat—felt soft, like good wool, and his shoes looked British-made.

"My mother owns the newspaper."

"Oh." He nodded. "That newspaper."

They walked on a little farther. "I thought when I told you my name, you might be induced to tell me yours."

"Didn't I tell it to you? It's Steven Miller. Steve."

Clara laughed. "Well, go on. I work on a newspaper, Steve. What do you do, Steve?"

"I write." Then he laughed too. At least that was what he seemed to be doing. It did not show on his face. "I'm sorry. Something came into my mind, a way to get over a tough spot in my book. I'm afraid I haven't been paying proper attention."

She thought but did not say, *That's not very flattering*. It was the kind of thing she would once have said to Fitz and had learned not to because he hated it.

"What's the book?" she asked instead.

"It's about De Gaulle."

He offered nothing more, and she let it go at that. She knew how reluctant writers could be to talk about work in progress. Perhaps it was partly superstition, like the unwillingness of primitive people to be photographed. As though some precious essence might be extracted and irretrievably lost.

Then he said, "Writing about De Gaulle is like climbing a mountain. You think you've reached the top, but there's always another peak rising out of the clouds. I suppose that's why he fascinates me.

Like Churchill. Such men can't be discounted as long as they're alive."

"Churchill." Clara stopped, pulling him back by his entwined arm. "Steven Miller. Are you *that* Steven Miller? *The King's First Minister?*"

"Well, I wrote it, yes," he said, looking fiercer than ever. "Don't say you've read it if you haven't."

"I wouldn't. I'm a congenital non-liar, though I'm trying to get over it." They were walking on again. His arm, which had stiffened at her mention of his book, relaxed a little. "Of course I've read it. At the bureau, it's practically required reading for anyone who wants to write any kind of story involving Churchill. I started dipping into it for some information I needed, and found myself reading it straight through. Staying up to read it when I should have been asleep."

They were stopped by a wide circle of people, three layers deep, that obstructed the sidewalk. By standing on tiptoe, Clara could glimpse the man in the center, his chest bare to the night. He was setting the end of a pole on fire and putting the flames into his mouth.

"Well," Clara said as they pushed past, "I guess some people just have an overpowering preference for outdoor work."

He responded to this by narrowing his eyes at her in a way that pulled up the corners of his straight mouth. It was more a look of appreciation than a smile.

They walked in silence for a time. She had no feeling that it was up to her to keep the conversation going. Why she should so often be oppressed by this responsibility with other people and not with this glowering stranger, she had no idea.

"Thanks for your comments on my book," he remarked after a block or two. "You said none of the idiotic things people say to writers."

"Maybe that's because I'm a writer myself."

"You don't mean a journalist." It was not a question.

"Maybe I should say a scribbler. I've never had anything published except, of course, in the Paper, and a poem in the *Times* when I was sixteen. What I want to write is a novel."

"Then write it."

"I'm trying, but I don't get very far. Plenty of journalists manage it. Half the reporters in the New York office and several correspondents here keep plays and books they're writing in their desks and work on them whenever they have a spare minute. I can't work like that. In bits and pieces, with my left hand. I'm an all-or-nothing person." It was too much to tell a man she had never met before. It was too much for her, ordinarily, to tell anyone.

"Then stop doing everything else," he said. "That's why I came over here. Not only to be close to my subject but to be away from distractions."

"Doesn't Paris distract you?"

"I work every morning from seven until noon. Sometimes, if I'm really hot, I go back to it for a couple of hours after lunch. While I'm working, nothing else exists for me. I take the phone off the hook and I don't answer the doorbell. I'm like you. I have to have long stretches like that every day. But then I need refreshment. A writer can't keep living off his own fat. Sooner or later he'd consume himself."

"I don't understand why it's refreshment in Paris but distraction in New York. It is New York you come from, isn't it?"

"Yes, it's New York."

He did not answer her other question until much later. By then they had been sitting in the café for more than two hours. His café, he called it. The front faced the Boulevard St. Germain and the side swung around the corner to the Boul' Mich'. A few students drifted in from time to time, but the regulars, Steve told her, were from the neighboring *Sénat* and *Faculté de Médecine* and *Institut de Chimie*.

Clara would have liked to do a piece for the Paper on the cafés of Paris, but that was not the kind of thing Mother wanted from her foreign correspondents. Well, that the foreign-news editor wanted, but Clara always thought of it as Mother. During the war, all kinds of stories with local color and human interest had been acceptable, but now the only foreign news the Paper printed was hard news, and not very much of that. According to Maggie Prout, the Paris Bureau chief, Americans had had their fill of Europe for a while. The last thing she needed, she implied every day without saying, was another correspondent on her staff, but when it was the publisher's daughter, there was unfortunately nothing she could do about it.

Steve said, "I don't understand why you stay. Particularly when this isn't what you really want to do with your life."

"It's complicated. You'd have to know all about me to understand it, and then I'm not sure you would. Or that I do myself. I tried to quit once, but I didn't. I came here instead. It has to do with being a Herzog."

"Herzog," he repeated. "That's what Hester told me your name was. And hers, before she translated it from the German. But it's not the name you told me before." Clara had not realized, until he sat down, how much there was of him. Under the little table, his legs were jammed against hers. Over it, his torso loomed like a tree trunk. "I wasn't abstracted enough to imagine that, was I?"

"No. I told you Clara Lowenthal. That's complicated too. It's my name, but I haven't been called it since I was three years old. From then until I came to Paris, I was Clara Herzog." She clasped her hands around her long-empty cup, from which the aroma of mint still drifted. "People in my family tend to discard other names in favor of Herzog."

Albert (she had always called him Father, but after the divorce it had seemed wrong because of Mother, as though she ought to divorce him too) would have liked to give her his name, either by adopting her—which Mother would not hear of—or just to use, as a convenience. One family, one name. That had been Mother's excuse after she divorced Clara's father. She intended to revert to her maiden name, and she had decided it would cause much less confusion if Clara had the same name. But when she became Mrs. Albert Kahn and Albert suggested it would be simpler if Clara became Clara Kahn, Mother said it would cause much less confusion if Clara remained Clara Herzog. The only difference it had made to Clara was that Herzog was easier than Lowenthal for her three-year-old tongue to fit around. Kahn would have been easier still, but she got no chance to use it.

"Of course I've always known my name was really Lowenthal. Yet I haven't known it. Not in a way that meant anything. I've heard Herzog all my life. My great-grandfather Herzog is a legend. My grandmother was born a Herzog and married a Herzog. My mother has called herself Herzog on and off for years. The Paper is a Herzog newspaper. I'm told I look like a Herzog and have the Herzog talent with words. We Herzogs. But it says Lowenthal on my birth certificate." He was bending his head to hear her, so she knew her voice was ebbing in that way that had so often irritated Mother when she was a child. "Speak up! No one can hear you," Mother would say in a stage whisper, after which Clara could not speak at all. "I never saw my birth certificate," she said, raising her voice a little for Steve, "or thought about what name would be on it, until I needed it to get a passport."

She had actually given her name as Clara Herzog, and not realized her error until she was told there was no record of a Clara Herzog, born in New York City on November 27, 1912. She probably could have explained to the Passport Office and had her passport issued in the name she had always used, but she had not done it. Now, since she had had to show the Clara Lowenthal passport at the Hotel Scribe, where she had stayed for a time until she found an apartment, it had been simpler to register that way and, finally, to use the name everywhere.

"I don't see what's simpler about it," Mother had said in her first letter, "when you've been Clara Herzog all your life." Mother still kept writing *Miss Clara Herzog* on all her envelopes and then scratching out the Herzog and writing *Lowenthal* above it. "But even if it is simpler, it's foolish and shortsighted. You have a heritage not only to be proud of but one that can open doors for you everywhere. Why you should choose to deny it, even if it seems simpler to you, is beyond me."

There was no use arguing with Mother about denying heritages. She was impatient with Clara's notion that it was simpler to use her own name, but at least not mortally wounded. Any other reason would have struck her as a denial of herself. Besides, Clara was not sure what reason she could have given.

She said to Steve: "I don't know why I'm telling you these basic things. It's not at all like me. At our first meeting, too. There won't be anything left for you to—" She stopped.

He had his arms on the table, leaving no room for anything else. The waiter had taken away the cups and Clara had shifted the ashtray, which neither of them needed, to another table.

"Why are you blushing?" he asked her.

"Because I was suggesting we're going to see more of each other." Saying it, she felt at ease again. "It just slipped out."

"Well, we are going to see more of each other."

"Yes, I thought so. But I was brought up to wait for the man to mention it." It was curious that she could smile so comfortably into that unsmiling face. "I was brought up to do a lot of things that are meaningless to me now, but it's not always easy to break out of them."

"Then, you're not a rebel by nature."

"I don't know. I ought to be. All the Herzogs— Oh, you see, there I go again." She must stop this now. It was indecent. "What about you? Are you a rebel by nature?"

The crowd in the café had changed, the earlier arrivals giving way to the movie-goers that poured out of the neighboring *cinémas*. Steve ordered another tisane for Clara, another pot of tea for himself. He began to talk about why, other than the need to be near his subject, he had left New York to write. She was to discover that he often did not answer a question at the moment of its asking, but was likely to return to it in his own time.

"My wife divorced me. I don't know whether you have any idea what a hideous thing a divorce can be, even when there are no children."

She knew one kind of hideousness. Sitting in the lawyer's office, being questioned about the things Albert had done to Mother. The things he had said. The lawyer had tried and tried to make her repeat the words.

"Dirty words," she had told him.

"*What* words, Clara? What were the words?"

Even for Mother's sake, she had not been able to say them. She could not say them to this day. The lawyer had finally let her write them down instead. There was nothing she could not write down.

But the hideousness Steve meant was something else, something Clara knew nothing about. She had been only a baby when Mother divorced her father. When the divorce from Albert was final, Mother had said, "Thank God!" and closed her eyes for a minute as though she were doing it, and then jumped up and danced around the room in a kind of pavan, stately yet joyous.

"It wasn't that I still loved her or wanted to hold on to her," Steve said. "She was young and much too malleable. She got in with a bohemian crowd in the Village that changed her into someone I couldn't live with, or she with me. But I had loved her. We had made a life together. It was all still there, waiting around any familiar corner or on the empty side of the bed. I suppose some people can slough it off like dead skin, but I couldn't."

"Is that why you hardly ever smile?"

He looked surprised. "I don't think so. It's finished now." He drew his eyebrows down still farther while he considered this. "No, it has nothing to do with anything like that. I think it's—well, what are some of the reasons people smile? To be ingratiating or apologetic or accommodating or congenial? I'm not often any of those things."

"Pleased?"

"I think I take most of my pleasures too seriously for easy smiling. You please me, for instance. So do Rilke's *Letters to a Young Poet* and Benét's *Litany for Dictatorships*. None jerk me into instant smiles." He paused, looked out through the glass at the stragglers along the boulevard and back at her again. "I rejected my family a long time ago. While I was still living at home. My mother was a well-meaning woman who said the wrong thing every time she opened her mouth. My father was a harsh man with no liking for children and no idea how to handle them. I have an older sister whose only concern was to get out of the house as soon as she could find someone to marry her. She and I never knew each other. None of us ever knew each other. I escaped into books and writing and a few good friends I made in school, and got out too, as soon as I could. My parents were always poor, but now I'm able to send them money, and clippings to show I'm a success. If they had me for any reason other than mindless convention, it was for that. So we're quits."

"That's sad."

"Most of it is commonplace."

They left finally. The Métro had long since closed down for the night. He took her across to her apartment on the Right Bank in a taxi, insisted on it, and then kept the taxi to take him back to where he lived, on the Ile St. Louis. She had half expected that he would want to come in with her and that she would have trouble handling him because she had told him so many intimate things. But he made no attempt even to kiss her.

"What time can you meet me at the café tomorrow?" he asked her.

They met there nearly every day at one o'clock, after she had had her necessary sleep and he had finished his morning's writing. For weeks, he scarcely touched her. Then one night—one morning, actually; it was three o'clock—she got home from the bureau and found him waiting for her, leaning against her door with his hands in his pockets, scowling at her as she got off the elevator.

"I couldn't sleep," he said. "I want to stay here with you tonight."

"All right," she said.

That September day, with the warm sun spilling prodigally across the city, they had been lovers for nearly two years. Usually they went to his apartment now, because it was closer to the Café Cluny, where they still met almost daily. Now and then he spent the night with her on the Rue St. Lazare, but it was not very satisfactory. If they slept long enough to be rested, he missed the best part of his working day. If he left early, he woke her too (she was a light sleeper and could never get back after he had gone), and neither of them was good for much the rest of the day.

Steve wanted her to give up her job and come and live with him on the Ile St. Louis and finish her novel. They agreed about most things, but they argued about this all the time. His anger was not the kind she was used to, or would have expected from his fierce Indian look. There was no heat in it, only an icy remoteness that she could not have endured if it had lasted. It never did. He unfroze as swiftly as Mother recovered from her screaming rages, took her hungrily in his arms as though he had been a long time away from her, and told her they must stop doing this to each other. But they kept doing it.

Clara had a number of reasons for opposing him, but she was not sure which of them were real. She had been ready to leave the Paper before she came to Paris, but she did not feel she could leave it now, from here; walk out on Mother, was the way she thought of it, when she was three thousand miles away and there was nothing Mother could do about it. Besides, if she quit her job she would have to live off Steve while she was finishing her novel—or longer if the novel was no good, was never published, made no money. That was distasteful to her. No matter what Steve said, she could not help thinking of such an arrangement as being kept.

Besides, his apartment was too small. One of them would have to work in the bedroom or the kitchen. Everything would always be in a mess, and they would fall over each other. Her apartment would be worse: it was what the French called a *studio*, one room with a minute kitchenette. There was no question of moving to a larger place. Apartments were almost impossible to find, even at the inflationary prices that were only now, with the help of America's European Recovery Act, beginning to level out.

"I had another letter from Mother this morning, asking me to come home. Begging me, really." Clara had avoided telling him this in the café. It was not a subject to bring up before making love. "She's never done that before. It's harder to handle than a demand."

"Why? Is it anything more than another face of the same coin?"

"Probably not, but—" She settled her head into the hollow between his shoulder and his breastbone. "You know I can't be strictly rational about Mother."

They were lying on his big double bed, covered by a quilt he had made by sewing together four of the little French quilts that seem designed to cover no one larger than a baby. She had never known a man who sewed. It surprised him that she should comment on it. Skills, he said, had no gender.

She had wondered about the size of the bed in a room that was hard to get around because of it. Not that she thought, or hoped, he had been celibate between his marriage and her. But he was not a man for casual sex. "I'm an all-or-nothing person too," he had said to her that time she had found him waiting outside her door to spend the night with her. Whoever had slept beside him in this bed had been important to him. This was one thing they had not told each other about themselves, a taboo agreed on without the need to mention it.

"Well, as long as you have no intention of going back," he was saying now, "you can be as irrational as you like."

"I'll have to go back sometime."

She had no idea why she had said that. It was true, but not imminent, and it could only start one of their arguments. She was not even sure it *was* true.

But he was not disposed to argue this time. "Your mother and I should meet," he said. "It would be interesting. She must have as inaccurate an impression of me as I probably have of her."

Mother had written that she had heard Clara was seeing a lot of a particular man. How she had heard it, Clara could not imagine. Hester swore she had said nothing to anyone.

"What would I say? That you met someone here that you've seen again since? What more do I know? Your mother's a *Hexe*," Hester said. "She finds out everything."

"Is it serious?" Mother had written. "Is he Jewish?"

That had amused Clara so much—that old question from her childhood—that she had told it to Steve. They had been walking on an early-December afternoon and were standing on the Pont du Carrousel, looking down the river at the marvel of Notre Dame.

"That reminds me," Clara said, and chuckled. "My mother wants to know whether you're Jewish."

It was windy on the bridge. They were standing close together, their arms around each other. "Why?"

"It's something Jewish mothers ask their children. It doesn't matter whether they're little mamas in *sheitels*, or publishers of newspapers."

They began walking again, their arms still around each other. "My mother never asked me," he said. "Or if she did, I didn't hear her. I started young not hearing her."

"This is a funny thing," Clara said, after a silence. "All those years of growing up with the question every time I met anybody new—like a litany—yet it never once came into my head until I got that letter. About you, I mean. And when it did, I assumed you weren't. I don't know why. Maybe because otherwise it would be too—well, pat."

"Pat?"

"Nice Jewish girl in Paris meets nice Jewish boy in Paris."

"You had reason to suspect me, you know."

"What? Oh, that. Yes. But these days that isn't conclusive. And I wasn't thinking about it anyway. Not at all. The whole business of dividing people up into little categories makes me sick."

"Especially when one of the categories gets stuffed into gas ovens."

She glanced up at him. He looked no angrier than usual. "Did you feel more strongly because they were Jews than if they'd been Christians or Moslems?"

"Probably," he said after a moment. "No more outraged, but sadder. A little. I've never really been a Jew. I've never been anything. But during the war I even went to temple now and then."

"That's like my uncle who thought of converting to please his Episcopalian wife but wouldn't do it until after the war. My Uncle Walter, my father's brother. He was once married to Hester, so he's my granduncle too."

She began telling him about Walter, which put an end to the other subject. But she wrote and told mother that she could relax, because the man was Jewish all right. Clara did not say whether or not it was serious, because serious to her was not the same thing as serious to Mother.

"The only way you'll meet her," Clara said to Steve now, "is if you go over there. She'll never come here. She could. The Paper would go on functioning perfectly well if she weren't there for a few weeks. She's the one who organized it so it isn't dependent on any one person. But she can't bear being away from it."

"Even for a wedding?"

Clara did not move. Then she sat up, pulling a corner of the quilt around her bare shoulders. It was colder in the apartment than in the sunny streets. "What wedding are you talking about?"

"Ours." He clasped his hands in back of his head and examined the ceiling. "It's insane to live this way. You know I've always thought so. I want you in my bed all night. I want to eat my meals with you. I want to share a life with you, not snatched hours, like guilty lovers who have no right to each other."

"But, Steve—" She had to stop and begin again. "Steve, this is nothing new. Why suddenly, now, are you talking about a—a wedding?"

"It isn't sudden. The night we met, and talked so much about ourselves in the café—" He turned his face toward her. "Remember?"

"I remember."

"That night," he said, looking back at the ceiling, "I knew that if I could ever think of marrying again, you would be the woman." He paused. "I'd like to have a child before I'm too old to be a suitable father. Your child."

She pushed the palms of her hands against her lids. "Steve, in three years I'll be forty."

"Women well past forty have children. You're built for it. You're strong and healthy."

"Oh, Lord!" She began to giggle. In a minute, if she was not careful, the tears and the giggling would both get away from her. "You make me sound like a horse. No, a mare." He said nothing. He was waiting. She drew up her knees and put her head down on them until she could talk calmly. "The problems are still the same. The Paper, a place to live—especially if there would be a—a baby—"

"No," he broke in sharply. "There are no problems. None. You'll leave the Paper. Your mother will reconcile herself to it, especially if you're getting married. We'll live here until we can get into a larger place. Even if that isn't until after the baby comes, we'll manage. You'll work on your novel. I have only a few more months' work on my book, and I won't start the new one right away. I can help you with the cooking, the baby, whatever needs to be done—"

"And I have nothing to say about it?"

"You do. You have a choice. You can marry me, or we can stop seeing each other. I don't want to continue this way. It's a travesty."

She lay down on her stomach and rested her cheek against the furry black hair of his chest. "You're saying what the woman is supposed to say," she murmured. "*I can't go on like this. Marry me, or else.* It's blackmail."

"Blackmail be damned. I have to live my love, that's all. If you don't, it's something less than I thought, or want."

"Marriage never entered my head. Any more than whether or not you were Jewish."

"Never entered your head?"

She had not let it. She had had enough of nourishing herself on fantasy. Her life with Steve had been no helpless acceptance, but her own choice. "It's too unexpected," she said. "You'll have to give me time to think about it."

She could feel the deep rumble of his "No" under her ear. "If you need time, it's no good. Time for what? To weigh me in the balance? No."

"You're pushing me. I don't want to be pushed."

He said nothing. He lay without moving, not touching her.

"I don't know what I think I'm doing," she said finally, in the almost inaudible voice. "The answer is yes. Of course yes, I'll marry you. Yes." She lifted her head to look at him. "You were sure I would."

"And now I'm triumphant?" He took her face between his large hands. "You've learned some wrong things about love."

Even on a blustery evening, it was an easy walk from Rue St. Lazare, where Clara lived, to Rue Caumartin, where she worked. All the way, she kept rewriting in her mind the letter she had begun on paper at four o'clock that morning.

> *My experience over here hasn't changed my mind about the Paper. I don't feel that just because I have Herzog blood, it's what I must devote my life to, any more than Samuel, for different reasons, felt he had to. I know it's what I once thought I wanted to do more than anything else, but that was partly because of some idealistic notions I had about the function of a newspaper. My disillusionment has nothing to do with you . . .*

No, that was no good. Mother would not believe it had nothing to do with her. Whatever Clara wrote in that vein would be wrong. She had better start with Steve.

Steven Miller, who wrote "The King's First Minister." He's finishing a book about De Gaulle now, and he has a contract for a new one on André Malraux, who has been the source of a lot of his material for the De Gaulle book and is a fascinating figure himself. Obviously Steve will have to continue living in France for the time being, and since my hours in the bureau here are so . . .

That wouldn't do either. It would take something more emotional than a recital of facts to appeal to Mother. If it was possible to appeal to her at all on the subject of quitting the Paper and staying in Paris.

He's the man I met at Hester's and have been seeing ever since. Steven Miller, the well-known writer. I didn't want to tell you about him until I was sure something would come of it. Now he's asked me to marry him and I've accepted. I'm very much in love with him, Mother, and I know you'd agree he's right for me. Since we're not young, we want to have a baby as soon as possible, so of course I'll have to leave the Paper, at least temporarily . . .

No, even Mother would gag at that. It sounded like a soap opera. She could put nothing into words for Mother to read that would not cheapen or distort what she felt for Steve. And she was not going to suggest that she might return to the Paper in time. It would only give Mother hopes Clara had no intention of fulfilling.

The letter was as far from taking satisfactory shape when she reached the building that housed the Paper's Paris Bureau as when she had left her apartment.

It was a small office building of stone, dingy gray with ancient city soil. The Paper occupied the third floor. There was an elevator, but like all Paris elevators, it functioned only when it felt like it, which was not often. This evening the usual dirty white card that said L'ASCENSEUR NE MARCHE PAS was stuck in the door. Clara trudged up the steep stairs, greeted the French receptionist in the outer office, and entered a miniature, shabbier version of the New York newsroom, with three short rows of desks and two glassed-in cubicles, one for the bureau chief and one for her assistant.

Maggie Prout was back at her desk after two weeks of interviews in eight countries where the North Atlantic Treaty had gone into effect at the end of August. The door of her cubicle was open.

"*Soyez la bienvenue!*" Clara said, sticking her head in. "*Comment ça va?*"

Maggie shrugged. She was large, dowdy, a little foolish-looking; a Helen Hokinson cartoon of a middle-aged, busty clubwoman; and one of the cleverest journalists in the business. Her French was fluent, but she made no concessions whatever to the appropriate accent, speaking every word in her native flat Midwesternese. "*Couci-couça,*" she said. "All this traipsing around the world is bad for my liver." She had lived in France so long that she had assimilated the French obsession with livers. "God knows what's in the water in those countries!"

"Come on, Maggie, you love traipsing around the world," Clara said. "Any excuse will do. Like getting reactions to NATO. As if you didn't know what they were before you went."

"Knew but could not quote, my girl. The American public, as only a partially baked journalist could fail to realize, is crazy about quotes. If I write that the Italian Communists hate NATO, our readers will pay it no mind. But if I write, *Signor Belloni says, 'The North Atlantic Treaty is a provocative act directed against the Soviet Union,'* they'll eat it up. I'm just some lines of print, but Signor Belloni is a real person saying real words."

"Gee!" Clara said. "Will I have to be old, too, before I learn all that?"

Maggie balled up a sheet of paper and threw it at her. "Get out of here and get to work or I'll string you up by your heels in the outer office, as an example to smart-ass newspaperwomen."

Clara waggled her fingers close to her nose and went to her own desk. She said good morning to the others on the way. Saying good morning at five in the evening was the same as calling the evening meal "lunch" on a New York morning newspaper. Humor among journalists tended to be either heavy-handed, childish, or obscene. Clara's working relationship with Maggie was a matter of silly, faintly barbed badinage, balanced with respect for her chief's talents, and laced with good reporting.

It had not been easy. Maggie had not needed or wanted another reporter on her staff, least of all one who probably had no qualifications except that she was the publisher's daughter. She could have been sent as much to snoop around and report back to her mother as to do a job. Clara had been under that kind of suspicion at the Washington Bureau too. There were always things to be uncovered if someone was looking for them, inefficiencies, irregularities, people whose eccentricities might appear inexcusable to an outsider.

If Clara had had Mother's instant magnetism, no doubt she could have charmed Maggie out of her obvious hostility. Clara simply endured it, accepted trivial assignments, worked to make something of them, and kept her mouth shut. She had come to Paris on the understanding with Mother that it was a trial, that she would not stay if she was dissatisfied. Those first months were miserable, but she did not think of leaving, not while Maggie wished she would.

After she met Steve, she bought some new clothes. "I like your suit," Maggie said to her one day. "Did you get it here?"

A few days later she expressed mild approval of something Clara had written.

"I think the war's over," Clara told Steve. "It's been a long siege."

He had not understood why she had gone through it. He had wondered, also, why Maggie had not been afraid Clara would complain and Mother would retaliate. Only someone who knew Mother and was aware of the complex politics and relationships that operated on the Paper could have realized how safe Maggie was even if Clara had chosen to complain. Maggie was not only the best type of foreign correspondent—a linguist, a scholar in the field of foreign affairs, and a fine writer—but she was shrewd enough to pretend humility in her dealings with the editors back in New York. Other bureau chiefs might ignore all directives from home and behave like prima donnas, but Maggie gave no trouble. Only Mother could have induced her superiors in New York to replace her, and it was Mother's unvarying policy not to interfere.

Clara had seen good journalists shunted aside because they did not know how to play on people in power, and incompetent ones pushed ahead because they did. It was part of her disillusionment with the Paper. But Maggie belonged where she was. When she assigned Clara to cover the Berlin airlift, and said of Clara's story about the end of the Russian blockade that she could not have written it better herself, Clara told Steve she felt as though she had won a Pulitzer.

That had been in May, four months back. It had taken all that time to get on a firm, insult-swapping footing with Maggie, and now Clara was going to leave. Well, no experience was a waste for a writer. Outlasting Maggie's antagonism would get into some story sometime, in one form or another.

She sat down at her desk and began working on a piece she was writing about the long-term effects of the Marshall Plan on the French economy. Since she knew little about economics, she was dealing with that aspect in only general terms. Instead her focus was on the thankless role of a beneficent United States, saving not only France but Europe as well as the United Kingdom from economic disaster, and being thoroughly detested for it. She quoted La Rochefoucauld, who had said that a man who was ungrateful was sometimes less to blame for it than his benefactor, but Maggie would probably take that out. Fitz had never entirely cured her of her tendency toward what he had called "fancy digressions."

Why was she thinking of Fitz? But it was better than thinking of Steve, because if she thought of Steve and what he had asked of her and what she had agreed to, she would get no work done.

Several of the desks around her were empty. One of the reporters was in the American Hospital, recovering from an appendectomy. Another was vacationing in Provence. Another had staggered in late, made a few stabs at his typewriter, and gradually sunk lower and lower in his chair until he was on the floor. Somebody had heaved him up and dragged him a couple of blocks to the Hotel Scribe, delivering him to the night porter. Since this happened on the average of once a week, it was fortunate that he was a small man. It was also fortunate, for him, that he was a first-class reporter. Otherwise Maggie would have had him left on the floor to be swept out.

The tension of the New York newsroom was not in evidence here. Telephones rang infrequently. Copy boys did not rush through the room. Nobody banged frantically at the typewriter, sweating to make a deadline. There was no deadline. None of the stories that the reporters were working on would be dispatched that night. Nothing that was going on in Europe at the moment could compete in news value with the astounding possibility that there really were traitors in the State Department in Washington.

Clara finished her report on the effects of the European Recovery Act and went home early. She got to bed before one, but it was daylight before she slept.

Steve is eager to meet you, and naturally we both want you here for our wedding. I can't imagine getting married without you. I can't, really, imagine getting married at all, after so many years of thinking I never would. I'm not troubled by any doubts about Steve, or about our belonging together, but I'm a little scared just the same. Marriage is so . . .

2

Although Clara had not slept until daylight, she was awake again before eleven. As soon as she had had her breakfast, she sat down at her desk and tried once more to write the letter to Mother. It was ridiculous to be having so much trouble. All her life she had written letters to Mother about everything, and now she could not find the right words to tell her the three simple facts that she was leaving the Paper, getting married, and staying in Paris.

"Of course they won't be simple facts to Mother," she said to Hester later. "No matter how I put it, she'll read things into it that aren't there."

"In that case, why agonize over it?"

"I don't know. I suppose I want to feel I did the best I could not to hurt her."

They were having coffee in Hester's apartment, a terrible brew that she made out of a French grind lavishly laced with chicory, and pressed on everyone under the delusion that this was her one culinary triumph. Clara was not meeting Steve at the café, but going straight to his place from here. He had been vague on the phone about this change in routine. When he was especially caught up in what he was writing, he was often vague, immersed in the world that emerged from his typewriter and absent from the real one. Clara understood how that was.

"She'll be all right. She'll get over it," Hester said. "She always gets over it, whatever it is."

"Yes, I know. I'm behaving like an idiot." Clara held her breath and swallowed a sip of the poisonous coffee. "I even feel guilty about telling you before I've told her."

Hester screwed a cigarette into a long, old-fashioned holder. She seldom dressed until evening, but what she had on—something in garnet velvet that flowed to the floor—was more court robe than negligee. With Mother, Clara always felt too commonplace in her clothes. With Hester, she felt too serviceable.

"Guilt," Hester said. "You know the necklaces grandparents often give to babies? They start with one pearl, and another is added each year until the string is complete? Some people wear such necklaces all their lives, adding stones instead of pearls, until they sag under the weight." She blew a puff of smoke toward the ceiling. "That metaphor didn't just come to me, in case you're wondering. I've given considerable thought to guilt in my time."

"Is there a way to take the necklace off?"

"If you can find the clasp— Oh, let's not carry this too far, for heaven's sake! You're engaged to be married and we're harping on stone necklaces. We ought to be celebrating, drinking a toast. There's half a bottle of sparkling wine in the refrigerator—just the thing."

Clara got the wine and glasses and they drank to the marriage. After the second glass, Clara felt she would no longer have difficulty with the letter to Mother. If she had a chance, she would write it this evening in the office and mail it on her way home.

"I don't think I've ever thanked you for bringing Steve and me together. I thank you now."

"It wasn't my doing. I'm not the matchmaker type. In fact, I shudder to think of the responsibility. No, it was happenstance. Fate, if one believes in the chessboard theory, which I reject."

"Of course you do. What Herzog would admit to helplessness?"

"Well, that's something else. When I was young, I thought I could make life happen, mold it to my heart's desire. I was wrong, but I don't think Fate had much to do with it. As Cassius said to Brutus, the fault isn't in our stars. It's in ourselves."

"That's only putting the same thing in another way. You're saying you couldn't control your own life, but you want to think the failure was under your direction. I wouldn't like to feel helpless either. But there must be a kind of comfort in it."

"And that could bring us full circle to guilt again, which we weren't going to discuss any more." Hester flicked ashes into her coffee cup, a practice that had always made Mother shudder. "A young French painter brought Steven here the first time, you know; recognized him in a café from a book-jacket photograph and dragged him along to me, wearing him like a rosette in his buttonhole."

"I can't imagine anyone dragging Steve anyplace he didn't want to be dragged."

"Well, he said he had no desire to come. Some pretentious old American woman, I believe he thought, imagining herself another

Madame de Staël. I suspect he was being kind to the Frenchman. He told me he'd intended to stay a polite twenty minutes, but he was here for hours, and came back the following week. The night you met him was his third visit."

"Yes, he told me. It was you he came for, not the others. I think he wants to marry me to make sure you don't escape him."

"I think he wants to marry you because he's a wise and discerning young man. He took one look at you when you came in and asked me who you were."

"You mean you didn't tell him to come over and rescue your poor niece who has trouble with entrances?"

"Good Lord! That's the kind of thing some of those bitches in Washington used to do when they wanted to kill a man's interest in another woman. I mentioned, as he started toward you, that you were still at the stage in French where everyone talking it at once bewildered you. That explained your lost look—which has its charms, incidentally, in case no one has ever told you so—without diminishing you."

Clara leaned over and kissed Hester's cheek. Her skin had a soft fragility not evident in anything else about her. Clara found it somehow touching. "You've always done the opposite of diminishing me." She sat back. "But I don't understand. The first thing Steve said to me was in French. Why, I wonder, after you told him I had trouble with it."

"Ah, can't you see the delicacy, Clara? The ordinary man would have spoken English to make you comfortable. He spoke French. A clear, understandable French, surely."

"Yes," Clara said. "Yes." She smiled up at the ceiling. "An ordinary man. I never thought he was that." She was silent a moment. "I wish Grandma could have known him."

It was a little after two when she left. She walked over to the river and strolled along the *quais*. The weather was still warm and sunny. All the *bouquinistes* had their stalls open, all displaying the same posters and color prints, old maps and dusty secondhand books that smelled of mildew. Below, on the bank of the Seine, a few fishermen sat with their long poles, watching the river or dozing, never catching anything. A *clocharde*, dressed in layers of ragged clothes, undoubtedly her entire wardrobe, had made a nest of newspapers under one of the bridges, and perched on it stoically with all her scruffy possessions around her. An occasional barge or pleasure boat glided along the still water, momentarily shattering the reflection of buildings that shimmered in golden light along the opposite bank.

At this hour, the streets were quiet. Parisians were still at their long lunches; most of them, even the businessmen, eating at home. No one hurried. It was hard to believe that only a few years before, these peaceful streets had erupted with gunshots and streamed with blood. But the bullet gouges were still visible in the stone of the buildings. And all along, engraved in the stone or on metal plaques, were the little memorials, many bearing a shelf with a vase of faded flowers, attesting to the bravery of Jean or Pierre or Paul, 20 or 23 or 24, who had fallen on that spot fighting for the liberation of Paris.

Clara crossed the river at the Pont de l'Archevêché, where she could see Notre Dame from the rear. It was, to her mind, the best view of the cathedral, its magnificent flying buttresses like a thrust of wings against the sky. She had tried to write a piece about it once, but everything she could think of to say had been said before. Reduced to words, or even pictures, the Cathedral of Notre Dame was a cliché. Steve, who had been to India, said the same of the Taj Mahal.

"I very nearly didn't go to Agra at all," he had told her. "A long trip to see some calendar art that every two-bit travel writer has mooned over. But then there it was, and nothing anyone has ever said about it or painted or photographed is true. If there is such a thing as objective beauty—a thing in the eye of all beholders through time and space—I think the Taj Mahal must be it. So of course it's a cliché. Unless, of course, you leave it alone and just look at it."

She had to cross another small bridge to reach the Ile St. Louis, and then walk down the Rue St. Louis en L'Ile to Steve's apartment. The concierge peered out from her curtained quarters just inside the front door, wearing the suspicious frown indigenous to concierges. When she saw it was Clara, her native approval of romance produced a nod. To get a smile, Clara thought it would have had to be a French romance.

Steve's apartment was on the first floor (the second floor, as Americans counted floors). Clara climbed the stairs, her heart racing expectantly. As a child she had often squealed with excitement over some imminent delight, a release that seemed needed to prevent her from exploding. Though she had learned to contain it, she was still capable of that intensity of anticipation.

"There are enjoyers and disenjoyers," Steve had said to her once. "You're an enjoyer."

"Disenjoyers!"

"That's right. These are my own categories. Disenjoyers are people who have no use for joy. If it seems inescapable, they kill themselves. Don't look so incredulous. What about Richard Cory? We're not told why he went home and put a bullet through his head, but possibly it was for the same reason some people in real life do it at the peak of their success. That much joy is alien to their natures, unmanageable. On the other hand, given enough for their basic needs, enjoyers enjoy. They may be interrupted, but never stopped. Nothing can stop them for long. Their enjoyment is built in."

"Which are you?"

"I'm an enjoyer too, of course. That's important. The one thing that can change an enjoyer into a disenjoyer is to team up with one."

"Why shouldn't it work the other way around?"

"The disenjoyers are too powerful. Their allies are everywhere. So be warned. Stick with me, and enjoy."

Clara rang Steve's bell. The door opened so quickly that she thought he must have been standing there listening for her. His face took on its special look of pleasure: the eyes narrowing, seeming to lift the corners of the mouth with the same muscles. "What are you amused about?" He drew her inside. "Or is that a smile of greeting?"

"I was thinking about enjoyers and disenjoyers."

He took her coat and hung it on a hook on the wall near the door. She was aware of something strange in him, a kind of nervous randomness to his movements, as though he were dancing around her. Ordinarily he pulled her into his arms the moment she stepped through the door, but he had not yet kissed her.

"What's the matter, Steve? You're acting funny."

"Am I? Yes I don't doubt I am. Come on in."

She followed him from the dark little hall into the room where he worked, ate, and entertained his friends. It was furnished for utility and comfort with the hideous, bulky, nondescript pieces sold in most Paris furniture stores. No curtains or draperies hung at the two windows that overlooked the river; only *volets*, inside shutters that could be closed against noise or adjusted to shut out the glare of the sun. Directly in front of them stood a low table holding an ancient portable typewriter, and next to it a larger table piled with books and a thick sheaf of papers. A partially typed sheet was in the typewriter.

Steve habitually left the portion he was working on unfinished, charged with momentum for the next session. His chair was placed so that while he worked he faced the room, not the distracting Seine.

"How did it go today?" She always asked him that.

"I haven't done much. I went out." He gave her a little push. "Sit down. Here. This chair, any chair . . . All right."

"Steve." She looked up at him, laughing. "What is it? I've never seen you like this."

"That's all right. Just—I think you'd better close your eyes . . . Yes . . . Now you can open them."

He was watching her with his fierce stare, holding something out to her. She looked down at his big hand. He had on his open palm a ring of dull gold, intricately twisted around an inset of small pearls. It had a solid look, and at the same time great delicacy.

"How beautiful!" Clara touched it with one finger, like a child who has been cautioned to be careful. "How very beautiful!"

"Do you like it?" He closed his fist over the ring, as though he meant to keep it from her. "Here. Give me your hand. Let me put it on." His booming voice softened. "Not that hand. Don't you know what it's for?"

"You mean—?"

"Yes, of course. Maybe you think it's all foolishness, but I believe in symbols. I believe in rites and myths and all the other inventions that bind what is to what was and what will be. I—" He stopped and pushed the ring on her finger. "There. It fits, doesn't it? I was afraid it might not. I saw it a week ago. I was afraid it might be gone when I went for it today. Then, when it wasn't, I was afraid you might not like it. You'd have pretended to, of course, but you're a poor pretender—"

She had never known him to be this vulnerable except in the helplessness of passion. It moved her so that she could not speak, only look from the ring to his angry Indian face and back again.

"It's very old," he said. "They told me it once belonged to a lady in the first Napoleon's court. An apocryphal story, probably, but I choose to believe it. I choose to imagine it was the lady's betrothal ring, and that her marriage was happy, as ours will be." Abruptly he reached for her and drew her up into his arms. "Don't mind my nonsense," he murmured into her hair. "I deal so much with figures that are larger than life. They tend to give me too strong a sense of occasion."

326

"No. I won't have you calling it nonsense."

"All right, I won't then. Let's go inside."

Afterward, he gave her tea. A fan in England had sent him an exotic assortment, which he was working through gradually. They were Churchill's favorites, according to the fan, though in all his interviews and research for his book, Steve had encountered no mention of Churchill's preferences in tea.

"They must all be vastly different to an educated palate," Steve said. "Mine doesn't understand the subtleties involved."

They were sitting at one end of his work table, the teapot before them. Steve had wrapped a dish towel around it to keep in the heat. He wore, in place of a shirt, the blue cotton garment, something between a blouse and a jacket, that had been worn for generations by the French workingman. His scorn for the appurtenances of success pleased Clara. They would live simply, bring up their child to ornament his life with grace, not things . . .

"Everybody must expect their marriage to be happy." She stared down into the tea leaves at the bottom of her cup. "Everybody must, at the start."

"But why should they? People take marriage like a pill to cure yearning or loneliness or childlessness or curiosity or the pity of their friends or whatever other pains unmarried life imposes. Why should they expect it to provide happiness too? Automatically. A panacea."

"You said ours—"

"Yes. We need each other for completeness, not escape. Husbands and wives hack pieces out of each other, trying to fill up their own gaps. You and I will be builders. We need each other whole." He paused. She did not look up, but she knew his eyes were on her. "Have you written to your mother?"

She longed to say she had. The letter would be on its way in a few hours, and he would never have to know how cowardly she was.

"I'm writing today."

He said nothing. She glanced at him. Now it was he who was staring into his cup. In disappointment? Anger? When he spoke, his voice showed neither. "Please," he said. "Today without fail. It will be long enough as it is, waiting for your mother's answer and then, if she's coming, waiting for her to arrive. I always thought I was a patient man. I find I'm not."

"I don't think she'll come. She'll want us to go there, to bring Hester, and have a big wedding. No, not big necessarily, but important. It wouldn't be for show, or for herself, but for me. Because I'm —a kind of crown princess, I suppose."

She could not have said what changed in that glowering face to signify tenderness, but it was manifest. "To think how unlovable you might have become, and how endearing you are," he said.

When she left him she felt heavy with love, as if with a child in her womb. Sitting at her desk on the Rue Caumartin, she tried to translate this for Mother, but when she read it back, it only sounded sexual, with none of the uniqueness of Steve, of Steve and her together. She pulled the sheet out of the typewriter, crumpled it up and threw it in the basket and then fished it out and tore it into small pieces. She did not believe the rumor that Maggie went around after everyone had left and examined the discarded miscellany in their wastebaskets. Still—

"Don't tell me you're writing a novel too!"

It was Maggie now, looming over her desk, arrived in the noiseless way very large people often have.

"No, a letter to my mother. The novel is in my desk at home, aging a lot faster than it grows. Do you want something, or are you just snooping?"

"Snooping. I'd as soon you didn't let Becky know you have nothing better to do than write letters during working hours. A picture of frenzied activity is what I want to give her." Maggie tucked a straggle of hair back behind her ear. In a moment it would escape again. "That piece you wrote about De Gaulle is pretty good, incidentally. I don't know whether I can use it, but it's pretty good. Who's your source?"

Clara grinned. Steve had given her an angle for an article that would not conflict with his book on De Gaulle, but she had no intention of telling this to Maggie. She had learned as a young reporter to keep her contacts to herself. Learned it from Fitz, who trusted no one and taught her not to trust everyone.

"I never reveal my sources," she said.

"Oh, poof! What do you think I'm going to do? Steal them from you?"

"In this particular case, you wouldn't stand a chance. But if it were important enough to you, I wouldn't put it past you to try."

Maggie tittered: a silly, small sound from that ample chest. "You boost my morale, Clara, you really do. I don't know how I ever got along without you."

328

Clara waited until Maggie was back in her cubicle before she rolled another sheet of paper into her typewriter. This time she made no attempt to describe her relationship with Steve beyond the banality that they loved each other. She was no more inventive with the rest of it. All to the good, probably. The more artless, the less Mother could read into it. She sealed and stamped the letter, ready to drop in the box on her way home.

But she did not drop it in the box. She wanted to read it over one more time first. This was something she did with everything she wrote. Read it over and over before she finally let it go. Usually she made changes at each reading, but sometimes not. Sometimes she just wanted to see it again, without knowing exactly why. She would have to take the letter home so she could steam it open and save the envelope with all the stamps, but as soon as she read it once more she would come out again and mail it. There was a box a block away from where she lived. The letter would not go out any later than if she mailed it now.

Clara's *studio* was three flights up. If the concierge felt like it, she brought the mail up. Otherwise she left it on a table in the lobby. There was nothing on the table now. One letter was pushed half under Clara's door, as though grudgingly. Clara could see the U.S. stamps. At the possibility that it was from Mother again, another plea or importunity so soon after the last, she yanked it out in irritation, almost tearing the envelope.

The handwriting was strange. She turned over the vellum envelope and saw Samuel's name and address on the back. To her recollection, Samuel had never written to her in her life. She had never even seen his signature on a check. For birthdays and other occasions, he had delighted her with carefully selected gifts of marvelous appropriateness to both her age and individuality. At four, a huge, comforting plush dog; at eleven, a first baseman's mitt; at sixteen, a perfume with the wicked name *Vierge Folle*. He had been a storybook uncle, handsome, charming, and witty, treating her with grave courtesy from babyhood, compensating wholly for David's failure in the role.

Hannah wanted me to telephone, he wrote, *but I feel that would be too raw and difficult for both of us, and there isn't quite that much urgency . . .*

Clara skimmed the letter before reading it through carefully line by line. She did not know she held her breath until it knifed her chest.

We've kept it from her. The doctor thinks that's kindest and we agree. A virus-caused weakness in the lung, he told her, necessitating rest and treatment for an indeterminate time. She must therefore make the same kinds of arrangements for the Paper as though she knew, and Hannah and I could think of no other reason to cause her the mental anguish of an irrevocable sentence. You may decide otherwise when you get here. Yours, needless to say, is the final word . . .

Clara sat in a chair beside the window, waiting for daylight. Once, she went to the kitchenette and made coffee, hoping vainly that it might warm her. Once, she rose to tear up the letter she had written in the office, destroying the stamps as well, because she did not feel it fitting to engage in the triviality of taking them off the envelope. Once, she fell asleep for an hour or so, and woke to guilty astonishment at her body's callousness. At six she made more coffee and forced down a slice of toast. She called Steve at seven and Hester at eight. At ten, after she had returned from the airline office, she called Steve again, and then Maggie. Then she packed.

"I wish we could have been married before you left," Steve said. "This way, I'm afraid—" He stopped.

"Afraid of what?"

"Nothing. You've enough to concern you without any of my fretting. Come back, that's all."

They were in the airport waiting room. In the seat next to Steve, a woman who looked almost as shabby as the *clocharde* Clara had seen the day before under the bridge poked distractedly into an overflowing cretonne bag. The well-dressed young woman beside Clara sat with her hands folded rigidly in her lap, staring straight ahead. An elderly couple walked back and forth, arm in arm, prattling like excited ducks. Several children ran around the bundles and suitcases on the floor, as though in an obstacle race, watched wide-eyed by a sedate small boy in short gray-flannel pants. Periodically, the chatter of voices rose in competition with the roar of propellers as a plane arrived or took off. "Of course I'll come back."

He leaned his head down to her, so close that his coarse black hair tickled her nose. "What?"

"Of course I'll be back. What do you think? As soon as—" She

330

choked, unable to finish. How could she make it seem a matter for impatience?

"Yes," he said, and stroked her hand. "I'll bury myself in work. I'll leave your shadow at our table at Cluny and find another café in the interim."

"Will you write to me every day? I will to you."

He shook his head. "I'm not good at letters. That's something I thought I could keep from you. Preposterous, isn't it? For a writer? I can make other people's lives vivid, but when I try to tell my own, it all dribbles away into commonplaces."

"I'll love your commonplaces."

"Let me send you a postcard every day. Nothing is expected of a postcard. Whatever it says, you'll understand the words that don't appear."

When she walked away from him, across the field to the waiting plane, it seemed to her she could feel the pull at her back, hear the tearing sound.

So layered over that she barely recognized it, something else stirred —a sense of reprieve, was it, from the finality Steve wanted of her?

3

She must have been about four, because she was small enough for Mother to pick up and hold while she ran around the bed, and yet old enough to ask, "Are you crazy, Mommy?"

She could not remember when she had started calling her "Mother."

"Are you crazy, Mommy?"

"No, baby, no. Don't cry. It's all right."

Someone else must have been there, chasing Mother around the bed. Surely not Albert, who, according to Mother, had adored her those first years, thought of her as a goddess. Could it have been Clara's real father, the meek, shrinking, faceless man Mother hoped Clara would not take after? She only remembered Mother snatching her up and holding her, gasping and sobbing and running, black hair straggling, eyes wild, the nightgown against Clara's cheek smelling of Mother and bed. Maybe it was a dream.

Afterward, tucked in again, she lay in the dark and heard them shouting at each other. Or maybe that was part of another night. Sometimes it was the noise of something being thrown that woke her. Once it was the smashing of the glass in the top half of the bathroom door. It must have been some years later that she began wondering whether it would be worse if Albert killed Mother or if she killed him and had to die for it. A child of four, even a precocious one, would not have wondered that.

She could read at four, and write a little. Fräulein taught her. Fräulein Mitzi Leschner. She was small and thin, but with a big soft bosom (*bossum* was the way Clara thought it was pronounced) and several stiff blond hairs growing out of a mole on her cheek. When Mother and Albert went out in the evening, she stayed all night, sleeping on the daybed in Clara's room. Otherwise, after Clara was in bed, she went home to some unimaginable place where Fräuleins lived. She liked to eat something called "clabber," which she made by leaving a bowl of milk on the warm top of a closet until it got sour and thick.

Mitzi Leschner was the first Fräulein Clara remembered, the first of a long series of Fräuleins and Mademoiselles. She loved Clara and Clara loved her. The nights she stayed and slept in Clara's room, Mother and Albert did not fight, or anyway not loud enough for Fräulein to hear. When she was not there, she was one of the things they fought about.

"Why the hell does a child that age need a fancy German governess? Can't you understand I don't have that kind of money? Why the hell don't you get her an ordinary nursemaid at half the wages?"

"Because she's not an ordinary child. She's too gifted to leave to the mercies of some ignorant nursemaid. She's Sigmund Herzog's great-granddaughter. Someday she may inherit the Paper. If you had an ounce of real feeling for her—"

"To hell with the goddam Paper! She's a nice, smart little girl, and I just want her to grow up into a nice, smart young lady and marry some nice, smart young man without putting me in the poorhouse in the meantime."

"*You* want her to? She's not *your* daughter. You don't even support her, except for extras."

Sometimes, when Mother said Clara wasn't Albert's daughter, he slapped her or called her a bad name. Sometimes he just said it was lucky he was willing to pay toward Clara's support, even though he was not supposed to, because where would she be if she had to depend on her good-for-nothing father? But it was the extras that were sending him to the poorhouse.

The two things that drove Albert wild were the Paper and the idea that he did not treat Clara as if she were his own daughter.

Clara knew he did treat her that way, in spite of what Mother sometimes said. When Mother was not mad at him, she said so herself, pointed out to Clara how good he was to her and how much he loved her. Clara knew it anyway. She called him Father, and usually forgot he wasn't really. Often she almost loved him, even though he joked too much and always asked her, "What's new?" instead of waiting for her to tell him, and gave her wet kisses that had an awful smell of cigars. She felt sorry for him because he wanted her to love him and she couldn't quite. But that must have been when she was older than four.

When she was four, and for some time after that, she did not understand what the Paper was, but she hated it. If she woke up in the night, with Fräulein not there, and saw a shape in the room that frightened her, she thought it was the Paper. She knew Mother was not frightened of the Paper. Mother was not frightened of anything. But Albert was. When he read *Little Orphant Annie* to Clara and came to the part about the goblins getting you if you didn't watch out, she could tell by his voice that he thought the goblins were the Paper. Mother did not want him to read stories like that to Clara, but Clara liked scary things as long as they were in books.

They lived in an apartment house on Riverside Drive and Ninety-fifth Street. It had two large glass globes on posts set into brown marble on either side of the front door. Down a few blocks there was a bronze statue of Joan of Arc on a horse, and down a little farther still and across the Drive was the Soldiers' and Sailors' Monument, surrounded by a walled-in marble-tiled plaza that made it a fine, smooth place for children to roller skate when they were old enough.

The apartment itself had a long hall with rooms on both sides. The bathroom was 'way at the end. No one could hear Clara call from there in her soft little voice. When she was finished, she blew on a pink whistle that she wore around her neck on a string, and Mother or Fräulein came to wipe her. Mother would never let anyone else bathe her, though. When the bath was over, Mother stood her on a towel on top of the toilet seat, dried her with another towel, rubbed her all over with alcohol until she was warm and pink, and powdered her with talcum powder.

Fräulein taught her to read and to count and to speak a little German, but not to dress herself. She did not go to school until she was seven. Mother wanted her to go to private school, but Albert, though he did not win many of the fights even though he could yell louder and throw better, won that one. Mother decided it was almost as nice as a private school. It was in a good neighborhood, on Eighty-second Street and West End Avenue, and most of the children came from well-to-do families. There were a few Italians from Amsterdam Avenue, and two or three colored, but Albert said Clara might as well know there were children in the world whose parents were not rich Jews. Mother must have thought he was right for once, because she did not argue about it.

The principal was a very old lady. At least she seemed very old to Clara. She gave Clara an easy arithmetic example to do, and then had her read a story about a man, a boy, and a donkey. The story was even easier than the arithmetic, and Clara read it with expression. She found out later that this was the difference between her and most of the other children. They could all read, but only a few of them knew how to read with expression.

The principal said Clara was 'way ahead of herself and belonged in the third grade.

"It's not altogether surprising," she said to Mother, "considering her heritage." She patted Clara on the head. "Perhaps she'll follow in your grandfather's footsteps. Who knows? By the time she's grown up, it may not be unusual for a woman to head a newspaper."

Clara knew the principal was talking about the Paper. At seven, she understood that the Paper was a newspaper. She saw it in the apartment every day. She even read a little of it once in a while, though it was hard and not very interesting. It no longer frightened her, of course, but she still did not like it much. She did not like the way it made Mother and Albert yell at each other. She hated the way everybody talked about it all the time—Mother and the principal and other people—mixing her up in it. Sometimes Mother talked almost as if she loved the Paper as much as she loved Clara. No, as if she loved Clara and the Paper mixed up together, instead of just Clara.

Clara liked school. It was easy, and there were a lot of girls to play with. In school, it was all right to play with anybody, even the Italian and colored girls, but outside you could only play with Jewish girls. Clara did not know which ones were Jewish unless they said so, but Mother could tell.

She was allowed to be best friends with a girl in her class whose

chauffeur brought her and called for her every day in a black automobile, and with a girl she played with in Riverside Park who went
to private school and lived in an apartment that had thirteen rooms.
One day when the teacher had to go out of the room, she made
Clara the monitor. The girl who was her best friend in the class
would not stop talking, so Clara had to report her. After that, she
had only one best friend. She could have had more. Everybody was
allowed to be friends with her because of the Paper. But she decided
one was enough.

Fräulein Leschner had left a long time before, but Clara still had a
governess who called for her at school and took her to Riverside
Park. It was never the same governess for long. Either Mother
thought they were unsatisfactory or Clara could not stand them.
Mother was very strict about things like telling the truth, not answering back, going to bed early, and manners, but she never forced
Clara to have a governess she could not stand.

Since the governess did not come until the afternoon, it was usually Mother who took her to school in the morning. Sometimes it
was Albert. Clara hated it when it was Albert, especially if the
weather was bad and they had to go on the streetcar. He joked all
the time, with everybody listening. He said he wasn't ready, he was
Reddy's brother. He made up stories, with silly faces, about a Jewish
elf called Shimcha Rice. He tickled her to make her laugh, and then
pretended she was being naughty and had to be sent away to Dr.
Krauskopf's Boarding School, which Clara knew was not a real place.
The worst part was when she left him at the corner on Broadway
and he waited while she walked down the block to school, waving
and calling, "Good-by, baby!" until she got to the door that said
GIRLS. She always made up her mind to pretend he was not anybody she knew, but when it came to it she always waved back once.

On Fräulein's or Mademoiselle's day off, Mother called for her at
school. If Mother was in a good humor, that was better than playing
with her best friend. Sometimes they went to Constantine's and sat
at elegant little marble tables and had ice cream or hot chocolate
and pastries and giggled as if they were both little girls. Sometimes
they went shopping on Broadway or rode downtown on the top of
the bus to the Fifth Avenue stores. If Mother and Albert had had a
fight the night before, Mother would buy something expensive for
the apartment, or a lot of clothes for Clara and herself, and ask
Clara's opinion about everything, just as if she were grown up.

When Clara was ten, they moved to Central Park West. Before that, they had lived on West End Avenue, and before that, between West End Avenue and Riverside Drive, always in the Seventies, Eighties, or Nineties. Every apartment was a little better than the one before, but the one on Central Park West was much better. There were more and bigger rooms and a view of the park. Mother hired an Interior Decorator, who said most of the things from the old apartment were no good and would have to be replaced.

"Won't Father be furious?" Clara asked Mother.

Mother did not exactly answer this. "He's doing very well now—" (that meant rich). "I want you to have the right setting for the people you'll meet as you get older."

Albert was a lawyer. Clara was allowed to tell that to people, but she was not allowed to tell other things. If anybody asked her why she had a different name, or whether he or someone else was her real father, or whether Mother had been married before, she was supposed to answer that she didn't know. This was the right answer to questions about secret family things, and not the same as a lie.

That year, when Clara was ten and they moved to Central Park West, she told Mother she did not need a governess any more. She told it to her in a note, the way she always told important things. They came out better in writing than when she tried to say them.

I'm getting too big for a governess. My friends laugh at me and call me a baby. It's very embarrassing. If you let me go to the park alone, I'll be very careful to look both ways when I cross the street and I won't play with anybody rough, so please PLEASE don't make me still have a governess and be embarrassed.

If Clara went into the closet and put her ear to the wall, she could hear Mother and Albert talking in the room next to hers.

"Of course she's too big," Albert said. "I told you it was asinine. You've always made a baby of her, hiring people to do everything for her. It's a wonder—"

"You don't know what you're talking about. I've brought her up the way a child with her background should be brought up. If you had your way, she'd probably be scrubbing floors." Clara could tell by Mother's voice that she was not going to make her have a governess any more. "Would anybody think a ten-year-old child had written that note? And every word perfectly spelled. Most children her age wouldn't even know how to use the word *embarrassed*, much less spell it."

336

The notes Clara wrote to Mother usually worked. Mother liked everything Clara wrote. She read out loud to all her friends the poems and descriptions Clara made up, and showed them the A's she always got on her school compositions. Mother said she had the Herzog talent and someday she would write for the Paper. That was the part Clara hated. She wanted to write what she felt like, not that boring stuff.

One of the best parts about not having a governess any more would be going alone to Central Park to play. Clara liked to climb on the rocks and shoot marbles and play baseball in Sheep's Meadow with the boys. One Mademoiselle had allowed her to, but when she told Mother that Clara was a *garçon manqué* and there was no harm in it, Mother discharged her and hired a strict Fräulein who agreed with Mother that boys were too rough for little girls.

Clara was supposed to tell Mother everything, but she did not tell her, even in a note, how she had got to play baseball with the boys in the first place. It was because they had made her so mad by saying she couldn't and making fun of her for being a girl (yaya-ya-yaYA-ya!) that she had punched one of them in the face and made his nose bleed. Clara thought Mother would not want to know about that.

Mother knew things, though, without being told. She did not mention the bloody-nose business, but she never did let Clara go alone to Central Park. Instead, she took her out of public school and sent her to a private one, where you stayed in the afternoon for athletics and dramatics and clubs that kept you busy until four o'clock.

Clara loved it. She played forward on the midget basketball team and took boys' parts in the plays because she was tall. Almost all the girls in the school were Jewish and came from good families, so she could be friends with anybody she liked. She had a teacher who let her write poems and stories while everybody else had to write dumb compositions about how they had spent their vacations. The teacher said she had talent too, and would probably grow up to be a writer, but she did not talk about the Paper. Clara loved her and never felt embarrassed with her the way she did with most grownups.

Mother and Albert fought worse than ever in the Central Park apartment. Clara was too busy to think about it in school. When she got home, she did her homework and wrote or read, and did not think about it then either. They never fought much at the dinner table, because of the maid, but that was the time Clara began watching for the signs. If anything came up about the rent or Clara's school or Albert's staying out late at night without Mother, she knew what to expect. Sometimes she would ask to go to Grandma's for overnight, and sometimes she was allowed to do that, and to walk to school by herself the next morning. There were no avenues to cross, only side streets.

Clara loved to stay at Grandma's. She could tell Grandma about the fights, because Grandma was in the family. She could even tell her about the way once in a while Mother yelled at her and spanked her for nothing. Grandma was always the same. She called Clara "Little One," and never scolded or lost her temper. After they were in bed, she let Clara talk as long as she wanted to, without saying it was time to go to sleep. They had conversations about school and friends and different thoughts Clara had, and the next thing Clara knew, it was morning. Another good part was that Grandma did not like the Paper either.

Until she was twelve, Clara went away with Mother for six weeks every summer. They went to a hotel in Lakewood or Asbury Park or Atlantic City that was not "restricted," which meant it took Jews. There were always a lot of children there with their mothers. The fathers came for their two-week vacations. Albert did not always come, which was a relief.

Clara loved the summers away. She was outdoors all day playing, and there was still time to read and write during the long evenings, with no fighting to worry about. She always had a best friend. One summer it was a girl all the way from Cleveland, Ohio, who had a glass eye. If the other children gave her Tootsie Rolls or lollipops, she would take the eye out and let them look at it in her hand while she closed her lid over the empty place. But she took it out for Clara for nothing.

The summer Clara was twelve, Mother stayed in the city and sent Clara to a camp for girls in Maine. Mother said it was one of the best Jewish camps in the country. It was very expensive. All the middies and bloomers had to be ordered from a special place, and name tags had to be sewed into every single thing. Overnight trips cost extra. So did horseback riding, but Mother would not allow Clara to ride anyway; she thought it was dangerous.

Mother warned Clara about being homesick, since this was her first time away for more than a night. But Clara wasn't. She thought the camp was the most beautiful place she had ever seen. She wrote

338

a poem about it in rest hour the second day, lying on her cot in her tent. The heads of the camp stressed athletics, sportsmanship, team spirit, and character, and Clara started working on all that right away. She seemed to be out of breath most of the summer, but she had a wonderful time. The last day, saying good-by to the friends she had made, was the saddest of her life. But when Mother saw her, all tanned and hard and pink-cheeked, getting off the train at Grand Central Station, she said, "Oh, baby, you look gorgeous!" and promised Clara she could go back the next summer. Clara felt better then. Mother never broke a promise.

When Clara was fifteen and came home from the same camp, Mother told her in the taxi that they were not going back to the apartment on Central Park West.

"I didn't want to write and upset you while you were at camp," she said. "I've left Albert, baby. I've rented a nice apartment on Seventy-fifth Street near the Drive for you and me."

Whenever Clara had come home after the summer, Albert and the yelling and fighting had settled down on her chest like a stone. Now she could have floated right up to the top of the taxi. But she was not supposed to feel like that. She was supposed to be upset. "Oh, Mother," she said. "What happened?"

Mother explained that Albert had used for himself money that a client had paid him for legal costs. It was called misappropriation of funds, and it was a very serious offense. "I think he has probably done it before, but this time he was found out before he could put the money back. He's going to be disbarred. That means he can never practice law again."

"How will he earn a living?"

"I'm sure he'll find something to do. There are plenty of jobs."

Clara wondered whether leaving Albert when he was in all this trouble was good sportsmanship, but she did not mention it. "We were well off," she said. "Why did he have to take anybody else's money?"

"We weren't as well off as it seemed. We could have been, if Albert had made the most of himself, but he isn't a worker. He always takes the easiest way. Often I've had to do without in order to provide things I thought you ought to have." She patted Clara's cheek, trailing a whiff of familiar perfume. "Not that I wasn't happy to do it for my baby. Anyway," she went on briskly, "he and I haven't gotten along for years. No one knows that better than you.

I've only stayed with him because I wanted you to have a father. But this was too much to stand, on top of everything else, and you're not a child any more." She leaned around to look into Clara's face. "You don't feel bad about it, do you? You never really cared much for him."

"I don't feel bad."

"No, of course not. We'll have fun, baby. We'll do a lot of things together."

"It will be peaceful, won't it? That's the best part."

The worst part was over. No terrible sounds and voices woke her in the night any more, stiffening her with the fear that this time one of them would kill the other. But it was not peaceful.

Clara thought Mother would never get angry and excited, now that Albert was gone, but she did. Grandma said it was her nature, part of what made her interesting, and that anyway Clara's age was a hard time for mothers and daughters to get through. It was true that Clara's friends were always telling her about arguments they had with their mothers. Some of them even said they hated their mothers, which Clara did not believe and thought was awful to say. Those mothers did not get into tempers and yell and scream about practically nothing. Sometimes Mother even slapped her, big as she was. Still, Clara never hated her, except maybe for a minute. Grandma said it would be better just to keep quiet and let Mother's rages burn themselves out, but Clara could not keep quiet. It was not fair to let Mother say any unreasonable thing she wanted to without answering. And in the end they both always cried and made up anyhow.

Mother was different from the mothers of her friends in good ways too. She did not even look like a mother. She was beautiful, wore stylish clothes, and smoked cigarettes. When Clara was younger, she had been a little embarrassed to have such an unusual kind of mother, but soon she began liking to show her off. Her friends all envied her. They were crazy about Mother, because she really listened to what they had to say and never spoke to them as if they were children. No matter how shy a girl was with other adults, Mother could get her talking.

Clara was the only one of her friends who had learned from her mother about the way babies grew in the womb and came out after nine months. Mother said it was the most beautiful thing in a woman's life. She described how it felt inside when the baby first moved—"like a little bird fluttering its wings"—and told Clara how she loved her even before she had seen her.

"Oh, it hurt, all right. I'll bet they could near me yelling all the way from the Hohenzollern down to the Battery." The Hohenzollern was the name of the apartment house, on Eighty-third Street and West End Avenue, where Clara was born. When the war started, they changed it to the Marlborough. "But you forget the pain as soon as it's over," Mother said. "That's another wonderful thing. You look at the miracle of your baby, and it's as though the pain had never been."

The only thing Mother did not tell her was how the baby got into the womb in the first place. She said she would tell her when she was older, but she forgot. Clara figured most of it out for herself her first summer at camp, from a joke one of the older girls told. She was not supposed to talk about it with her friends, because they would tell her all the wrong things, but when she was thirteen she had a friend whose father was a doctor and they looked it up in one of his medical books. That was not the same as talking about it.

When Clara was fourteen, she was allowed to go to parties where there were boys, as long as Mother knew the family that was giving the party. After she came home from camp that summer when Mother had left Albert, Mother said now that she was almost sixteen, she could have real dates. Mother talked again about the disgraceful way some girls behaved these days, and reminded her that boys did not respect girls like that and would never marry them. If the girls did somehow manage to get married, they would regret all their lives that they had not saved themselves for their husbands.

"A boy will go as far as a girl will let him. That's the way boys are. It's up to the girl to restrain him," Mother said. "I don't have to worry about you. With your character, I know I can trust you."

Clara was the only girl she knew who never let a boy kiss her. It was not so much character as lack of relish. The boys who liked her were either pimply or they perspired too much or their lips were too thick or they were stupid. With the boys she might have liked and been at least tempted to let kiss her, she was paralyzed. She blushed when they looked at her and could not think of anything to say if they spoke to her. It was peculiar, considering how much was always going on in her mind. When she wrote, the words came pouring out. She had filled a drawer full of notebooks with stories and poems on all kinds of subjects. At fourteen she had even written a novel, called

341

The Magnificent Fool, about a married woman who ran away with another man and was forgiven by her husband when she came back. But the only boys she could talk to were the ugly, stupid, perspiring ones that she would have died rather than kiss.

Mother was disappointed that Clara was not more popular with boys. At her age, Mother could have had any boy she wanted. Even now, she had more dates than Clara did. As soon as the divorce was final, she began going out all the time. It was not only because she was so beautiful, but because she had so much personality. If you had personality, you did not have to be beautiful to be popular. But there was no way to have personality without thinking of something to say.

Clara was popular enough with girls. All the nice Jewish girls in the square mile or so of New York where she grew up knew each other—it was like a small town—and the nicest of them were her friends. On Saturdays they went to matinees at the Shubert Riviera Theater on Ninety-sixth Street and Broadway and saw second runs of the best Broadway plays, paying fifty-five cents for a balcony seat. On Sundays they met at the street clock on Eighty-fourth Street and walked up Broadway to Walgreen's Drug Store at 110th Street, where a soda cost ten cents. Most of them did not have to practice these economies, but it was the style.

It was also the style to wear light tan camel's-hair coats, Roman striped scarves, felt hats with feathers, and, at all seasons, galoshes with the buckles left open; to cultivate a long, slouching stride called a "collegiate" walk; to belong to a secret society known as the Shifters, which had no secrets and no particular object except to wear a brass paper clip in the lapel of your coat.

Clara and her friends looked and acted like all the other girls in New York of their age and class. The only difference was that they were more serious. They talked about important things, not only boys, and exchanged books of poetry for their birthdays. All of them planned to get married, but one or two besides Clara wanted to do something else first, or at the same time; be an actress or a painter or even a scientist like Madame Curie or an aviatrix like Amelia Earhart. On Thanksgiving and Hanukkah they got somebody's chauffeur to drive them to the Lower East Side, where they distributed food and presents to poor Jewish families.

Mother and Clara were not as well off as they had been before the divorce from Albert. He was some kind of salesman, not making nearly as much money as when he had been a lawyer, and no better about alimony payments than Clara's real father was about payments for her support. Mother got some income from the Paper, but it was not what it should have been because Uncle David, Mother said, was running the Paper into the ground. It seemed to Clara that team spirit or good sportsmanship (she was not sure which) required her to suggest that she transfer to a public high school for this final year, but to her relief Mother would not hear of it.

"Over my dead body," Mother said. "You're going to stay right where you are, and next year you're going to Barnard College. If I can't get the money out of those two deadbeats, I'll scrub floors before I'll see you deprived of the proper background."

Mother did scrub the bathroom and kitchen floors, because they had to do without a maid, but she said she did not mind and it was good exercise. When she was in a good humor, she and Clara had fun together, as she had promised they would. They went to the Aquarium and rode to Staten Island on the ferry. They rode up Broadway on the streetcar until they saw a movie they liked and then got off and bought candy in the store that was always next to the theater—chocolate Plantations for Mother and chocolate-covered cherries for Clara—to eat while they watched Clara Bow or Joan Crawford or Rudolph Valentino. Once, one of the men who were always wanting to marry Mother invited Clara along to dinner at the Claremont Inn, on Riverside Drive near Grant's Tomb.

"He's trying to make up to you so you won't object to him as a stepfather," Mother said. "I'm going to object before you have a chance, but meanwhile you might as well have the fun of coming to the Inn with us. It's a beautiful place."

Claremont Inn was all right, but Clara would have had more fun alone with Mother. When they were alone, Mother laughed and joked with her, confided in her, talked to her as though she were another adult, but when other people were around, she treated her like a child.

Grandma always treated her the same. Sort of in between Mother's two ways. In the spring of that first year after the divorce, Clara stayed with Grandma for a month while Mother went to Europe with Uncle Samuel. It was a lovely month. Clara missed the excitement and fun a little, but she did not miss the raging arguments. She and Grandma never argued. They discussed ideas and literature and world problems. Grandma was very intelligent and knew a lot about a lot of things. She wrote letters to the New York *Times* almost every week, commenting on items they had printed, and her letters were published without one word changed or left out.

"Why do you write to the *Times* and not the Paper?" Clara asked her.

"I want nothing more to do with the Paper than I can help. That's part of a long, pretty dull history, Little One." She had a way of pulling in her lips that made you know she was not just a sweet, calm old lady. "Sometimes I wonder if, feeling as I do, it's altogether honest of me to take money from it."

Grandma was so honest that once when a storekeeper gave her two cents too much in change, she walked all the way back, seven blocks, to return it. She said that otherwise it would have troubled her conscience. Clara knew how that was. She often got annoyed with her conscience and wished it would let her alone. At one time she had believed it was God who was always bothering her about things she should or should not do, but she had stopped believing in God quite a while back.

She did not tell Grandma, because it would have made her feel bad. Grandma got a lot of pleasure out of God and religion. She liked to read the Bible and say prayers, and she went to temple every Friday night or Saturday morning or both. Clara had once been religious too, gone to Sunday school and everything, because she thought if Grandma said it was right, it must be. But she had been bored by Sunday school, and she had begun to notice that prayers did not work much of the time. It made more sense to her to think that there was no God than that there was one who had been mean to Grandma, made her first baby die, when Grandma was so religious and always did right.

During that month, though, Clara went to temple with her to please her. It was not bad. She liked the music, and during the other parts she thought about outside things and hardly knew she was there. Often, after the service, Grandma went up to the rabbi and talked and talked to him while other people waited impatiently.

"I'm sorry that took so long," she said to Clara once, on the way back to the hotel. "I thought it was time someone reminded that young rabbi that pride goeth before destruction. He always talks as though our people have a corner on righteousness, and as though only Christians can be fools. 'Young man, all religions have the same high goals,' I told him. 'And Judas in the New Testament was no

344

more of a rogue and a fool than Joseph's brothers in the Old. You would do far better to stress the equality of all men than to harp on the superiority of the Jews.'" Grandma's chuckle came from deep in her throat. "He didn't like it one bit, but I can't help that. Somebody had to tell him."

Clara wanted to know why, if Jews were no better than anyone else, it was so important to have only Jewish friends.

"We huddle together for warmth against a hostile world," Grandma said. "Most minorities have a choice between that and assimilation, but we have no choice. We're *sui generis*, a people as well as a religion. No matter how a Jew may try to assimilate, he can only become a Jew and something else; never something else instead of a Jew."

"I don't think the world is hostile."

"No, not to you, Little One. Maybe it never will be to you. You're one of the favored ones."

"What do you mean?"

"I suppose what I mean is that I'm very pleased to have you for a granddaughter."

That was one conversation with Grandma that Clara never forgot. Another was about her real father and Albert. Clara did not call him Albert to Grandma. "I feel a little sorry about Father," she said. "Not that I'd want him back. We're much happier without him. But I never even said good-by to him. The last I had to do with him was all that nasty stuff I had to tell the lawyer. He must think I hate him, and I don't."

"Have you thought of writing to him?"

"Yes, but I can't. It would be disloyal to Mother."

Mother always answered right away. A conversation with her was like a fast game of tennis, in which the ball was likely to come over the net before you could get in position for it. Grandma took her time, and never hurried you either. "I think perhaps he understands that," she said now. "He's not a stupid man. Far from it. Not a bad man, either. Weak, yes. Weak and driven."

There was another silence. They were eating dinner on Grandma's card table. Usually they went out to a neighborhood restaurant like C & L, but once or twice a week Grandma cooked something on her little, two-burner stove. Mother never let Clara help in the kitchen. She was too impatient. But Grandma let her, and did not mind if she made mistakes.

"Your own father too," Grandma went on. "I've always been fond of William, in spite of his weaknesses. You have his gentle heart, but more gumption. Take some more veal; there's plenty."

"Thanks." Clara ate for a while, thinking how to say what was in her mind. "If I could hide somewhere and watch him without his knowing I was there, I'd do it to see what he's like. That's as much as I'd want. But he knew me once. He must have cared about me. You'd think he'd want to see how I turned out, make a fuss so he could. I'm glad he doesn't, because it would be embarrassing and complicated, but you'd think he would."

"That's one of his weaknesses. He'll go to any lengths to avoid a fuss. But he's kind, and I'm not sure that isn't the cardinal virtue."

"Do you think Mother married him because of his kindness? And then found it wasn't enough?"

"I don't know. She may have married him because he was weak. We seem to lean toward weak men in our family. It takes skill to live with such a man. I hope you'll make a wiser choice and have a more rewarding marriage."

"I may not get married at all."

"Why don't we clear these things away and have our dessert?" Grandma said.

Clara was too old for camp, and they could not afford to go to the country. It was the first time in her life that Clara had stayed in the hot city all summer. All her friends were away. But she was a good sport about it. She decided it was a chance to try really being a writer, not just for her own pleasure but for money.

Mother rented a typewriter for her and she worked at it part of every day, no matter how hot it was. She wrote five stories during the summer. They all came back with rejection slips.

"Never mind, baby," Mother said. "You're a wonderful writer, but maybe this isn't the kind of writing you're cut out for."

"Five stories isn't anything. Some writers get thirty or forty rejection slips before they sell their first story. But I know you'd like to discourage me," Clara said, which was not fair. One thing Mother never did was try to discourage her. "I know all you care about is having me work on the Paper. But maybe I have other ideas."

Clara said these things instead of crying because the typewriter had gone back to the rental company and she was still not a real writer. But it would have been better to cry. Any suggestion that

Clara was not crazy to work on the Paper made Mother lose her temper. She threatened not to let her go to Barnard in January, but Clara knew she did not mean it. She had already paid part of the tuition.

During her first semester at Barnard Clara turned in the best of the five stories as an English assignment. The instructor gave her a B. It was the first time she had ever received a mark below an A in English.

"You have talent, but it's undisciplined," the instructor told her. "You should plan to go to the School of Journalism. Working on a newspaper is the best possible training for someone who wants to write."

He was young and fairly handsome. There was a rumor that he was secretly dating one of the sophomores. The superior, patronizing way he was talking to Clara reminded her of all the boys who had clogged her mind so she could think of nothing to say to them.

"I come from a family of journalists." She had never mentioned this to anyone before. "My great-grandfather was Sigmund Herzog."

His expression changed in a satisfying way. He gave her A's after that.

The following summer Clara worked at the Paper every afternoon. She helped the copy boys by going out for coffee and near beer for the reporters, and once in a while, when a deadline was near and everybody was very busy, ran around with copy or galley sheets. She did not stop to wonder how this was training her to be a writer. She did not care. Everything about the place was exciting to her. The people, the noises, the smells. When she thought about the Paper of her childhood nightmares, she had to laugh. Long after that, she had had some crazy ideas about it too. She could scarcely remember what they had been.

College, though she had enjoyed it and found it easy, seemed far off to her now, a puerile world to which she could not imagine returning in the fall. She was a working woman, earning a salary. She and Mother, who had started on the Paper only about a year before her, were both working women. Equals. Or almost.

"I think I already know more about running a newspaper," Mother said, "than David will ever know. At least three quarters of it is dealing with people, and he hasn't the faintest idea how to do that. If things go on the way they are, he's going to ruin us all. Grandpa must be turning over in his grave."

"Can't you do something?"

Mother smiled. "Don't worry, baby. Did you ever know me not to do what needed doing?"

Most of the copy boys wanted to be reporters someday. They were always trying to find mistakes in the galleys to get themselves noticed, and submitting items they hoped would be used at least as fillers. Some succeeded. Several of the reporters had once been copy boys.

Harry Whipple was a copy boy who had been graduated from Princeton that June. Harry was not handsome, but he was nice-looking, with red hair and reddish-brown eyes. He was one of the tall, self-assured ones, like the English teacher at Barnard, who usually behaved as though Clara should be grateful if they threw her a kind word in passing. But Harry asked her for a date. He came up to her in the newsroom and said he had two tickets for the Triangle show at Princeton, and he hoped she could go with him. Clara thought she was going to faint. The whole room began whirling around. The minute it stopped, she said yes, she would love to go, without thinking that he was not Jewish and Mother would object.

"You've got to let me! You've got to! The Princeton Triangle show, Mother!" She was half crying before she started, because if she couldn't go she would die. "What harm can it do? It's only a date. I'm not going to marry him. I don't even like him." Clara had no idea whether she liked him or not, but she thought it would help persuade Mother. And then an even better argument came to her. "He may have Jewish friends."

Mother told her all the things she had told her before about the dangers of going out with a gentile boy. You might fall in love with him, but he would never marry you. If he did ask you to marry him, you would have to refuse, because mixed marriages never worked out. Sooner or later, he or some member of his family would throw it up to you that you were Jewish. Besides, it would kill Grandma if you married outside your faith. Even if there was no question of love or marriage, it was dangerous, because gentile boys drank too much and were fast.

"Well, I've warned you," Mother said at the end. "If you still want to go—"

Clara went out with Harry a lot that summer. After the first time, she began to feel comfortable with him. They always had the Paper to talk about. Sometimes he brought her things he had written. She did not think they were very good, but she told him they were. She thought it was better to lie than to hurt his feelings. Besides, he might not like her as much if she found fault with his writing.

Clara never showed him her own writing, because she was afraid he would see how much better it was. She knew boys did not like girls to be better at things than they were. She was also careful not to let him spend too much money on her. Whenever he took her for a midnight snack, she ordered a Long Island Rarebit, which was always next to the cheapest dish on the menu. A Welsh Rarebit was cheaper, but she thought ordering the very cheapest thing might be a little too obvious. She ate so many Long Island Rarebits that summer that afterward the name on a menu was enough to nauseate her.

After the third time he took her out, Clara let Harry kiss her good night. Earlier that evening he had told her how pretty he thought she was, with skin like peaches and cream. He was not the first boy to say she was pretty, but he was the first one she thought must know what he was talking about. Nice-looking and a graduate of Princeton.

Kissing him was pleasant. She liked the way he smelled. At the end of the evening, he would stop his Stutz Torpedo (a graduation present from his father) a little away from the entrance of her apartment house, turn off the lights, and give her a long good-night kiss. He wanted her to open her mouth, but she wouldn't. She wouldn't let him do anything with his hands either, because she knew he would not respect her if she did.

One night he brought a flask of whisky along. He had never done that before. They went dancing at the Post Lodge in Westchester, and every little while he disappeared into the Men's Room and she knew he was taking a drink from the flask. Later, in the car, he tried to make her drink some, but she pushed it away.

"Aw, come on, don't be a flat tire," he said. "A little giggle water won't hurt you."

Clara hated the way he was acting. He was like somebody she had never met before. He even smelled different.

"I'm a little tired, Harry," she said. "I'd like to go home."

Instead of driving her home, he pulled the car into a dark side street, pushed her down on the seat, and got on top of her. She struggled, but he had her pinned so she could hardly move.

"Come on, Clara," he kept whispering. "Come on. You know I'm stuck on you."

349

Finally he shifted a little and she managed to free one leg and jab upward with her knee. It worked exactly as Mother had told her it would, in the unimaginable event that she would ever have to do it. He howled and rolled off her, clutching himself and screaming the same words at her that Albert had screamed at Mother. She left him there and walked back to the Post Lodge, where she got a taxi to take her home.

The next day, at the Paper, he tried to talk to her, but she walked right past him as though he were not there. Toward the end of the afternoon, she came out of the composing room and almost walked into him standing there waiting for her. He grabbed her by the arms and began babbling to her in a whiny voice, as though any minute he might cry.

"Listen, Clara . . . Listen . . . Oh, God, I'm so sorry about last night . . . I had too much to drink. I didn't know what I was doing . . . I'd have never . . . it was only because . . . Listen . . ." He began shaking her a little. "Listen, you won't tell your uncle, will you? I mean, there wouldn't be any sense . . ."

She pulled away from him. "I'm not going to tell anybody. Just don't ever speak to me again."

It surprised her that she did not mind a bit about its being over. She realized that what she must have liked was not Harry especially, just the idea of him. The only thing that bothered her was his worry about Uncle David. She had never had anything to say to Uncle David, or he to her. He seemed hardly to know who she was, or that she was working on the Paper. But Harry did not know that. She was afraid maybe he had asked her out not because he was attracted to her, but because he thought she had influence with Uncle David.

That part upset her for several days, but when Mother noticed and asked her what was wrong she said, "Nothing." It was the first important thing she had ever kept from Mother. She did not want Mother to say that it proved how right she was about gentile boys. Clara did not believe Harry's religion had anything to do with it, and she thought she might want to go out with a gentile boy again sometime.

It was one of the reporters who made her feel better. Most of the reporters were nice to her, but this one was the nicest. "What's the matter, kiddo?" he asked her. "Isn't the boy friend treating you right?"

He had an easy manner with her that made her feel easy too.

When he teased her, she got the feeling he did it because he liked her. Sometimes she even thought of something clever to say back. "What do you know about my boy friends?" she asked him.

"Reporters know everything." He crooked a finger at her to come closer. "That half-baked kid is lucky a girl like you looks at him twice," he said in a low voice that only pretended to be faking. "Tell him to go fly a kite."

"I already have."

"That's right," he said, and grinned as if he was delighted.

The reporter's name was Joseph Fitzsimmons. Everybody called him Fitz.

4

Mother was in the same hospital as the one where they had taken David. She had a large, sunny, corner room, so cluttered with flowers that Clara could scarcely find a place to put her handbag down.

"Go and have a drink with your boy friend," Mother said to the fat, gray-haired nurse. "My daughter can get me anything I need. Well, baby!" She stretched out her arms the moment the door had closed. The tears began to spurt from her eyes. "Well, it's about time!"

"I didn't know you were sick," Clara whispered into the pillow under Mother's head. "Not until night before last. As soon as I knew, I came."

"Shh-sh-shh! Don't cry. It's all right. I've got some kind of ridiculous virus, that's all. Sit up, now, and let me look at you. Give me one of those paper things to blow my nose in. You'd better blow your own too. Go stand over there in the light where I can see you."

Clara had come straight to the hospital from the plane. All the way, since Samuel's letter had not told her what to expect, she had braced herself for some dreadful change, some obvious ravagement. Except that Mother was a little thinner, she seemed much the same. If there were signs of disease in her face, they were concealed by make-up. Her voice was strong. Her perfume scented the air, unquenched by the pervasive hospital smells. Surely there was a mistake. Samuel had exaggerated. Or the doctors had misread the signs. Dr. Jimmy was, after all, an old man. Old Dr. Jimmy, who had pulled Clara through the influenza epidemic of 1918 but who might very well not know everything he should about modern medicine . . .

"You look marvelous," Mother said. "Chic." She pronounced the word with wonder. "Is that a Dior?"

"A copy."

"Well, it's becoming. That's a good length for you. About twelve inches, isn't it? Personally, of course, I'd rather have an original—"

"Yes. You'd rather have an original Anybody than a fake Dior."

They both laughed.

"But you wouldn't have known it wasn't an original."

"You know, though. Anyway, what are we talking about Dior for? Sit down. Wait. Crank up my bed a little first." As Clara did so, Mother made a faint grimace. Clara stopped, her hand frozen on the crank. "Go ahead. A little more. That was nothing. Dr. Jimmy said I'd have some pain from time to time. It's to be expected with a lung condition. They'll let me take something for it if I want it, but you know me. I'm not one to give in to myself. That's fine, baby. Sit down."

Clara seated herself in a pale green plastic armchair. It felt cool and slippery under her. Mother settled back against the pillows again. Cautiously, Clara thought. She wore a bed jacket that was not in the usual pale shade of bed jackets, but black, lacy, suggesting both elegance and daring. No trace of gray showed in her black hair. The eyes she fixed on Clara were still brilliantly green, their look familiar. The look that compelled complete disclosure.

"Now," she said, "the first thing I want to know is about this man, this Steven Miller you've been mentioning in your letters for the past year."

"Well, he's a successful—"

"I know all that. I know who he is. His family's nothing special, but all right. Not kikes, anyway. What I'm interested in—"

"Mother, don't use that word. I have less and less use all the time for fictitious distinctions based on—"

"All right, baby. We're not going to fight about a word, are we? After all this time apart?"

Clara was appalled at herself. How could it matter, now, what distinctions Mother made? What words she used? "No, of course not."

"Well. Now, tell me. He's divorced, isn't he? Free? So it's not another Fitz situation, is it? No reason for it to be, anyway, unless you're making a damn fool of yourself again." Clara shifted in her chair, and Mother held up her hand, the shapely red nails curved over the fingertips. "Now don't get back on your high horse. You and I don't have to mince words with each other. God knows I made a damn fool of myself too, in a different way, over two men, but I'd hate to see you do it twice."

Clara got up and went over to the bed. She held out her hand. "That's my engagement ring."

"Oh, baby, I'm so glad! You don't know how glad I am!" Mother pulled her down to hug her, released her and took her hand, examining the ring. Her fingers felt cold and dry. "It's beautiful, isn't it? Unusual. Is it old?"

"It belonged to a lady in the court of Napoleon I."

"Did it? Well. A great deal more panache than an ordinary solitaire, certainly. Your Steven has taste." Mother paused for an instant, looked away from Clara and back again. "Tell me all about him."

Clara tried, and failed, to think of some of the things she had said, mentally and on paper, in the several letters she had not sent. "I'm not sure I can. He's dark, big, a little taller than I am . . . I used to think he looked like an Indian—tight skin over prominent bones, and rather fierce—but now he just looks like Steve—" Mother's eyes had not shifted. She was waiting, as she had once waited when Clara came home from dates. "He's gentle, but no—Mother, I can't. I don't know the right words to wrap him up for you like a package."

"Your father was gentle."

"He's not like my father. He's not soft. Let's leave it that I love him and he loves me, and we're good for each other."

"You loved Fitz."

"Mother, don't keep mentioning Fitz. You don't really know anything about me and Fitz."

"Well, you never would talk to me about him. Maybe if you had—" She stopped to sigh. Or to get her breath. Clara looked away. Let her mention Fitz. Let her mention anything she wanted to mention, for God's sake. "All right, baby. That's not important any more. If you're happy now, with your Steve, I'm happy too. It seems funny, though, your being engaged to a man I've never even met, when we've always been so close."

"You'll meet him."

"What? Speak up, baby. No one can hear you when you mumble like that."

Clara laughed. "Oh, Mother! I said you'll meet him."

"Yes, of course. When is he coming? I'm surprised he didn't come with you."

"I came so suddenly . . . and he's working on the last part of a book—it's about De Gaulle, so he has to be there, where he can—I don't know exactly when—"

"You're mumbling again. I'll never understand why a girl with your brains, and all the advantages you've had, should speak as if—well, never mind. Now." She pushed herself up a little straighter, and did not go on for a moment. Her face was perfectly still. "Now. We'll put an announcement in Sunday's Paper, and send it to all the other newspapers, of course. CLARA HERZOG TO WED STEVEN MILLER. *Publisher's Daughter and Author Engaged. Mrs. Rebecca Herzog, publisher of the Paper, has announced*—Oh, we'll need a photo. You haven't a recent one, have you? You'll have to go to Bachrach and have one taken. That will delay the announcement a little, but I suppose it doesn't matter, since Steven isn't here for parties or anything—" She stopped abruptly. "I'm talking too much. I think I'll rest a while now. Come back in an hour."

"Shall I crank down your bed?"

"I'll ring for the nurse. You go. Have something to eat. They say the Coffee Shop isn't bad." She closed her eyes. As Clara bent to kiss her, she said, "I'm glad you're back, baby. You don't know how I missed you."

Clara went out in the hall and found a telephone booth. She closed the door and cried in there for a few minutes. Then she called Dr. Jimmy's office and was told that Dr. Hochmeier was at the hospital. When she came out of the booth, he was walking toward her, a short, big-nosed man with a fringe of kinky gray hair circling pink baldness, and a paunch so immense that he seemed to be preceded by another person. When he saw Clara, he beamed and embraced her.

"Clara! My favorite girl! I was just going in to see your mother."

"Can I talk to you a minute first? I was trying to get you on the phone."

His face sobered. "Of course. Of course." He peered through his thick glasses at one end of the hall and then the other, as though the place were strange to him. "We can go in the small waiting room. Usually it isn't crowded."

He always behaved as if he had all the time in the world. As if anyone else who might possibly be waiting for him was less important, less needful of his attention. He listened to Clara in the familiar way, his head tilted slightly toward her, nodding now and then with the totality of his understanding, his sympathy. When he answered he spoke slowly, waiting between sentences, letting the words settle before he added to them.

No, there was no possibility of error. There had been nothing the surgeon could do. If Mother had gone to him earlier? Ah, well, if she had a different physiology—if she had not taken up smoking—if—if—dwelling on ifs was fruitless self-torture.

"Isn't it a kind of insult not to tell her? She's such a strong woman. Not telling her implies we think she's too weak to stand it. And there might be things she'd want to say, or do, if she knew."

"Say? What? Can there be anything your mother ever wanted to say and didn't? Or wanted to do, either? Samuel told me the lawyer went over all the wills a few months ago, so that's taken care of, and she has accepted that she can't go back to the Paper for a long time." He shrugged his thick, round shoulders. "I don't know, Clara. Maybe she's strong enough. Maybe she'd want to be told, and would feel insulted to have it kept from her. Personally, I'd rather insult her, since she won't know I'm doing it. I'd rather take that chance than the other one. Seeing the spirit go out of her, I mean. Personally." He cleared his throat. "I love her very much, Clara. People either love her or hate her, I think. Personally, I love her. I wouldn't want to tell her. But I'm a simple man. I don't pretend to know all the ins and outs of such things. Only how I feel. You're the one who must decide." He waited for her to speak, but she could not. "Maybe I shouldn't even have told you how I feel."

"Yes, you should have. I'm glad you did. You've given me something to think through. I'd probably have said she should be told, without thinking about it at all." Clara looked at her hands, locked in her lap as though they would never come apart. "I'm not good at lying to her."

He leaned over to pat her hand. "If you want to do it, for this you'll learn."

They walked down the hall together. Clara had one more question. Just before he left her, she managed to ask it. "Will she suffer very much?"

"We won't let her," he said.

He went into Mother's room, and Clara took the elevator to the

Coffee Shop on the ground floor. She had had breakfast on the plane, but she had no idea what she had eaten. The sandwich she ate now had no distinguishable taste. The lack might have been in her rather than in the food. She felt as though she were not there, not inhabiting her body, watching herself from somewhere else. From where, she did not know. Not from Paris. That was another lifetime.

Mother looked refreshed when Clara returned to her room. She had had a nap, she said. Interrupted by Dr. Jimmy, who never did anything when he came but listen to her heart and take her blood pressure, which had already been done by some young house doctor, and stuff himself with the chocolates and cookies people brought her.

"Hannah called. She says you're going there for dinner. You and Samuel. I'm glad. They haven't seen you in a long time, and you look so chic. You ought to keep your hair blond, though. You always had such beautiful hair." She was doing what Hester called dithering. Undoubtedly it was the prelude to something else quite different. "Where are your bags, anyway? You might as well stay in my apartment while I'm in here. Afterward, too, if you think you can stand living with me for a little while again, until you get married. It doesn't make much sense for you to take a place for such a short time."

Under other circumstances, Mother might have asked her whether she had set the date for the wedding. "I planned to stay in your apartment," she said. "My bags are downstairs."

"Good. You'll find everything in order, naturally. You can call Gristede's for groceries, and charge them to my account. When you take the bedspread off at night, fold it just once lengthwise, and hang it over the—"

"Mother, you don't have to go into all this. I know about your bedspreads. I lived with you for twenty-seven years. Don't worry. Everything will be kept exactly as you like it."

"I know I'm a crank. It's a Herzog trait. Anyway, that's enough of that. What I must talk to you about is the Paper."

Clara had been hoping Mother would not return to the subject of Steve and their wedding. This was no better. She should have anticipated these things, prepared herself. Instead she had gone numb and blank, and left herself, and Mother, defenseless.

"They've told you, I suppose, that this business, this virus, may drag on, that it may be months before I can do anything approaching active work. It's a damn nuisance, but there's no use whining about it. You'll have to take over, baby."

"I don't know if I—"

"Of course you can. Why do you think I've seen to it that you had so many different kinds of experience? Copy girl, reporter, foreign desk, Paris Bureau . . . I've always prepared you to step into my shoes. You know that. Now you're just going to get a little advance practice. With my help. I'll be here to guide you. I can't work, but I can talk." She smiled. "Maybe not as much at a time, but enough."

Clara had a sudden strong urge to close her eyes. It occurred to her that she had scarcely slept for forty-eight hours. She had to concentrate now, on staying awake, and she missed part of what Mother was saying.

". . . more important than ever. They used to say Roosevelt made it the news capital of the country—"

Washington? Yes, she was talking about the Washington Bureau chief, newly appointed.

"He's good—tough—but he has to be watched—an opportunist—" Mother's voice turned sharp. "Are you listening to me, Clara?"

"I'm trying. The trouble is, I got no sleep on the plane, and I'm—"

"Why didn't you say so, for heaven's sake? Letting me waste my breath!"

Clara shuddered. "I'm sorry, Mother."

"Well, it's not a tragedy, baby, just silly. Go on over to the apartment now and take a nice, long nap, so you're fresh and rested for dinner. Get a good night's sleep tonight. If you get here about ten in the morning, they'll be finished with me for a few hours, and we can talk about Whipple and all the rest of it, before you go down to the Paper."

"Whipple?"

"You really didn't hear anything I said, did you? Whipple is the new chief of the Washington Bureau."

"*Harry* Whipple? The *copy boy?*"

"You really do need sleep, baby. I don't know what you're talking about. Harry Whipple was a political reporter for the *Times-Herald*. He got himself in solid with Roosevelt, but after Roosevelt's death, Cissy began one of her famous personal vendettas against him—"

Mother was referring to Eleanor Medill Patterson, the Washington publisher. A columnist had once called Mother "the Jewish

Cissy Patterson," but it was not a fair comparison. Rich, handsome, outrageous Cissy collected enemies the way Mother collected friends.

"He came to the Paper after you went to Paris," Mother was saying, "so you can't have known him."

"Came *back* to the Paper. I knew him all right." For the moment, Clara was diverted from her yearning for sleep. "I went out with him the first summer I worked on the Paper. Don't you remember? And he *was* a copy boy."

"My God, baby, that was a million years ago. How could I remember?" She frowned. "What was I doing, anyway, letting you go out with a goy?"

Clara got up to kiss her good-by. "I begged you to let me. You always hated to deprive me of anything."

"Well, maybe, but I didn't spoil you. Everyone says they've never seen such an unspoiled only child. Oh, listen," she said, as Clara went to the door. "You've got to wait a minute and listen to this. I forgot to tell you. Dr. Waldbaum, the chest surgeon—he's about the biggest in New York since poor Ted Rosenthal died—a man of maybe sixty, no more. The second time I went to his office, he tried to make love to me. He said I was the most fascinating woman he had ever met. Would you believe it, at my age? The damn fool! Do you suppose chest surgeons have a special susceptibility to old women?"

"You're no more an old woman than I am."

"No, I guess not." Mother closed her eyes and smiled. "We Herzogs keep our looks much longer than ordinary people."

Mother's apartment was on Sutton Place, overlooking the East River. Clara stumbled into it unseeingly, as though she were drunk. In the bedroom, she was so bewitched by the sight of the bed that it took all her will to keep from flinging herself down on it just as she was. But she took off the satin bedspread first, folded it carefully and hung it on the silk rope that stretched between two hooks on the inside of a closet door, and then undressed. She slept for five hours, and just made it to the Majestic by seven.

"I thought you were going to be late," Hannah said, sounding somewhat disappointed. "I don't tolerate lateness, you know."

Clara wondered whether Hannah would have refused to let her in. It was perfectly possible. She was a cranky, autocratic old woman who luxuriated in her eccentricities, and either had no interest in or

358

no conception of the feelings of others. Mother got along with her, but she had always made Clara uncomfortable. During her adolescent years, it had often appeared to Clara that Hannah resented her for being alive when her son, the superior Robert who had died before Clara was born, had been taken from her. Now she seemed merely indifferent, as though Clara were some acquaintance of Mother's who had to be accepted as a courtesy to Mother.

Samuel was there, having a drink with Hannah. When he saw Clara, he put down his glass and stood up with his arms outstretched. "There's a warm greeting for you after two years," he said, winking at Clara. "Come here and let your old uncle give you a proper welcome."

He changed only imperceptibly from year to year. At seventy-seven, he was still perfectly groomed, immaculate, jaunty, and handsome. Clara knew he was a useless, self-indulgent man who had, with obvious enjoyment, frittered his life away, and she adored him.

"You may kiss me, too," Hannah said, tilting a withered, brownish cheek toward Clara. "What's the matter? Do I smell bad? . . . Look at her blush! You're too old to blush. How old are you, anyway?" She turned away without waiting for an answer and held her glass out to Samuel. "Pour me another drink. My throat's dry. No wonder, after using it for eighty-four years." She gave a witch's cackle. "That's a hot one, isn't it? I hope you have my sense of humor when you're my age, girl."

She was, Clara realized, a little tipsy. As the evening progressed, she got more so. Dinner was an indifferent meal that she had had sent up from the hotel restaurant because her companion-maid could hardly boil water and was not worth a damn. She made this observation in a carrying voice that the woman in the kitchen could not have failed to hear. When Samuel suggested that she had had enough to drink, she told him to mind his own damn business.

"The worst it can do is kill me," she said, cackled again, and then looked blearily across the table at Clara. "I'm sorry about Rebecca. I always liked that girl."

By ten o'clock she seemed perfectly sober, having had nothing to drink for two hours. She had not mentioned Mother again. None of them had. Hannah had done most of the talking, delivering herself of pronouncements on Elsa, who had "always been mealy-mouthed with men and got stepped on for it"; Hester, who had "always thought she was smarter than anybody, and had ended up alone in a foreign country"; Ida, who had "gone so crazy with fear of Papa that she had run away with religion instead of a man" . . .

"At least Papa was somebody. You're nobody, Samuel. Nathan was nobody. David was nobody. Arthur made money, but he was nobody, too—"

"*I'm Nobody! Who are you?*" Clara murmured.

"What?"

"Nothing. A poem. Emily Dickinson."

"I have no use for poetry. Too mealy-mouthed for my taste. Besides, you interrupted me. Rude." She moistened her forefinger on her tongue and began scrubbing at a spot on her rusty black skirt, so vigorously that the aged fabric seemed in danger of wearing through. "My Robert would have been somebody."

A few moments later she announced that she was going to bed. "You two can stay if you want to, but keep your voices down so I can get my beauty sleep. Anyhow, I don't want to hear what you say about me." She poured a little whisky into her glass and went toward the bedroom with it, bawling for the woman in the kitchen. "I'm perfectly capable of getting myself to bed, but she's got to do something to earn her keep. She's no damn good for anything else. No use changing, though. None of them are any damn good. All I'd change is faces."

Clara caught a glimpse of a tall, strapping, fair-haired woman piloting Hannah by the arm that held the glass of whisky.

"Why does anyone stay with her?"

"A good many employees swallow insults for less pay and more work," Samuel said. "I tell you this of my own knowledge."

"What of all the drinking? It can't be good for her."

"Dr. Jimmy thinks if it's a comfort to her, at her age, we should leave her alone."

They had come around to it now.

"I saw Dr. Jimmy at the hospital today. This thing about not telling Mother the truth. I don't know. I'm not sure it's right."

"Of course you're not sure. Whatever you do, you won't be sure. You have to just do one thing or the other and forget about it." He smiled slightly. "Do you know, I believe there, in a nutshell, is my philosophy of life."

"How would you feel, Uncle Sammy?" She had not called him that since childhood. Why it had slipped out now, she did not know.

But it seemed to please him. His smile broadened. "If you were in Mother's place, would you want to be told?"

"My God, no! But don't go by me. I'm a devout coward."

"Mother's no coward. Still—"

"You don't have to decide right now. You have time." He placed two fingers on her forearm. The nails were scrupulously clean and smoothly filed. Did he do them himself, or did he still, incredibly, have what Mother called "one of his little manicurists"? "There's something to be said for procrastination, you know. I've always felt that things have their own flow and rhythm, and that if one doesn't interfere too much, they adjust themselves." He sat back. "Some might say that's a lazy man's outlook. They could well be right. God knows, I've always been a lazy man." He sat in silence for a moment. "I wish I could be more helpful to you."

"You are helpful, Uncle Sammy. Even without saying anything. Just by being here with me." She paused. "Just by being."

He looked a little away from her. "I'll cherish that. When I think too much about the senselessness of taking her and leaving me, I'll cherish what you said."

Clara wrote a letter to Steve before she went to bed. It was the first letter she had ever written to him. When she had finished and read it over, it seemed to her something written by another woman to a man she had known years ago. It said she longed for him, but Clara could not enter into the writer's yearning. She remembered a man and woman sitting with their knees bumping under a café table, walking close together through the streets of Paris, making love in a big bed in a small room, but it was like a montage on a movie screen, evoking the surrogate emotions of a viewer.

This letter is all wrong, she wrote in a post-script. *I should have waited with it. I'm too tired now. Or too numb. Or something. But I promised to write every day, so I've done the best I could.*

She thought she would not sleep well, especially after her long nap. In the dark, Mother's perfume was a presence, leaning to listen to the quality of her breathing. Long ago she had learned how to simulate the rhythm of sleep. She did it now, and thought Mother tiptoed out, satisfied, and felt—or dreamed she felt—the old unease for having fooled her.

When she arrived at the hospital, promptly at ten, the fat, gray-haired nurse was coming out of the room with a white basin covered by a towel.

"I wouldn't stay too long this morning," she said. "Mother had a restless night."

But Mother was sitting against the pillows, freshly made up, watching the door with lively anticipation.

"Hello, baby. I was hoping it was you. Sit down and tell me all about last night. How did Hannah and Samuel think you looked?"

Clara gave her a carefully embellished report. Once, after one of the first boy-girl parties she had ever attended, she had tried faithfully to recall for Mother a comment some boy had made about her hair. "He said it was like something, but I can't remember what."

Mother, smiling with advance gratification at this unknown's admiration of Clara's thick, springy blond hair, had suggested several possibilities. "Spun gold?"

"No . . . Oh, I know now! He said it was like steel wool."

Mother had declared the boy to be an idiot. A congenital idiot. She had been so furious that Clara had wished she had settled for spun gold, even though it would have been a lie.

Now Mother asked whether Hannah had had a lot to drink. "Did she get pie-eyed?"

"More or less."

"Mostly more, I'll bet," Mother said, with obvious relish. "She never did know how to drink. The rest of us are all moderate drinkers, but Hannah has always been different from the other Herzogs. Grandma used to say that once she left Great-Grandpa's house she didn't even seem Jewish any more. Jews aren't usually heavy drinkers, you know."

She closed her eyes for a minute, and Clara said quickly, "I'm tiring you. The nurse said you didn't sleep well. Why don't I—?"

"Nonsense. You never tire me." Mother's eyes snapped open. "The nurse is an ass. Well-meaning and kind, but an ass. Of course I didn't sleep well. Nobody sleeps well in a hospital. But I'll get plenty of rest after you go down to the Paper. I've got nothing to do but lie here."

Clara stayed for more than an hour. The nurse looked in several times, but Mother kept shooing her out.

"Beat it, Lizzie! I'm briefing my daughter . . . What are you looking so disapproving about? Lizzie? All right, then, beat it, Miss Lizlo! I'll call you anything to get rid of you . . . Wait a minute. Give me my handbag, Clara. It's in the top drawer . . . Here, Lizzie. Go have a beer on me."

"Oh, you shouldn't! Thank you, but you shouldn't." The nurse's pale lips slid apart, showing an improbable number of large, beige teeth. She stuffed the folded bill into the pocket of her uniform and wagged her head at Clara. "Beer! As if I would! And on duty, at that. Isn't Mother a terror?"

Clara had six pages of notes when she left. Mother's instructions were specific and detailed, down to the exact words Clara was to use in her approach to various people on the staff. "Mother, I'm not you," Clara had objected. "I have to do things in my own way."

"You'll do exactly as I tell you. Who do you think you are? Just because I'm stuck here in bed and I'm letting you sit in my office till I get out—"

"Please don't get excited, Mother. Look how hard you're breathing now. It's not good for you."

"How do you know what's good for me? I'll breathe any way I want to." She had paused for some time, her head turned away, and then looked back at Clara and smiled. "What the hell are we fighting about, baby? Come here and kiss me good-by and get down there. The Paper's gone long enough without a Herzog in the driver's seat."

The few people at the Paper who did not call her Clara greeted her as Miss Herzog. For two years, in Paris, she had been Clara Lowenthal, and now she was Clara Herzog again, and it was as though Clara Lowenthal had never existed. She shut the door of the publisher's office, the cool blue office that smelled of Mother, and sat behind the desk. She spread the pages of notes out on the desk and stared at them. In a little while she would have to do something, send for somebody, behave like the acting publisher of the Paper. The same kind of paralyzing panic seized her as when, in her adolescence and beyond, she had had to enter a room full of people she did not know. She had all Mother's instructions before her. But she could not think how to begin.

The knock on her door released her. Whoever it was, it would be a beginning. Some kind of beginning.

"Come in!" she called, and thought her voice sounded strong and authoritative.

He came in without haste. He had always moved like that, done everything as though there were no hurry, no importance to it. He shut the door behind him and leaned against it, looking at her and grinning. In the more than twenty years since she had first seen him, he must, of course, have changed, but she could not see the change in him.

"Well, Clara," he said. "Well . . ."

He had been leaning against another door, in another room, but he had said the same words in the same voice. She answered him now. Then, she had had no voice for it. "Hello, Fitz. How are you?"

5

After that summer working on the Paper, Clara never went back to Barnard. Grandma tried to persuade her that she was foolish, that she had plenty of time, that if the Paper was really what she wanted, the more education she got, the better. But, for once, she did not listen to Grandma. She did not want to wait three and a half years to begin living her real life. An education did not have to mean sitting in a classroom, letting a teacher stuff facts into you. Fitz had not been to college at all, not even for six months, but he knew a lot more than Harry Whipple, who was a graduate of Princeton. Fitz, at only twenty-four, was one of the best reporters on the Paper.

"Well, if you're sure," Mother said. "I wouldn't want you to regret, later, that you didn't finish college."

Clara had known she would have no trouble with Mother. A good education was, like good clothes, a good address, and a governess, something New York Jewish families provided for their children if they could possibly afford it. But between college and the Paper, Mother thought Clara was making a sensible choice. The daughters of her friends would be envious. College was all right, but for a girl it was really only a way to fill the time until a suitable man came along.

"Grandma thinks I'm making a mistake," Clara said. She had already rejected what Grandma thought, but it would do no harm to be fortified.

"Well, you have to realize," Mother said, "that Grandma is peculiar about the Paper. I think it's because Papa—my father—never got further than chief copyreader. That was Papa's fault, but I think Grandma blames the Paper."

Mother rarely spoke of her father, who had died the year before Clara was born. Nobody in the family mentioned him much, not even Grandma. It was almost as though he had never existed. That was what happened to people who were not remembered. One way to make your existence safe was to write a book that would be read long after you were dead.

Now and then, Clara thought of the novel she was going to write, but she knew she would not be ready to write it for a long time. She had too much to learn, not only about the Paper but about life. Now that she was out of school and working, she realized how little she had ever seen or done. She had never been anywhere, except in the summer to some not-restricted New Jersey hotel or to camp in Maine. She had gone out with a few boys, but she had never been in love, or even close to it. No one had ever fallen in love with her either. Some of the boys who called for her seemed more interested in Mother than in her. Mother knew how to talk to them, to draw them out.

"I hope you don't mind my saying so," one of them said to Clara one night, "but your mother has It."

Clara did not exactly mind. She thought there must be very few mothers of whom that could be said. She was only sorry that she evidently did not have It herself. Harry Whipple, of course, had acted as though she had, but she was not sure how Harry had really felt about her, and she never would be sure, because he left the Paper after that summer and she did not see him again.

He served a purpose, though.

Clara had a friend from high school named Sarah Heller. Sarah had always known she would be a painter, just as Clara had always known she would be a writer. All through school Sarah had saved part of her allowance and any other money she got so that someday she could go to Paris to study painting. The summer Clara started working on the Paper, Sarah went. When she told Clara she was going, Clara thought she was making it up. Sarah sometimes did make things up.

"Your parents will never let you," Clara said.

"Let me? How can they stop me? It's my money, isn't it?"

Clara knew that if it were she who wanted to go off to Europe all by herself, Mother would stop her no matter whose money it was. But Sarah's parents did not stop her. They were much more old-fashioned than Mother, too—a thin, pale little man and a thin, pale little woman who both sat around in house slippers all the time and called girls young ladies. But they let Sarah go. Maybe they really could not stop her. Maybe they were afraid of her. It had never before occurred to Clara that parents could be afraid of their children.

When Sarah got back from Europe after the summer, Clara met her at Schrafft's for lunch.

"Well," Sarah asked her, "are you still a virgin?"

Clara had a doughnut halfway to her mouth. She stared at Sarah, her hand in midair, feeling herself turn hot and red.

"What kind of a question is that?"

Sarah laughed. "So you still are."

"Aren't you?"

"Of course not. Nobody in Paris over eighteen is."

"Oh, come on, Sarah! They're stricter there than here. In good families, anyway. Girls have duennas and things who never leave them alone with men."

"Duennas are Spanish. It's different in Paris. You can believe me or not. Suit yourself. All I can say is, you're missing something."

Clara knew it was not true that nobody in Paris over eighteen was a virgin. She was less certain about Sarah, even though she could see no change in her. Sarah looked a little like both her father and her mother, except that she was robust and red-cheeked and full of energy. It was as if her parents had drained themselves to pour all their juices into her. She was attacking her Luxuro Chocolate Ice-cream Cake with a vigorous abandon that left gobs of fudge sauce around her mouth and on her chin. Somehow Clara was inclined to believe that she really was not a virgin any more.

"You're shocked, aren't you?"

Shocked was certainly one of the things Clara was. A few of her friends went in for fairly heavy necking, but none of them would have thought of going all the way. Like Clara, they were saving themselves for marriage, even if they weren't saving as much of themselves as she was. Men never married girls who went all the way beforehand.

Still, Clara said she was not shocked. She did not want Sarah, who had gone off to Europe and had an affair with a Frenchman, to think she had just stayed home all summer being unsophisticated.

"As a matter of fact, I was almost not a virgin myself," she said. "There was a boy—man—at the Paper who was crazy about me. A Princeton man. Harry Whipple. I had to fight him off one night—"

Clara told Sarah the story. She kept to the truth, and at the same time managed to give the impression that she had fought Harry off only because she did not like him enough.

Then Sarah told Clara all about the Frenchman and all about Paris. It was much better there than here, she said. People were freer there. You could do anything you wanted to and nobody cared. "I'm going back as soon as I can get enough money together again. You ought to come with me. We could rent a studio where I could paint and you could write. There are lots of American writers in Paris."

"Well, I'd love to, but I can't. I told you. I work at the Paper all the time now."

"You can quit, can't you? Why should you stay here and work for your uncle's dull old newspaper when you can have an exciting life in Paris? Be a real writer?"

"What do you mean, dull old newspaper? You don't know what you're talking about. The newspaper business is about the most exciting thing in the world. And if writing for one isn't being a real writer, I don't know what is."

Sarah only shrugged. At that moment, Clara realized that she and Sarah did not have much in common any more. They would go on seeing each other, but it would be at longer and longer intervals, and eventually one of them, to the relief of the other, would stop calling.

It was Sarah who stopped. Clara thought of her now and then. Occasionally she saw her name among a list of artists who were showing their paintings in a New York gallery, and she thought it likely that Sarah had never got back to Paris. Some years later, Clara spied her in Macy's, impatiently pulling a screaming little boy along by the arm. She wondered whether Sarah had ever seen her by-line in the Paper. For a moment she had an absurd impulse to go over and ask her, and then somehow, casually, to bring Fitz into it. Instead, she turned away and left the store before Sarah could catch sight of her.

That day in Schrafft's, though, Clara was a long way from any significant connection with Fitz, and even longer from a by-line. Some of the copy boys had small items printed in the Paper now and then, but nothing Clara wrote was ever used. Everyone on the staff was nice and friendly to her, but sometimes she felt that they thought of her more as a pet, or a mascot, than a newspaperwoman. Fitz was the only one who seemed to take her seriously, to realize she was there to learn the business. If he sent her out for coffee, he was apologetic, as though he understood she was destined for more important things. He encouraged her to keep writing and submitting items, even if they were not accepted. It was good practice, he told her. A writer had to write, no matter what.

Once, she got up enough courage to show him a short piece about a little boy who stood begging at the subway entrance at Seventy-second Street and Broadway every day. When he gave it back to her, there were black lines slashed all through it, leaving less than half of what she had written.

"But there's nothing to it now," she said, as furious at the absurd tears that rushed into her eyes as at him. "You've taken out all the good parts. You've spoiled it."

He turned his back on her. "Don't bother me, then," he said, "until you know enough to take the good parts out yourself."

Clara went off after that to cry in the ladies' room, because she thought it was the end of his being nice to her. But the next day he behaved the same as always.

Clara had expected her real life to start as soon as she left college and began working regularly at the Paper, but it did not seem to be starting. She did not see that she was any further than when she had worked there during the summer. She had imagined writing something so brilliant that it would appear on the front page. Everyone would talk about her remarkable talent (and so young, too!). They would realize she was wasted where she was and make her a reporter right away. Once she was a reporter, she would become poised and confident. You had to be poised and confident, or no attention would be paid to you.

"Maybe I don't have so much talent," she said to Mother. "Maybe I'm not cut out to be a newspaperwoman after all."

"Nonsense, baby," Mother said. "They're just wary of you because they don't know how you fit in. You're only the niece of the publisher, and they can see he has no interest in you. On the other hand, you're a Herzog, Sigmund Herzog's granddaughter, which means you may have certain ambitions that could get in somebody's way."

"What about you? Do they know how you—?"

Mother cut her off with a wave of her hand. "Oh, you know me. I can get away with anything. I think they have an idea I'm just a frivolous woman amusing myself with a new toy and when I get sick of it I'll go back to keeping house." She patted Clara's cheek. "Just don't worry, baby. Be patient. In time, everything will change."

Mother was talking about some kind of change for the better, but the changes others on the Paper talked about were different. There were people who tried to keep Clara from hearing what was said, but she always heard it from somebody. Everything got around eventually. Mother heard it too, but she just smiled.

"Don't worry," she said again. "The Paper isn't going under. It will be here for you and your children and your children's children, exactly as Great-Grandpa planned it."

"Is it true my—William Lowenthal thought it was going under?" Clara did not like to call him "my father" to Mother. "And that's why he left and went to work for Hearst?"

"So he apparently told David. I don't know what he thought. There was never much love lost between those two. Weak men never like each other. It doesn't matter, one way or the other. Whatever any of them think or say, believe me, the Paper is going to survive."

Mother told Clara everything—or almost everything—but not right away. She did not tell her Uncle David had left the Paper, or why, until it was all over. At the time, Mother said she had done the right thing, the only possible thing, to save the Paper. It was only two years later, after Uncle David's accident, that she blamed herself for anything. But she soon got over that. Mother was not one for looking back.

Whatever effect being ousted as publisher had had on Uncle David—and that they would never know—it had been a good thing for the Paper. There was no question that Mother had saved the Paper. When Clara thought of all the people who would have been out of work, and of Aunt Hester, who would not have been brought back to life, and of the collapse of everything Great-Grandpa had built, she could not feel it would have been better to save Uncle David. Even if getting him out had killed him, as Mother had extravagantly suggested for a time, Clara could not feel it. She was bothered by this, because she was not sure she would have felt the same way if she had loved him. She did not know whether or not Mother loved him. Some of her friends who had brothers hated them. Or said they did.

As soon as Mother became the publisher, everything did change. It was not only the practical improvements she effected that made the difference. It was Mother herself. If there was a slump—one of those dead periods when no important news was coming in and too many reporters were sitting around waiting for assignments—she had only to walk through the newsroom to electrify the atmosphere. If she spoke to a nervous young reporter or a lowly clerk, he was instantly transformed, convinced of his unique importance to the operation of the Paper. It was Mother, more than the Paper, for whom most of the staff enthusiastically worked.

"I think you've futzed around long enough," she said to Clara soon after she took over, "filling paste pots. I think it's time we began turning you into a journalist. Come on."

She was talking to Clara in the back of the newsroom. Now she turned and walked toward the front, said something to the city editor that Clara, following behind, could not hear, and then moved to Fitz's desk, beckoning to Clara to join her.

Fitz was typing in his indolent way. He looked up and smiled at Clara before he gave his attention to Mother. Clara thought no one else on the Paper would have done that.

"Fitz, I've got an assignment for you," Mother said. "I'd like you to make a reporter of this child of mine."

She waited for him to say something, but he was waiting, too. Finally he gave a little shrug. "Go on, please."

Mother looked annoyed. People did not often require elaboration before they said yes to her. But it was hard to stay annoyed with Fitz. There was nothing challenging in his face. A *used* face, was how Clara thought of it. The lines that in a few years would become deep grooves across his forehead and down the sides of his mouth were already sketched in. His bright blue eyes brimmed with knowledge that his quick, frequent Irish grin did not want told.

"I had in mind a kind of apprenticeship," Mother said. "Let her watch you, see the way you operate— You'll know better than I how to do it, Fitz." She lowered her voice, although no one at the other desks could have heard over the clatter of the typewriters. "For my money, there's not a reporter on the staff, regardless of age, who can teach her as much. If you tell any of the others I said so, I'll deny it."

Fitz shifted his gaze to Clara. "How does the idea strike you?"

"I think it's fine."

"Of course she does," Mother said. "She's dying to be a reporter. She has always written, you know. Since she could hold a pencil. All she needs is experience, and someone like you to direct her talent. I don't think you'll find it a hard job. Well," Mother went on, after a pause that Fitz did not fill, "you may as well start right away."

"Mother, he hasn't said he'll do it. Maybe he doesn't think—"

"Certainly I'll do it," Fitz said to Clara. "Do the best I can, anyhow. It will be a pleasure."

Mother did not seem to remember, afterward, that it was she who had thrown Clara and Fitz together. If she did, she never mentioned it. Clara had a notion that at the time Mother did not really think of Fitz as a man—simply as the means by which Clara would learn what she needed to know at this stage of her journey to eventual stewardship of the Paper. Either that, or to Mother, in the invulnerability of her rigid code, Fitz was sexless. It would have been inconceivable to her that she might not have transmitted to Clara her own absolute immunity to a man who was neither Jewish nor unmarried.

"We've been separated for three years," he told Clara. "We were only together for one. I'm not a man who should have married in the first place. Luckily there's no danger of my doing it again, since we're Catholic."

He talked little about himself, but he told her this at the beginning. Later she understood why. At the time she was pleased with what she thought of as personal communication. "Isn't it a lonely life?"

"Not very," he said, and grinned at her. "Oh, come on, now, don't blush. I was only—"

"I can't help blushing. It's physiological. I cry the same way. It's a nuisance, and I hate it, but I have no more control over it than I have over sneezing. Less."

"Well, don't let it worry you. It's cute." He tucked her hand into the crook of his arm. "You're a funny combination of old and young, do you know that?"

"Funny-haha, or funny-peculiar?"

He shook his head. "Funny-intriguing."

She was half in love with him then, but she did not recognize it. She only knew she felt happy. He was taking her with him on an assignment and letting her write it up afterward, though of course he would go over it before it went into the Paper. It was not the first time, but it was the most exciting. They were covering a dance marathon that had been going on for nearly two weeks in a ballroom on Seventh Avenue.

Fitz said twenty-five couples had entered the contest. When he and Clara got there, only six couples were holding each other up.

They looked bedraggled and dazed, like accident victims. One girl collapsed as they watched. Her partner tried desperately to haul her to her feet and get her moving again, but an orderly rushed out and shoved him aside so he could minister to her. The other couples slogged around her as though she were a log of wood. When she was carried out, her partner stood screaming curses after her until he was forcibly removed from the floor.

"He's off his rocker," Clara heard a spectator say. "They get that way. One guy thought his partner was after him with a hatchet. He looked like he could hardly move his feet no more, but I never see a guy light out so fast, yelling all the way."

Following Fitz's lead, Clara tried to interview a girl contestant during the hourly fifteen-minute recess. An attendant was massaging her feet while a nurse took her pulse.

"Go away," the girl said, as soon as Clara opened her mouth. "Go away, gowaygowaygoway—"

"You can't give up so easily," Fitz told Clara when they got outside. "One of them would have talked to you. A reporter has to have the persistence of a bulldog and the hide of an elephant."

Clara, who had been close to collapse herself in that steamy madhouse of a ballroom, shook her head despairingly.

"I'm nothing like that. I don't see how I'm ever going to be anything like that."

"Well, if you can't be, you can't," he said with a shrug. "You'll just have to learn to act as if you were."

He was sympathetic and tolerant about everything except her writing. About that he was ruthless.

The marathon dance craze continues all over the country. Men and women, staggering around countless dance floors to the tune of the latest fox-trot, go through agony trying to outlast each other, trying to prove that in one thing, at least, however absurd, they are better than anybody else . . .

Fitz read that far, and tore it up. He used a dirty word to describe what he thought of it. "What do you think you're writing? A sociological study? Tell what you saw, what they did, what they said. In that ballroom. Last night. News. N-E-W-S. In short sentences." He was sitting at his desk, looking at it, not at her, hitting the wood softly with his fist to punctuate each phrase. "If that last sentence ever got as far as the city editor, he'd chew you up and spit you out. Besides, it's hooey. *Trying to prove . . . !*" He broke off and looked up at her, shaking his head. "You dumb, overprivileged kid. Haven't you ever heard of the Depression? Those poor slobs you saw tonight aren't trying to prove anything. They're trying to win the prize money so they can eat a little longer."

Clara had been standing next to his chair. Now she leaned over and gripped the edge of his desk, furiously blinking back tears. "Don't you call me dumb," she whispered. "I may have a lot to learn about being a reporter. If I didn't have, I wouldn't be trailing around after you. But don't you ever call me dumb."

She stalked away from him, found an empty desk at the back of the room, rolled a sheet of paper into the typewriter, and began jabbing ferociously at the keys. At the next desk sat one of the younger reporters, slouching in boredom, enduring his second day of waiting for the city editor to find an assignment trivial enough for his humble status. He glanced gloomily across at Clara and then sat up a little. "Hey, what's the matter with *you?*"

She looked at him in surprise. "What do you mean? Nothing's the matter with me."

"Do you generally sit typing with the tears streaming down your face?"

Clara felt her cheeks. "Oh, that," she said, using her palms as blotters. "That's only this story I'm writing. It's so sad."

She finished her new piece about the dance marathon, put it on Fitz's desk, and started to walk away. He caught her by the sleeve. "Wait a minute." He was always grinning. When a person grinned that much, it was not even attractive. "I meant dumb-ignorant, not dumb-stupid. Ignorance can be cured." He held on to her while he read what she had written. "This is okay," he said then, not grinning. "You're going to make a damn good reporter someday."

She stood stiffly in his grasp. "What do you mean, someday? Ten years?"

"Well, let's not hurry it too much," he said in a low voice. "Once you've learned everything I know, what excuse will we have for you to trail around after me?"

Looking back afterward, she understood that he had had his eye on her from the beginning. It did not then, or later, interfere with the job he had undertaken to do. He took her everywhere, showed her a New York she had not known existed, made her interview Bowery bums and prostitutes, ward heelers, patrons of bread lines, barbers with nobody to shave at ten cents a face, slum landlords, families living in Hooverville shacks on Riverside Drive. He taught her how to call a story in to the Paper, giving the essentials to a rewrite man. He slashed away at stories she wrote herself, until she learned how to say what she had to say in lean, clear prose. He bullied, badgered, and hammered her into the shape of a journalist. Whether he did it out of pride, because he had said he would, out of love for the profession, or because he sensed how it would bind her to him, she was never sure.

She was so ripe for him. All she knew were the routine kisses and fumblings custom demanded—the involuntary, unfocused response of her resistant body.

One evening, after they had finished an assignment, he took her to a meeting in an apartment in Greenwich Village. About twenty girls and men were crowded into the small living room, most of them sitting on the floor. They kept shouting and interrupting each other, so that it was hard to understand what they were talking about. Something to do with the weaknesses of American democracy and the need for an alternative system of government. After a while she began to get the drift. Most of them were members of the Communist Party. They were trying to persuade the others to join. Clara thought some of the ideas were interesting, but it was not clear to her why Fitz had brought her.

When it was over and they all started to leave, she got up too.

"Wait awhile," Fitz said. "It's early."

She did not know what he wanted her to wait for, but she sat down again. In a few minutes everybody had gone.

"Would you like a drink?" Fitz asked her. "Or a cup of coffee?"

He was standing in front of her chair. She stared up at him.

"What is this? Where are the people who live here?"

"I live here. This is my apartment."

She had a faint memory of his telling her he had an apartment in the Village, but it had made no impression. She had not thought of him as living anywhere, except maybe at his desk at the Paper. "But how did those people get in?"

"I left the key."

"Do you belong to the—?"

"No. I'm sympathetic, but I'm not much of a joiner. I let them meet here because I'm hardly ever home and it's central for most of them. What about that drink?"

She said, "All right." While he went off somewhere to get it—to the kitchen, she supposed—she sat on her hands because they began to feel cold. The room looked larger, now that it was empty. There was not much furniture. A studio couch covered with a brown corduroy throw and a lot of big cushions, two overstuffed chairs and one straight-backed maple chair, a maple table in front of the sofa, a maple desk, bookshelves between the two windows. Everywhere there were dirty glasses and ashtrays full of butts.

"What a mess!" Fitz said, coming in with two orange blossoms. "Usually one of the girls cleans up, but I guess—" He did not finish. "Try your drink. I didn't make it too strong."

She took a sip. "No. It's good. Well, relatively, anyhow." She held the glass with both hands, afraid that otherwise she would spill the contents. "I don't really like the taste of any drink. Only the effect."

This was not the way she talked to Fitz. She seemed to have forgotten how to do that. She wished he would sit down, instead of standing in the middle of the room, watching her over the top of his glass. "The air's not fit to breathe in here," he said when she had finished. "Come on in the other room."

"I really ought to go home."

He pulled her gently to her feet and led her into the bedroom. He closed the door and leaned against it, looking at her. "Well, Clara," he said. "Well—it's about time for you and me, isn't it?"

Grandma was the only one who had no idea, who would not have believed it if anyone had told her. When Clara was with Grandma, she felt like another person disguised as Clara.

"Take some chocolate peppermints, Little One."

She knew the right drawer to open. She knew beforehand the bittersweet crispness, the tangy, sugary creaminess. But Little One was somebody else.

"I know it's right," she said to Fitz. "Loving you makes it right."

"Christ, kiddo, stop talking it to death. You always did use too many words."

She thought the time might come when he would want to hear her say she loved him, but it never did. He never told her he loved her. All she could do was endow him with an ethical reticence, and then believe in it.

He broke it off the first time because he said he was becoming too important to her. "I don't want to be responsible for your happiness."

Other times he gave other reasons. Eventually she knew that none of them was true, though he might have thought so. On occasion she was the one to break it off, the reasons she gave him no more genuine than his.

They stayed apart for long intervals—several months, a year, more. She tried, each time. She saw other men, attracted them now in a way she never had before, as though they smelled some emanation she had not previously exuded. To Clara, they might as well have been paper cutouts, representations of a species that had Fitz as its sole living member.

She knew early that their separations did not empty Fitz's bed. In time she knew women were his preoccupation. Still she did not rewrite the piece to edit out love. What else was it that always brought him back to her in the end? Back and back and back, through the years?

She had enough. Fitz and the Paper. She became an able reporter, and knew it, knew she was not sent out on big stories and given a by-line because she was the publisher's daughter, but because she had ability, the Herzog talent. She was part of a great tradition, dedicated to promoting justice, preserving freedom, ferreting out the truth for all to know.

"Nuts," Fitz said. "It's a business like any other. If you happen to be good at it and to think it's more fun than most lines of work, it's the thing to do. Why do you have to clutter everything up with marshmallow frosting?"

Clara paid no attention when he talked like that. It was his way. Sentiment embarrassed him. He pretended to be tough. She knew he was different inside.

Some things she learned quickly. She learned the world was not bounded by 110th Street and Seventy-second Street on the north and south, by Park Avenue and the Hudson River on the east and west. She learned why America was not the land of opportunity for everybody that it had been for Sigmund Herzog. She learned that the impeccable heroes of school history books were largely figments, and that even Franklin Roosevelt, with his bold imagination, his brilliant leadership, his compassion for the unfortunate, could be Machiavellian.

It took her much longer to learn about the Paper. A slow accumulation. Stories she phoned in garbled into misstatements by a rewrite man without firsthand knowledge of the facts and more concerned with pleasing sentence structure than with truth. Stories chosen or eliminated by editors to appeal to the tastes of the hypothetical average reader of the Paper. A man made bureau chief, and a more capable one passed over, because of internal politics and personal animosity. Editorials that wept for the terrible poverty of one third of the nation while advertisements invited lavish spending on luxury items. A moving piece on the plight of the Negro, but no Negro employees on the Paper except the janitor, Ronald, the husband of Aunt Hannah's maid. Policies adopted and changed out of expediency rather than conviction . . .

She was always preparing herself to write her novel, and was never prepared. When Fitz was actively in her life, he absorbed her. When he was out of it, she could not sit in solitude confronting herself.

"I've been trying to do too many things for too many years. The Paper always had to come first," she told Mother.

And Fitz, she did not say. Fitz and the Paper. The Paper and Fitz.

"I want out," she told Mother.

"I want out," she told Fitz.

"The door's wide open. It always has been."

"Open is for coming in as well as going out. I want it shut. Kept shut."

He grinned at her. "If you need a door monitor, don't pick me. You ought to know I'm not reliable. I never pretended I was."

"You've sometimes pretended to have scruples."

"I do have scruples. My trouble is the same as yours. Only, I know what it is and you've always tried to fancy it up into something it isn't."

The night before she left for Paris, it was as always when they had separated. Even the touch of the sheets was painful, as though she had no skin.

Halfway across the ocean, she looked down from the plane window at a floor of cotton clouds that disconnected the world, and felt —with astonishment, some reluctance, and a little embarrassment— relieved.

6

He shut the door behind him and leaned against it, looking at her and grinning.

"Well, Clara. Well . . ."

"Hello, Fitz. How are you?"

"The same as ever." He let that hang for a minute. "You haven't changed. A little Paris gloss, maybe, but I'd know you anywhere."

"One of several changes is that I'm in this office. For the time being." It came out all right. Impersonal, but not unfriendly. A touch of wry. "I intended to speak to some of the editors first, but as long as you're here, sit down, and we'll go over a few things."

He did not move. "When will Becky be back?"

"The doctor can't give me a date. It won't be soon. Let's get down to business, Fitz. I do have a lot of other people to see, and a lot of work to do."

He took his time ambling to the chair, sliding his long body down until he was half off it. Mother would have told him with fake severity to sit up. He might have done it, and he might not. "Shoot."

As soon as she began, he interrupted her.

"Just a minute, before we get into this. Will you have dinner with me tonight?"

"No," she said. "I'm engaged, Fitz. I'm going to be married. Now please let me—"

"That's fine. Congratulations. Are you having dinner with him?"

"He's in Paris."

"Well, then, what's to keep you from having dinner with me? For old time's sake? Christ, Clara, I haven't seen you for more than two years!"

She picked up the notes she had made in the hospital and looked at them without knowing what she read.

"I understand you feel you're going stale on your column," she said.

Oct. 8, 1949

Dear Steve:

I know my letters so far must have been disappointing to you. They have been to me. I wanted to talk to you through them. How we always talked, didn't we? From the first evening. But I can't seem to find that voice. It's like something I once knew in a dream, and can only recover if I dream it again.

Or maybe this, now, is the dream. At times I think it must be. I move from the apartment to the hospital to the Paper to the hospital without any sense that I am in control of my life, or even of my muscles. Often when I walk down the hall to Mother's room in the morning, not knowing how I will find her, I have that dreamlike sense of pressing against an impeding current, with a pursuer on my heels.

One day, sitting at Mother's desk, I felt all at once that I had changed into her, and that if I looked in the mirror I would see her face. For a second or two, I was actually afraid to look.

All this is probably nothing more than strain. I've come back to a familiar place where so much has turned unfamiliar (that's like a dream, too, of course) and it's easy to get lost. I don't remember ever seeing Mother sick in bed before, and now they say she's dying. I try to believe it, so I'll be prepared, but it isn't possible. She even infuriates me on occasion, the way she did when I thought there was as much time for anger as for love. Then I go down and try to run the Paper, knowing that whatever fantasies I may have, I'm not her, and that no one else imagines, for even an illusory second, that I am.

Your postcards are a comfort, reminding me another world exists somewhere and I once existed in it, at home in this same skin. Please keep sending them. Please be patient with me.

Love,
Clara

November 28, 1949

Dear Hester:

Thanks for the letter, which arrived *on* my birthday. Even the erratic French postal system gives way before Herzog punctilio.

I'm glad you think we've made the right decision about not telling Mother. We'll never be sure, of course, but we wouldn't be the other way either. As long as all of us who know her best feel this is what she'd choose if she could, there's no reason ever to regret it.

No, it really isn't hard to—well, fool her is the way to put it, I suppose, though it's not a comfortable concept. Except for the doctors and nurses, only Hannah, Samuel, and I know, and we all seem to take naturally to the deception. For me, at least, this is partly explained by my eagerness to deceive myself. We're helped, according to Dr. Jimmy, by the psychology of the gravely ill, who are deaf to anything less explicit than a blunt announcement of their condition, and sometimes deaf even to that.

Though she tires very easily now, she still wants detailed reports of what's happening at the Paper, and she still tells me how to handle everything. My decisions and methods would often be different, but though I know she'll never sit in the publisher's office again, I keep thinking of it as her Paper, and myself as her deputy. I always feel her looking over my shoulder. I suppose I always have.

Steve writes that he sees you often, but not what you talk about. He writes only postcards. They give me no sense of him. Tell me what he says, how he looks. I know it sounds insane, after only two months, but I don't clearly remember his face. I can't hear his voice. For more than a year, I was happier with him than I've ever been in my life, yet the shape of that happiness eludes me now. Does he talk to you about me?

You've read in the newspapers, I'm sure, that Walter died a few days ago. I went to the funeral with Samuel, partly because he asked me to—you know how he hates to go anywhere alone—and partly to pay my respects to a remarkable man. I'd had an idea I could somehow manage it without having to meet my father, but of course that was ridiculous. He knew who I was immediately, and waited outside for me after the service so he and I could ride in the same car to the cemetery. Samuel, who went in another car, could hardly wait to hear about it afterward. He's as curious and fond of gossip as he ever was.

Considering the inherent drama, it was pretty pedestrian. I could tell he was my father. I have his coloring, his mouth, his soft way of speaking. But I didn't feel any shock of recognition, or of anything else. It wasn't even as embarrassing or difficult as I'd have expected. He might have been a pleasant, mild-mannered old friend of the family catching up on what's been happening. I liked him and I think he liked me, but neither of us suggested another meeting. It's much too late for me to acquire a father, or he a daughter. We'd muff the roles. But I'm glad I met him. I didn't, incidentally, mention it to Mother.

Tell me about Steve.

Love,
Clara

December 15, 1949

Dear Steve:

Hester thinks, though she says you've never told her so, that you believe you may have lost me. It isn't true. If I say nothing about eventually going back to Paris, it's because I have so much to deal with here that I can't see beyond it yet. All I can do is handle one day at a time.

I asked you in an earlier letter to be patient with me. You've told me, and I know, you're not a patient man. But I'm still in that dream, stumbling and pursued. Steve, don't give me up before I wake.

Love,
Clara

Just after Christmas, Rick Schuman came up to Mother's office and told Clara he wanted to resign from the Paper.

"I'd have preferred to wait until Becky got back so I could give my notice to her," he said, "but I'd rather not put it off any longer. Naturally I'll stay until I'm replaced."

Clara looked away from him. He had been managing editor of the Paper for over twenty years. Mother said he knew more about handling the news, and the staff of newsmen under him, than any other managing editor in New York. With Rick there, Mother said, Clara had nothing to worry about. In an emergency, he could probably run the Paper singlehanded.

"Is anything wrong?" Clara asked him.

"Wrong? No. Unless getting old is wrong." He still looked like an amiable countryman, but his face was stitched with criss-cross lines and his loose, shambling movements were turning stiff. "I've been here too long as it is. The Paper needs younger people, with fresh ideas."

"And that's why you want to leave?"

"That's a side benefit to the Paper. I want to leave because I'm tired, and my wife hates the cold New York winters now. If it weren't for Becky's illness, we'd have been in Florida by Christmas."

Clara sighed. "There's nothing I can say to that, is there? I've never thought of your not being here. It's a shock." She paused. "Have you any ideas about who should succeed you?"

"Well, you'd better talk that over with Becky first." He gave her a sharp look. "She's not too sick, is she?"

"No, of course not."

Clara knew there were rumors that Mother was sicker than the family was admitting, and she did not want to give substance to them. But she had no intention of letting Mother know Rick was resigning. It would upset her to think of Clara there without him to

381

lean on. Nothing Clara could control was ever going to upset Mother again.

"It wouldn't hurt to give me your suggestions, though," Clara said, "and let me put them to her."

"She knows what I think. We've talked about it."

"You mean you told her you were going to resign?"

"Everybody resigns eventually, willingly or not. We've discussed the eventuality."

"I'd be interested in hearing what names came up."

Rick got to his feet. "Well, you ask Becky," he said in his deceptive, easygoing drawl. "Give her my love. Tell her I'll be in to see her as soon as she can have company."

It was not like Rick Schuman to be so wary of expressing his preferences. Clara puzzled over this for a few minutes after he had left the office, but she had more urgent concerns. If she tried to find out from Mother whom she and Rick had discussed, Mother would know at once that Rick was resigning. Even now, sick as she was, she would know. She was, as Hester always said, a *Hexe*. Only in the matter of her illness, was it possible to deceive her.

"Your Steve isn't coming, is he?"

"What are you talking about, Mother? I told you he has to finish his book before he can come. It just isn't going as fast as he expected."

"You never used to lie to me, baby."

In effect, the choice of a new managing editor was up to Clara. It should not have been difficult. The post would ordinarily have gone to one of the two assistant managing editors. But one worked on special assignments for Rick and had neither the experience nor the personality to handle Rick's job, and the other was almost old enough for retirement himself. They were surely not among the possibilities Mother and Rick had discussed.

Who, then? The national-news editor? Carter Hoag was a good newsman who worked well with his own staff, but he was old-womanish, jealous of his authority, forever squabbling with the city editor, Frank Nolan, over the jurisdiction of stories. Morris Fishman had presided over the bull pen for so many years that he could not be imagined in any other role. What Rick said was true. Most of those in key positions had been in them so long their jobs had hardened around them. Maybe Mother and Rick had thought of bringing in somebody from the outside, trying to hire an able man away from one of the other newspapers. Or—

She knew Fitz's knock. Light, minimal, a bone to the convention of knocking on doors. He was in before she had finished the admissive words, moving without haste to her desk, settling on a corner of it with one foot touching the floor, so that he half stood, half sat.

"You look bothered, kiddo. Pretty, but bothered."

Kiddo. The deliberate hark-back. No one called anybody kiddo any more. "I'm very busy, Fitz. If you've come on newspaper business, let's hear what it is. Otherwise, it will have to wait."

"Otherwise has been waiting, lo, these many weeks. It can wait a little longer." He leaned toward her. "Remember how long it waited in the first place? Making a reporter of you in the meantime? Until you were ready for otherwise?"

She pushed her chair back on its casters, away from him. "Get out, Fitz, will you? I have work to do."

"But I can't go before I tell you why I'm here. I didn't come for otherwise." He grinned. "You were the one who brought that up."

Clara tried to think her face into the throttling look that Mother would have used, but Fitz had slid off the desk to move to a chair, and did not notice.

"Rick Schuman has talked to you, hasn't he?"

"About what?"

"Come on, Clara. You don't have to be cagey with me. About resigning."

"And if he has?"

"And if he has, he must also have talked to you about his successor."

Clara sat up. "No," she said. "He wouldn't. First he wants to hear what Mother has to say."

"Rick knows damn well what Mother has to say."

Clara could not guess why he was angry, but his anger helped her. It separated him from her, cooled her. "Rick may know. I don't."

"You don't? I'll tell you. Mother has to say ability doesn't count, years of experience don't count, working your tail off doesn't count." He kept slamming his fist into his palm. "That's what Mother has to say. None of it counts. Not if you've been too friendly with Daughter."

"I don't know what you're talking about," Clara said, although she thought she probably did. "None of it counts for what?"

He let his arms fall away from each other and inched down in his chair until he was in his usual, spine-end position. "For me, kiddo. For me to be managing editor. Christ knows, the job is coming to me, and I'm the man for it. Rick knows it too. So does Becky. Only, she won't hear of it. Mother won't hear of it. Put that sonofabitch mick in the managing editor's chair after he had the gall to make up to her girl? Not a chance!"

She had never felt so calm. It was like floating on a cool, motionless surface. Somewhere beneath was an ebullition, but nothing to do with her. "You're talking nonsense. Whatever Mother's personal feelings may be, they'd never influence her where the Paper is concerned. If they could, you wouldn't be sitting here. You'd have been gone long ago." He tried to say something, but she rode serenely over him. "If she thought you were the best choice to replace Rick, nothing would prevent her from making you managing editor."

"No? Is it her judgment that's warped, then?"

"What arrogance!"

His eyes appeared hard and shining, their surface reflecting the blue of the room. "Look, let's stop playing word games, huh? I want this job, and the only one who can get it for me is you. I don't care why she doesn't want me to have it. If you ask, she'll give it to me. She'd jump off the Brooklyn Bridge if you asked her to."

"Don't tell me what she'd do. You don't know anything about it." Her eyes felt as hard as his looked, as though if she were to cry, the tears would be dammed behind them. "And if you think I'd ask her unless I felt it was right for the Paper, you don't know anything about me."

His voice changed pitch. "After twenty years? I know the little scar between your shoulder blades and the mole above your navel and the wonderland inside your skull. Of course you feel it's right for the Paper. Who else is there with my qualifications? But here's a thing I know about you that you don't." He grinned at her. "If you didn't feel it was right, you'd tell yourself you did and ask her anyway."

Invisibly, she shivered. "Would I? Well, we'll see. Rick just told me he'd have to be replaced. I haven't had a chance to give it much thought."

He pushed himself up from the chair, reached across the desk, and stroked the back of her neck lightly, once. "You go ahead and give it thought. Then if Becky should be a little stubborn when you ask her, you might want to tell her I'd have to quit the Paper if I didn't get the job. I wouldn't want to do that after all these years, but I'd have no choice. I'd have to go where I'd be appreciated."

In January 1950 the second trial of Alger Hiss, a well-born and respected State Department official who had denied charges that he had transmitted documents to the Russians, ended in his conviction for perjury.

In February, a vulgar, flamboyant, virtually unknown politician named Joseph McCarthy announced in a speech at Wheeling, West Virginia, that the State Department was full of Communists working and making policy, and that he and the Secretary of State had their names.

In March, Communist power in the Far East began to mobilize for war in Korea.

On the Paper, the rivalry between the Washington Bureau and the New York office was so acute that when a New York newsman got an early tip to the effect that President Truman planned to send American troops to Korea, no one on the Washington staff would help him confirm it. The New York man worked on it himself, at long distance. When the story appeared prominently in the Paper, Harry Whipple went to great lengths to get it discredited as a baseless rumor so that New York would learn its lesson and leave Washington news to the Washington Bureau.

April 2, 1950

Dear Hester:

Mother died two nights ago. In her sleep, the nurse said. Peacefully. Dr. Jimmy says it would have done no good for me to be there, and yet it seems wrong that I wasn't. So lonely. She wouldn't have known, he said. But wouldn't she?

I saw her last in the afternoon. She was in considerable pain for the first time. Or for the first time she couldn't help letting me see it. I went out of the room for a few minutes, and was standing in the hall with my forehead against the wall when Dr. Jimmy came along. He asked me what was the matter and I reminded him he had promised not to let her suffer. He patted my shoulder without saying anything and went into the room. When he came out, I went back in. She seemed more comfortable and told me she thought she'd take a nap. I kissed her, and then I said, without knowing I was going to

385

say it, that I'd had a letter from Steve that morning, and that he'd finished his book and was coming in a few days and we'd be married in June. I said I'd meant to surprise her, but I couldn't keep it to myself. She smiled and said, "I'm so glad, baby," and closed her eyes. I didn't see her again. It's a good way to remember her. But I have no idea what explanation I'd have given her if she had lived to know Steve wasn't coming.

The funeral was today at Temple Emanu-El. I'd have liked a small gathering of family and close friends, with those who loved her and knew her best saying what she meant to them. Samuel said it wasn't possible for someone in her position, and I suppose he was right. The whole temple was filled—that huge place. The music was beautiful and the service was all right, but the eulogy was awful. I'd said I didn't want a eulogy, but apparently that wasn't possible either. The rabbi, who had never met her, of course, since she hasn't been inside a temple since Grandma died, took the facts we gave him and embroidered them so wildly that there wasn't much resemblance to anyone we knew. He kept referring to her as "this sainted mother." I could hear her laughing. "I'll sainted-mother him right in the eye!" she'd have said.

Hester, I can't believe she's dead. I know she is. I cry because she is. But when the phone rings, I think it's going to be her, saying, "Hello, baby. It was all a mistake." I really think that. It's crazy.

Love,
Clara

April 25, 1950

Dear Steve:

This is my third try at this letter. Now I'm going ahead with it. I have two things to tell you—two things I know, after these months back in New York—and I'm going to have to trust the words of telling to come right.

I'll start with the hardest. It's quickly said: I can't return to Paris. I must stay here and publish the Paper. I've known it from the first, but I've faced it only since Mother's death.

To say why will take much longer.

Because Sigmund Herzog had a dream, and Mother carried it on, and I can't let it die.

Yes, I was going to leave the Paper. I would have. That was something else. I never thought of Mother's not living on for years, the

386

way the Herzogs do. Twenty years. By then, newspapers could be obsolete, taken over by radio and television. Or you and I might have had a son who wanted to be a journalist.

Now it's too soon, and I'm the only Herzog left to keep the dream alive.

I still hate the things I always hated, but I have the power to change them now. Or try to change them. Some of them. And what I loved, what I thought made the Paper great, made me proud to be a part of it, can still be. Must be, in this unsettling time for America.

Over there, away from it, you may not sense what's happening. Ever since the conviction of Hiss and the rise of that charlatan McCarthy, the whole tone of the country has begun to change. McCarthy is frightening the people into believing the government is in the hands of traitors. His methods are putting American democracy in terrible danger. If the Paper ever had a mission, it is to fight him.

One mission, soon over, maybe. It's only an example. There will be other missions. As long as the Paper is, as the masthead promises, and as I intend to keep it—or make it—independent of any man or party, and without fear, there will be missions.

Maybe I deceive myself with grandiloquent notions, the way I did when I was much younger. But then it was out of my hands. Now I have a chance—at least a chance—to reshape the dream. I have to try.

The second thing to tell, I said was easier. Now that I've come to it, I think it may be harder. It needs new words. The old ones have staled away into meaninglessness.

I love you, for instance. So stale. Except that until now I haven't said it to you, or written it, since I left you. Carefully not. As you've surely noticed. It would have been easy to say. I remembered loving you. But I didn't want to say it that way, like the lines of a popular song.

You see, I came home again. There were changes—Mother, lying in a hospital bed; I, in her chair at her desk in her office—but so much was so familiar. I wasn't sure I had ever left. Really left, I mean.

Now I know. Now I can write it to you. I love you. Love you, and yet not going back to you? How I've worried that one! If I loved you, I wouldn't feel I'm not free. I wouldn't give a hoot for the Herzog heritage, if I loved you. It's what we're taught. Love comes first, or it isn't love. For a woman. Only, I know it isn't true. We're taught wrong. If a man lets love drive out his dream, we're taught something different, aren't we?

I love you, yes. And need you. Need you, as you once said, for completeness. Still, I'm staying here. Alone, because without you is alone. Not writing the novel I want to write. Incomplete.

It's what I have to do, my love.

Clara

She stayed in the Sutton Place apartment. It held no memories of Mother. When the clothes were gone, Mother's perfume went with them. She replaced the satin bedspread and a few of the more elaborate furnishings, and moved the gate-leg table up between the windows so that she could look out at the river while she ate. Night, with indistinguishable boats sliding along the water and undefined lights studding the dark, obscured geography. She could have been at a table in the Tour d'Argent, overlooking the Seine.

As soon as she could get through the day without unexpected gusts of weeping, she went back to work. Meanwhile, she had herself moved out of Mother's office and into the one David had occupied on the newsroom floor. She wrote out and memorized what she wanted to say to the staff. It was hard to remember that she would not have to explain to Mother. When she did remember, grief and guilt hustled to smother relief. She knew those busybodies from long years back. Escaped, the first time, through the bushes on Riverside Drive, seven years old and running free along the waterfront, they had pursued her until she was caught; until she felt the hard smack of Mother's silver-backed hairbrush on her bottom, and would not cry.

"I want to be something other than an administrative publisher, separated from the working, writing core of the Paper," she told the staff. "This doesn't mean anyone else's function will be changed. Only the publisher's. And I'm changing that not because I think I have a better concept of the job, but because of what I am. I'm a writer and a trained reporter, neither of which my mother was or wanted to be. I've always had ink on my fingers. Now I'll be a publisher with ink on my fingers."

It was, after all, as much an explanation to Mother as to the staff. Most of them cared very little for her reasons. They had had twenty years of Mother, who had swept through the building in her black dress and pearls, leaving a glittering trail of charm, and gone away upstairs to run things. Now they had Clara. She could have been anybody. An ordinary woman in a skirt and cashmere sweater sitting on an empty desk to talk to them. She had her office right here, on the periphery of the newsroom. Peculiar, to those who had come since David's time. Troubling, to those who remembered David. No one was left who knew that Sigmund Herzog had had his office on the newsroom floor too.

"In my great-grandfather's day, this was a crusading newspaper," she told them. "I think the time for crusading has come again. I think we need more investigative reporting. Our reporting of the news is magnificent—as complete, accurate, and unbiased as I believe it's possible, given the human factor, for news reporting to be. What I'd like to see is more digging behind the news by reporters and correspondents, and more analysis and interpretation of the news by editors and columnists."

What are you saying, baby? That I didn't know how to run the Paper?

"All this seems to me of particular importance now, because of what I see as a crisis of confidence in our government and our democratic processes."

She stopped and looked around the room, saw a blur of politely upturned bored faces, and deled the remainder of her memorized lines.

"One thing I always found tough as a reporter was to be objective. Now that I'm a publisher, I don't have to be objective any more. You'll find me screaming on the editorial page, whenever I have something to scream about. Nobody has to agree with me, or reflect my views, to hold his job, but if some conservative stomachs aren't strong enough to digest what I have to say, I'll understand their wanting to move out. One of my first screams will be about Joseph McCarthy. I'm going to expose him if I have to fly down to Washington myself and find out how to take him apart . . ."

She had in the back of her mind to add that Mother, though she would have been unlikely to go herself, would surely have sent somebody else. But they applauded before she could say it, and she decided that was a good place to stop. She might not have said it anyway.

"That was a smart little speech," Fitz said. "Telling them you're not Becky before they could say it. Taking their lines away."

"Do you think I invented myself for the purpose?"

He pretended not to know what she meant. Or did not know. She had once believed he had an invisible center of tender perception, but she had endowed him with a number of qualities that Nature had never had in mind for him. "Let me know when you have something to tell me," he said. "I don't want to bother you too soon."

She waited two weeks before she sent for him. First she talked to Rick Schuman and to some of the executives upstairs, where Mother's former office was occupied by Lleland Winston, once business manager of the Paper and now its general manager. Winston, a clever, even-featured, socially prominent man in his late fifties, had been one of Mother's casual conquests. He tried, with impeccable manners, to patronize Clara and was thrown off balance by her disregard.

"You're very wise to go slowly, my dear; to ask for advice along the way. You are, after all, quite new to all this. Quite young, too, for such an important position."

"In this instance, I'm asking for comment rather than advice. Simply to make sure that in coming to my decision I haven't overlooked something I should have considered. I find I haven't."

He leaned an ear toward her. "I beg your pardon?"

"I said I haven't heard anything to change my decision."

Fitz, when he came into her office, would not sit down. She wondered whether he thought it gave him an advantage, a handhold on her memory, to lean against the wall, all the blueness of his eyes concentrated on hers. He started to say something, but she cut him off.

"Let's not waste words, Fitz. Let's get it over with."

"You make it sound like an ordeal. It shouldn't be. I'm the next managing editor or I'm not."

She looked straight back at him. "You're not."

"I'm not." He seemed to be tasting the words, rolling them on his tongue to identify the flavor. "You must be saying you couldn't convince Becky. But you're the publisher now, Clara. You don't have to—"

"I didn't try to convince Mother. I never mentioned it to her."

"I see. Then you're doing what you think she would have wanted."

He was astute, but not astute enough. He would never have recognized that child who gave her governess the slip and ran among the yacht clubs on the Hudson, frightened, crying for Mother's tears, but running anyway.

"I don't know what she would have wanted, Fitz. This is what I want." She waved a hand at him. "Come and sit down. There's more. I think you'll—"

"Is it for spite, Clara?" he broke in, not moving. "Because I couldn't be, never said I was, what you turned me into in your head? Because you think I wasted your years?" He shook his head slowly, as though he were easing an itch against the hard surface of the wall. "There's no fiancé, is there? You made him up out of pride, and now you've got a chance to settle the score with me. But I never wanted to harm you. All these years, you were the one I kept coming back to. That's a kind of love, maybe. I don't know. Anyhow, it's my only kind." He grinned at her. "I guess it's the best I can leave you with when I go."

"Shut up, Fitz," she said. "Sentimentality doesn't suit you, and it tends to make me cry. Sit down and be sensible. Listen to me. It would never work, you in the next office, managing editor, and me, here, your boss. Me, the kid you taught to be a journalist." She waited while he moved, now, sauntered, to show it was his own idea, to a chair across the room from her. "You may think it would end with you the boss and me a figurehead, but it wouldn't. We'd—"

"Just for the sake of curiosity, have you somebody else in mind?"

"I put in a trans-Atlantic call to Maggie Prout a few days ago. She'll be here next week, as soon as she can turn the Paris Bureau over to her assistant."

He raised his eyebrows. "A woman managing editor?"

"Why not? We have a woman publisher. Maggie's one of the best journalists in the business. She's a top-notch executive too. I saw her in action."

"Well," he said, "that's bully. You and Maggie cozy it up. This journalist will take his reputation and his Pulitzer and all that junk and go be a big executive for some other—"

"How about Washington?"

He came up from his limp slouch like a puppet pulled by slow strings. "What?"

"We need a good man there now as never before. Harry Whipple isn't it." She reached for a pencil to fidget with, and returned her hand empty to her lap. "You'll have complete autonomy. If your staff doesn't suit you, get rid of anybody you want to and hire your own people. Handle the news your own way. Nobody here in New York will challenge you. That doesn't mean no co-operation with New York. The kind of power struggle that's been going on, even before Whipple, is intolerable. But no one in this office will interfere with the way you run the bureau, or with the material that comes out of it."

"Not even you?" The mockery sounded flat, a tired joke.

"Not even me. You still know more about reporting than I'll ever know. If you—"

"That's right, I do. You're too well-bred. It takes a thick-skinned, street-wise snoop. You did all right, considering."

"As I was going to say, nobody, not even I, will interfere with the material you send us. Or with your management of the bureau, either. If you botch it, of course, you'll lose it. But I don't think you'll botch it."

"No, I don't think I will." He sat examining his feet for a minute. "I never seriously thought of being away from New York. I could go to any newspaper in this city and get a top spot. You've offered me the one other job, the only terms, I can't turn down." He looked at her. "Whose idea was all this, kiddo?"

She laughed. "Oh, Fitz! You really never did see beyond the mole, did you?"

May 10, 1950

Dear Hester:

Thank you for understanding why I can't let the Paper go. You're the only one, knowing the choice I made, who doesn't think I'm a fool. Samuel thinks I am. "Will the Paper comfort you when you're old?" he asks me. He can't see that it will. And yet I know he wonders, in *his* old age, what he might have been or done that he never tried for.

I was foolish enough to speak of it to Hannah as a trust. She didn't know what I was talking about. Grandma would have known, for all her antipathy for the Paper. But Hannah's perceptive enough in some ways. Old and sick as she is, her Herzog shrewdness hasn't deserted her.

"What are you doing? Trying to prove something to Becky?" she asked me. "Do you think she's up there in the sky, watching you?"

That isn't it. But it isn't altogether *not* it, either. I never had to prove anything to Mother, only to myself. I do still feel her looking over my shoulder. I hear her saying, "That's wonderful, baby," the way she did when I brought my marks home from school. It worried me at first, but it doesn't any more. Her voice is fainter than it was. I don't want it fading altogether, taking her immortality with it. I never want that.

The Paper is a trust. I even like the way the words look when I write them. The Herzog trust. Not many families have anything but money to hand down.

I wanted Steve to understand. I don't know whether he did, whether it's possible. He hasn't answered my letter. There was nothing to answer, I suppose. Still, I'd have liked to know whether he understood.

Love,
Clara

The postcard came the day after she had mailed that letter to Hester. Except for a date and a flight number, all it said was:

The mountain is coming to Mohammed.

She watched herself go through the two intervening days as though she had stepped outside her own skin and had no dominion over what moved within it. She had no recollection of stuffing the postcard inside her brassiere, but there it remained, idiotically, except at night, when it rested on her bedside table. What the card meant, she could not think. Did not want to think. Words floated by. Fragments of questions. *How long—? To see— Persuade— Can I stand—?* She let them go, made no attempt to grasp them. A dozen times, on both days, she looked at her watch and could not have said why. If she had been asked what she was feeling, she would not have known how to answer. But no one asked her. No one was aware, apparently, that there was anything unusual about the construct that moved around in her shape, uninhabited.

At the airport, she could not sit down. She was more than an hour early, but she stood the whole time. Cold as snow on the mild late-May evening, and something somewhere throbbing like a dozen pulses let loose.

He was first through the gate, with his scowl centered on her face as though he had located her from the sky. When she felt his arms around her, she began to cry.

"I hope it's joy," he boomed. "Is it joy?"

After a little while, she answered, hiccuping like a child. "If this is me, and that's you, it's joy."

"What?" He began rocking her, stopping at intervals to kiss her wet cheek. Nobody, in that place of diversified meetings and partings, paid any attention to them. "What, Clara? What?"

"Nothing. I don't know. You're as crazy as I am."

They sat close in the taxi, holding hands, and talked about May in New York as compared with May in Paris, and the kind of flight he had had, and Hester, and how long she had been waiting at the airport.

"Did you finish your book?"

"Yes. I have it with me to take to the publisher."

She did not ask him if that was why he had come. She did not want to know yet.

"How are you doing with the Paper?"

"All right, I think. It's too soon to tell."

He sat forward to peer out the window at Franklin D. Roosevelt Drive. "Where are we? I've been away too long. I don't know where we are." He did not wait for her to tell him. "We're going to your apartment, aren't we?"

"Yes, of course. You gave the driver the address yourself."

"Did I?" He sat back again, still clutching her hand. He sighed. "I don't know what I'm doing."

"I don't either. Know what I'm doing, I mean."

She watched him pay the cab driver. He took some limp, dirty francs from his wallet, stuffed them back impatiently, and found a crackling American bill in another compartment. She watched the movements of his large, hairy hands as though they were the movements of a pianist. He picked up the dispatch case he had put down on the sidewalk between his feet. He started to lift the suitcase the driver had taken from the trunk of the taxi, and then relinquished it to the doorman who came running out for it.

"Good evening, Miss Herzog."

"Yes," Clara said meaninglessly. She was looking at the suitcase now, trying to gauge the size of it. But she could not tell how many clothes it would hold. She had never packed a man's suitcase.

They went up in the elevator. She stabbed her key at the keyhole twice before she got it in. Part of that morning's Paper was sprawled out on the dark gold living-room rug, so counter to her customary orderliness that for a moment she thought someone must have been in the apartment.

"I don't know how this got here," she murmured, stooping to pick it up. "I must have—"

He had dropped his luggage and crossed the long room to stand at the windows with his back to her. "It could be the Seine," he said.

"Yes," she said. "Yes. I always think that."

He turned as she started toward him. They came together in a rush. He whispered something, and she heard not one word of it. Their hands kept colliding. They moved together into the other room, stumbling over each other's feet. The memory of Mother's satin bedspread flickered in her mind . . . she must take it off and fold it . . . no, the satin bedspread was gone; this one was her own, and it did not matter . . .

She lay with her face against his chest, his breathing a steady rhythm under her cheek.

"Say something. I want to feel your voice."

His hand, that huge hand, had scarcely any weight on her hair. "*Feel* my voice?"

"Yes, like that. Like the vibration of a drum. When I was little, it always seemed exciting and mysterious. The best part of a parade. Say something else."

"My love." The hand on her hair moved to join the other one, spanning her back. "That's what brought me."

"What's what brought you?"

" 'My love.' In your letter. *It's what I have to do, my love.* That— cry."

"I didn't know it was a cry."

"There are so many things you don't know. I've come to teach you."

For a time, neither of them spoke. Then Clara sighed. "I suppose you might as well tell me what you're talking about, and how long you're staying."

"How long—?" He pushed her gently away from him and got up on his elbow to look down at her. "Did you think I came for a quick roll in the hay? Is that what you thought my postcard meant?"

"Don't roar so. You're shaking the whole bed. I didn't know what it meant. How could I know? You've brought your book for the publisher. Naturally, while you're here, you'd come and see me and—"

"Shut up, you half-wit," he said, as softly as his booming voice allowed. "You said you had to stay here. *It's what I have to do, my love.* All right. I didn't have to stay where I was. So here I am."

She had to close her eyes. "Your new book—"

"What?"

"Your book about Malraux."

"I don't have to write a book about Malraux."

"But it's what you've wanted—what you've planned."

"What I've wanted and planned is to marry you."

Her eyes opened. His were so close that they swam into a multiplication of eyes. "Marry—"

"Do you think, once I knew you still wanted me, I'd let Malraux stand in the way?"

She could not seem to bring her thoughts into focus. "But I'm— the Paper—"

"That's different," he answered, as though she had said something intelligible. "I have no dream or mission that demands I write about Malraux. I have to write, that's all."

"You don't like New York."

"I like wherever you are."

She moved her head on the pillow, away from all the fierce black eyes. "I left you. I gave up marriage. It was settled." She stopped. "I thought it was settled." She stopped again. "You'll have to give me time to—"

"No," he said. "No more time."

They were married, as she had promised Mother, in June. A judge, a friend of Mother's, performed the ceremony in his chambers. Hannah could not come—she never went out any more—but Samuel was there, so dapper Steve looked slovenly by contrast. The story took less than half a column in the Paper. It was not what Mother had wanted. She would have understood, though, however regretfully, that any more splash would have been inappropriate so soon after her death.

The week following the wedding, North Korean troops invaded South Korea. The week after that, President Truman sent American troops to help defend South Korea against the Communists. The Paper, in its coverage of the war, was temporarily diverted from its full-scale attack on Senator McCarthy.

The Soviet Union had three times as many combat planes as the United States, four times as many troops, thirty times as many tank divisions, and the atomic bomb. The United States had the jitters. Early in 1951 the first bomb shelter was built, for a Los Angeles housewife. People discussed whether, in case of an atomic attack, they ought to allow friends and neighbors into their shelters to share the food hoarded for their own families, or shoot them to keep them out. Letters to the Paper leaned heavily toward self-preservation—"a basic instinct, shared even by animals," as one writer put it.

In April, General Douglas MacArthur was relieved of his command by President Truman for flouting United States policy. The Paper supported Truman's action. McCarthy said, "The son of a bitch ought to be impeached."

That May, a boy was born to Clara and Steve. They named him Simon, after Sigmund Herzog. Simon Herzog Miller. Clara worked at home for a while. She returned to the Paper full time when Simon was eight months old, leaving him in the care of a housekeeper and Steve, who was writing a history of the Rockefeller family. But she bathed the baby herself every morning before she left the apartment, and came home in time to play with him before he went to bed.

As the war in Korea ground on to a stalemate, the Paper resumed its all-out war against McCarthy. He was seemingly unstoppable.

The Paper endorsed Adlai Stevenson for President of the United States. General Eisenhower won the election.

7

Clara stood Simon on top of the toilet seat, dried him, and sprinkled him with baby powder.

"This is the way my mother used to dry and powder me," she said.

He chortled and reached for the can of powder, almost knocking it out of her hand and himself off the seat.

"Only, I used to stand still," she said.

"Wooo!" he answered, patting the top of her head. "I'm a BIG boy!"

"You bet. And you don't know or care what I'm talking about, but that's all right. Just listen. One of these days you'll learn the language."

"Garbitch!" he shouted, and began jigging from one foot to the other.

"No garbage. Language. Sometimes it's the same thing, at that."

She changed her tone. "Okay, now, Simon. Stand still so I can dress you."

He peered into her face to see if she was serious. "Okay," he said.

She wanted to giggle at the subdued tone, but that would set him off again. His energy astonished her. Everything about him astonished and diverted her. She thought it comical that he looked so much like Steve; a small, dark, not-quite-so-fierce Indian, yet with her mouth (and William Lowenthal's) and her long-legged build. His growing verbal and physical accomplishments made him new to her every day. She wondered whether, if she were younger, had not lived so long beyond any expectation of motherhood, she would have taken him more in stride.

"I must leave him free," she told Steve. "I mustn't dote on him. If you see me doing it, kick me."

But he understood only from hearsay what she meant. "Is it all right if *I* dote on him?"

"I don't know. I don't know much about fathers."

Excuse me, Albert . . .

Simon had breakfast with them every morning. It was a noisy, food-smeared occasion, disapproved of by the housekeeper, who thought adults should eat in peace. Peace means different things to different people.

Marriage had been easier for Steve than for Clara. He had done it before. She was not used to a man in her bathroom every morning and in her bed every night. The male sounds and smells she had known only intermittently now permeated her living quarters. She could not use all the closets, all the space. It was more than twenty years since she had had to make room for somebody else, and then it had been Mother, with whom she had always lived, not a strange husband.

But Steve, in his own way, was as much of an astonishment as Simon. She had known what he was like, yet it took her months to stop waiting for him to rage with his displeasures, months more to stop expecting him at her shoulder. She had been unable to imagine living a life in which tempers and intrusions were no part of love. Steve was sometimes angry, but he never raged. He loved her, but he let her alone.

They lived in a large, high-ceilinged apartment on Fifth Avenue and Sixty-eighth Street, overlooking Central Park. It was too much for the housekeeper and a once-a-week cleaning man to keep immaculate, but Steve was not used to servants and wanted as few as possible around. He did not care, or notice, that the apartment was not immaculate. In time, Clara did not care or notice either. She gave up imagining Mother's disapproval.

When they had finished breakfast, the housekeeper came and took Simon away. If Clara left while he was still sitting there, he cried, but if it was he who was leaving her, he went willingly enough. He and Mrs. Hammond, the housekeeper, were devoted to each other. She was a small, wiry, gray-haired no-nonsense woman, who reminded Clara a little of Grandma. It seemed sad to Clara that Simon would never have the benefits of a real Grandma, of the close Herzog family. Hannah, who had never been a real Herzog anyway, was dead; Hester was in Paris. There was only Samuel, and he was frank to say that, except for Clara, he had never cared very much for children. On the other hand, Simon had a full-time father.

"Anybody like more coffee?"

Rose, the large, grim-looking colored cook, had come in with the percolator. She could have left it plugged in on the buffet, but she had taken that suggestion to mean she was not wanted in the dining room.

"Yes, please, Rose," Clara said, although she had had all the coffee she wanted.

No one could foresee the richly various possibilities of Rose's touchiness. They seemed to have no common base. Clara, thinking she recognized a demand for dignity, had introduced her to Mrs. Hammond as Mrs. Cuthbert.

"My name is Rose," the cook had snapped.

Mrs. Hammond and Steve tried to stay out of her way. She tolerated Simon, who assumed she adored him, like everyone else in the household. Because she was a magnificent cook, Clara wanted to keep her and managed to deal with her.

"No one else could," Steve had remarked.

"It's easy. I simply capitulate. Mother would have found out what was eating her."

"Not everybody wants to be found out."

Now, Rose having returned to the kitchen with the coffee pot, Clara dared to laugh.

"Where were you when she came in?"

"Where was—? Oh." He smiled more since their marriage, but not with a show of teeth. "I don't remember exactly. Maybe counting John D's dimes. Why?"

"Because we both jumped, startled out of our separate bemusements. I used to think— You know those couples you see in restaurants sometimes, not exchanging a word during the meal except to ask for the salt? I used to think how dead their marriages must be, but maybe—"

"Comparing marriages will get you nowhere. Just tend to your own, madam."

They kissed good-by. He held her a little longer than necessary. She felt a small pain when she shut the front door behind her. In half an hour, she would not be thinking of him, nor he of her, but the marriage would be there, waiting.

Sometimes, riding down to her office in a cab, she could feel herself changing, as though she had drunk something, like Dr. Jekyll, that gradually transformed her into the publisher of the Paper. Steve had come with her to the Paper once to see what it was like and to be shown off, but there was no reason for him to come again. Someday she would bring Simon to work during his summer vacation, as Mother had brought her. Meanwhile, they were there and she was here. Clara Herzog, publisher. Mrs. Herzog to the few who did not call her Clara and took the Mrs. from her wedding ring. Steve never forgot, on the few occasions when he telephoned, not to ask for Mrs. Miller.

Maggie Prout, who had ears like a deer, heard Clara walk by her office and came to the door. Most of the day, she kept her door open so she could see out into the newsroom—a practice that had immediately earned her the nickname "Duenna"—but early in the morning she could not, she said, stand the sight of human faces, including her own.

"What are you looking like the Queen of the May for?" she asked Clara sourly. "All hell has broken loose."

Clara, having just walked through a relatively calm newsroom, suspected that no major catastrophe had overtaken the nation or the world since she had left home. Still, Maggie was not given to exaggerated alarms.

"What's happened? Has somebody upstairs exploded over my last jab at McCarthy?"

Upstairs—sometimes referred to as Mount Olympus by the staff—was where all the top management executives, except for

Clara, had their offices. Most of them were holdovers from Mother's era—good, sound, conservative men with whom Clara seldom saw eye to eye except in their devotion to the Paper. She did not think of herself as one of them. Here, on the newsroom floor, she said *we*. She referred to those upstairs as *they*.

"You're lukewarm," Maggie said. "Lleland has exploded, but not over you." She kicked the door wider. "Come on in."

Clara sat down in a leather armchair in Maggie's large, well-appointed, workmanlike office. Her own office was similar, a little larger but not enough to make a point of the differences in status. Even without the blue office upstairs, Mother's status had been evident. It had breathed from her pores. Clara did not always remember that she was no longer working for Maggie. They got along more easily than when she had been.

"It's Fitz," Maggie said.

"Fitz? A new anti-McCarthy piece?"

"All the anti-McCarthy pieces, I imagine." Maggie sat down at her desk and lit a cigarette. She always smoked as though she had never done it before, the cigarette in the exact center of her mouth, her eyes tearing because she left it there too long, ashes falling unnoticed on her prominent front. "McCarthy has called him to his star chamber. As you can imagine, that's enough to give Lleland the wind up. 'It's appalling to think that a man in one of the most influential positions on the Paper might be a Communist,' quote, unquote."

"Lleland is an ass," Clara said, and then thought it was what Mother would have said, though not about Lleland.

"Only, of course he isn't." Maggie industriously tucked a wisp of escaping hair behind her ear. "He's a shrewd businessman."

"Yes, I know he is. Which makes it worse, doesn't it? That lying monster, stunning men like Lleland Winston out of their senses."

"What worries me is the morale of the staff. If McCarthy is going to start witch-hunting in the press, and anybody he calls from the Paper is immediately under suspicion upstairs—"

"Yes," Clara said. "I'll have to take care of that."

Maggie did not seem to doubt that she could, and would. The Herzog name, Clara thought, carried its own authority. Mother, whose presence had had authority before she opened her mouth, had not needed the name. But Clara had no intrinsic seignoral attitudes. When she talked to a clerk or a young reporter or a linotype operator, nothing in her manner or tone of voice effected a natural distance between them. Part of Mother's power had derived from the charm of her unbending. The endearing incongruity of a queen with a cigarette behind her ear. In Clara, who often did not remember her elevated status, it would not have seemed incongruous.

She had no trouble with the staff, however. If they were not mesmerized by her, as they had been by Mother, they liked her and respected her position. Upstairs, it was another matter. To the men in the executive offices—especially to Lleland Winston—she was Mother's wrongheaded child. It was infuriating, yet gave a certain fillip of exhilaration to opposing them.

"We can't keep this man on our staff. This Communist," Winston said. "Surely you must see that, Clara."

It was a week or so after Clara's conversation with Maggie. Fitz had appeared before the House Un-American Activities Committee and answered McCarthy's questions either with typical Fitz scorn, or not at all. As soon as Lleland Winston heard of it, he wanted to see Clara in his office. She had made the mistake before of allowing herself to be summoned. This time she told him she would be available in her office for the next half hour. He sat across from her desk now, looking distinguished and disgruntled.

"If he were a Communist, I might see it," Clara said. "I have no reason to think he is."

"No *reason?*" Winston made a show of shaking his head in slow motion. "My dear girl, if he were not a Communist, why wouldn't he have answered Senator McCarthy's questions frankly and openly?"

"Why? Because they were preposterous questions, loaded with McCarthy's usual unverified and unverifiable insinuations. To answer them with anything but contempt would be to dignify them."

"You consider it preposterous to ask a man in Fitzsimmons' position, in these times, whether or not he is a Communist?"

"It depends on who asks it, and why. McCarthy has been demoralizing the country for three years, ruining careers, driving people to suicide. He has yet to back up one of his charges with legal evidence. There's no doubt in my mind that he got after Fitz only because Fitz has been after him."

Winston, abandoning avuncular condescension, gave a small, cold smile and fingered a sheet of paper on his knee. "You discount the fact that Fitzsimmons' connection with the Communist Party came to the senator's attention?" He lifted the paper a little, as though tendering it to her. "Fitzsimmons didn't deny, you know, that party meetings were held in his apartment."

Clara knew what Fitz had not denied. The report, of which Winston held a copy, was on her desk.

Did you or did you not, for a period of several years, hold meetings of the Communist Party in your own apartment in Greenwich Village in New York City?

I held no meetings. A few people I knew met in the apartment sometimes. Usually I wasn't there myself . . .

A few people you knew. What are the names of these few people you knew?

I don't remember. I'm very bad at names. Especially names from twenty years ago. Ancient history . . .

Clara wondered what expression would occupy Lleland's face if she told him she had attended one of those meetings herself, and, after it was over, lost her virginity in Fitz's bed. "Ancient history," she said. "McCarthy battens on it. How do I know *you* weren't interested in communism in the thirties? A good many young people were back then, before they learned better."

"I? My dear Clara, don't be ridiculous!"

It was ridiculous. Impossible to imagine Lleland Winston, however young, enticed by any such off-center concept. He was the archetypal high-caste WASP, valuable to the Paper not only for his business acumen but as a showpiece. Certain circles were closed even to a Herzog, but Winston had entree everywhere. "No, Lleland, you wouldn't have been, of course, but not everyone was so wise so young." She smiled and sat back with what she hoped was an air of finality. "Anyway, we certainly can't fire a man as valuable as Fitz because of some possible vague indiscretion twenty years ago."

"What assurance have you that the indiscretion hasn't continued? That he isn't a Communist now, at this moment?"

"As much assurance as I have about Maggie Prout or Morris Fishman or Carter Hoag. The fact that Joe McCarthy has singled out Fitz makes me not one iota less sure about him. He's the finest bureau chief we've ever had in Washington, and that's what I want him to go right on being."

She had made Lleland angry. Mother would have been the one to get angry. She would have had him appeasing her.

"I can't submit to that without a strong protest," he said. "Not only my own protest, but that of the other executives. I'm here as their representative as well as on my own behalf. We all feel that the Paper, responsible as it is to the public, cannot properly employ any journalist whose loyalty to our country is in doubt."

"It's only in doubt because McCarthy says it is, because he wants to get Fitz out of his hair. I won't have the Paper giving in to the man's smear tactics. Go back and tell your colleagues I said no."

He stood up. "Very well." His suit had been made to fit smoothly over the slight stoop of his habitual carriage. Now, as he walked to the door, the fabric was pleated between the stiffness of his shoulders. Almost at the threshold, he turned.

"Forgive me if I suggest—as an older man, a great admirer and friend of your mother's—that you think this over more carefully, Clara; make certain you aren't being swayed by—how shall I put it? —personal considerations." He gave her a formal little bow and went out.

Clara felt the heat coming up into her face—the absurd blush of a forty-year-old woman. She wanted to hurl something at the door Lleland had shut behind him. Her hand closed around the nearest heavy object. Feeling its smooth coolness under her hand, she loosened her grip. It was the Baccarat paperweight Steve had seen in a shop window and bought her for no special occasion, for what he called a "walking-around present." There were other things she might have thrown, but she did not do it. She never did it.

If Lleland Winston, in his remote office, knew about her and Fitz, everyone on the Paper must know. Or maybe Mother had told Lleland, confided in him, pretending to ask him what to do. Mother had used all kinds of ploys to bind men to her without sleeping with them or marrying them. But no, she would not have used Clara. No.

It did not matter anyway. Ancient history. The question now was how to temper the effect she had made on Lleland, and through him to the others upstairs, without surrendering to them. It was stupid to antagonize them. She needed them too much. Mother had had a flair for the business end of the Paper, but Clara had none. She wanted to be free of it, to use her talents as an editor and a writer, to effectuate her convictions as a policy maker. The co-operation of her top executives was essential, yet she was always undermining it. She could not resist pitting herself against them.

After a little thought, she put in a call to Washington.

Fitz came three days later. He ambled into her office and started to close the door behind him; to lean against it, she was sure, in the immemorial eye-contact pose.

"Leave it open, Fitz," she said. "Sit down."

He had not changed in three years. He did not change. If the lines around his eyes had multiplied, or the grooves down his cheeks were deeper, the aging was imperceptible. He had never looked young. "Are you afraid of something, too?" Though she had not seen it for so long, she was already wearied by his grin. "My friends in the newsroom either pretended not to see me or greeted me with such fake heartiness it was pathetic. Now you want the door open."

She ignored most of this. "I'm sure you know McCarthy's accusations don't weigh with me. If they did, you'd be out of a job."

"Yes." He slid down in his chair. "I understand you went to bat for me."

"Where did you hear that?"

She should not have asked him, walked into it. "A good newspaperman never reveals his sources," he said.

"Your source is inaccurate. I went to bat for a principle."

"Are you sure?"

She glanced out at the newsroom beyond the open door. No one could hear their voices over the clatter of typewriters, the stutter of wire machines, the ringing phones. No one, at least at the moment, was looking in. His question was confined to the space between them. "You're due upstairs in half an hour. Perhaps you'd better tell me what you propose to say to them."

"What do you want me to say?" He was like a well-preserved actor, endlessly repeating the lines of his youthful triumphs, playing the same scene over and over.

"I told you on the phone what I want, Fitz. McCarthy has them frightened. Or convinced. It's—"

She had forgotten his trick of interrupting her when she was in full spate. Now he was saying something about fools, but she did not let him finish.

"There's no use calling them fools. William Buckley isn't a fool. Neither is the congressman from Massachusetts, Joseph Kennedy's son. Neither are a lot of other people who believe McCarthy is really onto something. That's what's terrifying. I thought the Paper could demolish him. The power of the press. Sometimes I wonder—" She interrupted herself now. "Anyway, I asked you here to do personally what can't be done for you. To—"

"Prove I'm not a Communist?" The grin was gone. Without it, he looked less indestructible. "We keep saying in the Paper that for all the people McCarthy has accused, he hasn't proved it on one of them. That's true, but it isn't worth a damn. Not to the converts. Because the people he accuses can't prove they're not Communists. Can you prove you're not?"

"I've said nothing about proof. Talk to them, that's all. They have only your contemptuous answers to McCarthy to go by."

"If I'd answered him any other way, he'd have swarmed all over me. I gave him as good as I got." The grin was back. "A lying, bullying Irishman is no match whatever for a fine, upstanding, fighting Irishman."

"Tell them that upstairs, then. How fine and upstanding you are, and that McCarthy was no match for you because—"

"Because I'm really not a Communist?"

She was silent.

"I'm not, you know." He paused. "That's what you had to hear, isn't it? That's why you asked me to come."

"No, of course not. I've known you too long—" She broke off and looked away from him. "Yes, partly . . ."

"What?"

"Yes, I had to hear it," she said. "Damn McCarthy!"

She took Fitz home with her for dinner. She was not sure why. In penance, or pride, or to change the scenery and the players . . .

"Are they satisfied?" she had asked him when he came downstairs again.

"Well, appeased. I reminded them of the jump in circulation since I've been in Washington. That helped. And the fact my appearance before the committee isn't being played up in the press, because any journalist on any newspaper could be next."

"We shouldn't play up anything McCarthy does. Almost every day, our headlines scream that he's charged somebody, or that he has a mystery witness who will prove something about somebody else. We know there probably is no witness and the charges are false, but the public thinks if it's in the Paper there must be something to it. We ought to refuse to publish it, the way we refuse advertising we know to be fraudulent."

"Refuse to publish the charges of a United States senator? Besides, suppose one of his charges happens to be on target? Or he really does turn up with a bona fide witness? You're talking through your hat, kiddo."

She had been, of course. The duty of the Paper was not to protect its readers by withholding news. She was forever chafing at the conflicts involved in keeping the public informed. The conflicts between news and truth.

"Why can't you learn to accept things as they are?" Fitz had asked her years before. He had been talking about their relationship, but the question was not confined. Why couldn't she?

"I'm not used to meeting husbands," Fitz was saying now, going uptown in the cab. "I don't know why I said I'd come."

"I was just wondering why I asked you."

"Oh, I can tell you that."

"Don't."

He laughed. What he said next had no relevance that she could see to either the laugh or their conversation. "That's the thing about you that kept me coming back. You always had to be seduced all over again. Each time was a fresh conquest."

There was nothing to say to that except that it was nonsense. He had had only to whistle. Or did she remember it wrong? The cab pulled over to the curb. "Here we are," she said unnecessarily.

"I was forgetting," he said, peering out at the large, canopied apartment house, "that you'd live in a place like this. You don't look rich. Becky did, even when she wasn't."

"She couldn't help it. I can. Anyway, that's a vulgar thing to say."

"I'm a vulgar man. Didn't you know?"

In the elevator, she was suddenly nervous. No, she had been nervous all along. It made no sense to bring Fitz and Steve together. Steve knew who Fitz was—everybody who read the Paper knew who Fitz was—and that he had trained her as a reporter when she was very young. Nothing more. She should have left it that way. Fitz, in a new act and an unlearned part, was unpredictable.

Steve came out into the entrance hall when he heard her key. He had on his old blue French workman's smock and the pants of a long-dead suit he had once had made in London. Simon, freshly scrubbed, in spotless canary-yellow Dentons, sat astride one arm. Clara introduced Fitz, unseated Simon, and fled with him to the kitchen, where she wheedled Rose into accepting an unexpected guest for dinner.

When she came back, Simon trotting beside her, the men were still in the hall. Simon, who had asked twice who the man was, and appeared not to listen to the answer, ran out to them calling, "Here I am, Daddy! Here I am, Fitz!" taking it for granted they were both waiting breathlessly for his return. No one whose name he knew was a stranger to him.

Clara puttered around the room, wondering what they were doing out there so long. She made a neat pile of a strewing of books on the coffee table. She plumped a dent out of a sofa cushion. A dried-up pine needle was stuck in the cushion's underside. From the last Christmas tree. Or maybe from the one before the last. It might have stayed there forever, but for her fidgety poking.

"Jews don't have Christmas trees, baby."

It had seemed acceptable at the time. Sad, but acceptable. Jews did not do a number of things that regular people did. Especially things about Jesus. When all the children sang Christmas carols in assembly, Jews, or anyway Clara, did not sing the parts with Jesus in them out loud, but only mouthed the words. If you did not say it out loud it did not count.

"I'd like a tree," she said to Steve the first Christmas of their marriage. "A great big fat tree with lots of lights and tinsel and decorations."

"Why not?" Steve said.

She heard his booming bass now, and Fitz's drier, lighter voice, along with Simon's chirping obbligato. They were coming into the living room, Simon between the two men like a companionable dwarf.

"I've been hearing what it's like to be grilled by McCarthy," Steve said. "Any man who succeeds in confounding that menace, even a little, should be toasted in champagne. Will scotch do, Fitz? Or something else?" He moved toward the dining room, where they kept their liquor on a shelf of the buffet. "Champagne doesn't happen to be one of our staples."

Mrs. Hammond came in to take Simon to bed. He clung artfully to Fitz, the least likely of them to deliberately detach himself, and drew his sparse brows together in imitation of his father's scowl. Clara plucked him off Fitz and took him to bed herself, talking steadily above his loud indignation. "I know. It's hard to go to bed when everybody else is up. You're angry. You wish you could stay with us. I know."

Halfway down the hall, he stopped his noise and planted a wet, inexpert kiss on her cheek.

"I'm usually not much good with kids," Fitz said when she got back. "I can talk to presidents, but kids strike me dumb. Yours is different. *He* put *me* at ease."

"Now you can see," Clara said to Steve, "why Fitz is such a successful journalist. He always has a novel approach."

"Is the kid going to be a journalist?"

They both answered him. "Fitz, he's not two years old," Clara said. "Well," Steve said, "his middle name is Herzog."

All of them had scotch. Fitz refused the third one. "I'm an anomaly," he said. "An Irishman, a newspaperman, and a moderate drinker."

She tried to detach herself, to float between them in some omniscient sphere from which she could see each as he appeared to the other. Steve, his smock discarded now for a tweedy jacket that made him look even bulkier than he was, his coarse black hair in need of cutting, said little. He was not, except with her, a talker, but a foil for talkers, feeding them lines, listening with care to their responses. She had never heard Fitz talk so well. His explicit magnetism seemed to acquire a patina. He found less use for the grin. Even his disheveled, skewed-tie mode of dress looked, not so much studied, as, like Steve's indifference to appearance, a disregard for superficialities. It was as though Steve were creating him.

"I'm not sure I know what you mean by aristocracy, Fitz. A family like the Rockefellers?"

"The Rockefellers, yes. A prime example. The use of wealth and power for leadership and service. The recognition of *noblesse oblige*. But I mean something more. An aristocracy not limited by caste. Open to you and me, if we can qualify."

"Open in what sense?"

"No amount of wealth, power, education, achievement, character —no qualification you can name—will admit a Catholic or a Jew into the top levels of society. In a true aristocracy, religious or ethnic origins would be irrelevant. A Herzog could be elected President." He looked at Clara. "A Jew founded the Union League Club, but if your great-grandfather were alive today, he couldn't get into it."

"You've made a study of this," Steve said.

"No. I'm not a student of anything except—" Clara was sure he was about to say women. The ordinary Fitz, the Fitz she knew, would have said it. With the grin. This Fitz let it die. "A newspaperman swims in a sea of information. Some of it sticks. Some of it translates into ideas."

They had a simple dinner of grilled salmon, fresh asparagus, a salad, and Brie cheese. The perfection of Rose's preparation, the runny ripeness of the Brie, Mother's Royal Doulton and silver, made it, like all their meals, extraordinary.

"You set a fine table," this Steve-created Fitz said to Clara.

"I have to. Steve is used to French food. If the asparagus is overcooked, he beats me." She could feel, without seeing, the narrowing of Steve's eyes, the slight up-pull of his mouth, that composed his singular smile.

"It's a rare necessity. She comes from a family of gourmet publishers, raised on Grandpa's Meat."

"What the hell," Fitz asked, "is Grandpa's Meat?"

Clara looked at him. He was grinning. She had never, in all those years, told him about Grandpa's Meat.

"What made you mention that?" she asked Steve when Fitz had gone.

He had his back to her, putting the scotch away on the buffet shelf. "Mention what?"

"Grandpa's Meat," she said, though she was sure he knew.

"It just came to me."

"Did you think Fitz had heard of it?"

"I didn't think so."

"No, only a husband would hear of Grandpa's Meat." She put her arms around him from the back. "I'm glad it came to you."

They looked in on Simon, pulled the kicked-off blanket over his upthrust rump, and went to their own room.

"He's an interesting man," Steve said.

"It was you. You made him more interesting than he is."

He got into bed beside her. It always took him longer. Sometimes he went into his study in the midst of undressing to correct a page in the typewriter. Sometimes he stood for ten minutes with a shoe in his hand. She could not sleep until he was next to her. "That sounds like Alice-in-Wonderland nonsense," he said.

"Yes," she said. "Profound like that."

410

The end of McCarthy was depressing to Clara, an uneasy foreshadowing. Not the end itself, certainly, nor the manner of it, but the means. For four years the Paper had been fighting him. From the day he had waved an old letter at a group of Republican women in West Virginia, claiming it was a list of known Communists in the State Department, Clara had made a mission, a crusade, of his exposure. He had only grown more powerful, thrived on the publicity.

It was television that exposed him. In a few days, to twenty million viewers.

I think we should tell Mr. Welch that he has in his law firm a young man named Fisher who has been for a number of years a member of an organization named as the legal bulwark of the Communist Party . . .

Until this moment, Senator, I think I never really gauged your cruelty or your recklessness. Fred Fisher is starting what looks to be a brilliant career with us . . . I fear he shall always bear a scar needlessly inflicted by you . . . Have you no sense of decency, sir, at long last? Have you left no sense of decency?

At long last, millions knew he had no sense of decency. They did not learn it from the Paper. They saw it for themselves.

8

Lleland Winston's office, once Mother's, needed painting. He kept saying it could wait. What he meant was that, one way or another, he probably would not be using it long enough to bother. Clara should not have expected his devotion to the Paper to extend beyond his own foreseeable association with it.

"I'm afraid we're fighting a losing battle," he said. At least he still said *we*.

She came to his office these days, instead of asking him to hers. He was, physically, an old sixty-four, worn-looking, partly crippled by arthritis. For a Herzog, fifty was still young. She had no ailments, no gray hair. The mothers of some of Simon's friends looked almost as old as she did, though they were more than fifteen years younger.

She said, "That's what the business office told my mother when she became the publisher, in 1931."

"These are different times. The newspaper business has changed."

"Yes, I know it has, but the Paper could have resisted some of the changes. Can still. The Paper wasn't founded as a business institution. My great-grandfather conceived of it as a vehicle for expressing a passionate point of view, rousing the country to social and political action, explaining the world to its readers. Look at it now." She picked up the morning issue of the Paper from Lleland's desk and riffled through its pages. "Fourteen pages of news and twenty-four of advertising. The news is being squeezed down until it's hard to find among the ads. Columns and editorials that offend big business are being squeezed out on the grounds of limited space." The newspaper crackled for several seconds after she had thrown it down, as though with a life of its own. "I'm as much to blame as anyone else." More, she thought. More. She had a trust. "I let it happen. I didn't want to bother with the business end. I had competent executives for that. But the Paper can't be operated by the business office and fulfill its purpose. From now on, things will be different."

Lleland's face twitched with pain, whether from his arthritis or her remarks, there was no way of knowing. "Clara, my dear, you're ignoring the realities. I admire your idealism, but it won't pay the bills. We're plagued by factors totally beyond our control. With the constantly rising costs in material and labor, we need an even greater increase in advertising revenue, but television and other mass media make it virtually impossible to get. Our circulation isn't keeping pace with the growth in population. We can't raise our price any more, because the public won't pay it. We can't cut costs with more automation and labor-saving devices, because the unions won't stand for it." He gave a great sigh, as though exhausted by his own words. "You know all this, Clara."

"They told my mother what you call the realities thirty years ago. She ignored them too. If she hadn't, you and I wouldn't be sitting here today, with the presses rolling downstairs. You're too far away to hear them."

But she admitted to Steve that she was frightened.

"If it's too late—if it all slips away from under me—nothing left of the Herzog dream after all these years, nothing left for Simon, because I wasn't vigilant—"

"Stop that," he said. "Whatever happens, you're not to blame yourself. Do you think you can control the flow of events single-handed? You're one woman."

His indignation made her smile. She might have been someone else, unjustly holding his wife accountable. The transferences of love still charmed her, after twelve years of marriage. "One Herzog," she said.

"Maybe one Herzog could change the course of history eighty years ago. It's somewhat less manageable now."

"Yes, now it may take two." She looked at herself in the mirror of her dressing table, and at Steve, sitting behind her on the bed. Mother had never allowed beds to be sat on. "Sigmund did his best. He started us off with seven Herzogs. We've let him down there too, dying, procreating feebly or not at all, dwindling away to Simon and me . . ."

"Not dwindling. Culminating."

"Yes, he'd have been glad of Simon." She went and sat beside Steve on the bed. "All it needed to produce a good Herzog boy was to mix him with an equal quantity of Miller." He put his arm around her. They sat in silence for a moment. "Do you know he's keeping a diary?"

"He calls it a journal. A diary, he claims, is only what happens every day. In a journal he can put down ideas and comments on any subject that interests him. I'm sure there's no such distinction, except in his own mind."

"Maybe he thinks journal sounds more imposing. Or more masculine. Girls keep diaries." She felt suddenly quite happy and confident. "Anyway, it will be good practice for him."

September 5, 1962

School started today. It's not so good. Bill moved to Long Island and Timmy's parents took him out of public school. He has to go to some school way up in Riverdale. It's not so bad, though, because Pud didn't move or anything, and he's in my homeroom. Also I have Mr. Richardson for math, and he's the best math teacher in the whole school.

Mom thinks it's great I'm good in math. She says I'm a word person, like all the Herzogs and Dad, and word people usually aren't. She says it's also lucky, because even parents who are good at math learned a whole different way to do it and can't help their kids.

Mom talks a lot about the Herzogs. There was this one called Sigmund that I'm named after. He was my great-great-grandfather, who started the Paper about a million years ago. Then there was Grandma, my great-grandmother, and Mother, my grandmother. She's the one Mom talks about most. She was the publisher of the

413

Paper before Mom, and she had two different married names, but she called herself Mrs. Herzog, which wasn't either of them. Mom is only called Mrs. Herzog in the office.

All those Herzogs and a lot more were dead before I was born. I was nothing then and they're nothing now. It's creepy to think about being nothing. I think about a lot of creepy things sometimes. I wrote a science-fiction story in school last term that Miss Ostrander said gave her goose pimples.

Also there's this great-great-aunt who was alive until last summer, but I never saw her because she lived in Paris. The only one I ever saw was this very old man, Uncle Samuel. He died Friday, but I couldn't be sad because I didn't know him very well.

The reason I wrote all that about the Herzogs is because Mom says you can sort of keep people alive by remembering them, and we two are the only ones left to do it. I don't mind doing it, but there's one thing. I'm always going to keep my real name.

November 9, 1962

Dad asked me last night if I was still keeping this journal. I told him yes and I write in it almost every day. He said that was fine, because most kids don't stick to things. He said a lot of people who want to be writers could be if they stuck to it, but they get discouraged and give it up. I told him I wasn't sure yet if I wanted to be a writer or what, and he said I had plenty of time to decide and anything I wanted to be was okay with him and Mom. Grown people don't always mean what they say. It's not that they're liars or anything. It's that they have these rules about what's right to say and what isn't, but the way they feel is different sometimes. Like if I said I love football, which I hate, just because there's sort of a rule boys are supposed to say they love it. Some kids don't mean what they say either, but not so much. The sport I like is swimming. I'm a good swimmer. Baseball is okay too.

I almost got to go to a basketball game Friday night. Clarence Washington said he could bring three kids from the class to watch his brother's team play, and did I want to go. I said I did, but I had to ask Mom and Dad first. When I phoned him up to tell him it was okay, he said he already had the three kids, which made me mad. Mom heard me call him a stinker for not waiting till I phoned him up, and she said that was no way to talk, especially to a black boy. I told her he was a stinker because he ought to have waited after he asked me to go, so why not say so, and what did being black have to do with it. Mom said, "Nothing," and that I was light-years ahead of her. I know what light-years are but I don't know what she meant.

December 2, 1962
Fitz wrote me a letter to invite me down to Washington next weekend. I'll stay with him in his apartment and he'll show me around Washington. One of the best parts is I'll go down on the train by myself. We'll be a couple of bachelors together, Fitz said. You'd think maybe some boys eleven years and seven months old are married. Fitz always makes me laugh a lot. Mom and Dad said they were sort of hoping to take me to Washington themselves my first time, but they guessed this would be more of an adventure for me and nice for Fitz, who doesn't have any family. Mom said he'd show me around the Paper's Washington Bureau too. Fitz is the head of it.

I've been to the New York office of the Paper quite a lot with Mom. When she was a little girl, she heard everybody talking about it all the time, but she didn't know what it was. She thought it was some kind of monster or something. That's the reason she says she started taking me down there when I was a little kid, so it wouldn't scare me the way it did her. I think it's sort of a dopey thing to be scared of, but I wouldn't tell her.

One time in the summer she had me go around all morning with this copy boy. She said most people start out being copy boys. I don't think it's very interesting. I don't know why they're called boys either. This one I was with was a grown-up man. He kept reading the galley proofs before he took them to the bull pen. He said he was trying to find a mistake, because if he did he'd be noticed and maybe get to be a reporter. I wouldn't have to do any of that, he said. I could be a reporter without doing anything but grow up. I didn't tell him I wasn't even sure I wanted to be one. I was afraid he might tell Mom. What I did was ask him why it was called a bull pen, but he didn't know. Nobody knows. The person who made up the name must not have told anybody the reason. That was a dopey thing to do.

None of my friends have been to Washington yet.

December 18, 1962
Well, I didn't get to go. There's this strike that loused everything up. Mom gave me the idea to write about it for extra credit in So-

cial Studies, so what I'm doing is put it down in my journal as it goes along, and later I'll write the whole thing for school, only leave out the personal parts.

It started on December 8. What happened was, the printers' union wants the printers to get higher pay, more sick leave with pay, bigger pensions, part of the money the publishers are saving with automatic machines, and like that. The publishers say they can't give the printers all that and stay in business, but the printers don't believe them. Maybe some of them do, but they've got to go along with the union. There's this boss of the union, Mr. Powers, who tells them they ought to have more money and everything and the only way to get it is to go on strike. He picked right before Christmas, because that's when the newspapers get the most advertising and they'll lose a whole lot of money unless they give up. So far, nobody has given up.

I showed that much to Mom. She thought it was so good she made me read it to Dad. She said I was a born newspaperman, and then she ran out of the room. That's what she does when she wants to cry. Dad said it's because she's very worried about the Paper. She thinks if there's a long strike it may lose so much money it will have to go out of business. I asked Dad if we'd be poor then, but he said we wouldn't be. He said we have plenty of money saved, and also a lot he makes from writing his books. It isn't the money that worries Mom. It's that the Paper was always supposed to be in the family. It was supposed to go on forever, and Mom's afraid maybe now it won't.

Anyway, we won't be poor. Timmy asked me once if we were, because we don't even have two in help any more, only Rose, and Dad wears old clothes. I asked Mom and Dad and they said no. They said some people enjoy showing they have a lot of money, but they don't. What they enjoy showing is what they work at, like the Paper and Dad's books and me. I thought putting me in was a joke, but they said it wasn't.

I forgot to say the reason I didn't get to go to Washington is on account of the strike Fitz came to New York. He knows this Mr. Powers and he thought maybe he could talk to him. It wasn't any good, though. Mr. Powers said Fitz doesn't care about the printers, only about his own job. He said nobody cares about the printers but the union. Mom said she didn't think making the newspapers lose all this money so maybe they'll have to go out of business and the printers will be out of work is caring so much about them.

One good thing is Fitz is going to stay in New York over Christmas. Mom invited him for Christmas dinner. We always have one person who wasn't invited anyplace else. Mostly you can tell why they weren't. I'd a lot rather have Fitz.

January 6, 1963

I didn't get a chance to write anything long in this journal the whole Christmas vacation. You'd think I'd have more time then, but I didn't. I only really like to write in it at night when there's nothing else I have to do, like homework. It doesn't take long to do homework. It's easy. My guidance counselor said I should be in eighth grade, only I'm not socially ready. Mrs. Bowman, my English teacher this year, said it's no wonder I get all A's, especially in English, with the family I come from. You'd think it was the family that got the A's.

Anyway, about Christmas vacation. The reason I didn't have much time to write is we were always going someplace. We went ice-skating, to the Christmas show at the Music Hall, to see the tree lit up in Rockefeller Center, to a hockey game, and some other places. It was cool. The ice-skating was in the daytime and even Mom went. She was home on account of the strike, and she still is. It's funny to have her home all the time. I mean, I like it but I'm not used to it. When I come back from school or playing with my friends I always forget she's going to be there, and then she is.

The strike's been on for over a month and Mom said there's no sign it's going to be over soon. She took me down once to see the picket lines in front of all the newspaper buildings. That's where the printers walk up and down with signs that say they're on strike because the publishers aren't fair. Mom talked to a couple of the printers from the Paper and asked them if they really thought she wasn't fair, but they wouldn't say anything except they had to do what the union told them because the union would look out for them. Mom told me there didn't used to be a union at the Paper. The publisher always knew every printer's name and all about his family and gave him more pay when he did good work. The printers were proud to work for the Paper. Now they don't care. There are so many of them and the Paper is so big they're like in a separate world.

Another thing I have to say about the strike is it's hurting mostly the publishers. Everybody else gets unemployment insurance and money from the unions. People can hear the news on radio and television, so they don't care so much. Mom said some of them might get out of the habit of reading the Paper and never go back to it when the strike is over.

March 14, 1963

I'm letting my hair grow so I can wear it like Ringo Starr. A lot of the kids' parents won't let them. Pud's Mom would but his Dad won't. I think when a kid gets to be almost thirteen, like Pud, or almost twelve, like me, he has a right to wear his own hair any way he wants to. Mom and Dad said okay as long as I keep it clean, which I would anyway because it itches when it's dirty.

Mom and Dad are pretty good about not bugging me much. The only thing is the Paper. I mean, Mom doesn't exactly bug me about it. She says I can make up my own mind what I want to be. Except, the way she takes me down to the Paper all the time and the way she talks all that Herzog stuff, I know she wants me to make up my mind to want to be on the Paper. I think Dad would like it if I wrote books. Maybe I don't want to do either one. I don't see why a kid has to do the same as his parents. I might be a scientist. Mom says there never was a Herzog scientist, or a Miller one either. So what? There never was a Simon Miller before. Well, maybe there was, but not this Simon Miller. Me.

I might get to go down to Washington Easter vacation and meet President Kennedy. Fitz knows him, and he said he would try to fix it. I like President Kennedy a lot, except about the war.

The strike isn't over yet. I got used to Mom being home. She's writing a novel, but when I get home from school she stops for a while. So does Dad. They have coffee and I have a coke or something. I'm supposed to tell them about school and stuff, which is okay if I feel like it, but sometimes I don't. I mean, they don't say I have to, but I can tell they're waiting. Mom is, anyway. A lot of times Dad has his mind more on his book. What I want to say is it's nice they stop writing to talk to me and everything, and in a way I like it, but in another way I don't.

Dad sort of bugged Mom into writing the novel. He told her it's what she always wanted to do and now she has no excuse she's too busy so why doesn't she do it, so she is. It's about the Herzogs, natch, only she's changing the names and the people around and

418

making up a lot of it, because she doesn't want to tell the real, private, family things. She said it would be sort of in memory of the Herzogs anyway, in case the Paper has to go out of business. Every time she talks about the Paper maybe going out of business she runs out of the room to cry. Dad said I shouldn't worry because she'll be all right even if it happens, but he didn't tell me how he knows she will.

April 2, 1963

The strike ended yesterday. It lasted 114 days. The printers are getting more money, they don't have to work so many hours, the publishers can't use all the automatic machines they feel like, and a few more things. Mom said she doesn't know if the Paper can stay in business or not, but she's going to keep it going until she's sure there's no chance. Mom said Mr. Winston, he's the general manager, thinks she's crazy. Dad said to hell with Mr. Winston.

Kathy Phillips said my hair looks just like Ringo's, not that I care what a girl says.

November 24, 1963

I didn't write much in this journal for a long time. I was busy in school and everything, and anyway I got sort of sick of it. I'm writing this now because something happened I want to tell about. I have all these feelings I want to put down. Mom said if I wrote it she might print it in the Paper, but I'm not doing it for that. I might not even let her or anybody ever see it. Well, here goes.

Mom asked me last week if I wanted to see what it's like to be a reporter traveling with the President. She said if I did she would arrange for her and me to go with the Washington press corps when President Kennedy spoke in Dallas, Texas. I met him in Easter vacation, the way it says back a few pages in this journal, so I thought it would be cool to see him again, and I told Mom I wanted to go.

We left Thursday after school, so I only missed Friday. We were in this motorcade Friday that drove along to where the President was going to speak. There were a lot of motorcycle cops and Secret Service agents, and the President's car, which was a Lincoln with the top open so people could see him. The press cars and buses came in back. We were in a bus about nine cars behind the Lincoln. It was so hot you'd have thought it was the middle of summer.

Mom told me the people in Dallas don't like President Kennedy. I found that out. The ones along the sidewalk cheered him, but

419

nobody looking out the office windows did. We heard some teachers wouldn't let their classes out to see him because they said he wasn't a good President, which is a lie.

It was so hot I started wishing I wasn't there. I couldn't even see President Kennedy, he was so far up ahead. I started wishing I was in swimming or something. I was thinking Mom probably took me there to show me how much fun it was to be a reporter, but I sure couldn't see where crawling along in a bus in the hot sun with all those people staring out the windows and not even cheering was any fun.

We got to this place called Dealey Plaza. I didn't know the name of it then but I do now. I kept looking out, trying to see the President, but all I could see was his car. I saw a lot of pigeons woosh up in the air, but I didn't think that was anything. Pigeons do that in Central Park sometimes for no reason anybody can see except the pigeons. All of a sudden the Lincoln, the President's car, took off fast. I told Mom, and she said she didn't know why, maybe the President wanted a little extra time before everybody got there to hear his speech. The buses just kept crawling along to where he was supposed to talk, and we got out.

The way we knew something happened was the people in the crowd kept turning and talking from one to the other and looking scared, but we didn't know what it was. We just stood there until some reporter came along, running, and told us somebody shot the President.

We got back in the press bus and went to the hospital where he was. Mom went in but I had to stay outside and wait. A lot of people were around and more kept coming and going. I heard a lot of stuff about who shot the President and how many shots there were and how bad he was hurt, all different. Somebody said he wasn't hurt much. Somebody else said he was dead, and there was this fourth-grade class that when they heard it they clapped. Some reporter went running inside the hospital with this look on his face like when somebody's going to shoot the winning basket and you want to be in time to see it.

All of a sudden I started shaking, not so anybody could tell, I don't think, but sort of inside. I got this feeling the President really was dead, somebody shot him to death, and those little fourth-grade kids were glad. I mean, you have to hate a person a terrible lot to kill him, but you have to hate him a lot to clap because he's dead too, and what are those little kids doing with all that hate inside them in only fourth grade? Mom said later it might not be true about the kids, but even so. Here was this great President that people all over the world admired and he was killed because there's all this hate going around. I mean, something's the matter.

A lot of people were crying in the plane going home. Mom kept crying and stopping and starting over again. After a while I thought of something to make her feel better, so I told her. I said she shouldn't worry, I'd be on the Paper if she wanted me to. Well, that stopped her all right, but she looked at me in a funny way and said something like she sure should have learned you shouldn't try to force a person to dream another person's dream, but people keep making the same mistakes and don't even know they're doing it. I think that's about what she said. I told her I didn't get it, and she said the only important part was for me to be what I wanted to be, a scientist or whatever I want. She always says that, but I could tell she really meant it this time. I don't know why it has anything to do with President Kennedy getting shot, but I think it does.

The first edition of this newspaper was published eighty-eight years ago, on October 17, 1875. With this edition of December 27, 1963, it goes to press for the last time.

Sigmund Herzog, the founder, was the grandfather of David Herzog and Rebecca Herzog, who succeeded him as publisher in that order, and the great-grandfather of the present publisher. He dreamed and planned that the stewardship of the newspaper would be handed down in perpetuity to successive generations of his family, who would continue to accomplish his purposes and principles. He believed in the power of the press to influence for the better the course of human events. For this reason, he believed in personal journalism, the leadership of one individual who would make certain that awesome power was used wisely, with absolute integrity, without fear or favor. His successors, beset by human failings and the inexorable tide of history, have tried to carry on his beliefs. In these days of bigness, it is no longer possible. After eighty-eight years, the experiment has come to an end.

It is a time of endings. In a few days the year will end. Something over a month ago, the first President of the United States to be born in this century was cut down in the midst of his

421

dream of exploring the stars and lighting the world. Camelot ended. An era ended.

Now, it has been said, although we will laugh again, we will never be young again. No, we never will be. But others coming after us will be young. They will dream their own new dreams, and fail, and dream again.

Every ending is a beginning.

Clara Herzog Miller